Smoke Bellew

Smoke Bellew
Jack London

MINT EDITIONS

Smoke Bellew was first published in 1912.

This edition published by Mint Editions 2021.

ISBN 9781513270227 | E-ISBN 9781513275222

Published by Mint Editions®

 MINT
EDITIONS

minteditionbooks.com

Publishing Director: Jennifer Newens
Design & Production: Rachel Lopez Metzger
Typesetting: Westchester Publishing Services

Contents

I. The Taste of the Meat 7

II. The Meat 27

III. The Stampede to Squaw Creek 47

IV. Shorty Dreams 65

V. The Man on the Other Bank 78

VI. The Race for Number Three 94

VII. The Little Man 111

VIII. The Hanging of Cultus George 127

IX. The Mistake of Creation 141

X. A Flutter in Eggs 159

XI. The Town-Site of Tra-Lee 179

XII. Wonder of Woman 201

I

The Taste of the Meat

In the beginning he was Christopher Bellew. By the time he was at college he had become Chris Bellew. Later, in the Bohemian crowd of San Francisco, he was called Kit Bellew. And in the end he was known by no other name than Smoke Bellew. And this history of the evolution of his name is the history of his evolution. Nor would it have happened had he not had a fond mother and an iron uncle, and had he not received a letter from Gillet Bellamy.

"I have just seen a copy of The Billow," Gillet wrote from Paris. "Of course O'Hara will succeed with it. But he's missing some tricks." Here followed details in the improvement of the budding society weekly. "Go down and see him. Let him think they're your own suggestions. Don't let him know they're from me. If you do, he'll make me Paris correspondent, which I can't afford, because I'm getting real money for my stuff from the big magazines. Above all, don't forget to make him fire that dub who's doing the musical and art criticism. Another thing. San Francisco has always had a literature of her own. But she hasn't any now. Tell him to kick around and get some gink to turn out a live serial, and to put into it the real romance and glamour and colour of San Francisco."

And down to the office of The Billow went Kit Bellew faithfully to instruct. O'Hara listened. O'Hara debated. O'Hara agreed. O'Hara fired the dub who wrote criticisms. Further, O'Hara had a way with him—the very way that was feared by Gillet in distant Paris. When O'Hara wanted anything, no friend could deny him. He was sweetly and compellingly irresistible. Before Kit Bellew could escape from the office, he had become an associate editor, had agreed to write weekly columns of criticism till some decent pen was found, and had pledged himself to write a weekly instalment of ten thousand words on the San Francisco serial—and all this without pay. The Billow wasn't paying yet, O'Hara explained; and just as convincingly had he exposited that there was only one man in San Francisco capable of writing the serial and that man Kit Bellew.

"Oh, Lord, I'm the gink!" Kit had groaned to himself afterward on the narrow stairway.

And thereat had begun his servitude to O'Hara and the insatiable columns of The Billow. Week after week he held down an office chair, stood off creditors, wrangled with printers, and turned out twenty-five thousand words of all sorts. Nor did his labours lighten. The Billow was ambitious. It went in for illustration. The processes were expensive. It never had any money to pay Kit Bellew, and by the same token it was unable to pay for any additions to the office staff.

"This is what comes of being a good fellow," Kit grumbled one day.

"Thank God for good fellows then," O'Hara cried, with tears in his eyes as he gripped Kit's hand. "You're all that's saved me, Kit. But for you I'd have gone bust. Just a little longer, old man, and things will be easier."

"Never," was Kit's plaint. "I see my fate clearly. I shall be here always."

A little later he thought he saw his way out. Watching his chance, in O'Hara's presence, he fell over a chair. A few minutes afterwards he bumped into the corner of the desk, and, with fumbling fingers, capsized a paste pot.

"Out late?" O'Hara queried.

Kit brushed his eyes with his hands and peered about him anxiously before replying.

"No, it's not that. It's my eyes. They seem to be going back on me, that's all."

For several days he continued to fall over and bump into the office furniture. But O'Hara's heart was not softened.

"I tell you what, Kit," he said one day, "you've got to see an oculist. There's Doctor Hassdapple. He's a crackerjack. And it won't cost you anything. We can get it for advertizing. I'll see him myself."

And, true to his word, he dispatched Kit to the oculist.

"There's nothing the matter with your eyes," was the doctor's verdict, after a lengthy examination. "In fact, your eyes are magnificent—a pair in a million."

"Don't tell O'Hara," Kit pleaded. "And give me a pair of black glasses."

The result of this was that O'Hara sympathized and talked glowingly of the time when The Billow would be on its feet.

Luckily for Kit Bellew, he had his own income. Small it was, compared with some, yet it was large enough to enable him to belong to several clubs and maintain a studio in the Latin Quarter. In point of fact, since his associate-editorship, his expenses had decreased prodigiously. He had no time to spend money. He never saw the studio any more, nor entertained the local Bohemians with his famous chafing-dish suppers. Yet he was always broke, for The Billow, in perennial distress, absorbed his cash as well as his brains. There were the illustrators, who periodically refused to illustrate, the printers, who periodically refused to print, and the office-boy, who frequently refused to officiate. At such times O'Hara looked at Kit, and Kit did the rest.

When the steamship Excelsior arrived from Alaska, bringing the news of the Klondike strike that set the country mad, Kit made a purely frivolous proposition.

"Look here, O'Hara," he said. "This gold rush is going to be big—the days of '49 over again. Suppose I cover it for The Billow? I'll pay my own expenses."

O'Hara shook his head.

"Can't spare you from the office, Kit. Then there's that serial. Besides, I saw Jackson not an hour ago. He's starting for the Klondike to-morrow, and he's agreed to send a weekly letter and photos. I wouldn't let him get away till he promised. And the beauty of it is, that it doesn't cost us anything."

The next Kit heard of the Klondike was when he dropped into the club that afternoon, and, in an alcove off the library, encountered his uncle.

"Hello, avuncular relative," Kit greeted, sliding into a leather chair and spreading out his legs. "Won't you join me?"

He ordered a cocktail, but the uncle contented himself with the thin native claret he invariably drank. He glanced with irritated disapproval at the cocktail, and on to his nephew's face. Kit saw a lecture gathering.

"I've only a minute," he announced hastily. "I've got to run and take in that Keith exhibition at Ellery's and do half a column on it."

"What's the matter with you?" the other demanded. "You're pale. You're a wreck."

Kit's only answer was a groan.

"I'll have the pleasure of burying you, I can see that."

Kit shook his head sadly.

"No destroying worm, thank you. Cremation for mine."

John Bellew came of the old hard and hardy stock that had crossed the plains by ox-team in the fifties, and in him was this same hardness and the hardness of a childhood spent in the conquering of a new land.

"You're not living right, Christopher. I'm ashamed of you."

"Primrose path, eh?" Kit chuckled.

The older man shrugged his shoulders.

"Shake not your gory locks at me, avuncular. I wish it were the primrose path. But that's all cut out. I have no time."

"Then what in—?"

"Overwork."

John Bellew laughed harshly and incredulously.

"Honest."

Again came the laughter.

"Men are the products of their environment," Kit proclaimed, pointing at the other's glass. "Your mirth is thin and bitter as your drink."

"Overwork!" was the sneer. "You never earned a cent in your life."

"You bet I have—only I never got it. I'm earning five hundred a week right now, and doing four men's work."

"Pictures that won't sell? Or—er—fancy work of some sort? Can you swim?"

"I used to."

"Sit a horse?"

"I have essayed that adventure."

John Bellew snorted his disgust. "I'm glad your father didn't live to see you in all the glory of your gracelessness," he said. "Your father was a man, every inch of him. Do you get it? A man. I think he'd have whaled all this musical and artistic tom foolery out of you."

"Alas! these degenerate days," Kit sighed.

"I could understand it, and tolerate it," the other went on savagely, "if you succeeded at it. You've never earned a cent in your life, nor done a tap of man's work."

"Etchings, and pictures, and fans," Kit contributed unsoothingly.

"You're a dabbler and a failure. What pictures have you painted? Dinky water-colours and nightmare posters. You've never had one exhibited, even here in San Francisco—"

"Ah, you forget. There is one in the jinks room of this very club."

"A gross cartoon. Music? Your dear fool of a mother spent hundreds on lessons. You've dabbled and failed. You've never even earned a five-dollar piece by accompanying some one at a concert. Your songs?—rag-time rot that's never printed and that's sung only by a pack of fake Bohemians."

"I had a book published once—those sonnets, you remember," Kit interposed meekly.

"What did it cost you?"

"Only a couple of hundred."

"Any other achievements?"

"I had a forest play acted at the summer jinks."

"What did you get for it?"

"Glory."

"And you used to swim, and you have essayed to sit a horse!" John Bellew set his glass down with unnecessary violence. "What earthly good are you anyway? You were well put up, yet even at university you didn't play football. You didn't row. You didn't—"

"I boxed and fenced—some."

"When did you box last?"

"Not since, but I was considered an excellent judge of time and distance, only I was—er—"

"Go on."

"Considered desultory."

"Lazy, you mean."

"I always imagined it was an euphemism."

"My father, sir, your grandfather, old Isaac Bellew, killed a man with a blow of his fist when he was sixty-nine years old."

"The man?"

"No, your—you graceless scamp! But you'll never kill a mosquito at sixty-nine."

"The times have changed, oh, my avuncular! They send men to prison for homicide now."

"Your father rode one hundred and eighty-five miles, without sleeping, and killed three horses."

"Had he lived to-day, he'd have snored over the course in a Pullman."

The older man was on the verge of choking with wrath, but swallowed it down and managed to articulate:

"How old are you?"

"I have reason to believe—"

"I know. Twenty-seven. You finished college at twenty-two. You've dabbled and played and frilled for five years. Before God and man, of what use are you? When I was your age I had one suit of underclothes. I was riding with the cattle in Coluso. I was hard as rocks, and I could sleep on a rock. I lived on jerked beef and bear-meat. I am a better man physically right now than you are. You weigh about one hundred and sixty-five. I can throw you right now, or thrash you with my fists."

"It doesn't take a physical prodigy to mop up cocktails or pink tea," Kit murmured deprecatingly. "Don't you see, my avuncular, the times have changed. Besides, I wasn't brought up right. My dear fool of a mother—"

John Bellew started angrily.

"—As you described her, was too good to me; kept me in cotton wool and all the rest. Now, if when I was a youngster I had taken some of those intensely masculine vacations you go in for—I wonder why you didn't invite me sometimes? You took Hal and Robbie all over the Sierras and on that Mexico trip."

"I guess you were too Lord-Fauntleroyish."

"Your fault, avuncular, and my dear—er—mother's. How was I to know the hard? I was only a chee-ild. What was there left but etchings and pictures and fans? Was it my fault that I never had to sweat?"

The older man looked at his nephew with unconcealed disgust. He had no patience with levity from the lips of softness.

"Well, I'm going to take another one of those what-you-call masculine vacations. Suppose I asked you to come along?"

"Rather belated, I must say. Where is it?"

"Hal and Robert are going in to Klondike, and I'm going to see them across the Pass and down to the Lakes, then return—"

He got no further, for the young man had sprung forward and gripped his hand.

"My preserver!"

John Bellew was immediately suspicious. He had not dreamed the invitation would be accepted.

"You don't mean it?" he said.

"When do we start?"

"It will be a hard trip. You'll be in the way."

"No, I won't. I'll work. I've learned to work since I went on The Billow."

"Each man has to take a year's supplies in with him. There'll be such a jam the Indian packers won't be able to handle it. Hal and Robert will have to pack their outfits across themselves. That's what I'm going along for—to help them pack. If you come you'll have to do the same."

"Watch me."

"You can't pack," was the objection.

"When do we start?"

"To-morrow."

"You needn't take it to yourself that your lecture on the hard has done it," Kit said, at parting. "I just had to get away, somewhere, anywhere, from O'Hara."

"Who is O'Hara? A Jap?"

"No; he's an Irishman, and a slave-driver, and my best friend. He's the editor and proprietor and all-round big squeeze of The Billow. What he says goes. He can make ghosts walk."

That night Kit Bellew wrote a note to O'Hara. "It's only a several weeks' vacation," he explained. "You'll have to get some gink to dope out instalments for that serial. Sorry, old man, but my health demands it. I'll kick in twice as hard when I get back."

KIT BELLEW LANDED THROUGH THE madness of the Dyea beach, congested with thousand-pound outfits of thousands of men. This immense mass of luggage and food, flung ashore in mountains by the steamers, was beginning slowly to dribble up the Dyea Valley and across Chilkoot. It was a portage of twenty-eight miles, and could be accomplished only on the backs of men. Despite the fact that the Indian packers had jumped the freight from eight cents a pound to forty, they were swamped with the work, and it was plain that winter would catch the major portion of the outfits on the wrong side of the divide.

Tenderest of the tenderfeet was Kit. Like many hundreds of others he carried a big revolver swung on a cartridge-belt. Of this, his uncle, filled with memories of old lawless days, was likewise guilty. But Kit Bellew was romantic. He was fascinated by the froth and sparkle of the gold rush, and viewed its life and movement with an artist's eye. He did not take it seriously. As he said on the steamer, it was not his funeral. He was merely on a vacation, and intended to peep over the top of the pass for a "look see" and then to return.

Leaving his party on the sand to wait for the putting ashore of the freight, he strolled up the beach toward the old trading-post. He did not swagger, though he noticed that many of the be-revolvered individuals did. A strapping, six-foot Indian passed him, carrying an unusually large pack. Kit swung in behind, admiring the splendid calves of the man, and the grace and ease with which he moved along under his burden. The Indian dropped his pack on the scales in front of the post, and Kit joined the group of admiring gold-rushers who surrounded him. The pack weighed one hundred and twenty-five pounds, which fact was uttered back and forth in tones of awe. It was going some, Kit decided, and he wondered if he could lift such a weight, much less walk off with it.

"Going to Lake Linderman with it, old man?" he asked.

The Indian, swelling with pride, grunted an affirmative.

"How much you make that one pack?"

"Fifty dollar."

Here Kit slid out of the conversation. A young woman, standing in the doorway, had caught his eye. Unlike other women landing from the steamers, she was neither short-skirted nor bloomer-clad. She was dressed as any woman travelling anywhere would be dressed. What struck him was the justness of her being there, a feeling that somehow she belonged. Moreover, she was young and pretty. The bright beauty and colour of her oval face held him, and he looked over-long—looked till she resented, and her own eyes, long-lashed and dark, met his in cool survey.

From his face they travelled in evident amusement down to the big revolver at his thigh. Then her eyes came back to his, and in them was amused contempt. It struck him like a blow. She turned to the man beside her and indicated Kit. The man glanced him over with the same amused contempt.

"Chechako," the girl said.

The man, who looked like a tramp in his cheap overalls and dilapidated woollen jacket, grinned dryly, and Kit felt withered, though he knew not why. But anyway she was an unusually pretty girl, he decided, as the two moved off. He noted the way of her walk, and recorded the judgment that he would recognize it over the lapse of a thousand years.

"Did you see that man with the girl?" Kit's neighbor asked him excitedly. "Know who he is?"

Kit shook his head.

"Cariboo Charley. He was just pointed out to me. He struck it big on Klondike. Old-timer. Been on the Yukon a dozen years. He's just come out."

"What's 'chechako' mean?" Kit asked.

"You're one; I'm one," was the answer.

"Maybe I am, but you've got to search me. What does it mean?"

"Tenderfoot."

On his way back to the beach, Kit turned the phrase over and over. It rankled to be called tenderfoot by a slender chit of a woman.

Going into a corner among the heaps of freight, his mind still filled with the vision of the Indian with the redoubtable pack, Kit essayed to learn his own strength. He picked out a sack of flour which he knew weighed an even hundred pounds. He stepped astride it, reached down, and strove to get it on his shoulder. His first conclusion was that one hundred pounds were real heavy. His next was that his back was weak. His third was an oath, and it occurred at the end of five futile minutes, when he collapsed on top of the burden with which he was wrestling. He mopped his forehead, and across a heap of grub-sacks saw John Bellew gazing at him, wintry amusement in his eyes.

"God!" proclaimed that apostle of the hard. "Out of our loins has come a race of weaklings. When I was sixteen I toyed with things like that."

"You forget, avuncular," Kit retorted, "that I wasn't raised on bear-meat."

"And I'll toy with it when I'm sixty."

"You've got to show me."

John Bellew did. He was forty-eight, but he bent over the sack, applied a tentative, shifting grip that balanced it, and, with a quick heave, stood erect, the somersaulted sack of flour on his shoulder.

"Knack, my boy, knack—and a spine."

Kit took off his hat reverently.

"You're a wonder, avuncular, a shining wonder. D'ye think I can learn the knack?"

John Bellew shrugged his shoulders. "You'll be hitting the back trail before we get started."

"Never you fear," Kit groaned. "There's O'Hara, the roaring lion, down there. I'm not going back till I have to."

Kit's first pack was a success. Up to Finnegan's Crossing they had managed to get Indians to carry the twenty-five-hundred-pound outfit. From that point their own backs must do the work. They planned to move forward at the rate of a mile a day. It looked easy—on paper. Since John Bellew was to stay in camp and do the cooking, he would be unable to make more than an occasional pack; so to each of the three young men fell the task of carrying eight hundred pounds one mile each day. If they made fifty-pound packs, it meant a daily walk of sixteen miles loaded and of fifteen miles light—"Because we don't back-trip the last time," Kit explained the pleasant discovery. Eighty-pound packs meant nineteen miles travel each day; and hundred-pound packs meant only fifteen miles.

"I don't like walking," said Kit. "Therefore I shall carry one hundred pounds." He caught the grin of incredulity on his uncle's face, and added hastily: "Of course I shall work up to it. A fellow's got to learn the ropes and tricks. I'll start with fifty."

He did, and ambled gaily along the trail. He dropped the sack at the next camp-site and ambled back. It was easier than he had thought. But two miles had rubbed off the velvet of his strength and exposed the underlying softness. His second pack was sixty-five pounds. It was more difficult, and he no longer ambled. Several times, following the custom of all packers, he sat down on the ground, resting the pack behind him on a rock or stump. With the third pack he became bold. He fastened the straps to a ninety-five-pound sack of beans and started. At the end of a hundred yards he felt that he must collapse. He sat down and mopped his face.

"Short hauls and short rests," he muttered. "That's the trick."

Sometimes he did not make a hundred yards, and each time he struggled to his feet for another short haul the pack became undeniably heavier. He panted for breath, and the sweat streamed from him. Before he had covered a quarter of a mile he stripped off his woollen shirt and hung it on a tree. A little later he discarded his hat. At the end of half a mile he decided he was finished. He had never exerted himself so in his life, and he knew that he was finished. As he sat and panted, his gaze fell upon the big revolver and the heavy cartridge-belt.

"Ten pounds of junk!" he sneered, as he unbuckled it.

He did not bother to hang it on a tree, but flung it into the underbush. And as the steady tide of packers flowed by him, up trail and down, he noted that the other tenderfeet were beginning to shed their shooting-irons.

His short hauls decreased. At times a hundred feet was all he could stagger, and then the ominous pounding of his heart against his eardrums and the sickening totteriness of his knees compelled him to rest. And his rests grew longer. But his mind was busy. It was a twenty-eight-mile portage, which represented as many days, and this, by all accounts, was the easiest part of it. "Wait till you get to Chilkoot," others told him as they rested and talked, "where you climb with hands and feet."

"They ain't going to be no Chilkoot," was his answer. "Not for me. Long before that I'll be at peace in my little couch beneath the moss."

JACK LONDON

A slip and a violent, wrenching effort at recovery frightened him. He felt that everything inside him had been torn asunder.

"If ever I fall down with this on my back, I'm a goner," he told another packer.

"That's nothing," came the answer. "Wait till you hit the Canyon. You'll have to cross a raging torrent on a sixty-foot pine-tree. No guide-ropes, nothing, and the water boiling at the sag of the log to your knees. If you fall with a pack on your back, there's no getting out of the straps. You just stay there and drown."

"Sounds good to me," he retorted; and out of the depths of his exhaustion he almost meant it.

"They drown three or four a day there," the man assured him. "I helped fish a German out of there. He had four thousand in greenbacks on him."

"Cheerful, I must say," said Kit, battling his way to his feet and tottering on.

He and the sack of beans became a perambulating tragedy. It reminded him of the old man of the sea who sat on Sinbad's neck. And this was one of those intensely masculine vacations, he meditated. Compared with it, the servitude to O'Hara was sweet. Again and again he was nearly seduced by the thought of abandoning the sack of beans in the brush and of sneaking around the camp to the beach and catching a steamer for civilization.

But he didn't. Somewhere in him was the strain of the hard, and he repeated over and over to himself that what other men could do, he could. It became a nightmare chant, and he gibbered it to those that passed him on the trail. At other times, resting, he watched and envied the stolid, mule-footed Indians that plodded by under heavier packs. They never seemed to rest, but went on and on with a steadiness and certitude that were to him appalling.

He sat and cursed—he had no breath for it when under way—and fought the temptation to sneak back to San Francisco. Before the mile pack was ended he ceased cursing and took to crying. The tears were tears of exhaustion and of disgust with self. If ever a man was a wreck, he was. As the end of the pack came in sight, he strained himself in desperation, gained the camp-site, and pitched forward on his face, the beans on his back. It did not kill him, but he lay for fifteen minutes before he could summon sufficient shreds of strength to release himself from the straps. Then he became deathly sick, and was so found by

Robbie, who had similar troubles of his own. It was this sickness of Robbie that braced Kit up.

"What other men can do, we can do," Kit told Robbie, though down in his heart he wondered whether or not he was bluffing.

"AND I AM TWENTY-SEVEN YEARS old and a man," he privately assured himself many times in the days that followed. There was need for it. At the end of a week, though he had succeeded in moving his eight hundred pounds forward a mile a day, he had lost fifteen pounds of his own weight. His face was lean and haggard. All resilience had gone out of his body and mind. He no longer walked, but plodded. And on the back-trips, travelling light, his feet dragged almost as much as when he was loaded.

He had become a work animal. He fell asleep over his food, and his sleep was heavy and beastly, save when he was aroused, screaming with agony, by the cramps in his legs. Every part of him ached. He tramped on raw blisters; yet even this was easier than the fearful bruising his feet received on the water-rounded rocks of the Dyea Flats, across which the trail led for two miles. These two miles represented thirty-eight miles of travelling. He washed his face once a day. His nails, torn and broken and afflicted with hangnails, were never cleaned. His shoulders and chest, galled by the pack-straps, made him think, and for the first time with understanding, of the horses he had seen on city streets.

One ordeal that nearly destroyed him at first had been the food. The extraordinary amount of work demanded extraordinary stoking, and his stomach was unaccustomed to great quantities of bacon and of the coarse, highly poisonous brown beans. As a result, his stomach went back on him, and for several days the pain and irritation of it and of starvation nearly broke him down. And then came the day of joy when he could eat like a ravenous animal, and, wolf-eyed, ask for more.

When they had moved the outfit across the foot-logs at the mouth of the Canyon, they made a change in their plans. Word had come across the Pass that at Lake Linderman the last available trees for building boats were being cut. The two cousins, with tools, whipsaw, blankets, and grub on their backs, went on, leaving Kit and his uncle to hustle along the outfit. John Bellew now shared the cooking with Kit, and both packed shoulder to shoulder. Time was flying, and on the peaks the first snow was falling. To be caught on the wrong side of the Pass meant a delay of nearly a year. The older man put his iron back under a hundred pounds. Kit was shocked, but he gritted his teeth and fastened his own straps to a hundred pounds. It hurt, but he had learned the knack, and his body, purged of all softness and fat, was beginning to harden up with lean and bitter muscle. Also, he observed and devised. He took note of the head-straps worn by the Indians and manufactured one for himself, which he used in addition to the shoulder-straps. It made things easier, so that he began the practice of piling any light, cumbersome piece of luggage on top. Thus, he was soon able to bend along with a hundred pounds in the straps, fifteen or twenty more lying loosely on top of the pack and against his neck, an axe or a pair of oars in one hand, and in the other the nested cooking-pails of the camp.

But work as they would, the toil increased. The trail grew more rugged; their packs grew heavier; and each day saw the snow-line dropping down the mountains, while freight jumped to sixty cents. No word came from the cousins beyond, so they knew they must be at work chopping down the standing trees and whipsawing them into boat-planks. John Bellew grew anxious. Capturing a bunch of Indians back-tripping from Lake Linderman, he persuaded them to put their straps on the outfit. They charged thirty cents a pound to carry it to the summit of Chilkoot, and it nearly broke him. As it was, some four hundred pounds of clothes-bags and camp outfit were not handled. He remained behind to move it along, dispatching Kit with the Indians. At the summit Kit was to remain, slowly moving his ton until overtaken by the four hundred pounds with which his uncle guaranteed to catch him.

KIT PLODDED ALONG THE TRAIL with his Indian packers. In recognition of the fact that it was to be a long pack, straight to the top of Chilkoot, his own load was only eighty pounds. The Indians plodded under their loads, but it was a quicker gait than he had practised. Yet he felt no apprehension, and by now had come to deem himself almost the equal of an Indian.

At the end of a quarter of a mile he desired to rest. But the Indians kept on. He stayed with them, and kept his place in the line. At the half-mile he was convinced that he was incapable of another step, yet he gritted his teeth, kept his place, and at the end of the mile was amazed that he was still alive. Then, in some strange way, came the thing called second wind, and the next mile was almost easier than the first. The third mile nearly killed him, but, though half delirious with pain and fatigue, he never whimpered. And then, when he felt he must surely faint, came the rest. Instead of sitting in the straps, as was the custom of the white packers, the Indians slipped out of the shoulder-and head-straps and lay at ease, talking and smoking. A full half-hour passed before they made another start. To Kit's surprise he found himself a fresh man, and "long hauls and long rests" became his newest motto.

The pitch of Chilkoot was all he had heard of it, and many were the occasions when he climbed with hands as well as feet. But when he reached the crest of the divide in the thick of a driving snow-squall, it was in the company of his Indians, and his secret pride was that he had come through with them and never squealed and never lagged. To be almost as good as an Indian was a new ambition to cherish.

When he had paid off the Indians and seen them depart, a stormy darkness was falling, and he was left alone, a thousand feet above timber-line, on the backbone of a mountain. Wet to the waist, famished and exhausted, he would have given a year's income for a fire and a cup of coffee. Instead, he ate half a dozen cold flapjacks and crawled into the folds of the partly unrolled tent. As he dozed off he had time for only one fleeting thought, and he grinned with vicious pleasure at the picture of John Bellew in the days to follow, masculinely back-tripping his four hundred pounds up Chilcoot. As for himself, even though burdened with two thousand pounds, he was bound down the hill.

In the morning, stiff from his labours and numb with the frost, he rolled out of the canvas, ate a couple of pounds of uncooked bacon, buckled the straps on a hundred pounds, and went down the rocky way. Several hundred yards beneath, the trail led across a small glacier and down to Crater Lake. Other men packed across the glacier. All that day he dropped his packs at the glacier's upper edge, and, by virtue of the shortness of the pack, he put his straps on one hundred and fifty pounds each load. His astonishment at being able to do it never abated. For two dollars he bought from an Indian three leathery sea-biscuits, and out of these, and a huge quantity of raw bacon, made several meals. Unwashed, unwarmed, his clothing wet with sweat, he slept another night in the canvas.

In the early morning he spread a tarpaulin on the ice, loaded it with three-quarters of a ton, and started to pull. Where the pitch of the glacier accelerated, his load likewise accelerated, overran him, scooped him in on top, and ran away with him.

A hundred packers, bending under their loads, stopped to watch him. He yelled frantic warnings, and those in his path stumbled and staggered clear. Below, on the lower edge of the glacier, was pitched a small tent, which seemed leaping toward him, so rapidly did it grow larger. He left the beaten track where the packers' trail swerved to the left, and struck a patch of fresh snow. This arose about him in frosty smoke, while it reduced his speed. He saw the tent the instant he struck it, carrying away the corner guys, bursting in the front flaps, and fetching up inside, still on top of the tarpaulin and in the midst of his grub-sacks. The tent rocked drunkenly, and in the frosty vapour he found himself face to face with a startled young woman who was sitting up in her blankets—the very one who had called him a tenderfoot at Dyea.

"Did you see my smoke?" he queried cheerfully.

She regarded him with disapproval.

"Talk about your magic carpets!" he went on.

"Do you mind removing that sack from my foot?" she said coldly.

He looked, and lifted his weight quickly.

"It wasn't a sack. It was my elbow. Pardon me."

The information did not perturb her, and her coolness was a challenge.

"It was a mercy you did not overturn the stove," she said.

He followed her glance and saw a sheet-iron stove and a coffee-pot, attended by a young squaw. He sniffed the coffee and looked back to the girl.

"I'm a chechako," he said.

Her bored expression told him that he was stating the obvious. But he was unabashed.

"I've shed my shooting-irons," he added.

Then she recognized him, and her eyes lighted. "I never thought you'd get this far," she informed him.

Again, and greedily, he sniffed the air. "As I live, coffee!" He turned and directly addressed her: "I'll give you my little finger—cut it right off now; I'll do anything; I'll be your slave for a year and a day or any other old time, if you'll give me a cup out of that pot."

And over the coffee he gave his name and learned hers—Joy Gastell. Also, he learned that she was an old-timer in the country. She had been born in a trading-post on the Great Slave, and as a child had crossed the Rockies with her father and come down to the Yukon. She was going in, she said, with her father, who had been delayed by business in

Seattle, and who had then been wrecked on the ill-fated Chanter and carried back to Puget Sound by the rescuing steamer.

In view of the fact that she was still in her blankets, he did not make it a long conversation, and, heroically declining a second cup of coffee, he removed himself and his heaped and shifted baggage from her tent. Further, he took several conclusions away with him: she had a fetching name and fetching eyes; could not be more than twenty, or twenty-one or -two; her father must be French; she had a will of her own and temperament to burn; and she had been educated elsewhere than on the frontier.

OVER THE ICE-SCOURED ROCKS AND above the timber-line, the trail ran around Crater Lake and gained the rocky defile that led toward Happy Camp and the first scrub-pines. To pack his heavy outfit around would take days of heart-breaking toil. On the lake was a canvas boat employed in freighting. Two trips with it, in two hours, would see him and his ton across. But he was broke, and the ferryman charged forty dollars a ton.

"You've got a gold-mine, my friend, in that dinky boat," Kit said to the ferryman. "Do you want another gold-mine?"

"Show me," was the answer.

"I'll sell it to you for the price of ferrying my outfit. It's an idea, not patented, and you can jump the deal as soon as I tell you it. Are you game?"

The ferryman said he was, and Kit liked his looks.

"Very well. You see that glacier. Take a pick-axe and wade into it. In a day you can have a decent groove from top to bottom. See the point? The Chilkoot and Crater Lake Consolidated Chute Corporation, Limited. You can charge fifty cents a hundred, get a hundred tons a day, and have no work to do but collect the coin."

Two hours later, Kit's ton was across the lake, and he had gained three days on himself. And when John Bellew overtook him, he was well along toward Deep Lake, another volcanic pit filled with glacial water.

THE LAST PACK, FROM LONG Lake to Linderman, was three miles, and the trail, if trail it could be called, rose up over a thousand-foot hogback, dropped down a scramble of slippery rocks, and crossed a wide stretch of swamp. John Bellew remonstrated when he saw Kit arise with a hundred pounds in the straps and pick up a fifty-pound sack of flour and place it on top of the pack against the back of his neck.

"Come on, you chunk of the hard," Kit retorted. "Kick in on your bear-meat fodder and your one suit of underclothes."

But John Bellew shook his head. "I'm afraid I'm getting old, Christopher."

"You're only forty-eight. Do you realize that my grandfather, sir, your father, old Isaac Bellew, killed a man with his fist when he was sixty-nine years old?"

John Bellew grinned and swallowed his medicine.

"Avuncular, I want to tell you something important. I was raised a Lord Fauntleroy, but I can outpack you, outwalk you, put you on your back, or lick you with my fists right now."

John Bellew thrust out his hand and spoke solemnly. "Christopher, my boy, I believe you can do it. I believe you can do it with that pack on your back at the same time. You've made good, boy, though it's too unthinkable to believe."

Kit made the round trip of the last pack four times a day, which is to say that he daily covered twenty-four miles of mountain climbing, twelve miles of it under one hundred and fifty pounds. He was proud, hard, and tired, but in splendid physical condition. He ate and slept as he had never eaten and slept in his life, and as the end of the work came in sight, he was almost half sorry.

One problem bothered him. He had learned that he could fall with a hundred-weight on his back and survive; but he was confident, if he fell with that additional fifty pounds across the back of his neck, that it would break it clean. Each trail through the swamp was quickly churned bottomless by the thousands of packers, who were compelled continually to make new trails. It was while pioneering such a new trail, that he solved the problem of the extra fifty.

The soft, lush surface gave way under him; he floundered, and pitched forward on his face. The fifty pounds crushed his face in the mud and went clear without snapping his neck. With the remaining hundred pounds on his back, he arose on hands and knees. But he got no farther. One arm sank to the shoulder, pillowing his cheek in the slush. As he drew this arm clear, the other sank to the shoulder. In this position it was impossible to slip the straps, and the hundred-weight on his back would not let him rise. On hands and knees, sinking first one arm and then the other, he made an effort to crawl to where the small sack of flour had fallen. But he exhausted himself without advancing, and so churned and broke the grass surface, that a tiny pool of water began to form in perilous proximity to his mouth and nose.

He tried to throw himself on his back with the pack underneath, but this resulted in sinking both arms to the shoulders and gave him a foretaste of drowning. With exquisite patience, he slowly withdrew one sucking arm and then the other and rested them flat on the surface for the support of his chin. Then he began to call for help. After a time he heard the sound of feet sucking through the mud as some one advanced from behind.

"Lend a hand, friend," he said. "Throw out a life-line or something."

It was a woman's voice that answered, and he recognized it.

"If you'll unbuckle the straps I can get up."

The hundred pounds rolled into the mud with a soggy noise, and he slowly gained his feet.

"A pretty predicament," Miss Gastell laughed, at sight of his mud-covered face.

"Not at all," he replied airily. "My favourite physical-exercise stunt. Try it some time. It's great for the pectoral muscles and the spine."

He wiped his face, flinging the slush from his hand with a snappy jerk.

"Oh!" she cried in recognition. "It's Mr.—ah—Mr. Smoke Bellew."

"I thank you gravely for your timely rescue and for that name," he answered. "I have been doubly baptized. Henceforth I shall insist always on being called Smoke Bellew. It is a strong name, and not without significance."

He paused, and then voice and expression became suddenly fierce.

"Do you know what I'm going to do?" he demanded. "I'm going back to the States. I am going to get married. I am going to raise a large family of children. And then, as the evening shadows fall, I shall gather those children about me and relate the sufferings and hardships I endured on the Chilkoot Trail. And if they don't cry—I repeat, if they don't cry, I'll lambaste the stuffing out of them."

THE ARCTIC WINTER CAME DOWN apace. Snow that had come to stay lay six inches on the ground, and the ice was forming in quiet ponds, despite the fierce gales that blew. It was in the late afternoon, during a lull in such a gale, that Kit and John Bellew helped the cousins load the boat and watched it disappear down the lake in a snow-squall.

"And now a night's sleep and an early start in the morning," said John Bellew. "If we aren't storm-bound at the summit we'll make Dyea to-morrow night, and if we have luck in catching a steamer we'll be in San Francisco in a week."

"Enjoyed your vacation?" Kit asked absently.

Their camp for that last night at Linderman was a melancholy remnant. Everything of use, including the tent, had been taken by the cousins. A tattered tarpaulin, stretched as a wind-break, partially sheltered them from the driving snow. Supper they cooked on an open fire in a couple of battered and discarded camp utensils. All that was left them were their blankets, and food for several meals.

From the moment of the departure of the boat, Kit had become absent and restless. His uncle noticed his condition, and attributed it to the fact that the end of the hard toil had come. Only once during supper did Kit speak.

"Avuncular," he said, relevant of nothing, "after this, I wish you'd call me Smoke. I've made some smoke on this trail, haven't I?"

A few minutes later he wandered away in the direction of the village of tents that sheltered the gold-rushers who were still packing or building their boats. He was gone several hours, and when he returned and slipped into his blankets John Bellew was asleep.

In the darkness of a gale-driven morning, Kit crawled out, built a fire in his stocking feet, by which he thawed out his frozen shoes, then boiled coffee and fried bacon. It was a chilly, miserable meal. As soon as it was finished, they strapped their blankets. As John Bellew turned to lead the way toward the Chilcoot Trail, Kit held out his hand.

"Good-bye, avuncular," he said.

John Bellew looked at him and swore in his surprise.

"Don't forget, my name's Smoke," Kit chided.

"But what are you going to do?"

Kit waved his hand in a general direction northward over the storm-lashed lake.

"What's the good of turning back after getting this far?" he asked. "Besides, I've got my taste of meat, and I like it. I'm going on."

"You're broke," protested John Bellew. "You have no outfit."

"I've got a job. Behold your nephew, Christopher Smoke Bellew! He's got a job! He's a gentleman's man! He's got a job at a hundred and fifty per month and grub. He's going down to Dawson with a couple of dudes and another gentleman's man—camp-cook, boatman, and general all-around hustler. And O'Hara and The Billow can go to the devil. Good-bye."

But John Bellew was dazed, and could only mutter: "I don't understand."

"They say the baldface grizzlies are thick in the Yukon Basin," Kit explained. "Well, I've got only one suit of underclothes, and I'm going after the bear-meat, that's all."

II

The Meat

Half the time the wind blew a gale, and Smoke Bellew staggered against it along the beach. In the gray of dawn a dozen boats were being loaded with the precious outfits packed across Chilkoot. They were clumsy, home-made boats, put together by men who were not boat-builders, out of planks they had sawed by hand from green spruce-trees. One boat, already loaded, was just starting, and Kit paused to watch.

The wind, which was fair down the lake, here blew in squarely on the beach, kicking up a nasty sea in the shallows. The men of the departing boat waded in high rubber boots as they shoved it out toward deeper water. Twice they did this. Clambering aboard and failing to row clear, the boat was swept back and grounded. Kit noticed that the spray on the sides of the boat quickly turned to ice. The third attempt was a partial success. The last two men to climb in were wet to their waists, but the boat was afloat. They struggled awkwardly at the heavy oars, and slowly worked off shore. Then they hoisted a sail made of blankets, had it carry away in a gust, and were swept a third time back on the freezing beach.

Kit grinned to himself and went on. This was what he must expect to encounter, for he, too, in his new role of gentleman's man, was to start from the beach in a similar boat that very day.

Everywhere men were at work, and at work desperately, for the closing down of winter was so imminent that it was a gamble whether or not they would get across the great chain of lakes before the freeze-up. Yet, when Kit arrived at the tent of Messrs. Sprague and Stine, he did not find them stirring.

By a fire, under the shelter of a tarpaulin, squatted a short, thick man smoking a brown-paper cigarette.

"Hello," he said. "Are you Mister Sprague's new man?"

As Kit nodded, he thought he had noted a shade of emphasis on the *mister* and the *man*, and he was sure of a hint of a twinkle in the corner of the eye.

"Well, I'm Doc Stine's man," the other went on. "I'm five feet two inches long, and my name's Shorty, Jack Short for short, and sometimes known as Johnny-on-the-Spot."

Kit put out his hand and shook. "Were you raised on bear-meat?" he queried.

"Sure," was the answer; "though my first feedin' was buffalo-milk as near as I can remember. Sit down an' have some grub. The bosses ain't turned out yet."

And despite the one breakfast, Kit sat down under the tarpaulin and ate a second breakfast thrice as hearty. The heavy, purging toil of weeks had given him the stomach and appetite of a wolf. He could eat anything, in any quantity, and be unaware that he possessed a digestion. Shorty he found voluble and pessimistic, and from him he received surprising tips concerning their bosses and ominous forecasts of the expedition. Thomas Stanley Sprague was a budding mining engineer and the son of a millionaire. Doctor Adolph Stine was also the son of a wealthy father. And, through their fathers, both had been backed by an investing syndicate in the Klondike adventure.

"Oh, they're sure made of money," Shorty expounded. "When they hit the beach at Dyea, freight was seventy cents, but no Indians. There was a party from Eastern Oregon, real miners, that'd managed to get a team of Indians together at seventy cents. Indians had the straps on the outfit, three thousand pounds of it, when along comes Sprague and Stine. They offered eighty cents and ninety, and at a dollar a pound the Indians jumped the contract and took off their straps. Sprague and Stine came through, though it cost them three thousand, and the Oregon bunch is still on the beach. They won't get through till next year.

"Oh, they are real hummers, your boss and mine, when it comes to sheddin' the mazuma an' never mindin' other folks' feelin's. What did they do when they hit Linderman? The carpenters was just putting in the last licks on a boat they'd contracted to a 'Frisco bunch for six hundred. Sprague and Stine slipped 'em an even thousand, and they jumped their contract. It's a good-lookin' boat, but it's jiggered the other bunch. They've got their outfit right here, but no boat. And they're stuck for next year.

"Have another cup of coffee, and take it from me that I wouldn't travel with no such outfit if I didn't want to get to Klondike so blamed bad. They ain't hearted right. They'd take the crape off the door of a house in mourning if they needed it in their business. Did you sign a contract?"

Kit shook his head.

"Then I'm sorry for you, pardner. They ain't no grub in the country, and they'll drop you cold as soon as they hit Dawson. Men are going to starve there this winter."

"They agreed—" Kit began.

"Verbal," Shorty snapped him short. "It's your say-so against theirs, that's all. Well, anyway, what's your name, pardner?"

"Call me Smoke," said Kit.

"Well, Smoke, you'll have a run for your verbal contract just the same. This is a plain sample of what to expect. They can sure shed mazuma, but they can't work, or turn out of bed in the morning. We should have been loaded and started an hour ago. It's you an' me for the big work. Pretty soon you'll hear 'em shoutin' for their coffee—in bed, mind you, and them grown men. What d'ye know about boatin' on the water? I'm a cowman and a prospector, but I'm sure tenderfooted on water, an' they don't know punkins. What d'ye know?"

"Search me," Kit answered, snuggling in closer under the tarpaulin as the snow whirled before a fiercer gust. "I haven't been on a small boat since a boy. But I guess we can learn."

A corner of the tarpaulin tore loose, and Shorty received a jet of driven snow down the back of his neck.

"Oh, we can learn all right," he muttered wrathfully. "Sure we can. A child can learn. But it's dollars to doughnuts we don't even get started to-day."

It was eight o'clock when the call for coffee came from the tent, and nearly nine before the two employers emerged.

"Hello," said Sprague, a rosy-cheeked, well-fed young man of twenty-five. "Time we made a start, Shorty. You and—" Here he glanced interrogatively at Kit. "I didn't quite catch your name last evening."

"Smoke."

"Well, Shorty, you and Mr. Smoke had better begin loading the boat."

"Plain Smoke—cut out the Mister," Kit suggested.

Sprague nodded curtly and strolled away among the tents, to be followed by Doctor Stine, a slender, pallid young man.

Shorty looked significantly at his companion. "Over a ton and a half of outfit, and they won't lend a hand. You'll see."

"I guess it's because we're paid to do the work," Kit answered cheerfully, "and we might as well buck in."

To move three thousand pounds on the shoulders a hundred yards was no slight task, and to do it in half a gale, slushing through the snow in heavy rubber boots, was exhausting. In addition, there was the taking down of the tent and the packing of small camp equipage. Then came the loading. As the boat settled, it had to be shoved farther and farther out, increasing the distance they had to wade. By two o'clock it had all been accomplished, and Kit, despite his two breakfasts, was weak with the faintness of hunger. His knees were shaking under him. Shorty, in similar predicament, foraged through the pots and pans, and drew forth a big pot of cold boiled beans in which were imbedded large chunks of bacon. There was only one spoon, a long-handled one, and they dipped, turn and turn about, into the pot. Kit was filled with an immense certitude that in all his life he had never tasted anything so good.

"Lord, man," he mumbled between chews, "I never knew what appetite was till I hit the trail."

Sprague and Stine arrived in the midst of this pleasant occupation.

"What's the delay?" Sprague complained. "Aren't we ever going to get started?"

Shorty dipped in turn, and passed the spoon to Kit. Nor did either speak till the pot was empty and the bottom scraped.

"Of course we ain't been doin' nothing," Shorty said, wiping his mouth with the back of his hand. "We ain't been doin' nothing at all. And of course you ain't had nothing to eat. It was sure careless of me."

"Yes, yes," Stine said quickly. "We ate at one of the tents—friends of ours."

"Thought so," Shorty grunted.

"But now that you're finished, let us get started," Sprague urged.

"There's the boat," said Shorty. "She's sure loaded. Now, just how might you be goin' about to get started?"

"By climbing aboard and shoving off. Come on."

They waded out, and the employers got on board, while Kit and Shorty shoved clear. When the waves lapped the tops of their boots they clambered in. The other two men were not prepared with the oars, and the boat swept back and grounded. Half a dozen times, with a great expenditure of energy, this was repeated.

Shorty sat down disconsolately on the gunwale, took a chew of tobacco, and questioned the universe, while Kit baled the boat and the other two exchanged unkind remarks.

"If you'll take my orders, I'll get her off," Sprague finally said.

The attempt was well intended, but before he could clamber on board he was wet to the waist.

"We've got to camp and build a fire," he said, as the boat grounded again. "I'm freezing."

"Don't be afraid of a wetting," Stine sneered. "Other men have gone off to-day wetter than you. Now I'm going to take her out."

This time it was he who got the wetting and who announced with chattering teeth the need of a fire.

"A little splash like that!" Sprague chattered spitefully. "We'll go on."

"Shorty, dig out my clothes-bag and make a fire," the other commanded.

"You'll do nothing of the sort," Sprague cried.

Shorty looked from one to the other, expectorated, but did not move.

"He's working for me, and I guess he obeys my orders," Stine retorted. "Shorty, take that bag ashore."

Shorty obeyed, and Sprague shivered in the boat. Kit, having received no orders, remained inactive, glad of the rest.

"A boat divided against itself won't float," he soliloquized.

"What's that?" Sprague snarled at him.

"Talking to myself—habit of mine," he answered.

His employer favoured him with a hard look, and sulked several minutes longer. Then he surrendered.

"Get out my bag, Smoke," he ordered, "and lend a hand with that fire. We won't get off till morning now."

NEXT DAY THE GALE STILL blew. Lake Linderman was no more than a narrow mountain gorge filled with water. Sweeping down from the mountains through this funnel, the wind was irregular, blowing great guns at times and at other times dwindling to a strong breeze.

"If you give me a shot at it, I think I can get her off," Kit said, when all was ready for the start.

"What do you know about it?" Stine snapped at him.

"Search me," Kit answered, and subsided.

It was the first time he had worked for wages in his life, but he was learning the discipline of it fast. Obediently and cheerfully he joined in various vain efforts to get clear of the beach.

"How would you go about it?" Sprague finally half panted, half whined at him.

"Sit down and get a good rest till a lull comes in the wind, and then buck in for all we're worth."

Simple as the idea was, he had been the first to evolve it; the first time it was applied it worked, and they hoisted a blanket to the mast and sped down the lake. Stine and Sprague immediately became cheerful. Shorty, despite his chronic pessimism, was always cheerful, and Kit was too interested to be otherwise. Sprague struggled with the steering-sweep for a quarter of an hour, and then looked appealingly at Kit, who relieved him.

"My arms are fairly broken with the strain of it," Sprague muttered apologetically.

"You never ate bear-meat, did you?" Kit asked sympathetically.

"What the devil do you mean?"

"Oh, nothing; I was just wondering."

But behind his employer's back Kit caught the approving grin of Shorty, who had already caught the whim of his metaphor.

Kit steered the length of Linderman, displaying an aptitude that caused both young men of money and disinclination for work to name him boat-steerer. Shorty was no less pleased, and volunteered to continue cooking and leave the boat work to the other.

Between Linderman and Lake Bennett was a portage. The boat, lightly loaded, was lined down the small but violent connecting stream, and here Kit learned a vast deal more about boats and water. But when it came to packing the outfit, Stine and Sprague disappeared, and their men spent two days of back-breaking toil in getting the outfit across. And this was the history of many miserable days of the trip—Kit and Shorty working to exhaustion, while their masters toiled not and demanded to be waited upon.

But the iron-bound arctic winter continued to close down, and they were held back by numerous and unavoidable delays. At Windy Arm, Stine arbitrarily dispossessed Kit of the steering-sweep and within the hour wrecked the boat on a wave-beaten lee shore. Two days were lost here in making repairs, and the morning of the fresh start, as they came down to embark, on stern and bow, in large letters, was charcoaled "The Chechako."

Kit grinned at the appropriateness of the invidious word.

"Huh!" said Shorty, when accused by Stine. "I can sure read and spell, an' I know that chechako means tenderfoot, but my education never went high enough to learn me to spell a jaw-breaker like that."

Both employers looked daggers at Kit, for the insult rankled; nor did he mention that the night before, Shorty had besought him for the spelling of that particular word.

"That's 'most as bad as your bear-meat slam at 'em," Shorty confided later.

Kit chuckled. Along with the continuous discovery of his own powers had come an ever-increasing disapproval of the two masters. It was not so much irritation, which was always present, as disgust. He had got his taste of the meat, and liked it; but they were teaching him how not to eat it. Privily, he thanked God that he was not made as they. He came to dislike them to a degree that bordered on hatred. Their malingering bothered him less than their helpless inefficiency. Somewhere in him, old Isaac Bellew and all the rest of the hardy Bellews were making good.

"Shorty," he said one day, in the usual delay of getting started, "I could almost fetch them a rap over the head with an oar and bury them in the river."

"Same here," Shorty agreed. "They're not meat-eaters. They're fish-eaters, and they sure stink."

THEY CAME TO THE RAPIDS; first, the Box Canyon, and, several miles below, the White Horse. The Box Canyon was adequately named. It was a box, a trap. Once in it, the only way out was through. On either side arose perpendicular walls of rock. The river narrowed to a fraction of its width and roared through this gloomy passage in a madness of motion that heaped the water in the center into a ridge fully eight feet higher than at the rocky sides. This ridge, in turn, was crested with stiff, upstanding waves that curled over yet remained each in its unvarying place. The Canyon was well feared, for it had collected its toll of dead from the passing goldrushers.

Tying to the bank above, where lay a score of other anxious boats, Kit and his companions went ahead on foot to investigate. They crept to the brink and gazed down at the swirl of water. Sprague drew back, shuddering.

"My God!" he exclaimed. "A swimmer hasn't a chance in that."

Shorty touched Kit significantly with his elbow and said in an undertone:

"Cold feet. Dollars to doughnuts they don't go through."

Kit scarcely heard. From the beginning of the boat trip he had been learning the stubbornness and inconceivable viciousness of the elements, and this glimpse of what was below him acted as a challenge. "We've got to ride that ridge," he said. "If we get off it we'll hit the walls."

"And never know what hit us," was Shorty's verdict. "Can you swim, Smoke?"

"I'd wish I couldn't if anything went wrong in there."

"That's what I say," a stranger, standing alongside and peering down into the Canyon, said mournfully. "And I wish I were through it."

"I wouldn't sell my chance to go through," Kit answered.

He spoke honestly, but it was with the idea of heartening the man. He turned to go back to the boat.

"Are you going to tackle it?" the man asked.

Kit nodded.

"I wish I could get the courage to," the other confessed. "I've been here for hours. The longer I look, the more afraid I am. I am not a boatman, and I have with me only my nephew, who is a young boy, and my wife. If you get through safely, will you run my boat through?"

Kit looked at Shorty, who delayed to answer.

"He's got his wife with him," Kit suggested. Nor had he mistaken his man.

"Sure," Shorty affirmed. "It was just what I was stopping to think about. I knew there was some reason I ought to do it."

Again they turned to go, but Sprague and Stine made no movement.

"Good luck, Smoke," Sprague called to him. "I'll—er—" He hesitated. "I'll just stay here and watch you."

"We need three men in the boat, two at the oars and one at the steering-sweep," Kit said quietly.

Sprague looked at Stine.

"I'm damned if I do," said that gentleman. "If you're not afraid to stand here and look on, I'm not."

"Who's afraid?" Sprague demanded hotly.

Stine retorted in kind, and their two men left them in the thick of a squabble.

"We can do without them," Kit said to Shorty. "You take the bow with a paddle, and I'll handle the steering-sweep. All you'll have to do is just to help keep her straight. Once we're started, you won't be able to hear me, so just keep on keeping her straight."

They cast off the boat and worked out to middle in the quickening current. From the Canyon came an ever-growing roar. The river sucked in to the entrance with the smoothness of molten glass, and here, as the darkening walls received them, Shorty took a chew of tobacco and dipped his paddle. The boat leaped on the first crests of the ridge, and they were deafened by the uproar of wild water that reverberated from the narrow walls and multiplied itself. They were half-smothered with flying spray. At times Kit could not see his comrade at the bow. It was only a matter of two minutes, in which time they rode the ridge three-quarters of a mile and emerged in safety and tied to the bank in the eddy below.

Shorty emptied his mouth of tobacco juice—he had forgotten to spit—and spoke.

"That was bear-meat," he exulted, "the real bear-meat. Say, we want a few, didn't we? Smoke, I don't mind tellin' you in confidence that before we started I was the gosh-dangdest scaredest man this side of the Rocky Mountains. Now I'm a bear-eater. Come on an' we'll run that other boat through."

Midway back, on foot, they encountered their employers, who had watched the passage from above.

"There comes the fish-eaters," said Shorty. "Keep to win'ward."

AFTER RUNNING THE STRANGER'S BOAT through, whose name proved to be Breck, Kit and Shorty met his wife, a slender, girlish woman whose blue eyes were moist with gratitude. Breck himself tried to hand Kit fifty dollars, and then attempted it on Shorty.

"Stranger," was the latter's rejection, "I come into this country to make money outa the ground an' not outa my fellow critters."

Breck rummaged in his boat and produced a demijohn of whiskey. Shorty's hand half went out to it and stopped abruptly. He shook his head.

"There's that blamed White Horse right below, an' they say it's worse than the Box. I reckon I don't dast tackle any lightning."

Several miles below they ran in to the bank, and all four walked down to look at the bad water. The river, which was a succession of rapids, was here deflected toward the right bank by a rocky reef. The whole body of water, rushing crookedly into the narrow passage, accelerated its speed frightfully and was up-flung into huge waves, white and wrathful. This was the dread Mane of the White Horse, and here an even heavier toll of dead had been exacted. On one side of the Mane was a corkscrew curl-over and suck-under, and on the opposite side was the big whirlpool. To go through, the Mane itself must be ridden.

"This plum rips the strings outa the Box," Shorty concluded.

As they watched, a boat took the head of the rapids above. It was a large boat, fully thirty feet long, laden with several tons of outfit, and handled by six men. Before it reached the Mane it was plunging and leaping, at times almost hidden by the foam and spray.

Shorty shot a slow, sidelong glance at Kit and said: "She's fair smoking, and she hasn't hit the worst. They've hauled the oars in. There she takes it now. God! She's gone! No; there she is!"

Big as the boat was, it had been buried from sight in the flying smother between crests. The next moment, in the thick of the Mane, the boat leaped up a crest and into view. To Kit's amazement he saw the whole long bottom clearly outlined. The boat, for the fraction of an instant, was in the air, the men sitting idly in their places, all save one in the stern, who stood at the steering-sweep. Then came the downward plunge into the trough and a second disappearance. Three times the boat leaped and buried itself, then those on the bank saw its nose take the whirlpool as it slipped off the Mane. The steersman, vainly opposing with his full weight on the steering-gear, surrendered to the whirlpool and helped the boat to take the circle.

Three times it went around, each time so close to the rocks on which Kit and Shorty stood that either could have leaped on board. The steersman, a man with a reddish beard of recent growth, waved his hand to them. The only way out of the whirlpool was by the Mane, and on the third round the boat entered the Mane obliquely at its upper end. Possibly out of fear of the draw of the whirlpool, the steersman did not attempt to straighten out quickly enough. When he did, it was too late. Alternately in the air and buried, the boat angled the Mane and was sucked into and down through the stiff wall of the corkscrew on the opposite side of the river. A hundred feet below, boxes and bales began to float up. Then appeared the bottom of the boat and the scattered heads of six men. Two managed to make the bank in the eddy below. The others were drawn under, and the general flotsam was lost to view, borne on by the swift current around the bend.

There was a long minute of silence. Shorty was the first to speak.

"Come on," he said. "We might as well tackle it. My feet'll get cold if I stay here any longer."

"We'll smoke some," Kit grinned at him.

"And you'll sure earn your name," was the rejoinder. Shorty turned to their employers. "Comin'?" he queried.

Perhaps the roar of the water prevented them from hearing the invitation.

Shorty and Kit tramped back through a foot of snow to the head of the rapids and cast off the boat. Kit was divided between two impressions: one, of the caliber of his comrade, which served as a spur to him; the other, likewise a spur, was the knowledge that old Isaac Bellew, and all the other Bellews, had done things like this in their westward march of empire. What they had done, he could do. It was the meat, the strong meat, and he knew, as never before, that it required strong men to eat such meat.

"You've sure got to keep the top of the ridge," Shorty shouted at him, the plug of tobacco lifting to his mouth, as the boat quickened in the quickening current and took the head of the rapids.

Kit nodded, swayed his strength and weight tentatively on the steering-gear, and headed the boat for the plunge.

Several minutes later, half-swamped and lying against the bank in the eddy below the White Horse, Shorty spat out a mouthful of tobacco juice and shook Kit's hand.

"Meat! Meat!" Shorty chanted. "We eat it raw! We eat it alive!"

At the top of the bank they met Breck. His wife stood at a little distance. Kit shook his hand.

"I'm afraid your boat can't make it," he said. "It is smaller than ours and a bit cranky."

The man pulled out a row of bills.

"I'll give you each a hundred if you run it through."

Kit looked out and up the tossing Mane of the White Horse. A long, gray twilight was falling, it was turning colder, and the landscape seemed taking on a savage bleakness.

"It ain't that," Shorty was saying. "We don't want your money. Wouldn't touch it nohow. But my pardner is the real meat with boats, and when he says yourn ain't safe I reckon he knows what he's talkin' about."

Kit nodded affirmation, and chanced to glance at Mrs. Breck. Her eyes were fixed upon him, and he knew that if ever he had seen prayer in a woman's eyes he was seeing it then. Shorty followed his gaze and saw what he saw. They looked at each other in confusion and did not speak. Moved by the common impulse, they nodded to each other and turned to the trail that led to the head of the rapids. They had not gone a hundred yards when they met Stine and Sprague coming down.

"Where are you going?" the latter demanded.

"To fetch that other boat through," Shorty answered.

"No, you're not. It's getting dark. You two are going to pitch camp."

So huge was Kit's disgust that he forebore to speak.

"He's got his wife with him," Shorty said.

"That's his lookout," Stine contributed.

"And Smoke's and mine," was Shorty's retort.

"I forbid you," Sprague said harshly. "Smoke, if you go another step I'll discharge you."

"And you, too, Shorty," Stine added.

"And a hell of a pickle you'll be in with us fired," Shorty replied. "How'll you get your blamed boat to Dawson? Who'll serve you coffee in your blankets and manicure your finger-nails? Come on, Smoke. They don't dast fire us. Besides, we've got agreements. If they fire us they've got to divvy up grub to last us through the winter."

Barely had they shoved Breck's boat out from the bank and caught the first rough water, when the waves began to lap aboard. They were small waves, but it was an earnest of what was to come. Shorty cast back a quizzical glance as he gnawed at his inevitable plug, and Kit felt a strange rush of warmth at his heart for this man who couldn't swim and who couldn't back out.

The rapids grew stiffer, and the spray began to fly. In the gathering darkness, Kit glimpsed the Mane and the crooked fling of the current into it. He worked into this crooked current, and felt a glow of satisfaction as the boat hit the head of the Mane squarely in the middle. After that, in the smother, leaping and burying and swamping, he had no clear impression of anything save that he swung his weight on the steering-oar and wished his uncle were there to see. They emerged, breathless, wet through, the boat filled with water almost to the gunwale. Lighter pieces of baggage and outfit were floating inside the boat. A few careful strokes on Shorty's part worked the boat into the draw of the eddy, and the eddy did the rest till the boat softly touched the bank. Looking down from above was Mrs. Breck. Her prayer had been answered, and the tears were streaming down her cheeks.

"You boys have simply got to take the money," Breck called down to them.

Shorty stood up, slipped, and sat down in the water, while the boat dipped one gunwale under and righted again.

"Damn the money," said Shorty. "Fetch out that whiskey. Now that it's over I'm getting cold feet, an' I'm sure likely to have a chill."

In the morning, as usual, they were among the last of the boats to start. Breck, despite his boating inefficiency, and with only his wife and nephew for crew, had broken camp, loaded his boat, and pulled out at the first streak of day. But there was no hurrying Stine and Sprague, who seemed incapable of realizing that the freeze-up might come at any time. They malingered, got in the way, delayed, and doubled the work of Kit and Shorty.

"I'm sure losing my respect for God, seein' as he must 'a' made them two mistakes in human form," was the latter's blasphemous way of expressing his disgust.

"Well, you're the real goods, at any rate," Kit grinned back at him. "It makes me respect God the more just to look at you."

"He was sure goin' some, eh?" was Shorty's fashion of overcoming the embarrassment of the compliment.

The trail by water crossed Lake Labarge. Here was no fast current, but a tideless stretch of forty miles which must be rowed unless a fair wind blew. But the time for fair wind was past, and an icy gale blew in their teeth out of the north. This made a rough sea, against which it was almost impossible to pull the boat. Added to their troubles was driving snow; also, the freezing of the water on their oar-blades kept one man occupied in chopping it off with a hatchet. Compelled to take their turn at the oars, Sprague and Stine patently loafed. Kit had learned how to throw his weight on an oar, but he noted that his employers made a seeming of throwing their weights and that they dipped their oars at a cheating angle.

At the end of three hours, Sprague pulled his oar in and said they would run back into the mouth of the river for shelter. Stine seconded him, and the several hard-won miles were lost. A second day, and a third, the same fruitless attempt was made. In the river mouth, the continually arriving boats from White Horse made a flotilla of over two hundred. Each day forty or fifty arrived, and only two or three won to the northwest shore of the lake and did not come back. Ice was now forming in the eddies, and connecting from eddy to eddy in thin lines around the points. The freeze-up was very imminent.

"We could make it if they had the souls of clams," Kit told Shorty, as they dried their moccasins by the fire on the evening of the third day. "We could have made it to-day if they hadn't turned back. Another hour's work would have fetched that west shore. They're—they're babes in the woods."

"Sure," Shorty agreed. He turned his moccasin to the flame and debated a moment. "Look here, Smoke. It's hundreds of miles to Dawson. If we don't want to freeze in here, we've got to do something. What d'ye say?"

Kit looked at him, and waited.

"We've got the immortal cinch on them two babes," Shorty expounded. "They can give orders an' shed mazuma, but as you say, they're plum babes. If we're goin' to Dawson, we got to take charge of this here outfit."

They looked at each other.

"It's a go," said Kit, as his hand went out in ratification.

In the morning, long before daylight, Shorty issued his call. "Come on!" he roared. "Tumble out, you sleepers! Here's your coffee! Kick into it! We're goin' to make a start!"

Grumbling and complaining, Stine and Sprague were forced to get under way two hours earlier than ever before. If anything, the gale was stiffer, and in a short time every man's face was iced up, while the oars were heavy with ice. Three hours they struggled, and four, one man steering, one chopping ice, two toiling at the oars, and each taking his various turns. The northwest shore loomed nearer and nearer. The gale blew ever harder, and at last Sprague pulled in his oar in token of surrender. Shorty sprang to it, though his relief had only begun.

"Chop ice," he said, handing Sprague the hatchet.

"But what's the use?" the other whined. "We can't make it. We're going to turn back."

"We're going on," said Shorty. "Chop ice. An' when you feel better you can spell me."

It was heart-breaking toil, but they gained the shore, only to find it composed of surge-beaten rocks and cliffs, with no place to land.

"I told you so," Sprague whimpered.

"You never peeped," Shorty answered.

"We're going back."

Nobody spoke, and Kit held the boat into the seas as they skirted the forbidding shore. Sometimes they gained no more than a foot to the stroke, and there were times when two or three strokes no more than enabled them to hold their own. He did his best to hearten the two weaklings. He pointed out that the boats which had won to this shore had never come back. Perforce, he argued, they had found a shelter somewhere ahead. Another hour they labored, and a second.

"If you fellows'd put into your oars some of that coffee you swig in your blankets, we'd make it," was Shorty's encouragement. "You're just goin' through the motions an' not pullin' a pound."

A few minutes later, Sprague drew in his oar.

"I'm finished," he said, and there were tears in his voice.

"So are the rest of us," Kit answered, himself ready to cry or to commit murder, so great was his exhaustion. "But we're going on just the same."

"We're going back. Turn the boat around."

"Shorty, if he won't pull, take that oar yourself," Kit commanded.

"Sure," was the answer. "He can chop ice."

But Sprague refused to give over the oar; Stine had ceased rowing, and the boat was drifting backward.

"Turn around, Smoke," Sprague ordered.

And Kit, who never in his life had cursed any man, astonished himself.

"I'll see you in hell, first," he replied. "Take hold of that oar and pull."

It is in moments of exhaustion that men lose all their reserves of civilization, and such a moment had come. Each man had reached the breaking-point. Sprague jerked off a mitten, drew his revolver, and turned it on his steersman. This was a new experience to Kit. He had never had a gun presented at him in his life. And now, to his surprise, it seemed to mean nothing at all. It was the most natural thing in the world.

"If you don't put that gun up," he said, "I'll take it away and rap you over the knuckles with it."

"If you don't turn the boat around, I'll shoot you," Sprague threatened.

Then Shorty took a hand. He ceased chopping ice and stood up behind Sprague.

"Go on an' shoot," said Shorty, wiggling the hatchet. "I'm just aching for a chance to brain you. Go on an' start the festivities."

"This is mutiny," Stine broke in. "You were engaged to obey orders."

Shorty turned on him. "Oh, you'll get yours as soon as I finish with your pardner, you little hog-wallopin' snooper, you."

"Sprague," Kit said, "I'll give you just thirty seconds to put away that gun and get that oar out."

Sprague hesitated, gave a short hysterical laugh, put the revolver away, and bent his back to the work.

For two hours more, inch by inch, they fought their way along the edge of the foaming rocks, until Kit feared he had made a mistake. And then, when on the verge of himself turning back, they came abreast of a narrow opening, not twenty feet wide, which led into a land-locked enclosure where the fiercest gusts scarcely flawed the surface. It was the haven gained by the boats of previous days. They landed on a shelving beach, and the two employers lay in collapse in the boat, while Kit and Shorty pitched the tent, built a fire, and started the cooking.

"What's a hog-walloping snooper, Shorty?" Kit asked.

"Blamed if I know," was the answer; "but he's one just the same."

The gale, which had been dying quickly, ceased at nightfall, and it came on clear and cold. A cup of coffee, set aside to cool and forgotten, a few minutes later was found coated with half an inch of ice. At eight o'clock, when Sprague and Stine, already rolled in their blankets, were sleeping the sleep of exhaustion, Kit came back from a look at the boat.

"It's the freeze-up, Shorty," he announced. "There's a skin of ice over the whole pond already."

"What are you going to do?"

"There's only one thing. The lake of course freezes first. The rapid current of the river may keep it open for days. This time to-morrow any boat caught in Lake Labarge remains there until next year."

"You mean we got to get out to-night? Now?"

Kit nodded.

"Tumble out, you sleepers!" was Shorty's answer, couched in a roar, as he began casting off the guy-ropes of the tent.

The other two awoke, groaning with the pain of stiffened muscles and the pain of rousing from the sleep of exhaustion.

"What time is it?" Stine asked.

"Half-past eight."

"It's dark yet," was the objection.

Shorty jerked out a couple of guy-ropes, and the tent began to sag.

"It's not morning," he said. "It's evening. Come on. The lake's freezin'. We got to get acrost."

Stine sat up, his face bitter and wrathful. "Let it freeze. We're not going to stir."

"All right," said Shorty. "We're goin' on with the boat."

"You were engaged—"

"To take your outfit to Dawson," Shorty caught him up. "Well, we're takin' it, ain't we?" He punctuated his query by bringing half the tent down on top of them.

They broke their way through the thin ice in the little harbor, and came out on the lake, where the water, heavy and glassy, froze on their oars with every stroke. The water soon became like mush, clogging the stroke of the oars and freezing in the air even as it dripped. Later the surface began to form a skin, and the boat proceeded slower and slower.

Often afterwards, when Kit tried to remember that night and failed to bring up aught but nightmare recollections, he wondered what must have been the sufferings of Stine and Sprague. His one impression of himself was that he struggled through biting frost and intolerable exertion for a thousand years, more or less.

Morning found them stationary. Stine complained of frosted fingers, and Sprague of his nose, while the pain in Kit's cheeks and nose told him that he, too, had been touched. With each accretion of daylight they could see farther, and as far as they could see was icy surface. The water of the lake was gone. A hundred yards away was the shore of the north end. Shorty insisted that it was the opening of the river and that he could see water. He and Kit alone were able to work, and with their oars they broke the ice and forced the boat along. And at the last gasp of their strength they made the suck of the rapid river. One look back showed them several boats which had fought through the night and were hopelessly frozen in; then they whirled around a bend in a current running six miles an hour.

DAY BY DAY THEY FLOATED down the swift river, and day by day the shore-ice extended farther out. When they made camp at nightfall, they chopped a space in the ice in which to lay the boat and carried the camp outfit hundreds of feet to shore. In the morning, they chopped the boat out through the new ice and caught the current. Shorty set up the sheet-iron stove in the boat, and over this Stine and Sprague hung through the long, drifting hours. They had surrendered, no longer gave orders, and their one desire was to gain Dawson. Shorty, pessimistic, indefatigable, and joyous, at frequent intervals roared out the three lines of the first four-line stanza of a song he had forgotten. The colder it got the oftener he sang:

> "Like Argus of the ancient times,
> We leave this Modern Greece;
> Tum-tum, tum-tum, tum-tum, tum-tum,
> To shear the Golden Fleece."

As they passed the mouths of the Hootalinqua and the Big and Little Salmon, they found these streams throwing mush-ice into the main Yukon. This gathered about the boat and attached itself, and at night they found themselves compelled to chop the boat out of the current. In the morning they chopped the boat back into the current.

The last night ashore was spent between the mouths of the White River and the Stewart. At daylight they found the Yukon, half a mile wide, running white from ice-rimmed bank to ice-rimmed bank. Shorty cursed the universe with less geniality than usual, and looked at Kit.

"We'll be the last boat this year to make Dawson," Kit said.

"But they ain't no water, Smoke."

"Then we'll ride the ice down. Come on."

Futilely protesting, Sprague and Stine were bundled on board. For half an hour, with axes, Kit and Shorty struggled to cut a way into the swift but solid stream. When they did succeed in clearing the shore-ice, the floating ice forced the boat along the edge for a hundred yards, tearing away half of one gunwale and making a partial wreck of it. Then, at the lower end of the bend, they caught the current that flung off-shore. They proceeded to work farther toward the middle. The stream was no longer composed of mush-ice but of hard cakes. In between the cakes only was mush-ice, that froze solidly as they looked at it. Shoving with the oars against the cakes, sometimes climbing out on the cakes in order to force the boat along, after an hour they gained the middle. Five minutes after they ceased their exertions, the boat was frozen in. The whole river was coagulating as it ran. Cake froze to cake, until at last the boat was the center of a cake seventy-five feet in diameter. Sometimes they floated sideways, sometimes stern-first, while gravity tore asunder the forming fetters in the moving mass, only to be manacled by faster-forming ones. While the hours passed, Shorty stoked the stove, cooked meals, and chanted his war-song.

Night came, and after many efforts, they gave up the attempt to force the boat to shore, and through the darkness they swept helplessly onward.

"What if we pass Dawson?" Shorty queried.

"We'll walk back," Kit answered, "if we're not crushed in a jam."

The sky was clear, and in the light of the cold, leaping stars they caught occasional glimpses of the loom of mountains on either hand. At eleven o'clock, from below, came a dull, grinding roar. Their speed began to diminish, and cakes of ice to up-end and crash and smash about them. The river was jamming. One cake, forced upward, slid across their cake and carried one side of the boat away. It did not sink, for its own cake still upbore it, but in a whirl they saw dark water show for an instant within a foot of them. Then all movement ceased. At the end of half an hour the whole river picked itself up and began to move. This continued for an hour, when again it was brought to rest by a jam. Once again it started, running swiftly and savagely, with a great grinding. Then they saw lights ashore, and, when abreast, gravity and the Yukon surrendered, and the river ceased for six months.

On the shore at Dawson, curious ones, gathered to watch the river freeze, heard from out of the darkness the war-song of Shorty:

> *"Like Argus of the ancient times,*
> *We leave this Modern Greece;*
> *Tum-tum, tum-tum; tum-tum, tum-tum,*
> *To shear the Golden Fleece."*

For three days Kit and Shorty labored, carrying the ton and a half of outfit from the middle of the river to the log-cabin Stine and Sprague had bought on the hill overlooking Dawson. This work finished, in the warm cabin, as twilight was falling, Sprague motioned Kit to him. Outside the thermometer registered sixty-five below zero.

"Your full month isn't up, Smoke," Sprague said. "But here it is in full. I wish you luck."

"How about the agreement?" Kit asked. "You know there's a famine here. A man can't get work in the mines even, unless he has his own grub. You agreed—"

"I know of no agreement," Sprague interrupted. "Do you, Stine? We engaged you by the month. There's your pay. Will you sign the receipt?"

Kit's hands clenched, and for the moment he saw red. Both men shrank away from him. He had never struck a man in anger in his life, and he felt so certain of his ability to thrash Sprague that he could not bring himself to do it.

Shorty saw his trouble and interposed.

"Look here, Smoke, I ain't travelin' no more with a ornery outfit like this. Right here's where I sure jump it. You an' me stick together. Savvy? Now, you take your blankets an' hike down to the Elkhorn. Wait for me. I'll settle up, collect what's comin', an' give them what's comin'. I ain't no good on the water, but my feet's on terry-fermy now an' I'm sure goin' to make smoke."

Half an hour afterwards Shorty appeared at the Elkhorn. From his bleeding knuckles and the skin off one cheek, it was evident that he had given Stine and Sprague what was coming.

"You ought to see that cabin," he chuckled, as they stood at the bar. "Rough-house ain't no name for it. Dollars to doughnuts nary one of 'em shows up on the street for a week. An' now it's all figgered out for you an' me. Grub's a dollar an' a half a pound. They ain't no work for wages without you have your own grub. Moose-meat's sellin' for two dollars a pound an' they ain't none. We got enough money for a month's grub an' ammunition, an' we hike up the Klondike to the back country. If they ain't no moose, we go an' live with the Indians. But if we ain't got five thousand pounds of meat six weeks from now, I'll—I'll sure go back an' apologize to our bosses. Is it a go?"

Kit's hand went out, and they shook. Then he faltered. "I don't know anything about hunting," he said.

Shorty lifted his glass.

"But you're a sure meat-eater, an' I'll learn you."

III

THE STAMPEDE TO SQUAW CREEK

Two months after Smoke Bellew and Shorty went after moose for a grub-stake, they were back in the Elkhorn saloon at Dawson. The hunting was done, the meat hauled in and sold for two dollars and a half a pound, and between them they possessed three thousand dollars in gold dust and a good team of dogs. They had played in luck. Despite the fact that the gold-rush had driven the game a hundred miles or more into the mountains, they had, within half that distance, bagged four moose in a narrow canyon.

The mystery of the strayed animals was no greater than the luck of their killers, for within the day four famished Indian families, reporting no game in three days' journey back, camped beside them. Meat was traded for starving dogs, and after a week of feeding, Smoke and Shorty harnessed the animals and began freighting the meat to the eager Dawson market.

The problem of the two men now was to turn their gold-dust into food. The current price for flour and beans was a dollar and a half a pound, but the difficulty was to find a seller. Dawson was in the throes of famine. Hundreds of men, with money but no food, had been compelled to leave the country. Many had gone down the river on the last water, and many more, with barely enough food to last, had walked the six hundred miles over the ice to Dyea.

Smoke met Shorty in the warm saloon, and found the latter jubilant.

"Life ain't no punkins without whiskey an' sweetenin'," was Shorty's greeting, as he pulled lumps of ice from his thawing moustache and flung them rattling on the floor. "An' I sure just got eighteen pounds of that same sweetenin'. The geezer only charged three dollars a pound for it. What luck did you have?"

"I, too, have not been idle," Smoke answered with pride. "I bought fifty pounds of flour. And there's a man up on Adam Creek who says he'll let me have fifty pounds more to-morrow."

"Great! We'll sure live till the river opens. Say, Smoke, them dogs of ourn is the goods. A dog-buyer offered me two hundred apiece for the five of them. I told him nothin' doin'. They sure took on class when they got meat to get outside of; but it goes against the grain, feedin' dog-critters on grub that's worth two an' a half a pound. Come on an' have a drink. I just got to celebrate them eighteen pounds of sweetenin'."

Several minutes later, as he weighed in on the gold-scales for the drinks, he gave a start of recollection.

"I plum forgot that man I was to meet in the Tivoli. He's got some spoiled bacon he'll sell for a dollar an' a half a pound. We can feed it to the dogs an' save a dollar a day on each's board-bill. So long."

"So long," said Smoke. "I'm goin' to the cabin an' turn in."

Hardly had Shorty left the place, when a fur-clad man entered through the double storm-doors. His face lighted at sight of Smoke, who recognized him as Breck, the man whose boat they had run through the Box Canyon and White Horse Rapids.

"I heard you were in town," Breck said hurriedly, as they shook hands. "Been looking for you for half an hour. Come outside, I want to talk with you."

Smoke looked regretfully at the roaring, red-hot stove.

"Won't this do?"

"No; it's important. Come outside."

As they emerged, Smoke drew off one mitten, lighted a match, and glanced at the thermometer that hung beside the door. He remittened his naked hand hastily as if the frost had burned him. Overhead arched the flaming aurora borealis, while from all Dawson arose the mournful howling of thousands of wolf-dogs.

"What did it say?" Breck asked.

"Sixty below." Kit spat experimentally, and the spittle crackled in the air. "And the thermometer is certainly working. It's falling all the time. An hour ago it was only fifty-two. Don't tell me it's a stampede."

"It is," Breck whispered back cautiously, casting anxious eyes about in fear of some other listener. "You know Squaw Creek?—empties in on the other side of the Yukon thirty miles up?"

"Nothing doing there," was Smoke's judgment. "It was prospected years ago."

"So were all the other rich creeks. Listen! It's big. Only eight to twenty feet to bedrock. There won't be a claim that don't run to half a million. It's a dead secret. Two or three of my close friends let me in on it. I told my wife right away that I was going to find you before I started. Now, so long. My pack's hidden down the bank. In fact, when they told me, they made me promise not to pull out until Dawson was asleep. You know what it means if you're seen with a stampeding outfit. Get your partner and follow. You ought to stake fourth or fifth claim from Discovery. Don't forget—Squaw Creek. It's the third after you pass Swede Creek."

WHEN SMOKE ENTERED THE LITTLE cabin on the hillside back of Dawson, he heard a heavy familiar breathing.

"Aw, go to bed," Shorty mumbled, as Smoke shook his shoulder. "I'm not on the night shift," was his next remark, as the rousing hand became more vigorous. "Tell your troubles to the barkeeper."

"Kick into your clothes," Smoke said. "We've got to stake a couple of claims."

Shorty sat up and started to explode, but Smoke's hand covered his mouth.

"Ssh!" Smoke warned. "It's a big strike. Don't wake the neighborhood. Dawson's asleep."

"Huh! You got to show me. Nobody tells anybody about a strike, of course not. But ain't it plum amazin' the way everybody hits the trail just the same?"

"Squaw Creek," Smoke whispered. "It's right. Breck gave me the tip. Shallow bedrock. Gold from the grass-roots down. Come on. We'll sling a couple of light packs together and pull out."

Shorty's eyes closed as he lapsed back into sleep. The next moment his blankets were swept off him.

"If you don't want them, I do," Smoke explained.

Shorty followed the blankets and began to dress.

"Goin' to take the dogs?" he asked.

"No. The trail up the creek is sure to be unbroken, and we can make better time without them."

"Then I'll throw 'em a meal, which'll have to last 'em till we get back. Be sure you take some birch-bark and a candle."

Shorty opened the door, felt the bite of the cold, and shrank back to pull down his ear-flaps and mitten his hands.

Five minutes later he returned, sharply rubbing his nose.

"Smoke, I'm sure opposed to makin' this stampede. It's colder than the hinges of hell a thousand years before the first fire was lighted.

Besides, it's Friday the thirteenth, an' we're goin' to trouble as the sparks fly upward."

With small stampeding-packs on their backs, they closed the door behind them and started down the hill. The display of the aurora borealis had ceased, and only the stars leaped in the great cold and by their uncertain light made traps for the feet. Shorty floundered off a turn of the trail into deep snow, and raised his voice in blessing of the date of the week and month and year.

"Can't you keep still?" Smoke chided. "Leave the almanac alone. You'll have all Dawson awake and after us."

"Huh! See the light in that cabin? An' in that one over there? An' hear that door slam? Oh, sure Dawson's asleep. Them lights? Just buryin' their dead. They ain't stampedin', betcher life they ain't."

By the time they reached the foot of the hill and were fairly in Dawson, lights were springing up in the cabins, doors were slamming, and from behind came the sound of many moccasins on the hard-packed snow. Again Shorty delivered himself.

"But it beats hell the amount of mourners there is."

They passed a man who stood by the path and was calling anxiously in a low voice: "Oh, Charley; get a move on."

"See that pack on his back, Smoke? The graveyard's sure a long ways off when the mourners got to pack their blankets."

By the time they reached the main street a hundred men were in line behind them, and while they sought in the deceptive starlight for the trail that dipped down the bank to the river, more men could be heard arriving. Shorty slipped and shot down the thirty-foot chute into the soft snow. Smoke followed, knocking him over as he was rising to his feet.

"I found it first," he gurgled, taking off his mittens to shake the snow out of the gauntlets.

The next moment they were scrambling wildly out of the way of the hurtling bodies of those that followed. At the time of the freeze-up, a jam had occurred at this point, and cakes of ice were up-ended in snow-covered confusion. After several hard falls, Smoke drew out his candle and lighted it. Those in the rear hailed it with acclaim. In the windless air it burned easily, and he led the way more quickly.

"It's a sure stampede," Shorty decided. "Or might all them be sleep-walkers?"

"We're at the head of the procession at any rate," was Smoke's answer.

"Oh, I don't know. Mebbe that's a firefly ahead there. Mebbe they're all fireflies—that one, an' that one. Look at 'em! Believe me, they is a whole string of processions ahead."

It was a mile across the jams to the west bank of the Yukon, and candles flickered the full length of the twisting trail. Behind them, clear to the top of the bank they had descended, were more candles.

"Say, Smoke, this ain't no stampede. It's a exode-us. They must be a thousand men ahead of us an' ten thousand behind. Now, you listen to your uncle. My medicine's good. When I get a hunch it's sure right. An' we're in wrong on this stampede. Let's turn back an' hit the sleep."

"You'd better save your breath if you intend to keep up," Smoke retorted gruffly.

"Huh! My legs is short, but I slog along slack at the knees an' don't worry my muscles none, an' I can sure walk every piker here off the ice."

And Smoke knew he was right, for he had long since learned his comrade's phenomenal walking powers.

"I've been holding back to give you a chance," Smoke jeered.

"An' I'm plum troddin' on your heels. If you can't do better, let me go ahead and set pace."

Smoke quickened, and was soon at the rear of the nearest bunch of stampeders.

"Hike along, you, Smoke," the other urged. "Walk over them unburied dead. This ain't no funeral. Hit the frost like you was goin' somewheres."

Smoke counted eight men and two women in this party, and before the way across the jam-ice was won, he and Shorty had passed another party twenty strong. Within a few feet of the west bank, the trail swerved to the south, emerging from the jam upon smooth ice. The ice, however, was buried under several feet of fine snow. Through this the sled-trail ran, a narrow ribbon of packed footing barely two feet in width. On either side one sank to his knees and deeper in the snow. The stampeders they overtook were reluctant to give way, and often Smoke and Shorty had to plunge into the deep snow and by supreme efforts flounder past.

Shorty was irrepressible and pessimistic. When the stampeders resented being passed, he retorted in kind.

"What's your hurry?" one of them asked.

"What's yours?" he answered. "A stampede come down from Indian River yesterday afternoon an' beat you to it. They ain't no claims left."

"That being so, I repeat, what's your hurry?"

"*Who*? Me? I ain't no stampeder. I'm workin' for the government. I'm on official business. I'm just traipsin' along to take the census of Squaw Creek."

To another, who hailed him with: "Where away, little one? Do you really expect to stake a claim?" Shorty answered:

"Me? I'm the discoverer of Squaw Creek. I'm just comin' back from recordin' so as to see no blamed chechako jumps my claim."

The average pace of the stampeders on the smooth going was three miles and a half an hour. Smoke and Shorty were doing four and a half, though sometimes they broke into short runs and went faster.

"I'm going to travel your feet clean off, Shorty," Smoke challenged.

"Huh! I can hike along on the stumps an' wear the heels off your moccasins. Though it ain't no use. I've been figgerin'. Creek claims is five hundred feet. Call 'em ten to the mile. They's a thousand stampeders ahead of us, an' that creek ain't no hundred miles long. Somebody's goin' to get left, an' it makes a noise like you an' me."

Before replying, Smoke let out an unexpected link that threw Shorty half a dozen feet in the rear. "If you saved your breath and kept up, we'd cut down a few of that thousand," he chided.

"Who? Me? If you'd get outa the way I'd show you a pace what is."

Smoke laughed, and let out another link. The whole aspect of the adventure had changed. Through his brain was running a phrase of the mad philosopher—"the transvaluation of values." In truth, he was less interested in staking a fortune than in beating Shorty. After all, he concluded, it wasn't the reward of the game but the playing of it that counted. Mind, and muscle, and stamina, and soul, were challenged in a contest with this Shorty, a man who had never opened the books, and who did not know grand opera from rag-time, nor an epic from a chilblain.

"Shorty, I've got you skinned to death. I've reconstructed every cell in my body since I hit the beach at Dyea. My flesh is as stringy as whipcords, and as bitter and mean as the bite of a rattlesnake. A few months ago I'd have patted myself on the back to write such words, but I couldn't have written them. I had to live them first, and now that I'm living them there's no need to write them. I'm the real, bitter, stinging goods, and no scrub of a mountaineer can put anything over on me without getting it back compound. Now, you go ahead and set pace for half an hour. Do your worst, and when you're all in I'll go ahead and give you half an hour of the real worst."

"Huh!" Shorty sneered genially. "An' him not dry behind the ears yet. Get outa the way an' let your father show you some goin'."

Half-hour by half-hour they alternated in setting pace. Nor did they talk much. Their exertions kept them warm, though their breath froze on their faces from lips to chin. So intense was the cold that they almost continually rubbed their noses and cheeks with their mittens. A few minutes' cessation from this allowed the flesh to grow numb, and then most vigorous rubbing was required to produce the burning prickle of returning circulation.

Often they thought they had reached the lead, but always they overtook more stampeders who had started before them. Occasionally, groups of men attempted to swing in behind to their pace, but invariably they were discouraged after a mile or two and disappeared in the darkness to the rear.

"We've been out on trail all winter," was Shorty's comment. "An' them geezers, soft from layin' around their cabins, has the nerve to think they can keep our stride. Now, if they was real sour-doughs it'd be different. If there's one thing a sour-dough can do it's sure walk."

Once, Smoke lighted a match and glanced at his watch. He never repeated it, for so quick was the bite of the frost on his bared hands that half an hour passed before they were again comfortable.

"Four o'clock," he said, as he pulled on his mittens, "and we've already passed three hundred."

"Three hundred and thirty-eight," Shorty corrected. "I been keepin' count. Get outa the way, stranger. Let somebody stampede that knows how to stampede."

The latter was addressed to a man, evidently exhausted, who could no more than stumble along and who blocked the trail. This, and one other, were the only played-out men they encountered, for they were very near to the head of the stampede. Nor did they learn till afterwards the horrors of that night. Exhausted men sat down to rest by the way and failed to get up again. Seven were frozen to death, while scores of amputations of toes, feet, and fingers were performed in the Dawson hospitals on the survivors. For the stampede to Squaw Creek occurred on the coldest night of the year. Before morning, the spirit thermometers at

Dawson registered seventy degrees below zero. The men composing the stampede, with few exceptions, were new-comers in the country who did not know the way of the cold.

The other played-out man they found a few minutes later, revealed by a streamer of aurora borealis that shot like a searchlight from horizon to zenith. He was sitting on a piece of ice beside the trail.

"Hop along, sister Mary," Shorty gaily greeted him. "Keep movin'. If you sit there you'll freeze stiff."

The man made no response, and they stopped to investigate.

"Stiff as a poker," was Shorty's verdict. "If you tumbled him over he'd break."

"See if he's breathing," Smoke said, as, with bared hand, he sought through furs and woollens for the man's heart.

Shorty lifted one ear-flap and bent to the iced lips. "Nary breathe," he reported.

"Nor heart-beat," said Smoke.

He mittened his hand and beat it violently for a minute before exposing it to the frost to strike a match. It was an old man, incontestably dead. In the moment of illumination, they saw a long grey beard, massed with ice to the nose, cheeks that were white with frost, and closed eyes with frost-rimmed lashes frozen together. Then the match went out.

"Come on," Shorty said, rubbing his ear. "We can't do nothin' for the old geezer. An' I've sure frosted my ear. Now all the blamed skin'll peel off, and it'll be sore for a week."

A few minutes later, when a flaming ribbon spilled pulsating fire over the heavens, they saw on the ice a quarter of a mile ahead two forms. Beyond, for a mile, nothing moved.

"They're leading the procession," Smoke said, as darkness fell again. "Come on, let's get them."

At the end of half an hour, not yet having overtaken the two in front, Shorty broke into a run.

"If we catch 'em we'll never pass 'em," he panted. "Lord, what a pace they're hittin'. Dollars to doughnuts they're no chechakos. They're the real sour-dough variety, you can stack on that."

Smoke was leading when they finally caught up, and he was glad to ease to a walk at their heels. Almost immediately he got the impression that the one nearer him was a woman. How this impression came, he could not tell. Hooded and furred, the dark form was as any form; yet there was a haunting sense of familiarity about it. He waited for the next flame of the aurora, and by its light saw the smallness of the moccasined feet. But he saw more—the walk, and knew it for the unmistakable walk he had once resolved never to forget.

"She's a sure goer," Shorty confided hoarsely. "I'll bet it's an Indian."

"How do you do, Miss Gastell?" Smoke addressed her.

"How do you do," she answered, with a turn of the head and a quick glance. "It's too dark to see. Who are you?"

"Smoke."

She laughed in the frost, and he was certain it was the prettiest laughter he had ever heard. "And have you married and raised all those children you were telling me about?" Before he could retort, she went on. "How many chechakos are there behind?"

"Several thousand, I imagine. We passed over three hundred. And they weren't wasting any time."

"It's the old story," she said bitterly. "The new-comers get in on the rich creeks, and the old-timers, who dared and suffered and made this country, get nothing. Old-timers made this discovery on Squaw Creek—how it leaked out is the mystery—and they sent word up to all the old-timers on Sea Lion. But it's ten miles farther than Dawson, and when they arrive they'll find the creek staked to the skyline by the Dawson chechakos. It isn't right, it isn't fair, such perversity of luck."

"It is too bad," Smoke sympathized. "But I'm hanged if I know what you're going to do about it. First come, first served, you know."

"I wish I could do something," she flashed back at him. "I'd like to see them all freeze on the trail, or have everything terrible happen to them, so long as the Sea Lion stampede arrived first."

"You've certainly got it in for us hard," he laughed.

"It isn't that," she said quickly. "Man by man, I know the crowd from Sea Lion, and they are men. They starved in this country in the old days, and they worked like giants to develop it. I went through the hard times on the Koyukuk with them when I was a little girl. And I was with them in the Birch Creek famine, and in the Forty Mile famine. They are heroes, and they deserve some reward, and yet here are thousands of green softlings who haven't earned the right to stake anything, miles and miles ahead of them. And now, if you'll forgive my tirade, I'll save my breath, for I don't know when you and all the rest may try to pass dad and me."

No further talk passed between Joy and Smoke for an hour or so, though he noticed that for a time she and her father talked in low tones.

"I know 'em now," Shorty told Smoke. "He's old Louis Gastell, an' the real goods. That must be his kid. He come into this country so long ago they ain't nobody can recollect, an' he brought the girl with him, she only a baby. Him an' Beetles was tradin' partners an' they ran the first dinkey little steamboat up the Koyukuk."

"I don't think we'll try to pass them," Smoke said. "We're at the head of the stampede, and there are only four of us."

Shorty agreed, and another hour of silence followed, during which they swung steadily along. At seven o'clock, the blackness was broken by a last display of the aurora borealis, which showed to the west a broad opening between snow-clad mountains.

"Squaw Creek!" Joy exclaimed.

"Goin' some," Shorty exulted. "We oughtn't to been there for another half hour to the least, accordin' to my reckonin'. I must 'a' been spreadin' my legs."

It was at this point that the Dyea trail, baffled by ice-jams, swerved abruptly across the Yukon to the east bank. And here they must leave the hard-packed, main-travelled trail, mount the jams, and follow a dim trail, but slightly packed, that hovered the west bank.

Louis Gastell, leading, slipped in the darkness on the rough ice, and sat up, holding his ankle in both his hands. He struggled to his feet and went on, but at a slower pace and with a perceptible limp. After a few minutes he abruptly halted.

"It's no use," he said to his daughter. "I've sprained a tendon. You go ahead and stake for me as well as yourself."

"Can't we do something?" Smoke asked solicitously.

Louis Gastell shook his head. "She can stake two claims as well as one. I'll crawl over to the bank, start a fire, and bandage my ankle. I'll be all right. Go on, Joy. Stake ours above the Discovery claim; it's richer higher up."

"Here's some birch bark," Smoke said, dividing his supply equally. "We'll take care of your daughter."

Louis Gastell laughed harshly. "Thank you just the same," he said. "But she can take care of herself. Follow her and watch her."

"Do you mind if I lead?" she asked Smoke, as she headed on. "I know this country better than you."

"Lead on," Smoke answered gallantly, "though I agree with you it's a darned shame all us chechakos are going to beat that Sea Lion bunch to it. Isn't there some way to shake them?"

She shook her head. "We can't hide our trail, and they'll follow it like sheep."

After a quarter of a mile, she turned sharply to the west. Smoke noticed that they were going through unpacked snow, but neither he nor Shorty observed that the dim trail they had been on still led south. Had they witnessed the subsequent procedure of Louis Gastell, the history of the Klondike would have been written differently; for they would have seen that old-timer, no longer limping, running with his nose to the trail like a hound, following them. Also, they would have seen him trample and widen the turn to the fresh trail they had made to the west. And, finally, they would have seen him keep on the old dim trail that still led south.

A trail did run up the creek, but so slight was it that they continually lost it in the darkness. After a quarter of an hour, Joy Gastell was willing to drop into the rear and let the two men take turns in breaking a way through the snow. This slowness of the leaders enabled the whole stampede to catch up, and when daylight came, at nine o'clock, as far back as they could see was an unbroken line of men. Joy's dark eyes sparkled at the sight.

"How long since we started up the creek?" she asked.

"Fully two hours," Smoke answered.

"And two hours back make four," she laughed. "The stampede from Sea Lion is saved."

A faint suspicion crossed Smoke's mind, and he stopped and confronted her.

"I don't understand," he said.

"You don't? Then I'll tell you. This is Norway Creek. Squaw Creek is the next to the south."

Smoke was for the moment, speechless.

"You did it on purpose?" Shorty demanded.

"I did it to give the old-timers a chance." She laughed mockingly. The men grinned at each other and finally joined her. "I'd lay you across my knee an' give you a wallopin', if women folk wasn't so scarce in this country," Shorty assured her.

"Your father didn't sprain a tendon, but waited till we were out of sight and then went on?" Smoke asked.

She nodded.

"And you were the decoy?"

Again she nodded, and this time Smoke's laughter rang out clear and true. It was the spontaneous laughter of a frankly beaten man.

"Why don't you get angry with me?" she queried ruefully. "Or—or wallop me?"

"Well, we might as well be starting back," Shorty urged. "My feet's gettin' cold standin' here."

Smoke shook his head. "That would mean four hours lost. We must be eight miles up this creek now, and from the look ahead Norway is making a long swing south. We'll follow it, then cross over the divide somehow, and tap Squaw Creek somewhere above Discovery." He looked at Joy. "Won't you come along with us? I told your father we'd look after you."

"I—" She hesitated. "I think I shall, if you don't mind." She was looking straight at him, and her face was no longer defiant and mocking. "Really, Mr. Smoke, you make me almost sorry for what I have done. But somebody had to save the old-timers."

"It strikes me that stampeding is at best a sporting proposition."

"And it strikes me you two are very game about it," she went on, then added with the shadow of a sigh: "What a pity you are not old-timers!"

For two hours more they kept to the frozen creek-bed of Norway, then turned into a narrow and rugged tributary that flowed from the south. At midday they began the ascent of the divide itself. Behind them, looking down and back, they could see the long line of stampeders breaking up. Here and there, in scores of places, thin smoke-columns advertised the making of camps.

As for themselves, the going was hard. They wallowed through snow to their waists, and were compelled to stop every few yards to breathe. Shorty was the first to call a halt.

"We been hittin' the trail for over twelve hours," he said. "Smoke, I'm plum willin' to say I'm good an' tired. An' so are you. An' I'm free to shout that I can sure hang on to this here pasear like a starvin' Indian to a hunk of bear-meat. But this poor girl here can't keep her legs no time if she don't get something in her stomach. Here's where we build a fire. What d'ye say?"

So quickly, so deftly and methodically, did they go about making a temporary camp, that Joy, watching with jealous eyes, admitted to herself that the old-timers could not do it better. Spruce boughs, with a spread blanket on top, gave a foundation for rest and cooking operations.

But they kept away from the heat of the fire until noses and cheeks had been rubbed cruelly.

Smoke spat in the air, and the resultant crackle was so immediate and loud that he shook his head. "I give it up," he said. "I've never seen cold like this."

"One winter on the Koyukuk it went to eighty-six below," Joy answered. "It's at least seventy or seventy-five right now, and I know I've frosted my cheeks. They're burning like fire."

On the steep slope of the divide there was no ice, so snow, as fine and hard and crystalline as granulated sugar, was poured into the gold-pan by the bushel until enough water was melted for the coffee. Smoke fried bacon and thawed biscuits. Shorty kept the fuel supplied and tended the fire, and Joy set the simple table composed of two plates, two cups, two spoons, a tin of mixed salt and pepper, and a tin of sugar. When it came to eating, she and Smoke shared one set between them. They ate out of the same plate and drank from the same cup.

It was nearly two in the afternoon when they cleared the crest of the divide and began dropping down a feeder of Squaw Creek. Earlier in the winter some moose-hunter had made a trail up the canyon—that is, in going up and down he had stepped always in his previous tracks. As a result, in the midst of soft snow, and veiled under later snow falls, was a line of irregular hummocks. If one's foot missed a hummock, he plunged down through unpacked snow and usually to a fall. Also, the moose-hunter had been an exceptionally long-legged individual. Joy, who was eager now that the two men should stake, and fearing that they were slackening their pace on account of her evident weariness, insisted on taking her turn in the lead. The speed and manner in which she negotiated the precarious footing called out Shorty's unqualified approval.

"Look at her!" he cried. "She's the real goods an' the red meat. Look at them moccasins swing along. No high-heels there. She uses the legs God gave her. She's the right squaw for any bear-hunter."

She flashed back a smile of acknowledgment that included Smoke. He caught a feeling of chumminess, though at the same time he was bitingly aware that it was very much of a woman who embraced him in that comradely smile.

Looking back, as they came to the bank of Squaw Creek, they could see the stampede, strung out irregularly, struggling along the descent of the divide.

They slipped down the bank to the creek bed. The stream, frozen solidly to bottom, was from twenty to thirty feet wide and ran between six- and eight-foot earth banks of alluvial wash. No recent feet had disturbed the snow that lay upon its ice, and they knew they were above the Discovery claim and the last stakes of the Sea Lion stampeders.

"Look out for springs," Joy warned, as Smoke led the way down the creek. "At seventy below you'll lose your feet if you break through."

These springs, common to most Klondike streams, never cease at the lowest temperatures. The water flows out from the banks and lies in pools which are cuddled from the cold by later surface-freezings and snow falls. Thus, a man, stepping on dry snow, might break through half an inch of ice-skin and find himself up to the knees in water. In five minutes, unless able to remove the wet gear, the loss of one's foot was the penalty.

Though only three in the afternoon, the long grey twilight of the Arctic had settled down. They watched for a blazed tree on either bank, which would show the center-stake of the last claim located. Joy, impulsively eager, was the first to find it. She darted ahead of Smoke, crying: "Somebody's been here! See the snow! Look for the blaze! There it is! See that spruce!"

She sank suddenly to her waist in the snow.

"Now I've done it," she said woefully. Then she cried: "Don't come near me! I'll wade out."

Step by step, each time breaking through the thin skin of ice concealed under the dry snow, she forced her way to solid footing. Smoke did not wait, but sprang to the bank, where dry and seasoned twigs and sticks, lodged amongst the brush by spring freshets, waited the match. By the time she reached his side, the first flames and flickers of an assured fire were rising.

"Sit down!" he commanded.

She obediently sat down in the snow. He slipped his pack from his back, and spread a blanket for her feet.

From above came the voices of the stampeders who followed them.

"Let Shorty stake," she urged.

"Go on, Shorty," Smoke said, as he attacked her moccasins, already stiff with ice. "Pace off a thousand feet and place the two center-stakes. We can fix the corner-stakes afterwards."

With his knife Smoke cut away the lacings and leather of the moccasins. So stiff were they with ice that they snapped and crackled under the hacking and sawing. The Siwash socks and heavy woollen stockings were sheaths of ice. It was as if her feet and calves were encased in corrugated iron.

"How are your feet?" he asked, as he worked.

"Pretty numb. I can't move nor feel my toes. But it will be all right. The fire is burning beautifully. Watch out you don't freeze your own hands. They must be numb now from the way you're fumbling."

He slipped his mittens on, and for nearly a minute smashed the open hands savagely against his sides. When he felt the blood-prickles, he pulled off the mittens and ripped and tore and sawed and hacked at the frozen garments. The white skin of one foot appeared, then that of the other, to be exposed to the bite of seventy below zero, which is the equivalent of one hundred and two below freezing.

Then came the rubbing with snow, carried on with an intensity of cruel fierceness, till she squirmed and shrank and moved her toes, and joyously complained of the hurt.

He half-dragged her, and she half-lifted herself, nearer to the fire. He placed her feet on the blanket close to the flesh-saving flames.

"You'll have to take care of them for a while," he said.

She could now safely remove her mittens and manipulate her own feet, with the wisdom of the initiated, being watchful that the heat of the fire was absorbed slowly. While she did this, he attacked his hands. The snow did not melt nor moisten. Its light crystals were like so much sand. Slowly the stings and pangs of circulation came back into the chilled flesh. Then he tended the fire, unstrapped the light pack from her back, and got out a complete change of foot-gear.

Shorty returned along the creek bed and climbed the bank to them. "I sure staked a full thousan' feet," he proclaimed. "Number twenty-seven an' number twenty-eight, though I'd only got the upper stake of twenty-seven, when I met the first geezer of the bunch behind. He just straight declared I wasn't goin' to stake twenty-eight. An' I told him—"

"Yes, yes," Joy cried. "What did you tell him?"

"Well, I told him straight that if he didn't back up plum five hundred feet I'd sure punch his frozen nose into ice-cream an' chocolate eclaires. He backed up, an' I've got in the center-stakes of two full an' honest five-hundred-foot creek claims. He staked next, and I guess by now the bunch has Squaw Creek located to head-waters an' down the other side. Ourn is safe. It's too dark to see now, but we can put out the corner-stakes in the mornin'."

WHEN THEY AWOKE, THEY FOUND a change had taken place during the night. So warm was it, that Shorty and Smoke, still in their mutual blankets, estimated the temperature at no more than twenty below. The cold snap had broken. On top of their blankets lay six inches of frost crystals.

"Good morning! how are your feet?" was Smoke's greeting across the ashes of the fire to where Joy Gastell, carefully shaking aside the snow, was sitting up in her sleeping-furs.

Shorty built the fire and quarried ice from the creek, while Smoke cooked breakfast. Daylight came on as they finished the meal.

"You go an' fix them corner-stakes, Smoke," Shorty said. "There's gravel under where I chopped ice for the coffee, an' I'm goin' to melt water and wash a pan of that same gravel for luck."

Smoke departed, axe in hand, to blaze the stakes. Starting from the down-stream center-stake of 'twenty-seven,' he headed at right angles across the narrow valley towards its rim. He proceeded methodically, almost automatically, for his mind was alive with recollections of the night before. He felt, somehow, that he had won to empery over the delicate lines and firm muscles of those feet and ankles he had rubbed with snow, and this empery seemed to extend to the rest and all of this woman of his kind. In dim and fiery ways a feeling of possession mastered him. It seemed that all that was necessary was for him to walk up to this Joy Gastell, take her hand in his, and say "Come."

It was in this mood that he discovered something that made him forget empery over the white feet of woman. At the valley rim he blazed no corner-stake. He did not reach the valley rim, but, instead, he found himself confronted by another stream. He lined up with his eye a blasted willow tree and a big and recognizable spruce. He returned to the stream where were the center-stakes. He followed the bed of the creek around a wide horseshoe bend through the flat and found that the two creeks were the same creek. Next, he floundered twice through the snow from valley rim to valley rim, running the first line from the lower stake of 'twenty-seven,' the second from the upper stake of 'twenty-eight,' and he found that *The Upper Stake of the Latter was Lower than the Lower Stake of the Former*. In the gray twilight and half-darkness Shorty had located their two claims on the horseshoe.

Smoke plodded back to the little camp. Shorty, at the end of washing a pan of gravel, exploded at sight of him.

"We got it!" Shorty cried, holding out the pan. "Look at it! A nasty mess of gold. Two hundred right there if it's a cent. She runs rich from the top of the wash-gravel. I've churned around placers some, but I never got butter like what's in this pan."

Smoke cast an incurious glance at the coarse gold, poured himself a cup of coffee at the fire, and sat down. Joy sensed something wrong and looked at him with eagerly solicitous eyes. Shorty, however, was disgruntled by his partner's lack of delight in the discovery.

"Why don't you kick in an' get excited?" he demanded. "We got our pile right here, unless you're stickin' up your nose at two-hundred-dollar pans."

Smoke took a swallow of coffee before replying. "Shorty, why are our two claims here like the Panama Canal?"

"What's the answer?"

"Well, the eastern entrance of the Panama Canal is west of the western entrance, that's all."

"Go on," Shorty said. "I ain't seen the joke yet."

"In short, Shorty, you staked our two claims on a big horseshoe bend."

Shorty set the gold pan down in the snow and stood up. "Go on," he repeated.

"The upper stake of 'twenty-eight' is ten feet below the lower stake of 'twenty-seven.'"

"You mean we ain't got nothin', Smoke?"

"Worse than that; we've got ten feet less than nothing."

Shorty departed down the bank on the run. Five minutes later he returned. In response to Joy's look, he nodded. Without speech, he went over to a log and sat down to gaze steadily at the snow in front of his moccasins.

"We might as well break camp and start back for Dawson," Smoke said, beginning to fold the blankets.

"I am sorry, Smoke," Joy said. "It's all my fault."

"It's all right," he answered. "All in the day's work, you know."

"But it's my fault, wholly mine," she persisted. "Dad's staked for me down near Discovery, I know. I'll give you my claim."

He shook his head.

"Shorty," she pleaded.

Shorty shook his head and began to laugh. It was a colossal laugh. Chuckles and muffled explosions yielded to hearty roars.

"It ain't hysterics," he explained. "I sure get powerful amused at times, an' this is one of them."

His gaze chanced to fall on the gold-pan. He walked over and gravely kicked it, scattering the gold over the landscape.

"It ain't ourn," he said. "It belongs to the geezer I backed up five hundred feet last night. An' what gets me is four hundred an' ninety of them feet was to the good—his good. Come on, Smoke. Let's start the hike to Dawson. Though if you're hankerin' to kill me I won't lift a finger to prevent."

IV

SHORTY DREAMS

"Funny you don't gamble none," Shorty said to Smoke one night in the Elkhorn. "Ain't it in your blood?"

"It is," Smoke answered. "But the statistics are in my head. I like an even break for my money."

All about them, in the huge bar-room, arose the click and rattle and rumble of a dozen games, at which fur-clad, moccasined men tried their luck. Smoke waved his hand to include them all.

"Look at them," he said. "It's cold mathematics that they will lose more than they win to-night, that the big proportion are losing right now."

"You're sure strong on figgers," Shorty murmured admiringly. "An' in the main you're right. But they's such a thing as facts. An' one fact is streaks of luck. They's times when every geezer playin' wins, as I know, for I've sat in such games an' saw more'n one bank busted. The only way to win at gamblin' is wait for a hunch that you've got a lucky streak comin' and then play it to the roof."

"It sounds simple," Smoke criticized. "So simple I can't see how men can lose."

"The trouble is," Shorty admitted, "that most men gets fooled on their hunches. On occasion I sure get fooled on mine. The thing is to try an' find out."

Smoke shook his head. "That's a statistic, too, Shorty. Most men prove wrong on their hunches."

"But don't you ever get one of them streaky feelin's that all you got to do is put your money down an' pick a winner?"

Smoke laughed. "I'm too scared of the percentage against me. But I'll tell you what, Shorty. I'll throw a dollar on the 'high card' right now and see if it will buy us a drink."

Smoke was edging his way in to the faro table, when Shorty caught his arm.

"Hold on. I'm gettin' one of them hunches now. You put that dollar on roulette."

They went over to a roulette table near the bar.

"Wait till I give the word," Shorty counselled.

"What number?" Smoke asked.

"Pick it yourself. But wait till I say let her go."

"You don't mean to say I've got an even chance on that table?" Smoke argued.

"As good as the next geezer's."

"But not as good as the bank's."

"Wait an' see," Shorty urged. "Now! Let her go!"

The game-keeper had just sent the little ivory ball whirling around the smooth rim above the revolving, many-slotted wheel. Smoke, at the lower end of the table, reached over a player, and blindly tossed the dollar. It slid along the smooth, green cloth and stopped fairly in the center of "34."

The ball came to rest, and the game-keeper announced, "Thirty-four wins!" He swept the table, and alongside of Smoke's dollar, stacked thirty-five dollars. Smoke drew the money in, and Shorty slapped him on the shoulder.

"Now, that was the real goods of a hunch, Smoke! How'd I know it? There's no tellin'. I just knew you'd win. Why, if that dollar of yourn'd fell on any other number it'd won just the same. When the hunch is right, you just can't help winnin'."

"Suppose it had come 'double naught'?" Smoke queried, as they made their way to the bar.

"Then your dollar'd been on 'double naught,'" was Shorty's answer. "They's no gettin' away from it. A hunch is a hunch. Here's how. Come on back to the table. I got a hunch, after pickin' you for a winner, that I can pick some few numbers myself."

"Are you playing a system?" Smoke asked, at the end of ten minutes, when his partner had dropped a hundred dollars.

Shorty shook his head indignantly, as he spread his chips out in the vicinities of "3," "11," and "17," and tossed a spare chip on the green.

"Hell is sure cluttered with geezers that played systems," he exposited, as the keeper raked the table.

From idly watching, Smoke became fascinated, following closely every detail of the game from the whirling of the ball to the making and the paying of the bets. He made no plays, however, merely contenting himself with looking on. Yet so interested was he, that Shorty, announcing that he had had enough, with difficulty drew Smoke away from the table.

The game-keeper returned Shorty the gold-sack he had deposited as a credential for playing, and with it went a slip of paper on which was scribbled, "Out—$350.00." Shorty carried the sack and the paper across the room and handed them to the weigher, who sat behind a large pair of gold-scales. Out of Shorty's sack he weighed three hundred and fifty dollars, which he poured into the coffer of the house.

"That hunch of yours was another one of those statistics," Smoke jeered.

"I had to play it, didn't I, in order to find out?" Shorty retorted. "I reckon I was crowdin' some just on account of tryin' to convince you they's such a thing as hunches."

"Never mind, Shorty," Smoke laughed. "I've got a hunch right now—"

Shorty's eyes sparkled as he cried eagerly: "What is it? Kick in an' play it pronto."

"It's not that kind, Shorty. Now, what I've got is a hunch that some day I'll work out a system that will beat the spots off that table."

"System!" Shorty groaned, then surveyed his partner with a vast pity. "Smoke, listen to your side-kicker an' leave system alone. Systems is sure losers. They ain't no hunches in systems."

"That's why I like them," Smoke answered. "A system is statistical. When you get the right system you can't lose, and that's the difference between it and a hunch. You never know when the right hunch is going wrong."

"But I know a lot of systems that went wrong, an' I never seen a system win." Shorty paused and sighed. "Look here, Smoke, if you're gettin' cracked on systems this ain't no place for you, an' it's about time we hit the trail again."

DURING THE SEVERAL FOLLOWING WEEKS, the two partners played at cross purposes. Smoke was bent on spending his time watching the roulette game in the Elkhorn, while Shorty was equally bent on travelling trail. At last Smoke put his foot down when a stampede was proposed for two hundred miles down the Yukon.

"Look here, Shorty," he said, "I'm not going. That trip will take ten days, and before that time I hope to have my system in proper working order. I could almost win with it now. What are you dragging me around the country this way for, anyway?"

"Smoke, I got to take care of you," was Shorty's reply. "You're gettin' nutty. I'd drag you stampedin' to Jericho or the North Pole if I could keep you away from that table."

"It's all right, Shorty. But just remember I've reached full man-grown, meat-eating size. The only dragging you'll do, will be dragging home the dust I'm going to win with that system of mine, and you'll most likely have to do it with a dog-team."

Shorty's response was a groan.

"And I don't want you to be bucking any games on your own," Smoke went on. "We're going to divide the winnings, and I'll need all our money to get started. That system's young yet, and it's liable to trip me for a few falls before I get it lined up."

AT LAST, AFTER LONG HOURS and days spent at watching the table, the night came when Smoke proclaimed he was ready, and Shorty, glum and pessimistic, with all the seeming of one attending a funeral, accompanied his partner to the Elkhorn. Smoke bought a stack of chips and stationed himself at the game-keeper's end of the table. Again and again the ball was whirled, and the other players won or lost, but Smoke did not venture a chip. Shorty waxed impatient.

"Buck in, buck in," he urged. "Let's get this funeral over. What's the matter? Got cold feet?"

Smoke shook his head and waited. A dozen plays went by, and then, suddenly, he placed ten one-dollar chips on "26." The number won, and the keeper paid Smoke three hundred and fifty dollars. A dozen plays went by, twenty plays, and thirty, when Smoke placed ten dollars on "32." Again he received three hundred and fifty dollars.

"It's a hunch!" Shorty whispered vociferously in his ear. "Ride it! Ride it!"

Half an hour went by, during which Smoke was inactive, then he placed ten dollars on "34" and won.

"A hunch!" Shorty whispered.

"Nothing of the sort," Smoke whispered back. "It's the system. Isn't she a dandy?"

"You can't tell me," Shorty contended. "Hunches comes in mighty funny ways. You might think it's a system, but it ain't. Systems is impossible. They can't happen. It's a sure hunch you're playin'."

Smoke now altered his play. He bet more frequently, with single chips, scattered here and there, and he lost more often than he won.

"Quit it," Shorty advised. "Cash in. You've rung the bull's-eye three times, an' you're ahead a thousand. You can't keep it up."

At this moment the ball started whirling, and Smoke dropped ten chips on "26." The ball fell into the slot of "26," and the keeper again paid him three hundred and fifty dollars.

"If you're plum crazy an' got the immortal cinch, bet 'em the limit," Shorty said. "Put down twenty-five next time."

A quarter of an hour passed, during which Smoke won and lost on small scattering bets. Then, with the abruptness that characterized his big betting, he placed twenty-five dollars on the "double naught," and the keeper paid him eight hundred and seventy-five dollars.

"Wake me up, Smoke, I'm dreamin'," Shorty moaned.

Smoke smiled, consulted his notebook, and became absorbed in calculation. He continually drew the notebook from his pocket, and from time to time jotted down figures.

A crowd had packed densely around the table, while the players themselves were attempting to cover the same numbers he covered. It was then that a change came over his play. Ten times in succession he placed ten dollars on "18" and lost. At this stage he was deserted by the hardiest. He changed his number and won another three hundred and fifty dollars. Immediately the players were back with him, deserting again after a series of losing bets.

"Quit it, Smoke, quit it," Shorty advised. "The longest string of hunches is only so long, an' your string's finished. No more bull's-eyes for you."

"I'm going to ring her once again before I cash in," Smoke answered.

For a few minutes, with varying luck, he played scattering chips over the table, and then dropped twenty-five dollars on the "double naught."

"I'll take my slip now," he said to the dealer, as he won.

"Oh, you don't need to show it to me," Shorty said, as they walked to the weigher. "I been keepin' track. You're something like thirty-six hundred to the good. How near am I?"

"Thirty-six-sixty," Smoke replied. "And now you've got to pack the dust home. That was the agreement."

"Don't crowd your luck," Shorty pleaded with Smoke, the next night, in the cabin, as he evidenced preparations to return to the Elkhorn. "You played a mighty long string of hunches, but you played it out. If you go back you'll sure drop all your winnings."

"But I tell you it isn't hunches, Shorty. It's statistics. It's a system. It can't lose."

"System be damned. They ain't no such a thing as system. I made seventeen straight passes at a crap table once. Was it system? Nope. It was fool luck, only I had cold feet an' didn't dast let it ride. If it'd rid, instead of me drawin' down after the third pass, I'd 'a' won over thirty thousan' on the original two-bit piece."

"Just the same, Shorty, this is a real system."

"Huh! You got to show me."

"I did show you. Come on with me now, and I'll show you again."

When they entered the Elkhorn, all eyes centered on Smoke, and those about the table made way for him as he took up his old place at the keeper's end. His play was quite unlike that of the previous night. In the course of an hour and a half he made only four bets, but each bet was for twenty-five dollars, and each bet won. He cashed in thirty-five hundred dollars, and Shorty carried the dust home to the cabin.

"Now's the time to jump the game," Shorty advised, as he sat on the edge of his bunk and took off his moccasins. "You're seven thousan' ahead. A man's a fool that'd crowd his luck harder."

"Shorty, a man would be a blithering lunatic if he didn't keep on backing a winning system like mine."

"Smoke, you're a sure bright boy. You're college-learnt. You know more'n a minute than I could know in forty thousan' years. But just the same you're dead wrong when you call your luck a system. I've been around some, an' seen a few, an' I tell you straight an' confidential an' all-assurin', a system to beat a bankin' game ain't possible."

"But I'm showing you this one. It's a pipe."

"No, you're not, Smoke. It's a pipe-dream. I'm asleep. Bimeby I'll wake up, an' build the fire, an' start breakfast."

"Well, my unbelieving friend, there's the dust. Heft it."

So saying, Smoke tossed the bulging gold-sack upon his partner's knees. It weighed thirty-five pounds, and Shorty was fully aware of the crush of its impact on his flesh.

"It's real," Smoke hammered his point home.

"Huh! I've saw some mighty real dreams in my time. In a dream all things is possible. In real life a system ain't possible. Now, I ain't never been to college, but I'm plum justified in sizin' up this gamblin' orgy of ourn as a sure-enough dream."

"Hamilton's 'Law of Parsimony,'" Smoke laughed.

"I ain't never heard of the geezer, but his dope's sure right. I'm dreamin', Smoke, an' you're just snoopin' around in my dream an' tormentin' me with system. If you love me, if you sure do love me, you'll just yell, 'Shorty! Wake up!' An' I'll wake up an' start breakfast."

THE THIRD NIGHT OF PLAY, as Smoke laid his first bet, the game-keeper shoved fifteen dollars back to him.

"Ten's all you can play," he said. "The limit's come down."

"Gettin' picayune," Shorty sneered.

"No one has to play at this table that don't want to," the keeper retorted. "And I'm willing to say straight out in meeting that we'd sooner your pardner didn't play at our table."

"Scared of his system, eh?" Shorty challenged, as the keeper paid over three hundred and fifty dollars.

"I ain't saying I believe in system, because I don't. There never was a system that'd beat roulette or any percentage game. But just the same I've seen some queer strings of luck, and I ain't going to let this bank go bust if I can help it."

"Cold feet."

"Gambling is just as much business, my friend, as any other business. We ain't philanthropists."

Night by night, Smoke continued to win. His method of play varied. Expert after expert, in the jam about the table, scribbled down his bets and numbers in vain attempts to work out his system. They complained of their inability to get a clew to start with, and swore that it was pure luck, though the most colossal streak of it they had ever seen.

It was Smoke's varied play that obfuscated them. Sometimes, consulting his note-book or engaging in long calculations, an hour elapsed without his staking a chip. At other times he would win three limit-bets and clean up a thousand dollars and odd in five or ten minutes. At still other times, his tactics would be to scatter single chips prodigally and amazingly over the table. This would continue for from ten to thirty minutes of play, when, abruptly, as the ball whirled through the last few of its circles, he would play the limit on column, colour, and number, and win all three. Once, to complete confusion in the minds of those that strove to divine his secret, he lost forty straight bets, each at the limit. But each night, play no matter how diversely, Shorty carried home thirty-five hundred dollars for him.

"It ain't no system," Shorty expounded at one of their bed-going discussions. "I follow you, an' follow you, but they ain't no figgerin' it out. You never play twice the same. All you do is pick winners when you want to, an' when you don't want to, you just on purpose don't."

"Maybe you're nearer right than you think, Shorty. I've just got to pick losers sometimes. It's part of the system."

"System—hell! I've talked with every gambler in town, an' the last one is agreed they ain't no such thing as system."

"Yet I'm showing them one all the time."

"Look here, Smoke." Shorty paused over the candle, in the act of blowing it out. "I'm real irritated. Maybe you think this is a candle. It ain't. No, sir! An' this ain't me neither. I'm out on trail somewheres, in my blankets, lyin' flat on my back with my mouth open, an' dreamin' all this. That ain't you talkin', any more than this candle is a candle."

"It's funny, how I happen to be dreaming along with you then," Smoke persisted.

"No, it ain't. You're part of my dream, that's all. I've hearn many a man talk in my dreams. I want to tell you one thing, Smoke. I'm gettin' mangy an' mad. If this here dream keeps up much more I'm goin' to bite my veins an' howl."

ON THE SIXTH NIGHT OF play at the Elkhorn, the limit was reduced to five dollars.

"It's all right," Smoke assured the game-keeper. "I want thirty-five hundred to-night, as usual, and you only compel me to play longer. I've got to pick twice as many winners, that's all."

"Why don't you buck somebody else's table?" the keeper demanded wrathfully.

"Because I like this one." Smoke glanced over to the roaring stove only a few feet away. "Besides, there are no draughts here, and it is warm and comfortable."

On the ninth night, when Shorty had carried the dust home, he had a fit. "I quit, Smoke, I quit," he began. "I know when I got enough. I ain't dreamin'. I'm wide awake. A system can't be, but you got one just the same. There's nothin' in the rule o' three. The almanac's clean out. The world's gone smash. There's nothin' regular an' uniform no more. The multiplication table's gone loco. Two is eight, nine is eleven, and two-times-six is eight hundred an' forty-six—an'—an' a half. Anything is everything, an' nothing's all, an' twice all is cold-cream, milk-shakes, an' calico horses. You've got a system. Figgers beat the figgerin'. What ain't is, an' what isn't has to be. The sun rises in the west, the moon's a pay-streak, the stars is canned corn-beef, scurvy's the blessin' of God, him that dies kicks again, rocks floats, water's gas, I ain't me, you're somebody else, an' mebbe we're twins if we ain't hashed-brown potatoes fried in verdigris. Wake me up! Somebody! Oh! Wake me up!"

THE NEXT MORNING A VISITOR came to the cabin. Smoke knew him, Harvey Moran, the owner of all the games in the Tivoli. There was a note of appeal in his deep gruff voice as he plunged into his business.

"It's like this, Smoke," he began. "You've got us all guessing. I'm representing nine other game-owners and myself from all the saloons in town. We don't understand. We know that no system ever worked against roulette. All the mathematic sharps in the colleges have told us gamblers the same thing. They say that roulette itself is the system, the one and only system, and, therefore, that no system can beat it, for that would mean arithmetic has gone bug-house."

Shorty nodded his head violently.

"If a system can beat a system, then there's no such thing as system," the gambler went on. "In such a case anything could be possible—a thing could be in two different places at once, or two things could be in the same place that's only large enough for one at the same time."

"Well, you've seen me play," Smoke answered defiantly; "and if you think it's only a string of luck on my part, why worry?"

"That's the trouble. We can't help worrying. It's a system you've got, and all the time we know it can't be. I've watched you five nights now, and all I can make out is that you favour certain numbers and keep on winning. Now the ten of us game-owners have got together, and we want to make a friendly proposition. We'll put a roulette-table in a back room of the Elkhorn, pool the bank against you, and have you buck us. It will be all quiet and private. Just you and Shorty and us. What do you say?"

"I think it's the other way around," Smoke answered. "It's up to you to come and see me. I'll be playing in the barroom of the Elkhorn to-night. You can watch me there just as well."

THAT NIGHT, WHEN SMOKE TOOK up his customary place at the table, the keeper shut down the game. "The game's closed," he said. "Boss's orders."

But the assembled game-owners were not to be balked. In a few minutes they arranged a pool, each putting in a thousand, and took over the table.

"Come on and buck us," Harvey Moran challenged, as the keeper sent the ball on its first whirl around.

"Give me the twenty-five limit," Smoke suggested.

"Sure; go to it."

Smoke immediately placed twenty-five chips on the "double naught," and won.

Moran wiped the sweat from his forehead. "Go on," he said. "We got ten thousand in this bank."

At the end of an hour and a half, the ten thousand was Smoke's.

"The bank's bust," the keeper announced.

"Got enough?" Smoke asked.

The game-owners looked at one another. They were awed. They, the fatted proteges of the laws of chance, were undone. They were up against one who had more intimate access to those laws, or who had invoked higher and undreamed laws.

"We quit," Moran said. "Ain't that right, Burke?"

Big Burke, who owned the games in the M. and G. Saloon, nodded. "The impossible has happened," he said. "This Smoke here has got a system all right. If we let him go on we'll all bust. All I can see, if we're goin' to keep our tables running, is to cut down the limit to a dollar, or to ten cents, or a cent. He won't win much in a night with such stakes."

All looked at Smoke.

He shrugged his shoulders. "In that case, gentlemen, I'll have to hire a gang of men to play at all your tables. I can pay them ten dollars for a four-hour shift and make money."

"Then we'll shut down our tables," Big Burke replied. "Unless—" He hesitated and ran his eye over his fellows to see that they were with him. "Unless you're willing to talk business. What will you sell the system for?"

"Thirty thousand dollars," Smoke answered. "That's a tax of three thousand apiece."

They debated and nodded.

"And you'll tell us your system?"

"Surely."

"And you'll promise not to play roulette in Dawson ever again?"

"No, sir," Smoke said positively. "I'll promise not to play this system again."

"My God!" Moran exploded. "You haven't got other systems, have you?"

"Hold on!" Shorty cried. "I want to talk to my pardner. Come over here, Smoke, on the side."

Smoke followed into a quiet corner of the room, while hundreds of curious eyes centered on him and Shorty.

"Look here, Smoke," Shorty whispered hoarsely. "Mebbe it ain't a dream. In which case you're sellin' out almighty cheap. You've sure got the world by the slack of its pants. They's millions in it. Shake it! Shake it hard!"

"But if it's a dream?" Smoke queried softly.

"Then, for the sake of the dream an' the love of Mike, stick them gamblers up good and plenty. What's the good of dreamin' if you can't dream to the real right, dead sure, eternal finish?"

"Fortunately, this isn't a dream, Shorty."

"Then if you sell out for thirty thousan', I'll never forgive you."

"When I sell out for thirty thousand, you'll fall on my neck an' wake up to find out that you haven't been dreaming at all. This is no dream, Shorty. In about two minutes you'll see you have been wide awake all the time. Let me tell you that when I sell out it's because I've got to sell out."

Back at the table, Smoke informed the game-owners that his offer still held. They proffered him their paper to the extent of three thousand each.

"Hold out for the dust," Shorty cautioned.

"I was about to intimate that I'd take the money weighed out," Smoke said.

The owner of the Elkhorn cashed their paper, and Shorty took possession of the gold-dust.

"Now, I don't want to wake up," he chortled, as he hefted the various sacks. "Toted up, it's a seventy thousan' dream. It'd be too blamed expensive to open my eyes, roll out of the blankets, an' start breakfast."

"What's your system?" Big Burke demanded. "We've paid for it, and we want it."

Smoke led the way to the table. "Now, gentlemen, bear with me a moment. This isn't an ordinary system. It can scarcely be called legitimate, but its one great virtue is that it works. I've got my suspicious, but I'm not saying anything. You watch. Mr. Keeper, be ready with the ball. Wait. I am going to pick '26.' Consider I've bet on it. Be ready, Mr. Keeper—Now!"

The ball whirled around.

"You observe," Smoke went on, "that '9' was directly opposite."

The ball finished in "26."

Big Burke swore deep in his chest, and all waited.

"For 'double naught' to win, '11' must be opposite. Try it yourself and see."

"But the system?" Moran demanded impatiently. "We know you can pick winning numbers, and we know what those numbers are; but how do you do it?"

"By observed sequences. By accident I chanced twice to notice the ball whirled when '9' was opposite. Both times '26' won. After that I saw it happen again. Then I looked for other sequences, and found them. 'Double naught' opposite fetches '32,' and '11' fetches 'double naught.' It doesn't always happen, but it *usually* happens. You notice, I say 'usually.' As I said before, I have my suspicions, but I'm not saying anything."

Big Burke, with a sudden flash of comprehension reached over, stopped the wheel, and examined it carefully. The heads of the nine other game-owners bent over and joined in the examination. Big Burke straightened up and cast a glance at the near-by stove.

"Hell," he said. "It wasn't any system at all. The table stood close to the fire, and the blamed wheel's warped. And we've been worked to a frazzle. No wonder he liked this table. He couldn't have bucked for sour apples at any other table."

Harvey Moran gave a great sigh of relief and wiped his forehead. "Well, anyway," he said, "it's cheap at the price just to find out that it wasn't a system." His face began to work, and then he broke into laughter and slapped Smoke on the shoulder. "Smoke, you had us going for a while, and we patting ourselves on the back because you were letting our tables alone! Say, I've got some real fizz I'll open if you'll all come over to the Tivoli with me."

Later, back in the cabin, Shorty silently overhauled and hefted the various bulging gold-sacks. He finally piled them on the table, sat down on the edge of his bunk, and began taking off his moccasins.

"Seventy thousan'," he calculated. "It weighs three hundred and fifty pounds. And all out of a warped wheel an' a quick eye. Smoke, you eat'm raw, you eat'm alive, you work under water, you've given me the jim-jams; but just the same I know it's a dream. It's only in dreams that the good things comes true. I'm almighty unanxious to wake up. I hope I never wake up."

"Cheer up," Smoke answered. "You won't. There are a lot of philosophy sharps that think men are sleep-walkers. You're in good company."

Shorty got up, went to the table, selected the heaviest sack, and cuddled it in his arms as if it were a baby. "I may be sleep-walkin'," he said, "but as you say, I'm sure in mighty good company."

V

THE MAN ON THE OTHER BANK

I t was before Smoke Bellew staked the farcical town-site of Tra-Lee, made the historic corner of eggs that nearly broke Swiftwater Bill's bank account, or won the dog-team race down the Yukon for an even million dollars, that he and Shorty parted company on the Upper Klondike. Shorty's task was to return down the Klondike to Dawson to record some claims they had staked.

Smoke, with the dog-team, turned south. His quest was Surprise Lake and the mythical Two Cabins. His traverse was to cut the headwaters of the Indian River and cross the unknown region over the mountains to the Stewart River. Here, somewhere, rumour persisted, was Surprise Lake, surrounded by jagged mountains and glaciers, its bottom paved with raw gold. Old-timers, it was said, whose very names were forgotten in the frosts of earlier years, had dived into the icy waters of Surprise Lake and fetched lump-gold to the surface in both hands. At different times, parties of old-timers had penetrated the forbidding fastness and sampled the lake's golden bottom. But the water was too cold. Some died in the water, being pulled up dead. Others died later of consumption. And one who had gone down never did come up. All survivors had planned to return and drain the lake, yet none had ever gone back. Disaster always smote them. One man fell into an air-hole below Forty Mile; another was killed and eaten by his dogs; a third was crushed by a falling tree. And so the tale ran. Surprise Lake was a hoodoo; its location was unremembered; and the gold still paved its undrained bottom.

Two Cabins, no less mythical, was more definitely located. "Five sleeps," up the McQuestion River from the Stewart, stood two ancient cabins. So ancient were they that they must have been built before ever the first known gold-hunter had entered the Yukon Basin. Wandering moose-hunters, whom even Smoke had met and talked with, claimed to have found the two cabins in the old days, but to have sought vainly for the mine which those early adventurers must have worked.

"I wish you was goin' with me," Shorty said wistfully, at parting. "Just because you got the Indian bug ain't no reason for to go pokin' into trouble. They's no gettin' away from it, that's loco country you're bound for. The hoodoo's sure on it, from the first flip to the last call, judgin' from all you an' me has hearn tell about it."

"It's all right, Shorty," replied Smoke. "I'll make the round trip and be back in Dawson in six weeks. The Yukon trail is packed, and the first hundred miles or so of the Stewart ought to be packed. Old-timers from Henderson have told me a number of outfits went up last fall after the freeze-up. When I strike their trail I ought to hit her up forty or fifty miles a day. I'm likely to be back inside a month, once I get across."

"Yep, once you get acrost. But it's the gettin' acrost that worries me. Well, so long, Smoke. Keep your eyes open for that hoodoo, that's all. An' don't be ashamed to turn back if you don't kill any meat."

A WEEK LATER, SMOKE FOUND himself among the jumbled ranges south of Indian River. On the divide from the Klondike he had abandoned the sled and packed his wolf-dogs. The six big huskies each carried fifty pounds, and on his own back was an equal burden. Through the soft snow he led the way, packing it down under his snow-shoes, and behind, in single file, toiled the dogs.

He loved the life, the deep arctic winter, the silent wilderness, the unending snow-surface unpressed by the foot of any man. About him towered icy peaks unnamed and uncharted. No hunter's camp-smoke, rising in the still air of the valleys, ever caught his eye. He, alone, moved through the brooding quiet of the untravelled wastes; nor was he oppressed by the solitude. He loved it all, the day's toil, the bickering wolf-dogs, the making of the camp in the long twilight, the leaping stars overhead, and the flaming pageant of the aurora borealis.

Especially he loved his camp at the end of the day, and in it he saw a picture which he ever yearned to paint and which he knew he would never forget—a beaten place in the snow, where burned his fire; his bed, a couple of rabbit-skin robes spread on fresh-chopped spruce-boughs; his shelter, a stretched strip of canvas that caught and threw back the heat of the fire; the blackened coffee-pot and pail resting on a length of log, the moccasins propped on sticks to dry, the snow-shoes up-ended in the snow; and across the fire the wolf-dogs snuggling to it for the warmth, wistful and eager, furry and frost-rimed, with bushy tails curled protectingly over their feet; and all about, pressed backward but a space, the wall of encircling darkness.

At such times San Francisco, The Billow, and O'Hara seemed very far away, lost in a remote past, shadows of dreams that had never happened. He found it hard to believe that he had known any other life than this of the wild, and harder still was it for him to reconcile himself to the fact that he had once dabbled and dawdled in the Bohemian drift of city life. Alone, with no one to talk to, he thought much, and deeply, and simply. He was appalled by the wastage of his city years, by the cheapness, now, of the philosophies of the schools and books, of the clever cynicism of the studio and editorial room, of the cant of the business men in their clubs. They knew neither food, nor sleep, nor health; nor could they ever possibly know the sting of real appetite, the goodly ache of fatigue, nor the rush of mad strong blood that bit like wine through all one's body as work was done.

And all the time this fine, wise, Spartan Northland had been here, and he had never known. What puzzled him was, that, with such intrinsic fitness, he had never heard the slightest calling whisper, had not himself gone forth to seek. But this, too, he solved in time.

"Look here, Yellow Face, I've got it clear!"

The dog addressed lifted first one forefoot and then the other with quick, appeasing movements, curled his bush of a tail about them again, and laughed across the fire.

"Herbert Spencer was nearly forty before he caught the vision of his greatest efficiency and desire. I'm none so slow. I didn't have to wait till I was thirty to catch mine. Right here is my efficiency and desire. Almost, Yellow Face, do I wish I had been born a wolf-boy and been brother all my days to you and yours."

For days he wandered through a chaos of canyons and divides which did not yield themselves to any rational topographical plan. It was as if they had been flung there by some cosmic joker. In vain he sought for a creek or feeder that flowed truly south toward the McQuestion and the Stewart. Then came a mountain storm that blew a blizzard across the riff-raff of high and shallow divides. Above timber-line, fireless, for two days, he struggled blindly to find lower levels. On the second day he came out upon the rim of an enormous palisade. So thickly drove the snow that he could not see the base of the wall, nor dared he attempt the descent. He rolled himself in his robes and huddled the dogs about him in the depths of a snow-drift, but did not permit himself to sleep.

In the morning, the storm spent, he crawled out to investigate. A quarter of a mile beneath him, beyond all mistake, lay a frozen, snow-covered lake. About it, on every side, rose jagged peaks. It answered the description. Blindly, he had found Surprise Lake.

"Well named," he muttered, an hour later, as he came out upon its margin. A clump of aged spruce was the only woods. On his way to it, he stumbled upon three graves, snow-buried, but marked by hand-hewn head-posts and undecipherable writing. On the edge of the woods was a small ramshackle cabin. He pulled the latch and entered. In a corner, on what had once been a bed of spruce-boughs, still wrapped in mangy furs that had rotted to fragments, lay a skeleton. The last visitor to Surprise Lake, was Smoke's conclusion, as he picked up a lump of gold as large as his doubled fist. Beside the lump was a pepper-can filled with nuggets of the size of walnuts, rough-surfaced, showing no signs of wash.

So true had the tale run that Smoke accepted without question that the source of the gold was the lake's bottom. Under many feet of ice and inaccessible, there was nothing to be done, and at midday, from the rim of the palisade, he took a farewell look back and down at his find.

"It's all right, Mr. Lake," he said. "You just keep right on staying there. I'm coming back to drain you—if that hoodoo doesn't catch me. I don't know how I got here, but I'll know by the way I go out."

IN A LITTLE VALLEY, BESIDE a frozen stream and under beneficent spruce trees, he built a fire four days later. Somewhere in that white anarchy he had left behind him was Surprise Lake—somewhere, he knew not where; for a hundred hours of driftage and struggle through blinding, driving snow had concealed his course from him, and he knew not in what direction lay *behind*. It was as if he had just emerged from a nightmare. He was not sure whether four days or a week had passed. He had slept with the dogs, fought across a forgotten number of shallow divides, followed the windings of weird canyons that ended in pockets, and twice had managed to make a fire and thaw out frozen moose-meat. And here he was, well-fed and well-camped. The storm had passed, and it had turned clear and cold. The lay of the land had again become rational. The creek he was on was natural in appearance, and tended as it should toward the southwest. But Surprise Lake was as lost to him as it had been to all its seekers in the past.

Half a day's journey down the creek brought him to the valley of a larger stream which he decided was the McQuestion. Here he shot a moose, and once again each wolf-dog carried a full fifty-pound pack of meat. As he turned down the McQuestion, he came upon a sled-trail. The late snows had drifted over, but underneath, it was well packed by travel. His conclusion was that two camps had been established on the McQuestion, and that this was the connecting trail. Evidently, Two Cabins had been found, and it was the lower camp, so he headed down the stream.

It was forty below zero when he camped that night, and he fell asleep wondering who were the men who had rediscovered the Two Cabins, and if he would fetch it next day. At the first hint of dawn he was under way, easily following the half-obliterated trail and packing the recent snow with his webbed shoes so that the dogs should not wallow.

And then it came, the unexpected, leaping out upon him on a bend of the river. It seemed to him that he heard and felt simultaneously. The crack of the rifle came from the right, and the bullet, tearing through and across the shoulders of his drill parka and woollen coat, pivoted him half around with the shock of its impact. He staggered on his twisted snow-shoes to recover balance, and heard a second crack of the rifle. This time it was a clean miss. He did not wait for more, but plunged across the snow for the sheltering trees of the bank a hundred feet away. Again and again the rifle cracked, and he was unpleasantly aware of a trickle of warm moisture down his back.

He climbed the bank, the dogs floundering behind, and dodged in among the trees and brush. Slipping out of his snow-shoes, he wallowed forward at full length and peered cautiously out. Nothing was to be seen. Whoever had shot at him was lying quiet among the trees of the opposite bank.

"If something doesn't happen pretty soon," he muttered at the end of half an hour, "I'll have to sneak away and build a fire or freeze my feet. Yellow Face, what'd you do, lying in the frost with circulation getting slack and a man trying to plug you?"

He crawled back a few yards, packed down the snow, danced a jig that sent the blood back into his feet, and managed to endure another half hour. Then, from down the river, he heard the unmistakable jingle of dog-bells. Peering out, he saw a sled round the bend. Only one man was with it, straining at the gee-pole and urging the dogs along. The effect on Smoke was one of shock, for it was the first human he had seen since he parted from Shorty three weeks before. His next thought was of the potential murderer concealed on the opposite bank.

Without exposing himself, Smoke whistled warningly. The man did not hear, and came on rapidly. Again, and more sharply, Smoke whistled. The man whoa'd his dogs, stopped, and had turned and faced Smoke when the rifle cracked. The instant afterwards, Smoke fired into the wood in the direction of the sound. The man on the river had been struck by the first shot. The shock of the high velocity bullet staggered him. He stumbled awkwardly to the sled, half-falling, and pulled a rifle out from under the lashings. As he strove to raise it to his shoulder, he crumpled at the waist and sank down slowly to a sitting posture on the sled. Then, abruptly, as the gun went off aimlessly, he pitched backward and across a corner of the sled-load, so that Smoke could see only his legs and stomach.

From below came more jingling bells. The man did not move. Around the bend swung three sleds, accompanied by half a dozen men. Smoke cried warningly, but they had seen the condition of the first sled, and they dashed on to it. No shots came from the other bank, and Smoke, calling his dogs to follow, emerged into the open. There were exclamations from the men, and two of them, flinging off the mittens of their right hands, levelled their rifles at him.

"Come on, you red-handed murderer, you," one of them, a black-bearded man, commanded. "An' jest pitch that gun of yourn in the snow."

Smoke hesitated, then dropped his rifle and came up to them.

"Go through him, Louis, an' take his weapons," the black-bearded man ordered.

Louis was a French-Canadian voyageur, Smoke decided, as were four of the others. His search revealed only Smoke's hunting knife, which was appropriated.

"Now, what have you got to say for yourself, stranger, before I shoot you dead?" the black-bearded man demanded.

"That you're making a mistake if you think I killed that man," Smoke answered.

A cry came from one of the voyageurs. He had quested along the trail and found Smoke's tracks where he had left it to take refuge on the bank. The man explained the nature of his find.

"What'd you kill Joe Kinade for?" he of the black beard asked.

"I tell you I didn't—" Smoke began.

"Aw, what's the good of talkin'? We got you red-handed. Right up there's where you left the trail when you heard him comin'. You laid among the trees an' bushwhacked him. A short shot. You couldn't 'a' missed. Pierre, go an' get that gun he dropped."

"You might let me tell what happened," Smoke objected.

"You shut up," the man snarled at him. "I reckon your gun'll tell the story."

All the men examined Smoke's rifle, ejecting and counting the cartridges, and examining the barrel at muzzle and breech.

"One shot," Blackbeard concluded.

Pierre, with nostrils that quivered and distended like a deer's, sniffed at the breech.

"Him one fresh shot," he said.

"The bullet entered his back," Smoke said. "He was facing me when he was shot. You see, it came from the other bank."

Blackbeard considered this proposition for a scant second, and shook his head. "Nope. It won't do. Turn him around to face the other bank—that's how you whopped him in the back. Some of you boys run up an' down the trail, and see if you can see any tracks making for the other bank."

Their report was that on that side the snow was unbroken. Not even a snow-shoe rabbit had crossed it. Blackbeard, bending over the dead man, straightened up, with a woolly, furry wad in his hand. Shredding this, he found imbedded in the center the bullet which had perforated the body. Its nose was spread to the size of a half dollar, its butt-end, steel-jacketed, was undamaged. He compared it with a cartridge from Smoke's belt.

"That's plain enough evidence, stranger, to satisfy a blind man. It's soft-nosed an' steel-jacketed; yourn is soft-nosed and steel-jacketed. It's thirty-thirty; yourn is thirty-thirty. It's manufactured by the J. and T. Arms Company; yourn is manufactured by the J. and T. Arms Company. Now you come along, an' we'll go over to the bank an' see jest how you done it."

"I was bushwhacked myself," Smoke said. "Look at the hole in my parka."

While Blackbeard examined it, one of the voyageurs threw open the breech of the dead man's gun. It was patent to all that it had been fired once. The empty cartridge was still in the chamber.

"A damn shame poor Joe didn't get you," Blackbeard said bitterly. "But he did pretty well with a hole like that in him. Come on, you."

"Search the other bank first," Smoke urged.

"You shut up an' come on, an' let the facts do the talkin'."

They left the trail at the same spot he had, and followed it on up the bank and then in among the trees.

"Him dance that place keep him feet warm," Louis pointed out. "That place him crawl on belly. That place him put one elbow w'en him shoot."

"And by God there's the empty cartridge he done it with!" was Blackbeard's discovery. "Boys, there's only one thing to do—"

"You might ask me how I came to fire that shot," Smoke interrupted.

"An' I might knock your teeth into your gullet if you butt in again. You can answer them questions later on. Now, boys, we're decent an' law-abidin', an' we got to handle this right an' regular. How far do you reckon we've come, Pierre?"

"Twenty mile, I t'ink for sure."

"All right. We'll cache the outfit an' run him an' poor Joe back to Two Cabins. I reckon we've seen an' can testify to what'll stretch his neck."

It was three hours after dark when the dead man, Smoke, and his captors arrived at Two Cabins. By the starlight, Smoke could make out a dozen or more recently built cabins snuggling about a larger and older cabin on a flat by the river bank. Thrust inside this older cabin, he found it tenanted by a young giant of a man, his wife, and an old blind man. The woman, whom her husband called "Lucy," was herself a strapping creature of the frontier type. The old man, as Smoke learned afterwards, had been a trapper on the Stewart for years, and had gone finally blind the winter before. The camp of Two Cabins, he was also to learn, had been made the previous fall by a dozen men who arrived in half as many poling-boats loaded with provisions. Here they had found the blind trapper, on the site of Two Cabins, and about his cabin they had built their own. Later arrivals, mushing up the ice with dog teams, had tripled the population. There was plenty of meat in camp, and good low-pay dirt had been discovered and was being worked.

In five minutes, all the men of Two Cabins were jammed into the room. Smoke, shoved off into a corner, ignored and scowled at, his hands and feet tied with thongs of moose-hide, looked on. Thirty-eight men he counted, a wild and husky crew, all frontiersmen of the States or voyageurs from Upper Canada. His captors told the tale over and over, each the center of an excited and wrathful group. There were mutterings of: "Lynch him now! Why wait?" And, once, a big Irishman was restrained only by force from rushing upon the helpless prisoner and giving him a beating.

It was while counting the men that Smoke caught sight of a familiar face. It was Breck, the man whose boat Smoke had run through the rapids. He wondered why the other did not come and speak to him, but himself gave no sign of recognition. Later, when with shielded face Breck passed him a significant wink, Smoke understood.

Blackbeard, whom Smoke heard called Eli Harding, ended the discussion as to whether or not the prisoner should be immediately lynched.

"Hold on," Harding roared. "Keep your shirts on. That man belongs to me. I caught him an' I brought him here. D'ye think I brought him all the way here to be lynched? Not on your life. I could 'a' done that myself when I found him. I brought him here for a fair an' impartial trial, an' by God, a fair an' impartial trial he's goin' to get. He's tied up safe an' sound. Chuck him in a bunk till morning, an' we'll hold the trial right here."

SMOKE WOKE UP. A DRAUGHT that possessed all the rigidity of an icicle was boring into the front of his shoulders as he lay on his side facing the wall. When he had been tied into the bunk there had been no such draught, and now the outside air, driving into the heated atmosphere of the cabin with the pressure of fifty below zero, was sufficient advertizement that some one from without had pulled away the moss-chinking between the logs. He squirmed as far as his bonds would permit, then craned his neck forward until his lips just managed to reach the crack.

"Who is it?" he whispered.

"Breck," came the almost inaudible answer. "Be careful you don't make a noise. I'm going to pass a knife in to you."

"No good," Smoke said. "I couldn't use it. My hands are tied behind me and made fast to the leg of the bunk. Besides, you couldn't get a knife through that crack. But something must be done. Those fellows are of a temper to hang me, and, of course, you know I didn't kill that man."

"It wasn't necessary to mention it, Smoke. And if you did you had your reasons. Which isn't the point at all. I want to get you out of this. It's a tough bunch of men here. You've seen them. They're shut off from the world, and they make and enforce their own law—by miner's meeting, you know. They handled two men already—both grub-thieves. One they hiked from camp without an ounce of grub and no matches.

He made about forty miles and lasted a couple of days before he froze stiff. Two weeks ago they hiked the second man. They gave him his choice: no grub, or ten lashes for each day's ration. He stood for forty lashes before he fainted. And now they've got you, and every last one is convinced you killed Kinade."

"The man who killed Kinade shot at me, too. His bullet broke the skin on my shoulder. Get them to delay the trial till some one goes up and searches the bank where the murderer hid."

"No use. They take the evidence of Harding and the five Frenchmen with him. Besides, they haven't had a hanging yet, and they're keen for it. You see, things have been pretty monotonous. They haven't located anything big, and they got tired of hunting for Surprise Lake. They did some stampeding the first part of the winter, but they've got over that now. Scurvy is beginning to show up amongst them, too, and they're just ripe for excitement."

"And it looks like I'll furnish it," was Smoke's comment. "Say, Breck, how did you ever fall in with such a God-forsaken bunch?"

"After I got the claims at Squaw Creek opened up and some men to working, I came up here by way of the Stewart, hunting for Two Cabins. They'd beaten me to it, so I've been higher up the Stewart. Just got back yesterday out of grub."

"Find anything?"

"Nothing much. But I think I've got a hydraulic proposition that'll work big when the country's opened up. It's that, or a gold-dredger."

"Hold on," Smoke interrupted. "Wait a minute. Let me think."

He was very much aware of the snores of the sleepers as he pursued the idea that had flashed into his mind.

"Say, Breck, have they opened up the meat-packs my dogs carried?" he asked.

"A couple. I was watching. They put them in Harding's cache."

"Did they find anything?"

"Meat."

"Good. You've got to get into the brown-canvas pack that's patched with moose-hide. You'll find a few pounds of lumpy gold. You've never seen gold like it in the country, nor has anybody else. Here's what you've got to do. Listen."

A quarter of an hour later, fully instructed and complaining that his toes were freezing, Breck went away. Smoke, his own nose and one cheek frosted by proximity to the chink, rubbed them against the blankets for half an hour before the blaze and bite of the returning blood assured him of the safety of his flesh.

"My mind's made up right now. There ain't no doubt but what he killed Kinade. We heard the whole thing last night. What's the good of goin' over it again? I vote guilty."

In such fashion, Smoke's trial began. The speaker, a loose-jointed, hard-rock man from Colorado, manifested irritation and disgust when Harding set his suggestion aside, demanded the proceedings should be regular, and nominated one Shunk Wilson for judge and chairman of the meeting. The population of Two Cabins constituted the jury, though, after some discussion, the woman, Lucy, was denied the right to vote on Smoke's guilt or innocence.

While this was going on, Smoke, jammed into a corner on a bunk, overheard a whispered conversation between Breck and a miner.

"You haven't fifty pounds of flour you'll sell?" Breck queried.

"You ain't got the dust to pay the price I'm askin'," was the reply.

"I'll give you two hundred."

The man shook his head.

"Three hundred. Three-fifty."

At four hundred, the man nodded, and said, "Come on over to my cabin an' weigh out the dust."

The two squeezed their way to the door, and slipped out. After a few minutes Breck returned alone.

Harding was testifying, when Smoke saw the door shoved open slightly, and in the crack appear the face of the man who had sold the flour. He was grimacing and beckoning emphatically to some one inside, who arose from near the stove and started to work toward the door.

"Where are you goin', Sam?" Shunk Wilson demanded.

"I'll be back in a jiffy," Sam explained. "I jes' got to go."

Smoke was permitted to question the witnesses, and he was in the middle of the cross-examination of Harding when from without came the whining of dogs in harness, and the grind and churn of sled-runners. Somebody near the door peeped out.

"It's Sam an' his pardner an' a dog-team hell-bent down the trail for Stewart River," the man reported.

Nobody spoke for a long half-minute, but men glanced significantly at one another, and a general restlessness pervaded the packed room.

JACK LONDON

Out of the corner of his eye, Smoke caught a glimpse of Breck, Lucy, and her husband whispering together.

"Come on, you," Shunk Wilson said gruffly to Smoke. "Cut this questionin' short. We know what you're tryin' to prove—that the other bank wa'n't searched. The witness admits it. We admit it. It wa'n't necessary. No tracks led to that bank. The snow wa'n't broke."

"There was a man on the other bank just the same," Smoke insisted.

"That's too thin for skatin', young man. There ain't many of us on the McQuestion, an' we got every man accounted for."

"Who was the man you hiked out of camp two weeks ago?" Smoke asked.

"Alonzo Miramar. He was a Mexican. What's that grub-thief got to do with it?"

"Nothing, except that you haven't accounted for *him*, Mr. Judge."

"He went down the river, not up."

"How do you know where he went?"

"Saw him start."

"And that's all you know of what became of him?"

"No, it ain't, young man. I know, we all know, he had four days' grub an' no gun to shoot meat with. If he didn't make the settlement on the Yukon he'd croaked long before this."

"I suppose you've got all the guns in this part of the country accounted for, too," Smoke observed pointedly.

Shunk Wilson was angry. "You'd think I was the prisoner the way you slam questions into me. Now then, come on with the next witness. Where's French Louis?"

While French Louis was shoving forward, Lucy opened the door.

"Where you goin'?" Shunk Wilson shouted.

"I reckon I don't have to stay," she answered defiantly. "I ain't got no vote, an' besides, my cabin's so jammed up I can't breathe."

In a few minutes her husband followed. The closing of the door was the first warning the judge received of it.

"Who was that?" he interrupted Pierre's narrative to ask.

"Bill Peabody," somebody spoke up. "Said he wanted to ask his wife something and was coming right back."

Instead of Bill, it was Lucy who re-entered, took off her furs, and resumed her place by the stove.

"I reckon we don't need to hear the rest of the witnesses," was Shunk Wilson's decision, when Pierre had finished. "We already know they only can testify to the same facts we've already heard. Say, Sorensen, you go an' bring Bill Peabody back. We'll be votin' a verdict pretty short. Now, stranger, you can get up an' say your say concernin' what happened. In the meantime, we'll just be savin' delay by passin' around the two rifles, the ammunition, an' the bullet that done the killin'."

Midway in his story of how he had arrived in that part of the country, and at the point in his narrative where he described his own ambush and how he had fled to the bank, Smoke was interrupted by the indignant Shunk Wilson.

"Young man, what sense is there in you testifyin' that way? You're just takin' up valuable time. Of course you got the right to lie to save your neck, but we ain't goin' to stand for such foolishness. The rifle, the ammunition, an' the bullet that killed Joe Kinade is against you. What's that? Open the door, somebody!"

The frost rushed in, taking form and substance in the heat of the room, while through the open door came the whining of dogs that decreased rapidly with distance.

"It's Sorensen an' Peabody," some one cried, "a-throwin' the whip into the dawgs an' headin' down river!"

"Now, what the hell—!" Shunk Wilson paused, with dropped jaw, and glared at Lucy. "I reckon you can explain, Mrs. Peabody."

She tossed her head and compressed her lips, and Shunk Wilson's wrathful and suspicious gaze passed on and rested on Breck.

"An' I reckon that newcomer you've been chinning with could explain if *he* had a mind to."

Breck, now very uncomfortable, found all eyes centered on him.

"Sam was chewing the rag with him, too, before he hit out," some one said.

"Look here, Mr. Breck," Shunk Wilson continued. "You've been interruptin' proceedings, and you got to explain the meanin' of it. What was you chinnin' about?"

Breck cleared his throat timidly and replied. "I was just trying to buy some grub."

"What with?"

"Dust, of course."

"Where'd you get it?"

Breck did not answer.

"He's been snoopin' around up the Stewart," a man volunteered. "I run across his camp a week ago when I was huntin'. An' I want to tell you he was almighty secretious about it."

"The dust didn't come from there," Breck said. "That's only a low-grade hydraulic proposition."

"Bring your poke here an' let's see your dust," Wilson commanded.

"I tell you it didn't come from there."

"Let's see it, just the same."

Breck made as if to refuse, but all about him were menacing faces. Reluctantly, he fumbled in his coat pocket. In the act of drawing forth a pepper-can, it rattled against what was evidently a hard object.

"Fetch it all out!" Shunk Wilson thundered.

And out came the big nugget, fist-size, yellow as no gold any onlooker had ever seen. Shunk Wilson gasped. Half a dozen, catching one glimpse, made a break for the door. They reached it at the same moment, and, with cursing and scuffling, jammed and pivoted through. The judge emptied the contents of the pepper-can on the table, and the sight of the rough lump-gold sent half a dozen more toward the door.

"Where are you goin'?" Eli Harding asked, as Shunk started to follow.

"For my dogs, of course."

"Ain't you goin' to hang him?"

"It'd take too much time right now. He'll keep till we get back, so I reckon this court is adjourned. This ain't no place for lingerin'."

Harding hesitated. He glanced savagely at Smoke, saw Pierre beckoning to Louis from the doorway, took one last look at the lump-gold on the table, and decided.

"No use you tryin' to get away," he flung back over his shoulder. "Besides, I'm goin' to borrow your dogs."

"What is it?—another one of them blamed stampedes?" the old blind trapper asked in a queer and petulant falsetto, as the cries of men and dogs and the grind of the sleds swept the silence of the room.

"It sure is," Lucy answered. "An' I never seen gold like it. Feel that, old man."

She put the big nugget in his hand. He was but slightly interested.

"It was a good fur-country," he complained, "before them danged miners come in an' scared back the game."

The door opened, and Breck entered. "Well," he said, "we four are all that are left in camp. It's forty miles to the Stewart by the cut-off I broke, and the fastest of them can't make the round trip in less than five or six days. But it's time you pulled out, Smoke, just the same."

Breck drew his hunting-knife across the other's bonds, and glanced at the woman. "I hope you don't object?" he said, with significant politeness.

"If there's goin' to be any shootin'," the blind man broke out, "I wish somebody'd take me to another cabin first."

"Go on, an' don't mind me," Lucy answered. "If I ain't good enough to hang a man, I ain't good enough to hold him."

Smoke stood up, rubbing his wrists where the thongs had impeded the circulation.

"I've got a pack all ready for you," Breck said. "Ten days' grub, blankets, matches, tobacco, an axe, and a rifle."

"Go to it," Lucy encouraged. "Hit the high places, stranger. Beat it as fast as God'll let you."

"I'm going to have a square meal before I start," Smoke said. "And when I start it will be up the McQuestion, not down. I want you to go along with me, Breck. We're going to search that other bank for the man that really did the killing."

"If you'll listen to me, you'll head down for the Stewart and the Yukon," Breck objected. "When this gang gets back from my low-grade hydraulic proposition, it will be seeing red."

Smoke laughed and shook his head.

"I can't jump this country, Breck. I've got interests here. I've got to stay and make good. I don't care whether you believe me or not, but I've found Surprise Lake. That's where that gold came from. Besides, they took my dogs, and I've got to wait to get them back. Also, I know what I'm about. There was a man hidden on that bank. He came pretty close to emptying his magazine at me."

Half an hour afterward, with a big plate of moose-steak before him and a big mug of coffee at his lips, Smoke half-started up from his seat. He had heard the sounds first. Lucy threw open the door.

"Hello, Spike; hello, Methody," she greeted the two frost-rimed men who were bending over the burden on their sled.

"We just come down from Upper Camp," one said, as the pair staggered into the room with a fur-wrapped object which they handled with exceeding gentleness. "An' this is what we found by the way. He's all in, I guess."

"Put him in the near bunk there," Lucy said. She bent over and pulled back the furs, disclosing a face composed principally of large, staring, black eyes, and of skin, dark and scabbed by repeated frost-bite, tightly stretched across the bones.

"If it ain't Alonzo!" she cried. "You pore, starved devil!"

"That's the man on the other bank," Smoke said in an undertone to Breck.

"We found it raidin' a cache that Harding must 'a' made," one of the men was explaining. "He was eatin' raw flour an' frozen bacon, an' when we got 'm he was cryin' an' squealin' like a hawg. Look at him! He's all starved, an' most of him frozen. He'll kick at any moment."

HALF AN HOUR LATER, WHEN the furs had been drawn over the face of the still form in the bunk, Smoke turned to Lucy. "If you don't mind, Mrs. Peabody, I'll have another whack at that steak. Make it thick and not so well done. I'm a meat-eater, I am."

VI

The Race for Number Three

"Huh! Get on to the glad rags!"

Shorty surveyed his partner with simulated disapproval, and Smoke, vainly attempting to rub the wrinkles out of the pair of trousers he had just put on, was irritated.

"They sure fit you close for a second-hand buy," Shorty went on. "What was the tax?"

"One hundred and fifty for the suit," Smoke answered. "The man was nearly my own size. I thought it was remarkably reasonable. What are you kicking about?"

"Who? Me? Oh, nothin'. I was just thinkin' it was goin' some for a meat-eater that hit Dawson in an ice-jam, with no grub, one suit of underclothes, a pair of mangy moccasins, an' overalls that looked like they'd been through the wreck of the Hesperus. Pretty gay front, pardner. Pretty gay front. Say—?"

"What do you want now?" Smoke demanded testily.

"What's her name?"

"There isn't any her, my friend. I'm to have dinner at Colonel Bowie's, if you want to know. The trouble with you, Shorty, is you're envious because I'm going into high society and you're not invited."

"Ain't you some late?" Shorty queried with concern.

"What do you mean?"

"For dinner. They'll be eatin' supper when you get there."

Smoke was about to explain with crudely elaborate sarcasm when he caught the twinkle in the other's eye. He went on dressing, with fingers that had lost their deftness, tying a Windsor tie in a bow-knot at the throat of his soft cotton shirt.

"Wisht I hadn't sent all my starched shirts to the laundry," Shorty murmured sympathetically. "I might 'a' fitted you out."

By this time Smoke was straining at a pair of shoes. The woollen socks were too thick to go into them. He looked appealingly at Shorty, who shook his head.

"Nope. If I had thin ones I wouldn't lend 'em to you. Back to the moccasins, pardner. You'd sure freeze your toes in skimpy-fangled gear like that."

"I paid fifteen dollars for them, second hand," Smoke lamented.

"I reckon they won't be a man not in moccasins."

"But there are to be women, Shorty. I'm going to sit down and eat with real live women—Mrs. Bowie, and several others, so the Colonel told me."

"Well, moccasins won't spoil their appetite none," was Shorty's comment. "Wonder what the Colonel wants with you?"

"I don't know, unless he's heard about my finding Surprise Lake. It will take a fortune to drain it, and the Guggenheims are out for investment."

"Reckon that's it. That's right, stick to the moccasins. Gee! That coat is sure wrinkled, an' it fits you a mite too swift. Just peck around at your vittles. If you eat hearty you'll bust through. An' if them women folks gets to droppin' handkerchiefs, just let 'em lay. Don't do any pickin' up. Whatever you do, don't."

As became a high-salaried expert and the representative of the great house of Guggenheim, Colonel Bowie lived in one of the most magnificent cabins in Dawson. Of squared logs, hand-hewn, it was two stories high, and of such extravagant proportions that it boasted a big living room that was used for a living room and for nothing else.

Here were big bear-skins on the rough board floor, and on the walls horns of moose and caribou. Here roared an open fireplace and a big wood-burning stove. And here Smoke met the social elect of Dawson—not the mere pick-handle millionaires, but the ultra-cream of a mining city whose population had been recruited from all the world—men like Warburton Jones, the explorer and writer; Captain Consadine of the Mounted Police; Haskell, Gold Commissioner of the Northwest Territory; and Baron Von Schroeder, an emperor's favourite with an international duelling reputation.

And here, dazzling in evening gown, he met Joy Gastell, whom hitherto he had encountered only on trail, befurred and moccasined. At dinner he found himself beside her.

"I feel like a fish out of water," he confessed. "All you folks are so real grand you know. Besides, I never dreamed such Oriental luxury existed in the Klondike. Look at Von Schroeder there. He's actually got a dinner jacket, and Consadine's got a starched shirt. I noticed he wore moccasins just the same. How do you like *my* outfit?"

He moved his shoulders about as if preening himself for Joy's approval.

"It looks as if you'd grown stout since you came over the Pass," she laughed.

"Wrong. Guess again."

"It's somebody else's."

"You win. I bought it for a price from one of the clerks at the A. C. Company."

"It's a shame clerks are so narrow-shouldered," she sympathized. "And you haven't told me what you think of *my* outfit."

"I can't," he said. "I'm out of breath. I've been living on trail too long. This sort of thing comes to me with a shock, you know. I'd quite forgotten that women have arms and shoulders. To-morrow morning, like my friend Shorty, I'll wake up and know it's all a dream. Now, the last time I saw you on Squaw Creek—"

"I was just a squaw," she broke in.

"I hadn't intended to say that. I was remembering that it was on Squaw Creek that I discovered you had feet."

"And I can never forget that you saved them for me," she said. "I've been wanting to see you ever since to thank you—" (He shrugged his shoulders deprecatingly). "And that's why you are here to-night."

"You asked the Colonel to invite me?"

"No! Mrs. Bowie. And I asked her to let me have you at table. And here's my chance. Everybody's talking. Listen, and don't interrupt. You know Mono Creek?"

"Yes."

"It has turned out rich—dreadfully rich. They estimate the claims as worth a million and more apiece. It was only located the other day."

"I remember the stampede."

"Well, the whole creek was staked to the sky-line, and all the feeders, too. And yet, right now, on the main creek, Number Three below Discovery is unrecorded. The creek was so far away from Dawson that the Commissioner allowed sixty days for recording after location. Every claim was recorded except Number Three below. It was staked by Cyrus Johnson. And that was all. Cyrus Johnson has disappeared. Whether he died, whether he went down river or up, nobody knows. Anyway, in six days, the time for recording will be up. Then the man who stakes it, and reaches Dawson first and records it, gets it."

"A million dollars," Smoke murmured.

"Gilchrist, who has the next claim below, has got six hundred dollars in a single pan off bedrock. He's burned one hole down. And the claim on the other side is even richer. I know."

"But why doesn't everybody know?" Smoke queried skeptically.

"They're beginning to know. They kept it secret for a long time, and it is only now that it's coming out. Good dog-teams will be at a premium in another twenty-four hours. Now, you've got to get away as decently as you can as soon as dinner is over. I've arranged it. An Indian will come with a message for you. You read it, let on that you're very much put out, make your excuses, and get away."

"I—er—I fail to follow."

"Ninny!" she exclaimed in a half-whisper. "What you must do is to get out to-night and hustle dog-teams. I know of two. There's Hanson's team, seven big Hudson Bay dogs—he's holding them at four hundred each. That's top price to-night, but it won't be to-morrow. And Sitka Charley has eight Malemutes he's asking thirty-five hundred for. To-morrow he'll laugh at an offer of five thousand. Then you've got your own team of dogs. And you'll have to buy several more teams. That's your work to-night. Get the best. It's dogs as well as men that will win this race. It's a hundred and ten miles, and you'll have to relay as frequently as you can."

"Oh, I see, you want me to go in for it," Smoke drawled.

"If you haven't the money for the dogs, I'll—" She faltered, but before she could continue, Smoke was speaking.

"I can buy the dogs. But—er—aren't you afraid this is gambling?"

"After your exploits at roulette in the Elkhorn," she retorted, "I'm not afraid that you're afraid. It's a sporting proposition, if that's what you mean. A race for a million, and with some of the stiffest dog-mushers and travellers in the country entered against you. They haven't entered yet, but by this time to-morrow they will, and dogs will be worth what the richest man can afford to pay. Big Olaf is in town. He came up from Circle City last month. He is one of the most terrible dog-mushers in the country, and if he enters he will be your most dangerous man. Arizona Bill is another. He's been a professional freighter and mail-carrier for years. If he goes in, interest will be centered on him and Big Olaf."

"And you intend me to come along as a sort of dark horse."

"Exactly. And it will have its advantages. You will not be supposed to stand a show. After all, you know, you are still classed as a chechako.

You haven't seen the four seasons go around. Nobody will take notice of you until you come into the home stretch in the lead."

"It's on the home stretch the dark horse is to show up its classy form, eh?"

She nodded, and continued earnestly: "Remember, I shall never forgive myself for the trick I played on the Squaw Creek stampede unless you win this Mono claim. And if any man can win this race against the old-timers, it's you."

It was the way she said it. He felt warm all over, and in his heart and head. He gave her a quick, searching look, involuntary and serious, and for the moment that her eyes met his steadily, ere they fell, it seemed to him that he read something of vaster import than the claim Cyrus Johnson had failed to record.

"I'll do it," he said. "I'll win it."

The glad light in her eyes seemed to promise a greater meed than all the gold in the Mono claim. He was aware of a movement of her hand in her lap next to his. Under the screen of the tablecloth he thrust his own hand across and met a firm grip of woman's fingers that sent another wave of warmth through him.

"What will Shorty say?" was the thought that flashed whimsically through his mind as he withdrew his hand. He glanced almost jealously at the faces of Von Schroeder and Jones, and wondered if they had not divined the remarkableness and deliciousness of this woman who sat beside him.

He was aroused by her voice, and realized that she had been speaking some moments.

"So you see, Arizona Bill is a white Indian," she was saying. "And Big Olaf is a bear wrestler, a king of the snows, a mighty savage. He can out-travel and out-endure an Indian, and he's never known any other life but that of the wild and the frost."

"Who's that?" Captain Consadine broke in from across the table.

"Big Olaf," she answered. "I was just telling Mr. Bellew what a traveller he is."

"You're right," the Captain's voice boomed. "Big Olaf is the greatest traveller in the Yukon. I'd back him against Old Nick himself for snow-bucking and ice-travel. He brought in the government dispatches in 1895, and he did it after two couriers were frozen on Chilkoot and the third drowned in the open water of Thirty Mile."

Smoke had travelled in a leisurely fashion up to Mono Creek, fearing to tire his dogs before the big race. Also, he had familiarized himself with every mile of the trail and located his relay camps. So many men had entered the race that the hundred and ten miles of its course was almost a continuous village. Relay camps were everywhere along the trail. Von Schroeder, who had gone in purely for the sport, had no less than eleven dog-teams—a fresh one for every ten miles. Arizona Bill had been forced to content himself with eight teams. Big Olaf had seven, which was the complement of Smoke. In addition, over two score of other men were in the running. Not every day, even in the golden north, was a million dollars the prize for a dog race. The country had been swept of dogs. No animal of speed and endurance escaped the fine-tooth comb that had raked the creeks and camps, and the prices of dogs had doubled and quadrupled in the course of the frantic speculation.

Number Three below Discovery was ten miles up Mono Creek from its mouth. The remaining hundred miles was to be run on the frozen breast of the Yukon. On Number Three itself were fifty tents and over three hundred dogs. The old stakes, blazed and scrawled sixty days before by Cyrus Johnson, still stood, and every man had gone over the boundaries of the claim again and again, for the race with the dogs was to be preceded by a foot and obstacle race. Each man had to relocate the claim for himself, and this meant that he must place two center-stakes and four corner-stakes and cross the creek twice, before he could start for Dawson with his dogs.

Furthermore, there were to be no "sooners." Not until the stroke of midnight of Friday night was the claim open for relocation, and not until the stroke of midnight could a man plant a stake. This was the ruling of the Gold Commissioner at Dawson, and Captain Consadine had sent up a squad of mounted police to enforce it. Discussion had arisen about the difference between sun-time and police-time, but Consadine had sent forth his fiat that police-time went, and, further, that it was the watch of Lieutenant Pollock that went.

The Mono trail ran along the level creek-bed, and, less than two feet in width, was like a groove, walled on either side by the snowfall of months. The problem of how forty-odd sleds and three hundred dogs were to start in so narrow a course was in everybody's mind.

"Huh!" said Shorty. "It's goin' to be the gosh-dangdest mix-up that ever was. I can't see no way out, Smoke, except main strength an' sweat an' to plow through. If the whole creek was glare-ice they ain't room for a dozen teams abreast. I got a hunch right now they's goin' to be a heap of scrappin' before they get strung out. An' if any of it comes our way, you got to let me do the punchin'."

Smoke squared his shoulders and laughed non-committally.

"No, you don't!" his partner cried in alarm. "No matter what happens, you don't dast hit. You can't handle dogs a hundred miles with a busted knuckle, an' that's what'll happen if you land on somebody's jaw."

Smoke nodded his head. "You're right, Shorty. I couldn't risk the chance."

"An' just remember," Shorty went on, "that I got to do all the shovin' for them first ten miles, an' you got to take it easy as you can. I'll sure jerk you through to the Yukon. After that it's up to you an' the dogs. Say—what d'ye think Schroeder's scheme is? He's got his first team a quarter of a mile down the creek, an' he'll know it by a green lantern. But we got him skinned. Me for the red flare every time."

THE DAY HAD BEEN CLEAR and cold, but a blanket of cloud formed across the face of the sky, and the night came on warm and dark, with the hint of snow impending. The thermometer registered fifteen below zero, and in the Klondike winter fifteen below is esteemed very warm.

At a few minutes before midnight, leaving Shorty with the dogs five hundred yards down the creek, Smoke joined the racers on Number Three. There were forty-five of them waiting the start for the thousand thousand dollars Cyrus Johnson had left lying in the frozen gravel. Each man carried six stakes and a heavy wooden mallet, and was clad in a smock-like parka of heavy cotton drill.

Lieutenant Pollock, in a big bearskin coat, looked at his watch by the light of a fire. It lacked a minute of midnight. "Make ready," he said, as he raised a revolver in his right hand and watched the second hand tick around.

Forty-five hoods were thrown back from the parkas. Forty-five pairs of hands unmittened, and forty-five pairs of moccasins pressed tensely into the packed snow. Also, forty-five stakes were thrust into the snow, and the same number of mallets lifted in the air.

The shot rang out, and the mallets fell. Cyrus Johnson's right to the million had expired. To prevent confusion, Lieutenant Pollock had insisted that the lower center-stake be driven first, next the south-eastern;

and so on around the four sides, including the upper center-stake on the way.

Smoke drove in his stake and was away with the leading dozen. Fires had been lighted at the corners, and by each fire stood a policeman, list in hand, checking off the names of the runners. A man was supposed to call out his name and show his face. There was to be no staking by proxy while the real racer was off and away down the creek.

At the first corner, beside Smoke's stake, Von Schroeder placed his. The mallets struck at the same instant. As they hammered, more arrived from behind and with such impetuosity as to get in one another's way and cause jostling and shoving. Squirming through the press and calling his name to the policeman, Smoke saw the Baron, struck in collision by one of the rushers, hurled clean off his feet into the snow. But Smoke did not wait. Others were still ahead of him. By the light of the vanishing fire, he was certain that he saw the back, hugely looming, of Big Olaf, and at the southwestern corner Big Olaf and he drove their stakes side by side.

It was no light work, this preliminary obstacle race. The boundaries of the claim totalled nearly a mile, and most of it was over the uneven surface of a snow-covered, niggerhead flat. All about Smoke men tripped and fell, and several times he pitched forward himself, jarringly, on hands and knees. Once, Big Olaf fell so immediately in front of him as to bring him down on top.

The upper center-stake was driven by the edge of the bank, and down the bank the racers plunged, across the frozen creek-bed, and up the other side. Here, as Smoke clambered, a hand gripped his ankle and jerked him back. In the flickering light of a distant fire, it was impossible to see who had played the trick. But Arizona Bill, who had been treated similarly, rose to his feet and drove his fist with a crunch into the offender's face. Smoke saw and heard as he was scrambling to his feet, but before he could make another lunge for the bank a fist dropped him half-stunned into the snow. He staggered up, located the man, half-swung a hook for his jaw, then remembered Shorty's warning and refrained. The next moment, struck below the knees by a hurtling body, he went down again.

It was a foretaste of what would happen when the men reached their sleds. Men were pouring over the other bank and piling into the jam. They swarmed up the bank in bunches, and in bunches were dragged back by their impatient fellows. More blows were struck, curses rose from the panting chests of those who still had wind to spare, and Smoke, curiously visioning the face of Joy Gastell, hoped that the mallets would not be brought into play. Overthrown, trod upon, groping in the snow for his lost stakes, he at last crawled out of the crush and attacked the bank farther along. Others were doing this, and it was his luck to have many men in advance of him in the race for the northwestern corner.

Reaching the fourth corner, he tripped headlong and in the long sprawling fall lost his remaining stake. For five minutes he groped in the darkness before he found it, and all the time the panting runners were passing him. From the last corner to the creek he began overtaking men for whom the mile run had been too much. In the creek itself Bedlam had broken loose. A dozen sleds were piled up and overturned, and nearly a hundred dogs were locked in combat. Among them men struggled, tearing the tangled animals apart, or beating them apart with clubs. In the fleeting glimpse he caught of it, Smoke wondered if he had ever seen a Dore grotesquery to compare.

Leaping down the bank beyond the glutted passage, he gained the hard-footing of the sled-trail and made better time. Here, in packed harbors beside the narrow trail, sleds and men waited for runners that were still behind. From the rear came the whine and rush of dogs, and Smoke had barely time to leap aside into the deep snow. A sled tore past, and he made out the man kneeling and shouting madly. Scarcely was it by when it stopped with a crash of battle. The excited dogs of a harbored sled, resenting the passing animals, had got out of hand and sprung upon them.

Smoke plunged around and by. He could see the green lantern of Von Schroeder and, just below it, the red flare that marked his own team. Two men were guarding Schroeder's dogs, with short clubs interposed between them and the trail.

"Come on, you Smoke! Come on, you Smoke!" he could hear Shorty calling anxiously.

"Coming!" he gasped.

By the red flare, he could see the snow torn up and trampled, and from the way his partner breathed he knew a battle had been fought. He staggered to the sled, and, in a moment he was falling on it, Shorty's whip snapped as he yelled: "Mush! you devils! Mush!"

The dogs sprang into the breast-bands, and the sled jerked abruptly ahead. They were big animals—Hanson's prize team of Hudson Bays— and Smoke had selected them for the first stage, which included the ten miles of Mono, the heavy going of the cut-off across the flat at the mouth, and the first ten miles of the Yukon stretch.

"How many are ahead?" he asked.

"You shut up an' save your wind," Shorty answered. "Hi! you brutes! Hit her up! Hit her up!"

He was running behind the sled, towing on a short rope. Smoke could not see him; nor could he see the sled on which he lay at full length. The fires had been left in the rear, and they were tearing through a wall of blackness as fast as the dogs could spring into it. This blackness was almost sticky, so nearly did it take on the seeming of substance.

Smoke felt the sled heel up on one runner as it rounded an invisible curve, and from ahead came the snarls of beasts and the oaths of men. This was known afterward as the Barnes-Slocum Jam. It was the teams of these two men which first collided, and into it, at full career, piled Smoke's seven big fighters. Scarcely more than semi-domesticated wolves, the excitement of that night on Mono Creek had sent every dog fighting mad. The Klondike dogs, driven without reins, cannot be stopped except by voice, so that there was no stopping this glut of struggle that heaped itself between the narrow rims of the creek. From behind, sled after sled hurled into the turmoil. Men who had their teams nearly extricated were overwhelmed by fresh avalanches of dogs—each animal well fed, well rested, and ripe for battle.

"It's knock down an' drag out an' plow through!" Shorty yelled in his partner's ear. "An' watch out for your knuckles! You drag dogs out an' let me do the punchin'!"

What happened in the next half hour Smoke never distinctly remembered. At the end he emerged exhausted, sobbing for breath, his jaw sore from a fist-blow, his shoulder aching from the bruise of a club, the blood running warmly down one leg from the rip of a dog's fangs, and both sleeves of his parka torn to shreds. As in a dream, while the battle still raged behind, he helped Shorty reharness the dogs. One, dying, they cut from the traces, and in the darkness they felt their way to the repair of the disrupted harness.

"Now you lie down an' get your wind back," Shorty commanded.

And through the darkness the dogs sped, with unabated strength, down Mono Creek, across the long cut-off, and to the Yukon. Here, at the junction with the main river-trail, somebody had lighted a fire, and here Shorty said good-bye. By the light of the fire, as the sled leaped behind the flying dogs, Smoke caught another of the unforgettable pictures of the Northland. It was of Shorty, swaying and sinking down limply in the snow, yelling his parting encouragement, one eye blackened and closed, knuckles bruised and broken, and one arm, ripped and fang-torn, gushing forth a steady stream of blood.

"How many ahead?" Smoke asked, as he dropped his tired Hudson Bays and sprang on the waiting sled at the first relay station.

"I counted eleven," the man called after him, for he was already away, behind the leaping dogs.

Fifteen miles they were to carry him on the next stage, which would fetch him to the mouth of White River. There were nine of them, but they composed his weakest team. The twenty-five miles between White River and Sixty Mile he had broken into two stages because of ice-jams, and here two of his heaviest, toughest teams were stationed.

He lay on the sled at full length, face-down, holding on with both hands. Whenever the dogs slacked from topmost speed he rose to his knees, and, yelling and urging, clinging precariously with one hand, threw his whip into them. Poor team that it was, he passed two sleds before White River was reached. Here, at the freeze-up, a jam had piled a barrier, allowing the open water, that formed for half a mile below, to freeze smoothly. This smooth stretch enabled the racers to make flying exchanges of sleds, and down all the course they had placed their relays below the jams.

Over the jam and out on to the smooth, Smoke tore along, calling loudly, "Billy! Billy!"

Billy heard and answered, and by the light of the many fires on the ice, Smoke saw a sled swing in from the side and come abreast. Its dogs were fresh and overhauled his. As the sleds swerved toward each other he leaped across, and Billy promptly rolled off.

"Where's Big Olaf?" Smoke cried.

"Leading!" Billy's voice answered; and the fires were left behind, and Smoke was again flying through the wall of blackness.

In the jams of that relay, where the way led across a chaos of up-ended ice-cakes, and where Smoke slipped off the forward end of the sled and with a haul-rope toiled behind the wheel-dog, he passed three sleds. Accidents had happened, and he could hear the men cutting out dogs and mending harnesses.

Among the jams of the next short relay into Sixty Mile, he passed two more teams. And that he might know adequately what had happened to them, one of his own dogs wrenched a shoulder, was unable to keep up, and was dragged in the harness. Its teammates, angered, fell upon it with their fangs, and Smoke was forced to club them off with the heavy butt of his whip. As he cut the injured animal out, he heard the whining cries of dogs behind him and the voice of a man that was familiar. It was Von Schroeder. Smoke called a warning to prevent a rear-end collision, and the Baron, hawing his animals and swinging on the gee-pole, went by a dozen feet to the side. Yet so impenetrable was the blackness that Smoke heard him pass but never saw him.

On the smooth stretch of ice beside the trading-post at Sixty Mile, Smoke overtook two more sleds. All had just changed teams, and for five minutes they ran abreast, each man on his knees and pouring whip and voice into the maddened dogs. But Smoke had studied out that portion of the trail, and now marked the tall pine on the bank that showed faintly in the light of the many fires. Below that pine was not merely darkness, but an abrupt cessation of the smooth stretch. There the trail, he knew, narrowed to a single sled-width. Leaning out ahead, he caught the haul-rope and drew his leaping sled up to the wheel-dog. He caught the animal by the hind legs and threw it. With a snarl of rage it tried to slash him with its fangs, but was dragged on by the rest of the team. Its body proved an efficient brake, and the two other teams, still abreast, dashed ahead into the darkness for the narrow way.

Smoke heard the crash and uproar of their collision, released his wheeler, sprang to the gee-pole, and urged his team to the right into the soft snow where the straining animals wallowed to their necks. It was exhausting work, but he won by the tangled teams and gained the hard-packed trail beyond.

On the relay out of Sixty Mile, Smoke had next to his poorest team, and though the going was good, he had set it a short fifteen miles. Two more teams would bring him into Dawson and to the gold-recorder's office, and Smoke had selected his best animals for the last two stretches. Sitka Charley himself waited with the eight Malemutes that would jerk Smoke along for twenty miles, and for the finish, with a fifteen-mile run, was his own team—the team he had had all winter and which had been with him in the search for Surprise Lake.

The two men he had left entangled at Sixty Mile failed to overtake him, and, on the other hand, his team failed to overtake any of the three that still led. His animals were willing, though they lacked stamina and speed, and little urging was needed to keep them jumping into it at their best. There was nothing for Smoke to do but to lie face downward and hold on. Now and again he would plunge out of the darkness into the circle of light about a blazing fire, catch a glimpse of furred men standing by harnessed and waiting dogs, and plunge into the darkness again. Mile after mile, with only the grind and jar of the runners in his ears, he sped on. Almost automatically he kept his place as the sled bumped ahead or half lifted and heeled on the swings and swerves of the bends. First one, and then another, without apparent rhyme or reason, three faces limned themselves on his consciousness: Joy Gastell's, laughing and audacious; Shorty's, battered and exhausted by the struggle down Mono Creek; and John Bellew's, seamed and rigid, as if cast in iron, so unrelenting was its severity. And sometimes Smoke wanted to shout aloud, to chant a paean of savage exultation, as he remembered the office of The Billow and the serial story of San Francisco which he had left unfinished, along with the other fripperies of those empty days.

The grey twilight of morning was breaking as he exchanged his weary dogs for the eight fresh Malemutes. Lighter animals than Hudson Bays, they were capable of greater speed, and they ran with the supple tirelessness of true wolves. Sitka Charley called out the order of the teams ahead. Big Olaf led, Arizona Bill was second, and Von Schroeder third. These were the three best men in the country. In fact, ere Smoke had left Dawson, the popular betting had placed them in that order. While they were racing for a million, at least half a million had been staked by others on the outcome of the race. No one had bet on Smoke, who, despite his several known exploits, was still accounted a chechako with much to learn.

As daylight strengthened, Smoke caught sight of a sled ahead, and, in half an hour, his own lead-dog was leaping at its tail. Not until the man turned his head to exchange greetings, did Smoke recognize him as Arizona Bill. Von Schroeder had evidently passed him. The trail, hard-packed, ran too narrowly through the soft snow, and for another half-hour Smoke was forced to stay in the rear. Then they topped an ice-jam and struck a smooth stretch below, where were a number of relay camps and where the snow was packed widely. On his knees, swinging his whip and yelling, Smoke drew abreast. He noted that Arizona Bill's right arm hung dead at his side, and that he was compelled to pour leather with his left hand. Awkward as it was, he had no hand left with which to hold on, and frequently he had to cease from the whip and clutch to save himself from falling off. Smoke remembered the scrimmage in the creek bed at Three Below Discovery, and understood. Shorty's advice had been sound.

"What's happened?" Smoke asked, as he began to pull ahead.

"I don't know," Arizona Bill answered. "I think I threw my shoulder out in the scrapping."

He dropped behind very slowly, though when the last relay station was in sight he was fully half a mile in the rear. Ahead, bunched together, Smoke could see Big Olaf and Von Schroeder. Again Smoke arose to his knees, and he lifted his jaded dogs into a burst of speed such as a man only can who has the proper instinct for dog-driving. He drew up close to the tail of Von Schroeder's sled, and in this order the three sleds dashed out on the smooth going below a jam, where many men and many dogs waited. Dawson was fifteen miles away.

Von Schroeder, with his ten-mile relays, had changed five miles back and would change five miles ahead. So he held on, keeping his dogs at full leap. Big Olaf and Smoke made flying changes, and their fresh teams immediately regained what had been lost to the Baron. Big Olaf led past, and Smoke followed into the narrow trail beyond.

"Still good, but not so good," Smoke paraphrased Spencer to himself.

Of Von Schroeder, now behind, he had no fear; but ahead was the greatest dog-driver in the country. To pass him seemed impossible. Again and again, many times, Smoke forced his leader to the other's sled-tail, and each time Big Olaf let out another link and drew away. Smoke contented himself with taking the pace, and hung on grimly. The race was not lost until one or the other won, and in fifteen miles many things could happen.

Three miles from Dawson something did happen. To Smoke's surprise, Big Olaf rose up and with oaths and leather proceeded to fetch out the last ounce of effort in his animals. It was a spurt that should have been reserved for the last hundred yards instead of being begun three miles from the finish. Sheer dog-killing that it was, Smoke followed. His own team was superb. No dogs on the Yukon had had harder work or were in better condition. Besides, Smoke had toiled with them, and eaten and bedded with them, and he knew each dog as an individual and how best to win in to the animal's intelligence and extract its last least shred of willingness.

They topped a small jam and struck the smooth going below. Big Olaf was barely fifty feet ahead. A sled shot out from the side and drew in toward him, and Smoke understood Big Olaf's terrific spurt. He had tried to gain a lead for the change. This fresh team that waited to jerk him down the home stretch had been a private surprise of his. Even the men who had backed him to win had had no knowledge of it.

Smoke strove desperately to pass during the exchange of sleds. Lifting his dogs to the effort, he ate up the intervening fifty feet. With urging and pouring of leather, he went to the side and on until his lead-dog was jumping abreast of Big Olaf's wheeler. On the other side, abreast, was the relay sled. At the speed they were going, Big Olaf did not dare try the flying leap. If he missed and fell off, Smoke would be in the lead and the race would be lost.

Big Olaf tried to spurt ahead, and he lifted his dogs magnificently, but Smoke's leader still continued to jump beside Big Olaf's wheeler. For half a mile the three sleds tore and bounced along side by side. The smooth stretch was nearing its end when Big Olaf took the chance. As the flying sleds swerved toward each other, he leaped, and the instant he struck he was on his knees, with whip and voice spurting the fresh team. The smooth stretch pinched out into the narrow trail, and he jumped his dogs ahead and into it with a lead of barely a yard.

A man was not beaten until he was beaten, was Smoke's conclusion, and drive no matter how, Big Olaf failed to shake him off. No team Smoke had driven that night could have stood such a killing pace and kept up with fresh dogs—no team save this one. Nevertheless, the pace *was* killing it, and as they began to round the bluff at Klondike City, he could feel the pitch of strength going out of his animals. Almost imperceptibly they lagged behind, and foot by foot Big Olaf drew away until he led by a score of yards.

A great cheer went up from the population of Klondike City assembled on the ice. Here the Klondike entered the Yukon, and half a mile away, across the Klondike, on the north bank, stood Dawson. An outburst of madder cheering arose, and Smoke caught a glimpse of a sled shooting out to him. He recognized the splendid animals that drew it. They were Joy Gastell's. And Joy Gastell drove them. The hood of her squirrel-skin parka was tossed back, revealing the cameo-like oval of her face outlined against her heavily-massed hair. Mittens had been discarded, and with bare hands she clung to whip and sled.

"Jump!" she cried, as her leader snarled at Smoke's.

Smoke struck the sled behind her. It rocked violently from the impact of his body, but she was full up on her knees and swinging the whip.

"Hi! You! Mush on! Chook! Chook!" she was crying, and the dogs whined and yelped in eagerness of desire and effort to overtake Big Olaf.

And then, as the lead-dog caught the tail of Big Olaf's sled, and yard by yard drew up abreast, the great crowd on the Dawson bank went mad. It *was* a great crowd, for the men had dropped their tools on all the creeks and come down to see the outcome of the race, and a dead heat at the end of a hundred and ten miles justified any madness.

"When you're in the lead I'm going to drop off!" Joy cried out over her shoulder.

Smoke tried to protest.

"And watch out for the dip curve half way up the bank," she warned.

Dog by dog, separated by half a dozen feet, the two teams were running abreast. Big Olaf, with whip and voice, held his own for a minute. Then, slowly, an inch at a time, Joy's leader began to forge past.

"Get ready!" she cried to Smoke. "I'm going to leave you in a minute. Get the whip."

And as he shifted his hand to clutch the whip, they heard Big Olaf roar a warning, but too late. His lead-dog, incensed at being passed, swerved in to the attack. His fangs struck Joy's leader on the flank. The rival teams flew at one another's throats. The sleds overran the fighting brutes and capsized. Smoke struggled to his feet and tried to lift Joy up. But she thrust him from her, crying: "Go!"

On foot, already fifty feet in advance, was Big Olaf, still intent on finishing the race. Smoke obeyed, and when the two men reached the foot of the Dawson bank, he was at the other's heels. But up the bank Big Olaf lifted his body hugely, regaining a dozen feet.

Five blocks down the main street was the gold-recorder's office. The street was packed as for the witnessing of a parade. Not so easily this time did Smoke gain to his giant rival, and when he did he was unable to pass. Side by side they ran along the narrow aisle between the solid walls of fur-clad, cheering men. Now one, now the other, with great convulsive jerks, gained an inch or so, only to lose it immediately after.

If the pace had been a killing one for their dogs, the one they now set themselves was no less so. But they were racing for a million dollars and greatest honour in Yukon Country. The only outside impression that came to Smoke on that last mad stretch was one of astonishment that there should be so many people in the Klondike. He had never seen them all at once before.

He felt himself involuntarily lag, and Big Olaf sprang a full stride in the lead. To Smoke it seemed that his heart would burst, while he had lost all consciousness of his legs. He knew they were flying under him, but he did not know how he continued to make them fly, nor how he put even greater pressure of will upon them and compelled them again to carry him to his giant competitor's side.

The open door of the Recorder's office appeared ahead of them. Both men made a final, futile spurt. Neither could draw away from the other, and side by side they hit the doorway, collided violently, and fell headlong on the office floor.

They sat up, but were too exhausted to rise. Big Olaf, the sweat pouring from him, breathing with tremendous, painful gasps, pawed the air and vainly tried to speak. Then he reached out his hand with unmistakable meaning; Smoke extended his, and they shook.

"It's a dead heat," Smoke could hear the Recorder saying, but it was as if in a dream, and the voice was very thin and very far away. "And all I can say is that you both win. You'll have to divide the claim between you. You're partners."

Their two arms pumped up and down as they ratified the decision. Big Olaf nodded his head with great emphasis, and spluttered. At last he got it out.

"You damn chechako," was what he said, but in the saying of it was admiration. "I don't know how you done it, but you did."

Outside, the great crowd was noisily massed, while the office was packing and jamming. Smoke and Big Olaf essayed to rise, and each helped the other to his feet. Smoke found his legs weak under him, and staggered drunkenly. Big Olaf tottered toward him.

"I'm sorry my dogs jumped yours."

"It couldn't be helped," Smoke panted back. "I heard you yell."

"Say," Big Olaf went on with shining eyes. "That girl—one damn fine girl, eh?"

"One damn fine girl," Smoke agreed.

VII

The Little Man

"I wisht you wasn't so set in your ways," Shorty demurred. "I'm sure scairt of that glacier. No man ought to tackle it by his lonely."

Smoke laughed cheerfully, and ran his eye up the glistening face of the tiny glacier that filled the head of the valley. "Here it is August already, and the days have been getting shorter for two months," he epitomized the situation. "You know quartz, and I don't. But I can bring up the grub, while you keep after that mother lode. So-long. I'll be back by to-morrow evening."

He turned and started.

"I got a hunch something's goin' to happen," Shorty pleaded after him.

But Smoke's reply was a bantering laugh. He held on down the little valley, occasionally wiping the sweat from his forehead, the while his feet crushed through ripe mountain raspberries and delicate ferns that grew beside patches of sun-sheltered ice.

In the early spring he and Shorty had come up the Stewart River and launched out into the amazing chaos of the region where Surprise Lake lay. And all of the spring and half of the summer had been consumed in futile wanderings, when, on the verge of turning back, they caught their first glimpse of the baffling, gold-bottomed sheet of water which had lured and fooled a generation of miners. Making their camp in the old cabin which Smoke had discovered on his previous visit, they had learned three things: first, heavy nugget gold was carpeted thickly on the lake bottom; next, the gold could be dived for in the shallower portions, but the temperature of the water was man-killing; and, finally, the draining of the lake was too stupendous a task for two men in the shorter half of a short summer. Undeterred, reasoning from the coarseness of the gold that it had not traveled far, they had set out in search of the mother lode. They had crossed the big glacier that frowned on the southern rim and devoted themselves to the puzzling maze of small valleys and canyons beyond, which, by most unmountainlike methods, drained, or had at one time drained, into the lake.

The valley Smoke was descending gradually widened after the fashion of any normal valley; but, at the lower end, it pinched narrowly between high precipitous walls and abruptly stopped in a cross wall. At the base of this, in a welter of broken rock, the streamlet disappeared, evidently finding its way out underground. Climbing the cross wall, from the top Smoke saw the lake beneath him. Unlike any mountain lake he had ever seen, it was not blue. Instead, its intense peacock-green tokened its shallowness. It was this shallowness that made its draining feasible. All about arose jumbled mountains, with ice-scarred peaks and crags, grotesquely shaped and grouped. All was topsyturvy and unsystematic—a Doré nightmare. So fantastic and impossible was it that it affected Smoke as more like a cosmic landscape-joke than a rational portion of earth's surface. There were many glaciers in the canyons, most of them tiny, and, as he looked, one of the larger ones, on the north shore, calved amid thunders and splashings. Across the lake, seemingly not more than half a mile, but, as he well knew, five miles away, he could see the bunch of spruce-trees and the cabin. He looked again to make sure, and saw smoke clearly rising from the chimney. Somebody else had surprised themselves into finding Surprise Lake, was his conclusion, as he turned to climb the southern wall.

From the top of this he came down into a little valley, flower-floored and lazy with the hum of bees, that behaved quite as a reasonable valley should, in so far as it made legitimate entry on the lake. What was wrong with it was its length—scarcely a hundred yards; its head a straight up-and-down cliff of a thousand feet, over which a stream pitched itself in descending veils of mist.

And here he encountered more smoke, floating lazily upward in the warm sunshine beyond an outjut of rock. As he came around the corner he heard a light, metallic tap-tapping and a merry whistling that kept the beat. Then he saw the man, an upturned shoe between his knees, into the sole of which he was driving hob-spikes.

"Hello!" was the stranger's greeting, and Smoke's heart went out to the man in ready liking. "Just in time for a snack. There's coffee in the pot, a couple of cold flapjacks, and some jerky."

"I'll go you if I lose," was Smoke's acceptance, as he sat down. "I've been rather skimped on the last several meals, but there's oodles of grub over in the cabin."

"Across the lake? That's what I was heading for."

"Seems Surprise Lake is becoming populous," Smoke complained, emptying the coffee-pot.

"Go on, you're joking, aren't you?" the man said, astonishment painted on his face.

Smoke laughed. "That's the way it takes everybody. You see those high ledges across there to the northwest? There's where I first saw it. No warning. Just suddenly caught the view of the whole lake from there. I'd given up looking for it, too.

"Same here," the other agreed. "I'd headed back and was expecting to fetch the Stewart last night, when out I popped in sight of the lake. If that's it, where's the Stewart? And where have I been all the time? And how did you come here? And what's your name?"

"Bellew. Kit Bellew."

"Oh! I know you." The man's eyes and face were bright with a joyous smile, and his hand flashed eagerly out to Smoke's. "I've heard all about you."

"Been reading police-court news, I see," Smoke sparred modestly.

"Nope." The man laughed and shook his head. "Merely recent Klondike history. I might have recognized you if you'd been shaved. I watched you putting it all over the gambling crowd when you were bucking roulette in the Elkhorn. My name's Carson—Andy Carson; and I can't begin to tell you how glad I am to meet up with you."

He was a slender man, wiry with health, with quick black eyes and a magnetism of camaraderie.

"And this is Surprise Lake?" he murmured incredulously.

"It certainly is."

"And its bottom's buttered with gold?"

"Sure. There's some of the churning." Smoke dipped in his overalls pocket and brought forth half a dozen nuggets. "That's the stuff. All you have to do is go down to bottom, blind if you want to, and pick up a handful. Then you've got to run half a mile to get up your circulation."

"Well, gosh-dash my dingbats, if you haven't beaten me to it," Carson swore whimsically, but his disappointment was patent. "An' I thought I'd scooped the whole caboodle. Anyway, I've had the fun of getting here."

"Fun!" Smoke cried. "Why, if we can ever get our hands on all that bottom, we'll make Rockefeller look like thirty cents."

"But it's yours," was Carson's objection.

"Nothing to it, my friend. You've got to realize that no gold deposit like it has been discovered in all the history of mining. It will take you and me and my partner and all the friends we've got to lay our hands on it. All Bonanza and Eldorado, dumped together, wouldn't be richer than half an acre down here. The problem is to drain the lake. It will take millions. And there's only one thing I'm afraid of. There's so much of it that if we fail to control the output it will bring about the demonetization of gold."

"And you tell me——" Carson broke off, speechless and amazed.

"And glad to have you. It will take a year or two, with all the money we can raise, to drain the lake. It can be done. I've looked over the ground. But it will take every man in the country that's willing to work for wages. We'll need an army, and we need right now decent men in on the ground floor. Are you in?"

"Am I in? Don't I look it? I feel so much like a millionaire that I'm real timid about crossing that big glacier. Couldn't afford to break my neck now. Wish I had some more of those hob-spikes. I was just hammering the last in when you came along. How's yours? Let's see."

Smoke held up his foot.

"Worn smooth as a skating-rink!" Carson cried. "You've certainly been hiking some. Wait a minute, and I'll pull some of mine out for you."

But Smoke refused to listen. "Besides," he said, "I've got about forty feet of rope cached where we take the ice. My partner and I used it coming over. It will be a cinch."

It was a hard, hot climb. The sun blazed dazzlingly on the ice-surface, and with streaming pores they panted from the exertion. There were places, criss-crossed by countless fissures and crevasses, where an hour of dangerous toil advanced them no more than a hundred yards. At two in the afternoon, beside a pool of water bedded in the ice, Smoke called a halt.

"Let's tackle some of that jerky," he said. "I've been on short allowance, and my knees are shaking. Besides, we're across the worst. Three hundred yards will fetch us to the rocks, and it's easy going, except for a couple of nasty fissures and one bad one that heads us down toward the bulge. There's a weak ice-bridge there, but Shorty and I managed it."

Over the jerky, the two men got acquainted, and Andy Carson unbosomed himself of the story of his life. "I just knew I'd find Surprise Lake," he mumbled in the midst of mouthfuls. "I had to. I missed the French Hill Benches, the Big Skookum, and Monte Cristo, and then it was Surprise Lake or bust. And here I am. My wife knew I'd strike it. I've got faith enough, but hers knocks mine galleywest. She's a corker, a crackerjack—dead game, grit to her finger-ends, never-say-die, a fighter from the drop of the hat, the one woman for me, true blue and all the rest. Take a look at that."

He sprung open his watch, and on the inside cover Smoke saw the small, pasted photograph of a bright-haired woman, framed on either side by the laughing face of a child.

"Boys?" he queried.

"Boy and girl," Carson answered proudly. "He's a year and a half older." He sighed. "They might have been some grown, but we had to wait. You see, she was sick. Lungs. But she put up a fight. What'd we know about such stuff? I was clerking, railroad clerk, Chicago, when we got married. Her folks were tuberculous. Doctors didn't know much in those days. They said it was hereditary. All her family had it. Caught it from each other, only they never guessed it. Thought they were born with it. Fate. She and I lived with them the first couple of years. I wasn't afraid. No tuberculosis in my family. And I got it. That set me thinking. It was contagious. I caught it from breathing their air.

"We talked it over, she and I. Then I jumped the family doctor and consulted an up-to-date expert. He told me what I'd figured out for myself, and said Arizona was the place for us. We pulled up stakes and went down—no money, nothing. I got a job sheep-herding, and left her in town—a lung town. It was filled to spilling with lungers.

"Of course, living and sleeping in the clean open, I started right in to mend. I was away months at a time. Every time I came back, she was worse. She just couldn't pick up. But we were learning. I jerked her out of that town, and she went to sheep-herding with me. In four years, winter and summer, cold and heat, rain, snow, and frost, and all the rest, we never slept under a roof, and we were moving camp all the time. You ought to have seen the change—brown as berries, lean as Indians, tough as rawhide. When we figured we were cured, we pulled out for San Francisco. But we were too previous. By the second month we both had slight hemorrhages. We flew the coop back to Arizona and the sheep. Two years more of it. That fixed us. Perfect cure. All her family's dead. Wouldn't listen to us.

"Then we jumped cities for keeps. Knocked around on the Pacific coast and southern Oregon looked good to us. We settled in the Rogue

River Valley—apples. There's a big future there, only nobody knows it. I got my land—on time, of course—for forty an acre. Ten years from now it'll be worth five hundred.

"We've done some almighty hustling. Takes money, and we hadn't a cent to start with, you know—had to build a house and barn, get horses and plows, and all the rest. She taught school two years. Then the boy came. But we've got it. You ought to see those trees we planted—a hundred acres of them, almost mature now. But it's all been outgo, and the mortgage working overtime. That's why I'm here. She'd 'a' come along only for the kids and the trees. She's handlin' that end, and here I am, a gosh-danged expensive millionaire—in prospect."

He looked happily across the sun-dazzle on the ice to the green water of the lake along the farther shore, took a final look at the photograph, and murmured:

"She's some woman, that. She's hung on. She just wouldn't die, though she was pretty close to skin and bone all wrapped around a bit of fire when she went out with the sheep. Oh, she's thin now. Never will be fat. But it's the prettiest thinness I ever saw, and when I get back, and the trees begin to bear, and the kids get going to school, she and I are going to do Paris. I don't think much of that burg, but she's just hankered for it all her life."

"Well, here's the gold that will take you to Paris," Smoke assured him. "All we've got to do is to get our hands on it."

Carson nodded with glistening eyes. "Say—that farm of ours is the prettiest piece of orchard land on all the Pacific coast. Good climate, too. Our lungs will never get touched again there. Ex-lungers have to be almighty careful, you know. If you're thinking of settling, well, just take a peep in at our valley before you settle, that's all. And fishing! Say!—did you ever get a thirty-five-pound salmon on a six-ounce rod? Some fight, bo', some fight!"

"I'm lighter than you by forty pounds," Carson said. "Let me go first."

They stood on the edge of the crevasse. It was enormous and ancient, fully a hundred feet across, with sloping, age-eaten sides instead of sharp-angled rims. At this one place it was bridged by a huge mass of pressure-hardened snow that was itself half ice. Even the bottom of this mass they could not see, much less the bottom of the crevasse. Crumbling and melting, the bridge threatened imminent collapse.

There were signs where recent portions had broken away, and even as they studied it a mass of half a ton dislodged and fell.

"Looks pretty bad," Carson admitted with an ominous head-shake. "And it looks much worse than if I wasn't a millionaire."

"But we've got to tackle it," Smoke said. "We're almost across. We can't go back. We can't camp here on the ice all night. And there's no other way. Shorty and I explored for a mile up. It was in better shape, though, when we crossed."

"It's one at a time, and me first." Carson took the part coil of rope from Smoke's hand. "You'll have to cast off. I'll take the rope and the pick. Gimme your hand so I can slip down easy."

Slowly and carefully he lowered himself the several feet to the bridge, where he stood, making final adjustments for the perilous traverse. On his back was his pack outfit. Around his neck, resting on his shoulders, he coiled the rope, one end of which was still fast to his waist.

"I'd give a mighty good part of my millions right now for a bridge-construction gang," he said, but his cheery, whimsical smile belied the words. Also, he added, "It's all right; I'm a cat."

The pick, and the long stick he used as an alpenstock, he balanced horizontally after the manner of a rope-walker. He thrust one foot forward tentatively, drew it back, and steeled himself with a visible, physical effort.

"I wish I was flat broke," he smiled up. "If ever I get out of being a millionaire this time, I'll never be one again. It's too uncomfortable."

"It's all right," Smoke encouraged. "I've been over it before. Better let me try it first."

"And you forty pounds to the worse," the little man flashed back. "I'll be all right in a minute. I'm all right now." And this time the nerving-up process was instantaneous. "Well, here goes for Rogue River and the apples," he said, as his foot went out, this time to rest carefully and lightly while the other foot was brought up and past. Very gently and circumspectly he continued on his way until two-thirds of the distance was covered. Here he stopped to examine a depression he must cross, at the bottom of which was a fresh crack. Smoke, watching, saw him glance to the side and down into the crevasse itself, and then begin a slight swaying.

"Keep your eyes up!" Smoke commanded sharply. "Now! Go on!"

The little man obeyed, nor faltered on the rest of the journey. The sun-eroded slope of the farther edge of the crevasse was slippery, but not steep, and he worked his way up to a narrow ledge, faced about, and sat down.

"Your turn," he called across. "But just keep a-coming and don't look down. That's what got my goat. Just keep a-coming, that's all. And get a move on. It's almighty rotten."

Balancing his own stick horizontally, Smoke essayed the passage. That the bridge was on its last legs was patent. He felt a jar under foot, a slight movement of the mass, and a heavier jar. This was followed by a single sharp crackle. Behind him he knew something was happening. If for no other reason, he knew it by the strained, tense face of Carson. From beneath, thin and faint, came the murmur of running water, and Smoke's eyes involuntarily wavered to a glimpse of the shimmering depths. He jerked them back to the way before him. Two-thirds over, he came to the depression. The sharp edges of the crack, but slightly touched by the sun, showed how recent it was. His foot was lifted to make the step across, when the crack began slowly widening, at the same time emitting numerous sharp snaps. He made the step quickly, increasing the stride of it, but the worn nails of his shoe skated on the farther slope of the depression. He fell on his face, and without pause slipped down and into the crack, his legs hanging clear, his chest supported by the stick which he had managed to twist crosswise as he fell.

His first sensation was the nausea caused by the sickening up-leap of his pulse; his first idea was of surprise that he had fallen no farther. Behind him was crackling and jar and movement to which the stick vibrated. From beneath, in the heart of the glacier, came the soft and hollow thunder of the dislodged masses striking bottom. And still the bridge, broken from its farthest support and ruptured in the middle, held, though the portion he had crossed tilted downward at a pitch of twenty degrees. He could see Carson, perched on his ledge, his feet braced against the melting surface, swiftly recoiling the rope from his shoulders to his hand.

"Wait!" he cried. "Don't move, or the whole shooting-match will come down."

He calculated the distance with a quick glance, took the bandana from his neck and tied it to the rope, and increased the length by a second bandana from his pocket. The rope, manufactured from sled-lashings and short lengths of plaited rawhide knotted together, was both light and strong. The first cast was lucky as well as deft, and Smoke's fingers clutched it. He evidenced a hand-over-hand intention of crawling out of the crack. But Carson, who had refastened the rope around his own waist, stopped him.

"Make it fast around yourself as well," he ordered.

"If I go I'll take you with me," Smoke objected.

The little man became very peremptory.

"You shut up," he ordered. "The sound of your voice is enough to start the whole thing going."

"If I ever start going—" Smoke began.

"Shut up! You ain't going to ever start going. Now do what I say. That's right—under the shoulders. Make it fast. Now! Start! Get a move on, but easy as you go. I'll take in the slack. You just keep a-coming. That's it. Easy. Easy."

Smoke was still a dozen feet away when the final collapse of the bridge began. Without noise, but in a jerky way, it crumbled to an increasing tilt.

"Quick!" Carson called, coiling in hand-over-hand on the slack of the rope which Smoke's rush gave him.

When the crash came, Smoke's fingers were clawing into the hard face of the wall of the crevasse, while his body dragged back with the falling bridge. Carson, sitting up, feet wide apart and braced, was heaving on the rope. This effort swung Smoke in to the side wall, but it jerked Carson out of his niche. Like a cat, he faced about, clawing wildly for a hold on the ice and slipping down. Beneath him, with forty feet of taut rope between them, Smoke was clawing just as wildly; and ere the thunder from below announced the arrival of the bridge, both men had come to rest. Carson had achieved this first, and the several pounds of pull he was able to put on the rope had helped bring Smoke to a stop.

Each lay in a shallow niche, but Smoke's was so shallow that, tense with the strain of flattening and sticking, nevertheless he would have slid on had it not been for the slight assistance he took from the rope. He was on the verge of a bulge and could not see beneath him. Several minutes passed, in which they took stock of the situation and made rapid strides in learning the art of sticking to wet and slippery ice. The little man was the first to speak.

"Gee!" he said; and, a minute later, "If you can dig in for a moment and slack on the rope, I can turn over. Try it."

Smoke made the effort, then rested on the rope again. "I can do it," he said. "Tell me when you're ready. And be quick."

"About three feet down is holding for my heels," Carson said. "It won't take a moment. Are you ready?"

"Go on."

It was hard work to slide down a yard, turn over and sit up; but it was even harder for Smoke to remain flattened and maintain a position that from instant to instant made a greater call upon his muscles. As it was, he could feel the almost perceptible beginning of the slip when the rope tightened and he looked up into his companion's face. Smoke noted the yellow pallor of sun-tan forsaken by the blood, and wondered what his own complexion was like. But when he saw Carson, with shaking fingers, fumble for his sheath-knife, he decided the end had come. The man was in a funk and was going to cut the rope.

"Don't m-mind m-m-me," the little man chattered. "I ain't scared. It's only my nerves, gosh-dang them. I'll b-b-be all right in a minute."

And Smoke watched him, doubled over, his shoulders between his knees, shivering and awkward, holding a slight tension on the rope with one hand while with the other he hacked and gouged holes for his heels in the ice.

"Carson," he breathed up to him, "you're some bear, some bear."

The answering grin was ghastly and pathetic. "I never could stand height," Carson confessed. "It always did get me. Do you mind if I stop a minute and clear my head? Then I'll make those heel-holds deeper so I can heave you up."

Smoke's heart warmed. "Look here, Carson. The thing for you to do is to cut the rope. You can never get me up, and there's no use both of us being lost. You can make it out with your knife."

"You shut up!" was the hurt retort. "Who's running this?"

And Smoke could not help but see that anger was a good restorative for the other's nerves. As for himself, it was the more nerve-racking strain, lying plastered against the ice with nothing to do but strive to stick on.

A groan and a quick cry of "Hold on!" warned him. With face pressed against the ice, he made a supreme sticking effort, felt the rope slacken, and knew Carson was slipping toward him. He did not dare look up until he felt the rope tighten and knew the other had again come to rest.

"Gee, that was a near go," Carson chattered. "I came down over a yard. Now you wait. I've got to dig new holds. If this danged ice wasn't so melty we'd be hunky-dory."

Holding the few pounds of strain necessary for Smoke with his left hand, the little man jabbed and chopped at the ice with his right. Ten minutes of this passed.

"Now, I'll tell you what I've done," Carson called down. "I've made heel-holds and hand-holes for you alongside of me. I'm going to heave the rope in slow and easy, and you just come along sticking an' not too fast. I'll tell you what, first of all. I'll take you on the rope and you worry out of that pack. Get me?"

Smoke nodded, and with infinite care unbuckled his pack-straps. With a wriggle of the shoulders he dislodged the pack, and Carson saw it slide over the bulge and out of sight.

"Now, I'm going to ditch mine," he called down. "You just take it easy and wait."

Five minutes later the upward struggle began. Smoke, after drying his hands on the insides of his arm-sleeves, clawed into the climb—bellied, and clung, and stuck, and plastered—sustained and helped by the pull of the rope. Alone, he could not have advanced. Despite his muscles, because of his forty pounds' handicap, he could not cling as did Carson. A third of the way up, where the pitch was steeper and the ice less eroded, he felt the strain on the rope decreasing. He moved slower and slower. Here was no place to stop and remain. His most desperate effort could not prevent the stop, and he could feel the down-slip beginning.

"I'm going," he called up.

"So am I," was the reply, gritted through Carson's teeth.

"Then cast loose."

Smoke felt the rope tauten in a futile effort, then the pace quickened, and as he went past his previous lodgment and over the bulge the last glimpse he caught of Carson he was turned over, with madly moving hands and feet striving to overcome the downward draw. To Smoke's surprise, as he went over the bulge, there was no sheer fall. The rope restrained him as he slid down a steeper pitch, which quickly eased until he came to a halt in another niche on the verge of another bulge. Carson was now out of sight, ensconced in the place previously occupied by Smoke.

"Gee!" he could hear Carson shiver. "Gee!"

An interval of quiet followed, and then Smoke could feel the rope agitated.

"What are you doing?" he called up.

"Making more hand- and foot-holds," came the trembling answer. "You just wait. I'll have you up here in a jiffy. Don't mind the way I talk. I'm just excited. But I'm all right. You wait and see."

"You're holding me by main strength," Smoke argued. "Soon or late, with the ice melting, you'll slip down after me. The thing for you to do is to cut loose. Hear me! There's no use both of us going. Get that? You're the biggest little man in creation, but you've done your best. You cut loose."

"You shut up. I'm going to make holes this time deep enough to haul up a span of horses."

"You've held me up long enough," Smoke urged. "Let me go."

"How many times have I held you up?" came the truculent query.

"Some several, and all of them too many. You've been coming down all the time."

"And I've been learning the game all the time. I'm going on holding you up until we get out of here. Savvy? When God made me a light-weight I guess he knew what he was about. Now, shut up. I'm busy."

Several silent minutes passed. Smoke could hear the metallic strike and hack of the knife and occasional driblets of ice slid over the bulge and came down to him. Thirsty, clinging on hand and foot, he caught the fragments in his mouth and melted them to water, which he swallowed.

He heard a gasp that slid into a groan of despair, and felt a slackening of the rope that made him claw. Immediately the rope tightened again. Straining his eyes in an upward look along the steep slope, he stared a moment, then saw the knife, point first, slide over the verge of the bulge and down upon him. He tucked his cheek to it, shrank from the pang of cut flesh, tucked more tightly, and felt the knife come to rest.

"I'm a slob," came the wail down the crevasse.

"Cheer up, I've got it," Smoke answered.

"Say! Wait! I've a lot of string in my pocket. I'll drop it down to you, and you send the knife up."

Smoke made no reply. He was battling with a sudden rush of thought.

"Hey! You! Here comes the string. Tell me when you've got it."

A small pocket-knife, weighted on the end of the string, slid down the ice. Smoke got it, opened the larger blade by a quick effort of his teeth and one hand, and made sure that the blade was sharp. Then he tied the sheath-knife to the end of the string.

"Haul away!" he called.

With strained eyes he saw the upward progress of the knife. But he saw more—a little man, afraid and indomitable, who shivered and chattered, whose head swam with giddiness, and who mastered his qualms and distresses and played a hero's part. Not since his meeting with Shorty had Smoke so quickly liked a man. Here was a proper meat-eater, eager with friendliness, generous to destruction, with a grit that shaking fear could not shake. Then, too, he considered the situation cold-bloodedly. There was no chance for two. Steadily, they were sliding into the heart of the glacier, and it was his greater weight that was dragging the little man down. The little man could stick like a fly. Alone, he could save himself.

"Bully for us!" came the voice from above, down and across the bulge of ice. "Now we'll get out of here in two shakes."

The awful struggle for good cheer and hope in Carson's voice decided Smoke.

"Listen to me," he said steadily, vainly striving to shake the vision of Joy Gastell's face from his brain. "I sent that knife up for you to get out with. Get that? I'm going to chop loose with the jack-knife. It's one or both of us. Get that?"

"Two or nothing," came the grim but shaky response. "If you'll hold on a minute—"

"I've held on for too long now. I'm not married. I have no adorable thin woman nor kids nor apple-trees waiting for me. Get me? Now, you hike up and out of that!"

"Wait! For God's sake, wait!" Carson screamed down. "You can't do that! Give me a chance to get you out. Be calm, old horse. We'll make the turn. You'll see. I'm going to dig holds that'll lift a house and barn."

Smoke made no reply. Slowly and gently, fascinated by the sight, he cut with the knife until one of the three strands popped and parted.

"What are you doing?" Carson cried desperately. "If you cut, I'll never forgive you—never. I tell you it's two or nothing. We're going to get out. Wait! For God's sake!"

And Smoke, staring at the parted strand, five inches before his eyes, knew fear in all its weakness. He did not want to die; he recoiled from the shimmering abyss beneath him, and his panic brain urged all the preposterous optimism of delay. It was fear that prompted him to compromise.

"All right," he called up. "I'll wait. Do your best. But I tell you, Carson, if we both start slipping again I'm going to cut."

"Huh! Forget it. When we start, old horse, we start up. I'm a porous plaster. I could stick here if it was twice as steep. I'm getting a sizable hole for one heel already. Now, you hush, and let me work."

The slow minutes passed. Smoke centered his soul on the dull hurt of a hang-nail on one of his fingers. He should have clipped it away that morning—it was hurting then—he decided; and he resolved, once clear of the crevasse, that it should immediately be clipped. Then, with short focus, he stared at the hang-nail and the finger with a new comprehension. In a minute, or a few minutes at best, that hang-nail, that finger, cunningly jointed and efficient, might be part of a mangled carcass at the bottom of the crevasse. Conscious of his fear, he hated himself. Bear-eaters were made of sterner stuff. In the anger of self-revolt he all but hacked at the rope with his knife. But fear made him draw back the hand and to stick himself again, trembling and sweating, to the slippery slope. To the fact that he was soaking wet by contact with the thawing ice he tried to attribute the cause of his shivering; but he knew, in the heart of him, that it was untrue.

A gasp and a groan and an abrupt slackening of the rope, warned him. He began to slip. The movement was very slow. The rope tightened loyally, but he continued to slip. Carson could not hold him, and was slipping with him. The digging toe of his farther-extended foot encountered vacancy, and he knew that it was over the straight-away fall. And he knew, too, that in another moment his falling body would jerk Carson's after it.

Blindly, desperately, all the vitality and life-love of him beaten down in a flashing instant by a shuddering perception of right and wrong, he brought the knife-edge across the rope, saw the strands part, felt himself slide more rapidly, and then fall.

What happened then, he did not know. He was not unconscious, but it happened too quickly, and it was unexpected. Instead of falling to his death, his feet almost immediately struck in water, and he sat violently down in water that splashed coolingly on his face. His first impression was that the crevasse was shallower than he had imagined and that he had safely fetched bottom. But of this he was quickly disabused. The opposite wall was a dozen feet away. He lay in a basin formed in an out-jut of the ice-wall by melting water that dribbled and trickled over the bulge above and fell sheer down a distance of a dozen feet. This had hollowed out the basin. Where he sat the water was two feet deep, and it was flush with the rim. He peered over the rim and looked down the narrow chasm hundreds of feet to the torrent that foamed along the bottom.

"Oh, why did you?" he heard a wail from above.

"Listen," he called up. "I'm perfectly safe, sitting in a pool of water up to my neck. And here's both our packs. I'm going to sit on them. There's room for a half-dozen here. If you slip, stick close and you'll land. In the meantime you hike up and get out. Go to the cabin. Somebody's there. I saw the smoke. Get a rope, or anything that will make rope, and come back and fish for me."

"Honest!" came Carson's incredulous voice.

"Cross my heart and hope to die. Now, get a hustle on, or I'll catch my death of cold."

Smoke kept himself warm by kicking a channel through the rim with the heel of his shoe. By the time he had drained off the last of the water, a faint call from Carson announced that he had reached the top.

After that Smoke occupied himself with drying his clothes. The late afternoon sun beat warmly in upon him, and he wrung out his garments and spread them about him. His match-case was water-proof, and he manipulated and dried sufficient tobacco and rice-paper to make cigarettes.

Two hours later, perched naked on the two packs and smoking, he heard a voice above that he could not fail to identify.

"Oh, Smoke! Smoke!"

"Hello, Joy Gastell!" he called back. "Where'd you drop from?"

"Are you hurt?"

"Not even any skin off!"

"Father's paying the rope down now. Do you see it?"

"Yes, and I've got it," he answered. "Now, wait a couple of minutes, please."

"What's the matter?" came her anxious query, after several minutes. "Oh, I know, you're hurt."

"No, I'm not. I'm dressing."

"Dressing?"

"Yes. I've been in swimming. Now! Ready? Hoist away!"

He sent up the two packs on the first trip, was consequently rebuked by Joy Gastell, and on the second trip came up himself.

Joy Gastell looked at him with glowing eyes, while her father and Carson were busy coiling the rope. "How could you cut loose in that splendid way?" she cried. "It was—it was glorious, that's all."

Smoke waved the compliment away with a deprecatory hand.

"I know all about it," she persisted. "Carson told me. You sacrificed yourself to save him."

"Nothing of the sort," Smoke lied. "I could see that swimming-pool right under me all the time."

VIII

THE HANGING OF CULTUS GEORGE

The way led steeply up through deep, powdery snow that was unmarred by sled-track or moccasin impression. Smoke, in the lead, pressed the fragile crystals down under his fat, short snow-shoes. The task required lungs and muscle, and he flung himself into it with all his strength. Behind, on the surface he packed, strained the string of six dogs, the steam-jets of their breathing attesting their labor and the lowness of the temperature. Between the wheel-dog and the sled toiled Shorty, his weight divided between the guiding gee-pole and the haul, for he was pulling with the dogs. Every half-hour he and Smoke exchanged places, for the snow-shoe work was even more arduous than that of the gee-pole.

The whole outfit was fresh and strong. It was merely hard work being efficiently done—the breaking of a midwinter trail across a divide. On this severe stretch, ten miles a day they called a decent stint. They kept in condition, but each night crawled well tired into their sleeping-furs. This was their sixth day out from the lively camp of Mucluc on the Yukon. In two days, with the loaded sled, they had covered the fifty miles of packed trail up Moose Creek. Then had come the struggle with the four feet of untouched snow that was really not snow, but frost-crystals, so lacking in cohesion that when kicked it flew with the thin hissing of granulated sugar. In three days they had wallowed thirty miles up Minnow Creek and across the series of low divides that separate the several creeks flowing south into Siwash River; and now they were breasting the big divide, past the Bald Buttes, where the way would lead them down Porcupine Creek to the middle reaches of Milk River. Higher up Milk River, it was fairly rumored, were deposits of copper. And this was their goal—a hill of pure copper, half a mile to the right and up the first creek after Milk River issued from a deep gorge to flow across a heavily timbered stretch of bottom. They would know it when they saw it. One-Eyed McCarthy had described it with sharp definiteness. It was impossible to miss it—unless McCarthy had lied.

Smoke was in the lead, and the small scattered spruce-trees were becoming scarcer and smaller, when he saw one, dead and bone-dry, that stood in their path. There was no need for speech. His glance to Shorty was acknowledged by a stentorian "Whoa!" The dogs stood in the traces till they saw Shorty begin to undo the sled-lashings and Smoke attack the dead spruce with an ax; whereupon the animals dropped in the snow and curled into balls, the bush of each tail curved to cover four padded feet and an ice-rimmed muzzle.

The men worked with the quickness of long practice. Gold-pan, coffee-pot, and cooking-pail were soon thawing the heaped frost-crystals into water. Smoke extracted a stick of beans from the sled. Already cooked, with a generous admixture of cubes of fat pork and bacon, the beans had been frozen into this portable immediacy. He chopped off chunks with an ax, as if it were so much firewood, and put them into the frying-pan to thaw. Solidly frozen sourdough biscuits were likewise placed to thaw. In twenty minutes from the time they halted, the meal was ready to eat.

"About forty below," Shorty mumbled through a mouthful of beans. "Say—I hope it don't get colder—or warmer, neither. It's just right for trail breaking."

Smoke did not answer. His own mouth full of beans, his jaws working, he had chanced to glance at the lead-dog, lying half a dozen feet away. That gray and frosty wolf was gazing at him with the infinite wistfulness and yearning that glimmers and hazes so often in the eyes of Northland dogs. Smoke knew it well, but never got over the unfathomable wonder of it. As if to shake off the hypnotism, he set down his plate and coffee-cup, went to the sled, and began opening the dried-fish sack.

"Hey!" Shorty expostulated. "What 'r' you doin'?"

"Breaking all law, custom, precedent, and trail usage," Smoke replied. "I'm going to feed the dogs in the middle of the day—just this once. They've worked hard, and that last pull to the top of the divide is before them. Besides, Bright there has been talking to me, telling me all untellable things with those eyes of his."

Shorty laughed skeptically. "Go on an' spoil 'em. Pretty soon you'll be manicurin' their nails. I'd recommend cold cream and electric massage—it's great for sled-dogs. And sometimes a Turkish bath does 'em fine."

"I've never done it before," Smoke defended. "And I won't again. But this once I'm going to. It's just a whim, I guess."

"Oh, if it's a hunch, go to it." Shorty's tones showed how immediately he had been mollified. "A man's always got to follow his hunches."

"It isn't a hunch, Shorty. Bright just sort of got on my imagination for a couple of twists. He told me more in one minute with those eyes of his than I could read in the books in a thousand years. His eyes were acrawl with the secrets of life. They were just squirming and wriggling there. The trouble is I almost got them, and then I didn't. I'm no wiser than I was before, but I was near them." He paused and then added, "I can't tell you, but that dog's eyes were just spilling over with cues to what life is, and evolution, and star-dust, and cosmic sap, and all the rest—everything."

"Boiled down into simple American, you got a hunch," Shorty insisted.

Smoke finished tossing the dried salmon, one to each dog, and shook his head.

"I tell you yes," Shorty argued. "Smoke, it's a sure hunch. Something's goin' to happen before the day is out. You'll see. And them dried fish'll have a bearin'."

"You've got to show me," said Smoke.

"No, I ain't. The day'll take care of itself an' show you. Now listen to what I'm tellin' you. I got a hunch myself out of your hunch. I'll bet eleven ounces against three ornery toothpicks I'm right. When I get a hunch I ain't a-scared to ride it."

"You bet the toothpicks, and I'll bet the ounces," Smoke returned.

"Nope. That'd be plain robbery. I win. I know a hunch when it tickles me. Before the day's out somethin' 'll happen, an' them fish'll have a meanin'."

"Hell," said Smoke, dismissing the discussion contemptuously.

"An' it'll be hell," Shorty came back. "An' I'll take three more toothpicks with you on them same odds that it'll be sure-enough hell."

"Done," said Smoke.

"I win," Shorty exulted. "Chicken-feather toothpicks for mine."

An hour later they cleared the divide, dipped down past the Bald Buttes through a sharp elbow-canyon, and took the steep open slope that dropped into Porcupine Creek. Shorty, in the lead, stopped abruptly, and Smoke whoaed the dogs. Beneath them, coming up, was a procession of humans, scattered and draggled, a quarter of a mile long.

"They move like it was a funeral," Shorty noted.

"They've no dogs," said Smoke.

"Yep; there's a couple of men pullin' on a sled."

"See that fellow fall down? There's something the matter, Shorty, and there must be two hundred of them."

"Look at 'em stagger as if they was soused. There goes another."

"It's a whole tribe. There are children there."

"Smoke, I win," Shorty proclaimed. "A hunch is a hunch, an' you can't beat it. There she comes. Look at her!—surgin' up like a lot of corpses."

The mass of Indians, at sight of the two men, had raised a weird cry of joy and accelerated its pace.

"They're sure tolerable woozy," commented Shorty. "See 'em fallin' down in lumps and bunches."

"Look at the face of that first one," Smoke said. "It's starvation—that's what's the matter with them. They've eaten their dogs."

"What'll we do? Run for it?"

"And leave the sled and dogs?" Smoke demanded reproachfully.

"They'll sure eat us if we don't. They look hungry enough for it. Hello, old skeeziks. What's wrong with you? Don't look at that dog that way. No cookin'-pot for him—savvy?"

The forerunners were arriving and crowding about them, moaning and plainting in an unfamiliar jargon. To Smoke the picture was grotesque and horrible. It was famine unmistakable. Their faces, hollow-cheeked and skin-stretched, were so many death's-heads. More and more arrived and crowded about, until Smoke and Shorty were hemmed in by the wild crew. Their ragged garments of skin and fur were cut and slashed away, and Smoke knew the reason for it when he saw a wizened child on a squaw's back that sucked and chewed a strip of filthy fur. Another child he observed steadily masticating a leather thong.

"Keep off there!—keep back!" Shorty yelled, falling back on English after futile attempts with the little Indian he did know.

Bucks and squaws and children tottered and swayed on shaking legs and continued to surge in, their mad eyes swimming with weakness and burning with ravenous desire. A woman, moaning, staggered past Shorty and fell with spread and grasping arms on the sled. An old man followed her, panting and gasping, with trembling hands striving to cast off the sled lashings, and get at the grub-sacks beneath. A young man, with a naked knife, tried to rush in, but was flung back by Smoke. The whole mass pressed in upon them, and the fight was on.

At first Smoke and Shorty shoved and thrust and threw back. Then they used the butt of the dog-whip and their fists on the food-mad crowd. And all this against a background of moaning and wailing women and children. Here and there, in a dozen places, the sled-lashings were cut. Men crawled in on their bellies, regardless of a rain of kicks and blows, and tried to drag out the grub. These had to be picked up bodily and flung back. And such was their weakness that they fell continually, under the slightest pressures or shoves. Yet they made no attempt to injure the two men who defended the sled.

It was the utter weakness of the Indians that saved Smoke and Shorty from being overborne. In five minutes the wall of up-standing, on-struggling Indians had been changed to heaps of fallen ones that moaned and gibbered in the snow, and cried and sniveled as their staring, swimming eyes focused on the grub that meant life to them and that brought the slaver to their lips. And behind it all arose the wailing of the women and children.

"Shut up! Oh, shut up!" Shorty yelled, thrusting his fingers into his ears and breathing heavily from his exertions. "Ah, you would, would you!" was his cry as he lunged forward and kicked a knife from the hand of a man who, bellying through the snow, was trying to stab the lead-dog in the throat.

"This is terrible," Smoke muttered.

"I'm all het up," Shorty replied, returning from the rescue of Bright. "I'm real sweaty. An' now what 'r' we goin' to do with this ambulance outfit?"

Smoke shook his head, and then the problem was solved for him. An Indian crawled forward, his one eye fixed on Smoke instead of on the sled, and in it Smoke could see the struggle of sanity to assert itself. Shorty remembered having punched the other eye, which was already swollen shut. The Indian raised himself on his elbow and spoke.

"Me Carluk. Me good Siwash. Me savvy Boston man plenty. Me plenty hungry. All people plenty hungry. All people no savvy Boston man. Me savvy. Me eat grub now. All people eat grub now. We buy 'm grub. Got 'm plenty gold. No got 'm grub. Summer, salmon no come Milk River. Winter, caribou no come. No grub. Me make 'm talk all people. Me tell 'em plenty Boston man come Yukon. Boston man have plenty grub. Boston man like 'm gold. We take 'm gold, go Yukon, Boston man give 'm grub. Plenty gold. Me savvy Boston man like 'm gold."

He began fumbling with wasted fingers at the draw-string of a pouch he took from his belt.

"Too much make 'm noise," Shorty broke in distractedly. "You tell 'm squaw, you tell 'm papoose, shut 'm up mouth."

Carluk turned and addressed the wailing women. Other bucks, listening, raised their voices authoritatively, and slowly the squaws stilled, and quieted the children near to them. Carluk paused from fumbling the draw-string and held up his fingers many times.

"Him people make 'm die," he said.

And Smoke, following the count, knew that seventy-five of the tribe had starved to death.

"Me buy 'm grub," Carluk said, as he got the pouch open and drew out a large chunk of heavy metal. Others were following his example, and on every side appeared similar chunks. Shorty stared.

"Great Jeminey!" he cried. "Copper! Raw, red copper! An' they think it's gold!"

"Him gold," Carluk assured them confidently, his quick comprehension having caught the gist of Shorty's exclamation.

"And the poor devils banked everything on it," Smoke muttered. "Look at it. That chunk there weighs forty pounds. They've got hundreds of pounds of it, and they've carried it when they didn't have strength enough to drag themselves. Look here, Shorty. We've got to feed them."

"Huh! Sounds easy. But how about statistics? You an' me has a month's grub, which is six meals times thirty, which is one hundred an' eighty meals. Here's two hundred Indians, with real, full-grown appetites. How the blazes can we give 'm one meal even?"

"There's the dog-grub," Smoke answered. "A couple of hundred pounds of dried salmon ought to help out. We've got to do it. They've pinned their faith on the white man, you know."

"Sure, an' we can't throw 'm down," Shorty agreed. "An' we got two nasty jobs cut out for us, each just about twicet as nasty as the other. One of us has got to make a run of it to Mucluc an' raise a relief. The other has to stay here an' run the hospital an' most likely be eaten. Don't let it slip your noodle that we've been six days gettin' here; an' travelin' light, an' all played out, it can't be made back in less 'n three days."

For a minute Smoke pondered the miles of the way they had come, visioning the miles in terms of time measured by his capacity for exertion. "I can get there to-morrow night," he announced.

"All right," Shorty acquiesced cheerfully. "An' I'll stay an' be eaten."

"But I'm going to take one fish each for the dogs," Smoke explained, "and one meal for myself."

"An' you'll sure need it if you make Mucluc to-morrow night."

Smoke, through the medium of Carluk, stated the program. "Make fires, long fires, plenty fires," he concluded. "Plenty Boston man stop Mucluc. Boston man much good. Boston man plenty grub. Five sleeps I come back plenty grub. This man, his name Shorty, very good friend of mine. He stop here. He big boss—savvy?"

Carluk nodded and interpreted.

"All grub stop here. Shorty, he give 'm grub. He boss—savvy?"

Carluk interpreted, and nods and guttural cries of agreement proceeded from the men.

Smoke remained and managed until the full swing of the arrangement was under way. Those who were able, crawled or staggered in the collecting of firewood. Long, Indian fires were built that accommodated all. Shorty, aided by a dozen assistants, with a short club handy for the rapping of hungry knuckles, plunged into the cooking. The women devoted themselves to thawing snow in every utensil that could be mustered. First, a tiny piece of bacon was distributed all around, and, next, a spoonful of sugar to cloy the edge of their razor appetites. Soon, on a circle of fires drawn about Shorty, many pots of beans were boiling, and he, with a wrathful eye for what he called renigers, was frying and apportioning the thinnest of flapjacks.

"Me for the big cookin'," was his farewell to Smoke. "You just keep a-hikin'. Trot all the way there an' run all the way back. It'll take you to-day an' to-morrow to get there, and you can't be back inside of three days more. To-morrow they'll eat the last of the dog-fish, an' then there'll be nary a scrap for three days. You gotta keep a-comin', Smoke. You gotta keep a-comin'."

Though the sled was light, loaded only with six dried salmon, a couple of pounds of frozen beans and bacon, and a sleeping-robe, Smoke could not make speed. Instead of riding the sled and running the dogs, he was compelled to plod at the gee-pole. Also, a day of work had already been done, and the freshness and spring had gone out of the dogs and himself. The long arctic twilight was on when he cleared the divide and left the Bald Buttes behind.

Down the slope better time was accomplished, and often he was able to spring on the sled for short intervals and get an exhausting six-mile clip out of the animals. Darkness caught him and fooled him in a wide-valleyed, nameless creek. Here the creek wandered in broad horseshoe curves through the flats, and here, to save time, he began short-cutting the flats instead of keeping to the creek-bed. And black dark found him back on the creek-bed feeling for the trail. After an hour of futile searching, too wise to go farther astray, he built a fire, fed each dog half a fish, and divided his own ration in half. Rolled in his robe, ere quick sleep came he had solved the problem. The last big flat he had short-cut was the one that occurred at the forks of the creek. He had missed the trail by a mile. He was now on the main stream and below where his and Shorty's trail crossed the valley and climbed through a small feeder to the low divide on the other side.

At the first hint of daylight he got under way, breakfastless, and wallowed a mile upstream to pick up the trail. And breakfastless, man and dogs, without a halt, for eight hours held back transversely across the series of small creeks and low divides and down Minnow Creek. By four in the afternoon, with darkness fast-set about him, he emerged on the hard-packed, running trail of Moose Creek. Fifty miles of it would end the journey. He called a rest, built a fire, threw each dog its half-salmon, and thawed and ate his pound of beans. Then he sprang on the sled, yelled, "Mush!" and the dogs went out strongly against their breast-bands.

"Hit her up, you huskies!" he cried. "Mush on! Hit her up for grub! And no grub short of Mucluc! Dig in, you wolves! Dig in!"

MIDNIGHT HAD GONE A QUARTER of an hour in the Annie Mine. The main room was comfortably crowded, while roaring stoves, combined with lack of ventilation, kept the big room unsanitarily warm. The click of chips and the boisterous play at the craps-table furnished a monotonous background of sound to the equally monotonous rumble of men's voices where they sat and stood about and talked in groups and twos and threes. The gold-weighers were busy at their scales, for dust was the circulating medium, and even a dollar drink of whiskey at the bar had to be paid for to the weighers.

The walls of the room were of tiered logs, the bark still on, and the chinking between the logs, plainly visible, was arctic moss. Through the open door that led to the dance-room came the rollicking strains of a Virginia reel, played by a piano and a fiddle. The drawing of Chinese lottery had just taken place, and the luckiest player, having cashed at the scales, was drinking up his winnings with half a dozen cronies. The faro- and roulette-tables were busy and quiet. The draw-poker and stud-poker tables, each with its circle of onlookers, were equally quiet. At another table, a serious, concentrated game of Black Jack was on. Only from the craps-table came noise, as the man who played rolled the dice, full sweep, down the green amphitheater of a table in pursuit of his elusive and long-delayed point. Ever he cried: "Oh! you Joe Cotton! Come a four! Come a Joe! Little Joe! Bring home the bacon, Joe! Joe, you Joe, you!"

Cultus George, a big strapping Circle City Indian, leaned distantly and dourly against the log wall. He was a civilized Indian, if living like a white man connotes civilization; and he was sorely offended, though the offense was of long standing. For years he had done a white man's work, had done it alongside of white men, and often had done it better than they did. He wore the same pants they wore, the same hearty woolens and heavy shirts. He sported as good a watch as they, parted his short hair on the side, and ate the same food—bacon, beans, and flour; and yet he was denied their greatest diversion and reward; namely, whiskey. Cultus George was a money-earner. He had staked claims, and bought and sold claims. He had been grub-staked, and he had accorded grub-stakes. Just now he was a dog-musher and freighter, charging twenty-eight cents a pound for the winter haul from Sixty Mile to Mucluc—and for bacon thirty-three cents, as was the custom. His poke was fat with dust. He had the price of many drinks. Yet no barkeeper would serve him. Whiskey, the hottest, swiftest, completest gratifier of civilization, was not for him. Only by subterranean and cowardly and expensive ways could he get a drink. And he resented this invidious distinction, as he had resented it for years, deeply. And he was especially thirsty and resentful this night, while the white men he had so sedulously emulated he hated more bitterly than ever before. The white men would graciously permit him to lose his gold across their gaming-tables, but for neither love nor money could he obtain a drink across their bars. Wherefore he was very sober, and very logical, and logically sullen.

The Virginia reel in the dance-room wound to a wild close that interfered not with the three camp drunkards who snored under the piano. "All couples promenade to the bar!" was the caller's last cry as the music stopped. And the couples were so promenading through the wide doorway into the main room—the men in furs and moccasins, the women in soft fluffy dresses, silk stockings, and dancing-slippers—when the double storm-doors were thrust open, and Smoke Bellew staggered wearily in.

Eyes centered on him, and silence began to fall. He tried to speak, pulled off his mittens (which fell dangling from their cords), and clawed at the frozen moisture of his breath which had formed in fifty miles of running. He halted irresolutely, then went over and leaned his elbow on the end of the bar.

Only the man at the craps-table, without turning his head, continued to roll the dice and to cry: "Oh! you Joe! Come on, you Joe!" The gamekeeper's gaze, fixed on Smoke, caught the player's attention, and he, too, with suspended dice, turned and looked.

"What's up, Smoke?" Matson, the owner of the Annie Mine, demanded.

With a last effort, Smoke clawed his mouth free. "I got some dogs out there—dead beat," he said huskily. "Somebody go and take care of them, and I'll tell you what's the matter."

In a dozen brief sentences, he outlined the situation. The craps-player, his money still lying on the table and his slippery Joe Cotton still uncaptured, had come over to Smoke, and was now the first to speak.

"We gotta do something. That's straight. But what? You've had time to think. What's your plan? Spit it out."

"Sure," Smoke assented. "Here's what I've been thinking. We've got to hustle light sleds on the jump. Say a hundred pounds of grub on each sled. The driver's outfit and dog-grub will fetch it up fifty more. But they can make time. Say we start five of these sleds pronto—best running teams, best mushers and trail-eaters. On the soft trail the sleds can take the lead turn about. They've got to start at once. At the best, by the time they can get there, all those Indians won't have had a scrap to eat for three days. And then, as soon as we've got those sleds off we'll have to follow up with heavy sleds. Figure it out yourself. Two pounds a day is the very least we can decently keep those Indians traveling on. That's four hundred pounds a day, and, with the old people and the children, five days is the quickest time we can bring them into Mucluc. Now what are you going to do?"

"Take up a collection to buy all the grub," said the craps-player.

"I'll stand for the grub," Smoke began impatiently.

"Nope," the other interrupted. "This ain't your treat. We're all in. Fetch a wash-basin somebody. It won't take a minute. An' here's a starter."

He pulled a heavy gold-sack from his pocket, untied the mouth, and poured a stream of coarse dust and nuggets into the basin. A man beside him caught his hand up with a jerk and an oath, elevating the mouth of the sack so as to stop the run of the dust. To a casual eye, six or eight ounces had already run into the basin.

"Don't be a hawg," cried the second man. "You ain't the only one with a poke. Gimme a chance at it."

"Huh!" sneered the craps-player. "You'd think it was a stampede, you're so goshdanged eager about it."

Men crowded and jostled for the opportunity to contribute, and when they were satisfied, Smoke hefted the heavy basin with both hands and grinned.

"It will keep the whole tribe in grub for the rest of the winter," he said. "Now for the dogs. Five light teams that have some run in them."

A dozen teams were volunteered, and the camp, as a committee of the whole, bickered and debated, accepted and rejected.

"Huh! Your dray-horses!" Long Bill Haskell was told.

"They can pull," he bristled with hurt pride.

"They sure can," he was assured. "But they can't make time for sour apples. They've got theirs cut out for them bringing up the heavy loads."

As fast as a team was selected, its owner, with half a dozen aids, departed to harness up and get ready.

One team was rejected because it had come in tired that afternoon. One owner contributed his team, but apologetically exposed a bandaged ankle that prevented him from driving it. This team Smoke took, overriding the objection of the crowd that he was played out.

Long Bill Haskell pointed out that while Fat Olsen's team was a crackerjack, Fat Olsen himself was an elephant. Fat Olsen's two hundred and forty pounds of heartiness was indignant. Tears of anger came into his eyes, and his Scandinavian explosions could not be stopped until he was given a place in the heavy division, the craps-player jumping at the chance to take out Olsen's light team.

Five teams were accepted and were being harnessed and loaded, but only four drivers had satisfied the committee of the whole.

"There's Cultus George," some one cried. "He's a trail-eater, and he's fresh and rested."

All eyes turned upon the Indian, but his face was expressionless, and he said nothing.

"You'll take a team," Smoke said to him.

Still the big Indian made no answer. As with an electric thrill, it ran through all of them that something untoward was impending. A restless shifting of the group took place, forming a circle in which Smoke and Cultus George faced each other. And Smoke realized that by common consent he had been made the representative of his fellows in what was taking place, in what was to take place. Also, he was angered. It was beyond him that any human creature, a witness to the scramble of volunteers, should hang back. For another thing, in what followed, Smoke did not have Cultus George's point of view—did not dream that the Indian held back for any reason save the selfish, mercenary one.

"Of course you will take a team," Smoke said.

"How much?" Cultus George asked.

A snarl, spontaneous and general, grated in the throats and twisted the mouths of the miners. At the same moment, with clenched fists or fingers crooked to grip, they pressed in on the offender.

"Wait a bit, boys," Smoke cried. "Maybe he doesn't understand. Let me explain it to him. Look here, George. Don't you see, nobody is charging anything. They're giving everything to save two hundred Indians from starving to death." He paused, to let it sink home.

"How much?" said Cultus George.

"Wait, you fellows! Now listen, George. We don't want you to make any mistake. These starving people are your kind of people. They're another tribe, but they're Indians just the same. Now you've seen what the white men are doing—coughing up their dust, giving their dogs and sleds, falling over one another to hit the trail. Only the best men can go with the first sleds. Look at Fat Olsen there. He was ready to fight because they wouldn't let him go. You ought to be mighty proud because all men think you are a number-one musher. It isn't a case of how much, but how quick."

"How much?" said Cultus George.

"Kill him!" "Bust his head!" "Tar and feathers!" were several of the cries in the wild medley that went up, the spirit of philanthropy and good fellowship changed to brute savagery on the instant.

In the storm-center Cultus George stood imperturbable, while Smoke thrust back the fiercest and shouted:

"Wait! Who's running this?" The clamor died away. "Fetch a rope," he added quietly.

Cultus George shrugged his shoulders, his face twisting tensely in a sullen and incredulous grin. He knew this white-man breed. He had toiled on trail with it and eaten its flour and bacon and beans too long not to know it. It was a law-abiding breed. He knew that thoroughly. It always punished the man who broke the law. But he had broken no law. He knew its law. He had lived up to it. He had neither murdered, stolen, nor lied. There was nothing in the white man's law against charging a price and driving a bargain. They all charged a price and drove bargains. He was doing nothing more than that, and it was the thing they had taught him. Besides, if he wasn't good enough to drink with them, then he was not good enough to be charitable with them, nor to join them in any other of their foolish diversions.

Neither Smoke nor any man there glimpsed what lay in Cultus George's brain, behind his attitude and prompting his attitude. Though they did not know it, they were as beclouded as he in the matter of mutual understanding. To them, he was a selfish brute; to him, they were selfish brutes.

When the rope was brought, Long Bill Haskell, Fat Olsen, and the craps-player, with much awkwardness and angry haste, got the slip-noose around the Indian's neck and rove the rope over a rafter. At the other end of the dangling thing a dozen men tailed on, ready to hoist away.

Nor had Cultus George resisted. He knew it for what it was—bluff. The whites were strong on bluff. Was not draw-poker their favorite game? Did they not buy and sell and make all bargains with bluff? Yes; he had seen a white man do business with a look on his face of four aces and in his hand a busted straight.

"Wait," Smoke commanded. "Tie his hands. We don't want him climbing."

More bluff, Cultus George decided, and passively permitted his hands to be tied behind his back.

"Now it's your last chance, George," said Smoke. "Will you take out the team?"

"How much?" said Cultus George.

Astounded at himself that he should be able to do such a thing, and at the same time angered by the colossal selfishness of the Indian, Smoke gave the signal. Nor was Cultus George any less astounded when he felt the noose tighten with a jerk and swing him off the floor. His stolidity broke on the instant. On his face, in quick succession, appeared surprise, dismay, and pain.

Smoke watched anxiously. Having never been hanged himself, he felt a tyro at the business. The body struggled convulsively, the tied hands strove to burst the bonds, and from the throat came unpleasant noises of strangulation. Suddenly Smoke held up his hand.

"Slack away" he ordered.

Grumbling at the shortness of the punishment, the men on the rope lowered Cultus George to the floor. His eyes were bulging, and he was tottery on his feet, swaying from side to side and still making a fight with his hands. Smoke divined what was the matter, thrust violent fingers between the rope and the neck, and brought the noose slack with a jerk. With a great heave of the chest, Cultus George got his first breath.

"Will you take that team out?" Smoke demanded.

Cultus George did not answer. He was too busy breathing.

"Oh, we white men are hogs," Smoke filled in the interval, resentful himself at the part he was compelled to play. "We'd sell our souls for gold, and all that; but once in a while we forget about it and turn loose and do something without a thought of how much there is in it. And when we do that, Cultus George, watch out. What we want to know now is: Are you going to take out that team?"

Cultus George debated with himself. He was no coward. Perhaps this was the extent of their bluff, and if he gave in now he was a fool. And while he debated, Smoke suffered from secret worry lest this stubborn aborigine would persist in being hanged.

"How much?" said Cultus George.

Smoke started to raise his hand for the signal.

"Me go," Cultus George said very quickly, before the rope could tighten.

"An' when that rescue expedition found me," Shorty told it in the Annie Mine, "that ornery Cultus George was the first in, beatin' Smoke's sled by three hours, an' don't you forget it, Smoke comes in second at that. Just the same, it was about time, when I heard Cultus George a-yellin' at his dogs from the top of the divide, for those blamed Siwashes had ate my moccasins, my mitts, the leather lacin's, my knife-sheath, an' some of 'em was beginnin' to look mighty hungry at me—me bein' better nourished, you see.

"An' Smoke? He was near dead. He hustled around a while, helpin' to start a meal for them two hundred sufferin' Siwashes; an' then he fell asleep, settin' on his haunches, thinkin' he was feedin' snow into a thawin'-pail. I fixed him my bed, an' dang me if I didn't have to help him into it, he was that give out. Sure I win the toothpicks. Didn't them dogs just naturally need the six salmon Smoke fed 'em at the noonin'?"

IX

THE MISTAKE OF CREATION

W hoa!" Smoke yelled at the dogs, throwing his weight back on the gee-pole to bring the sled to a halt.

"What's eatin' you now?" Shorty complained. "They ain't no water under that footing."

"No; but look at that trail cutting out to the right," Smoke answered. "I thought nobody was wintering in this section."

The dogs, on the moment they stopped, dropped in the snow and began biting out the particles of ice from between their toes. This ice had been water five minutes before. The animals had broken through a skein of ice, snow-powdered, which had hidden the spring water that oozed out of the bank and pooled on top of the three-foot winter crust of Nordbeska River.

"First I heard of anybody up the Nordbeska," Shorty said, staring at the all but obliterated track covered by two feet of snow, that left the bed of the river at right angles and entered the mouth of a small stream flowing from the left. "Mebbe they're hunters and pulled their freight long ago."

Smoke, scooping the light snow away with mittened hands, paused to consider, scooped again, and again paused. "No," he decided. "There's been travel both ways, but the last travel was up that creek. Whoever they are, they're there now—certain. There's been no travel for weeks. Now what's been keeping them there all the time? That's what I want to know."

"And what I want to know is where we're going to camp to-night," Shorty said, staring disconsolately at the sky-line in the southwest, where the mid-afternoon twilight was darkening into night.

"Let's follow the track up the creek," was Smoke's suggestion. "There's plenty of dead timber. We can camp any time."

"Sure we can camp any time, but we got to travel most of the time if we ain't goin' to starve, an' we got to travel in the right direction."

"We're going to find something up that creek," Smoke went on.

"But look at the grub! Look at them dogs!" Shorty cried. "Look at— oh, hell, all right. You will have your will."

"It won't make the trip a day longer," Smoke urged. "Possibly no more than a mile longer."

"Men has died for as little as a mile," Shorty retorted, shaking his head with lugubrious resignation. "Come on for trouble. Get up, you poor sore-foots, you—get up! Haw! You Bright! Haw!"

The lead-dog obeyed, and the whole team strained weakly into the soft snow.

"Whoa!" Shorty yelled. "It's pack trail."

Smoke pulled his snow-shoes from under the sled-lashings, bound them to his moccasined feet, and went to the fore to press and pack the light surface for the dogs.

It was heavy work. Dogs and men had been for days on short rations, and few and limited were the reserves of energy they could call upon. Though they followed the creek bed, so pronounced was its fall that they toiled on a stiff and unrelenting up-grade. The high rocky walls quickly drew near together, so that their way led up the bottom of a narrow gorge. The long lingering twilight, blocked by the high mountains, was no more than semi-darkness.

"It's a trap," Shorty said. "The whole look of it is rotten. It's a hole in the ground. It's the stampin'-ground of trouble."

Smoke made no reply, and for half an hour they toiled on in silence—a silence that was again broken by Shorty.

"She's a-workin'," he grumbled. "She's sure a-workin', an' I'll tell you if you're minded to hear an' listen."

"Go on," Smoke answered.

"Well, she tells me, plain an' simple, that we ain't never goin' to get out of this hole in the ground in days an' days. We're goin' to find trouble an' be stuck in here a long time an' then some."

"Does she say anything about grub?" Smoke queried unsympathetically. "For we haven't grub for days and days and days and then some."

"Nope. Nary whisper about grub. I guess we'll manage to make out. But I tell you one thing, Smoke, straight an' flat. I'll eat any dog in the team exceptin' Bright. I got to draw the line on Bright. I just couldn't scoff him."

"Cheer up," Smoke girded. "My hunch is working overtime. She tells me there'll be no dogs eaten, and, whether it's moose or caribou or quail on toast, we'll all fatten up."

Shorty snorted his unutterable disgust, and silence obtained for another quarter of an hour.

"There's the beginning of your trouble," Smoke said, halting on his snow-shoes and staring at an object that lay on one side of the old trail.

Shorty left the gee-pole and joined him, and together they gazed down on the body of a man beside the trail.

"Well fed," said Smoke.

"Look at them lips," said Shorty.

"Stiff as a poker," said Smoke, lifting an arm, that, without moving, moved the whole body.

"Pick 'm up an' drop 'm and he'd break to pieces," was Shorty's comment.

The man lay on his side, solidly frozen. From the fact that no snow powdered him, it was patent that he had lain there but a short time.

"There was a general fall of snow three days back," said Shorty.

Smoke nodded, bending over the corpse, twisting it half up to face them, and pointing to a bullet wound in the temple. He glanced to the side and tilted his head at a revolver that lay on top of the snow.

A hundred yards farther on they came upon a second body that lay face downward in the trail. "Two things are pretty clear," Smoke said. "They're fat. That means no famine. They've not struck it rich, else they wouldn't have committed suicide."

"If they did," Shorty objected.

"They certainly did. There are no tracks besides their own, and each is powder-burned." Smoke dragged the corpse to one side and with the toe of his moccasin nosed a revolver out of the snow into which it had been pressed by the body. "That's what did the work. I told you we'd find something."

"From the looks of it we ain't started yet. Now what'd two fat geezers want to kill theirselves for?"

"When we find that out we'll have found the rest of your trouble," Smoke answered. "Come on. It's blowing dark."

Quite dark it was when Smoke's snow-shoe tripped him over a body. He fell across a sled, on which lay another body. And when he had dug the snow out of his neck and struck a match, he and Shorty glimpsed a third body, wrapped in blankets, lying beside a partially dug grave. Also, ere the match flickered out, they caught sight of half a dozen additional graves.

"B-r-r," Shorty shivered. "Suicide Camp. All fed up. I reckon they're all dead."

"No—peep at that." Smoke was looking farther along at a dim glimmer of light. "And there's another light—and a third one there. Come on. Let's hike."

No more corpses delayed them, and in several minutes, over a hard-packed trail, they were in the camp.

"It's a city," Shorty whispered. "There must be twenty cabins. An' not a dog. Ain't that funny!"

"And that explains it," Smoke whispered back excitedly. "It's the Laura Sibley outfit. Don't you remember? Came up the Yukon last fall on the Port Townsend Number Six. Went right by Dawson without stopping. The steamer must have landed them at the mouth of the creek."

"Sure. I remember. They was Mormons."

"No—vegetarians." Smoke grinned in the darkness. "They won't eat meat and they won't work dogs."

"It's all the same. I knowed they was something funny about 'em. Had the allwise steer to the yellow. That Laura Sibley was goin' to take 'em right to the spot where they'd all be millionaires."

"Yes; she was their seeress—had visions and that sort of stuff. I thought they went up the Nordensjold."

"Huh! Listen to that!"

Shorty's hand in the darkness went out warningly to Smoke's chest, and together they listened to a groan, deep and long drawn, that came from one of the cabins. Ere it could die away it was taken up by another cabin, and another—a vast suspiration of human misery. The effect was monstrous and nightmarish.

"B-r-r-r," Shorty shivered. "It's gettin' me goin'. Let's break in an' find what's eatin' 'em."

Smoke knocked at a lighted cabin, and was followed in by Shorty in answer to the "Come in" of the voice they heard groaning. It was a simple log cabin, the walls moss-chinked, the earth floor covered with sawdust and shavings. The light was a kerosene-lamp, and they could make out four bunks, three of which were occupied by men who ceased from groaning in order to stare.

"What's the matter?" Smoke demanded of one whose blankets could not hide his broad shoulders and massively muscled body, whose eyes were pain-racked and whose cheeks were hollow. "Smallpox? What is it?"

In reply, the man pointed at his mouth, spreading black and swollen lips in the effort; and Smoke recoiled at the sight.

"Scurvy," he muttered to Shorty; and the man confirmed the diagnosis with a nod of the head.

"Plenty of grub?" Shorty asked.

"Yep," was the answer from a man in another bunk. "Help yourself. There's slathers of it. The cabin next on the other side is empty. Cache is right alongside. Wade into it."

In every cabin they visited that night they found a similar situation. Scurvy had smitten the whole camp. A dozen women were in the party, though the two men did not see all of them. Originally there had been ninety-three men and women. But ten had died, and two had recently disappeared. Smoke told of finding the two, and expressed surprise that none had gone that short distance down the trail to find out for themselves. What particularly struck him and Shorty was the helplessness of these people. Their cabins were littered and dirty. The dishes stood unwashed on the rough plank tables. There was no mutual aid. A cabin's troubles were its own troubles, and already they had ceased from the exertion of burying their dead.

"It's almost weird," Smoke confided to Shorty. "I've met shirkers and loafers, but I never met so many all at one time. You heard what they said. They've never done a tap. I'll bet they haven't washed their own faces. No wonder they got scurvy."

"But vegetarians hadn't ought to get scurvy," Shorty contended. "It's the salt-meat-eaters that's supposed to fall for it. And they don't eat meat, salt or fresh, raw or cooked, or any other way."

Smoke shook his head. "I know. And it's vegetable diet that cures scurvy. No drugs will do it. Vegetables, especially potatoes, are the only dope. But don't forget one thing, Shorty: we are not up against a theory but a condition. The fact is these grass-eaters have all got scurvy."

"Must be contagious."

"No; that the doctors do know. Scurvy is not a germ disease. It can't be caught. It's generated. As near as I can get it, it's due to an impoverished condition of the blood. Its cause is not something they've got, but something they haven't got. A man gets scurvy for lack of certain chemicals in his blood, and those chemicals don't come out of powders and bottles, but do come out of vegetables."

"An' these people eats nothin' but grass," Shorty groaned. "And they've got it up to their ears. That proves you're all wrong, Smoke. You're spielin' a theory, but this condition sure knocks the spots outa your theory. Scurvy's catchin', an' that's why they've all got it, an' rotten bad at that. You an' me'll get it too, if we hang around this diggin'. B-r-r-r!—I can feel the bugs crawlin' into my system right now."

Smoke laughed skeptically, and knocked on a cabin door. "I suppose we'll find the same old thing," he said. "Come on. We've got to get a line on the situation."

"What do you want?" came a woman's sharp voice.

"We want to see you," Smoke answered.

"Who are you?"

"Two doctors from Dawson," Shorty blurted in, with a levity that brought a punch in the short ribs from Smoke's elbow.

"Don't want to see any doctors," the woman said, in tones crisp and staccato with pain and irritation. "Go away. Good night. We don't believe in doctors."

Smoke pulled the latch, shoved the door open, and entered, turning up the low-flamed kerosene-lamp so that he could see. In four bunks four women ceased from groaning and sighing to stare at the intruders. Two were young, thin-faced creatures, the third was an elderly and very stout woman, and the fourth, the one whom Smoke identified by her voice, was the thinnest, frailest specimen of the human race he had ever seen. As he quickly learned, she was Laura Sibley, the seeress and professional clairvoyant who had organized the expedition in Los Angeles and led it to this death-camp on the Nordbeska. The conversation that ensued was acrimonious. Laura Sibley did not believe in doctors. Also, to add to her purgatory, she had wellnigh ceased to believe in herself.

"Why didn't you send out for help?" Smoke asked, when she paused, breathless and exhausted, from her initial tirade. "There's a camp at Stewart River, and eighteen days' travel would fetch Dawson from here."

"Why didn't Amos Wentworth go?" she demanded, with a wrath that bordered on hysteria.

"Don't know the gentleman," Smoke countered. "What's he been doing?"

"Nothing. Except that he's the only one that hasn't caught the scurvy. And why hasn't he caught the scurvy? I'll tell you. No, I won't." The thin lips compressed so tightly that through the emaciated transparency of them Smoke was almost convinced he could see the teeth and the roots of the teeth. "And what would have been the use? Don't I know? I'm not a fool. Our caches are filled with every kind of fruit juice and preserved vegetables. We are better situated than any other camp in

Alaska to fight scurvy. There is no prepared vegetable, fruit, and nut food we haven't, and in plenty."

"She's got you there, Smoke," Shorty exulted. "And it's a condition, not a theory. You say vegetables cures. Here's the vegetables, and where's the cure?"

"There's no explanation I can see," Smoke acknowledged. "Yet there is no camp in Alaska like this. I've seen scurvy—a sprinkling of cases here and there; but I never saw a whole camp with it, nor did I ever see such terrible cases. Which is neither here nor there, Shorty. We've got to do what we can for these people, but first we've got to make camp and take care of the dogs. We'll see you in the morning, er— Mrs. Sibley."

"*Miss* Sibley," she bridled. "And now, young man, if you come fooling around this cabin with any doctor stuff I'll fill you full of birdshot."

"This divine seeress is a sweet one," Smoke chuckled, as he and Shorty felt their way back through the darkness to the empty cabin next to the one they had first entered.

It was evident that two men had lived until recently in the cabin, and the partners wondered if they weren't the two suicides down the trail. Together they overhauled the cache and found it filled with an undreamed-of variety of canned, powdered, dried, evaporated, condensed, and desiccated foods.

"What in the name of reason do they want to go and get scurvy for?" Shorty demanded, brandishing to the light packages of egg-powder and Italian mushrooms. "And look at that! And that!" He tossed out cans of tomatoes and corn and bottles of stuffed olives. "And the divine steeress got the scurvy, too. What d'ye make of it?"

"Seeress," Smoke corrected.

"Steeress," Shorty reiterated. "Didn't she steer 'em here to this hole in the ground?"

Next morning, after daylight, Smoke encountered a man carrying a heavy sled-load of firewood. He was a little man, clean-looking and spry, who walked briskly despite the load. Smoke experienced an immediate dislike.

"What's the matter with you?" he asked.

"Nothing," the little man answered.

"I know that," Smoke said. "That's why I asked you. You're Amos Wentworth. Now why under the sun haven't you the scurvy like all the rest?"

"Because I've exercised," came the quick reply. "There wasn't any need for any of them to get it if they'd only got out and done something. What did they do? Growled and kicked and grouched at the cold, the long nights, the hardships, the aches and pains and everything else. They loafed in their beds until they swelled up and couldn't leave them, that's all. Look at me. I've worked. Come into my cabin."

Smoke followed him in.

"Squint around. Clean as a whistle, eh? You bet. Everything shipshape. I wouldn't keep those chips and shavings on the floor except for the warmth, but they're clean chips and shavings. You ought to see the floor in some of the shacks. Pig-pens. As for me, I haven't eaten a meal off an unwashed dish. No, sir. It meant work, and I've worked, and I haven't the scurvy. You can put that in your pipe and smoke it."

"You've hit the nail on the head," Smoke admitted. "But I see you've only one bunk. Why so unsociable?"

"Because I like to be. It's easier to clean up for one than two, that's why. The lazy blanket-loafers! Do you think that I could have stood one around? No wonder they got scurvy."

It was very convincing, but Smoke could not rid himself of his dislike of the man.

"What's Laura Sibley got it in for you for?" he asked abruptly.

Amos Wentworth shot a quick look at him. "She's a crank," was the reply. "So are we all cranks, for that matter. But Heaven save me from the crank that won't wash the dishes that he eats off of, and that's what this crowd of cranks are like."

A few minutes later, Smoke was talking with Laura Sibley. Supported by a stick in either hand, she had paused in hobbling by his cabin.

"What have you got it in for Wentworth for?" he asked, apropos of nothing in the conversation and with a suddenness that caught her off her guard.

Her green eyes flashed bitterly, her emaciated face for the second was convulsed with rage, and her sore lips writhed on the verge of unconsidered speech. But only a splutter of gasping, unintelligible sounds issued forth, and then, by a terrible effort, she controlled herself.

"Because he's healthy," she panted. "Because he hasn't the scurvy. Because he is supremely selfish. Because he won't lift a hand to help anybody else. Because he'd let us rot and die, as he is letting us rot and die, without lifting a finger to fetch us a pail of water or a load of

JACK LONDON

firewood. That's the kind of a brute he is. But let him beware! That's all. Let him beware!"

Still panting and gasping, she hobbled on her way, and five minutes afterward, coming out of the cabin to feed the dogs, Smoke saw her entering Amos Wentworth's cabin.

"Something rotten here, Shorty, something rotten," he said, shaking his head ominously, as his partner came to the door to empty a pan of dish-water.

"Sure," was the cheerful rejoinder. "An' you an' me'll be catchin' it yet. You'll see."

"I don't mean the scurvy."

"Oh, sure, if you mean the divine steeress. She'd rob a corpse. She's the hungriest-lookin' female I ever seen."

"Exercise has kept you and me in condition, Shorty. It's kept Wentworth in condition. You see what lack of exercise has done for the rest. Now it's up to us to prescribe exercise for these hospital wrecks. It will be your job to see that they get it. I appoint you chief nurse."

"What? Me?" Shorty shouted. "I resign."

"No, you don't. I'll be able assistant, because it isn't going to be any soft snap. We've got to make them hustle. First thing, they'll have to bury their dead. The strongest for the burial squad; then the next strongest on the firewood squad (they've been lying in their blankets to save wood); and so on down the line. And spruce-tea. Mustn't forget that. All the sour-doughs swear by it. These people have never even heard of it."

"We sure got ourn cut out for us," Shorty grinned. "First thing we know we'll be full of lead."

"And that's our first job," Smoke said. "Come on."

In the next hour, each of the twenty-odd cabins was raided. All ammunition and every rifle, shotgun, and revolver was confiscated.

"Come on, you invalids," was Shorty's method. "Shootin'-irons— fork 'em over. We need 'em."

"Who says so?" was the query at the first cabin.

"Two doctors from Dawson," was Shorty's answer. "An' what they say goes. Come on. Shell out the ammunition, too."

"What do you want them for?"

"To stand off a war-party of canned beef comin' down the canyon. And I'm givin' you fair warnin' of a spruce-tea invasion. Come across."

And this was only the beginning of the day. Men were persuaded, coaxed, bullied or dragged by main strength from their bunks and forced to dress. Smoke selected the mildest cases for the burial squad. Another squad was told off to supply the wood by which the graves were burned down into the frozen muck and gravel. Still another squad had to chop firewood and impartially supply every cabin. Those who were too weak for outdoor work were put to cleaning and scrubbing the cabins and washing clothes. One squad brought in many loads of spruce-boughs, and every stove was used for the brewing of spruce-tea.

But no matter what face Smoke and Shorty put on it, the situation was grim and serious. At least thirty fearful and impossible cases could not be taken from the beds, as the two men, with nausea and horror, learned; while one, a woman, died in Laura Sibley's cabin. Yet strong measures were necessary.

"I don't like to wallop a sick man," Shorty explained, his fist doubled menacingly. "But I'd wallop his block off if it'd make him well. And what all you lazy bums needs is a wallopin'. Come on! Out of that an' into them duds of yourn, double quick, or I'll sure muss up the front of your face."

All the gangs groaned, and sighed, and wept, the tears streaming and freezing down their cheeks as they toiled; and it was patent that their agony was real. The situation was desperate, and Smoke's prescription was heroic.

When the work-gangs came in at noon, they found decently cooked dinners awaiting them, prepared by the weaker members of their cabins under the tutelage and drive of Smoke and Shorty.

"That'll do," Smoke said at three in the afternoon. "Knock off. Go to your bunks. You may be feeling rotten now, but you'll be the better for it to-morrow. Of course it hurts to get well, but I'm going to get you well."

"Too late," Amos Wentworth sneered pallidly at Smoke's efforts. "They ought to have started in that way last fall."

"Come along with me," Smoke answered. "Pick up those two pails. You're not ailing."

From cabin to cabin the three men went, dosing every man and woman with a full pint of spruce-tea. Nor was it easy.

"You might as well learn at the start that we mean business," Smoke stated to the first obdurate, who lay on his back, groaning through set teeth. "Stand by, Shorty." Smoke caught the patient by the nose and tapped the solar-plexus section so as to make the mouth gasp open. "Now, Shorty! Down she goes!"

And down it went, accompanied with unavoidable splutterings and stranglings.

"Next time you'll take it easier," Smoke assured the victim, reaching for the nose of the man in the adjoining bunk.

"I'd sooner take castor oil," was Shorty's private confidence, ere he downed his own portion. "Great jumpin' Methuselem!" was his entirely public proclamation the moment after he had swallowed the bitter dose. "It's a pint long, but hogshead strong."

"We're covering this spruce-tea route four times a day, and there are eighty of you to be dosed each time," Smoke informed Laura Sibley. "So we've no time to fool. Will you take it or must I hold your nose?" His thumb and forefinger hovered eloquently above her. "It's vegetable, so you needn't have any qualms."

"Qualms!" Shorty snorted. "No, sure, certainly not. It's the deliciousest dope!"

Laura Sibley hesitated. She gulped her apprehension.

"Well?" Smoke demanded peremptorily.

"I'll—I'll take it," she quavered. "Hurry up!"

That night, exhausted as by no hard day of trail, Smoke and Shorty crawled into their blankets.

"I'm fairly sick with it," Smoke confessed. "The way they suffer is awful. But exercise is the only remedy I can think of, and it must be given a thorough trial. I wish we had a sack of raw potatoes."

"Sparkins he can't wash no more dishes," Shorty said. "It hurts him so he sweats his pain. I seen him sweat it. I had to put him back in the bunk, he was that helpless."

"If only we had raw potatoes," Smoke went on. "The vital, essential something is missing from that prepared stuff. The life has been evaporated out of it."

"An' if that young fellow Jones in the Brownlow cabin don't croak before morning I miss my guess."

"For Heaven's sake be cheerful," Smoke chided.

"We got to bury him, ain't we?" came the indignant snort. "I tell you that boy's something awful—"

"Shut up," Smoke said.

And after several more indignant snorts, the heavy breathing of sleep arose from Shorty's bunk.

In the morning, not only was Jones dead, but one of the stronger men who had worked on the firewood squad was found to have hanged himself. A nightmare procession of days set in. For a week, steeling himself to the task, Smoke enforced the exercise and the spruce-tea. And one by one, and in twos and threes, he was compelled to knock off the workers. As he was learning, exercise was the last thing in the world for scurvy patients. The diminishing burial squad was kept steadily at work, and a surplus half-dozen graves were always burned down and waiting.

"You couldn't have selected a worse place for a camp," Smoke told Laura Sibley. "Look at it—at the bottom of a narrow gorge, running east and west. The noon sun doesn't rise above the top of the wall. You can't have had sunlight for several months."

"But how was I to know?"

He shrugged his shoulders. "I don't see why not, if you could lead a hundred fools to a gold-mine."

She glared malevolently at him and hobbled on. Several minutes afterward, coming back from a trip to where a squad of groaning patients was gathering spruce-boughs, Smoke saw the seeress entering Amos Wentworth's cabin and followed after her. At the door he could hear her voice, whimpering and pleading.

"Just for me," she was begging, as Smoke entered. "I won't tell a soul."

Both glanced guiltily at the intruder, and Smoke was certain that he was on the edge of something, he knew not what, and he cursed himself for not having eavesdropped.

"Out with it," he commanded harshly. "What is it?"

"What is what?" Amos Wentworth asked sullenly. And Smoke could not name what was what.

Grimmer and grimmer grew the situation. In that dark hole of a canyon, where sunlight never penetrated, the horrible death list mounted up. Each day, in apprehension, Smoke and Shorty examined each other's mouths for the whitening of the gums and mucous membranes—the invariable first symptom of the disease.

"I've quit," Shorty announced one evening. "I've been thinkin' it over, an' I quit. I can make a go at slave-drivin', but cripple-drivin's too much for my stomach. They go from bad to worse. They ain't twenty men I can drive to work. I told Jackson this afternoon he could take to his bunk. He was gettin' ready to suicide. I could see it stickin' out all over him. Exercise ain't no good."

"I've made up my mind to the same thing," Smoke answered. "We'll knock off all but about a dozen. They'll have to lend a hand. We can relay them. And we'll keep up the spruce-tea."

"It ain't no good."

"I'm about ready to agree with that, too, but at any rate it doesn't hurt them."

"Another suicide," was Shorty's news the following morning. "That Phillips is the one. I seen it comin' for days."

"We're up against the real thing," Smoke groaned. "What would you suggest, Shorty?"

"Who? Me? I ain't got no suggestions. The thing's got to run its course."

"But that means they'll all die," Smoke protested.

"Except Wentworth," Shorty snarled; for he had quickly come to share his partner's dislike for that individual.

The everlasting miracle of Wentworth's immunity perplexed Smoke. Why should he alone not have developed scurvy? Why did Laura Sibley hate him, and at the same time whine and snivel and beg from him? What was it she begged from him and that he would not give?

On several occasions Smoke made it a point to drop into Wentworth's cabin at meal-time. But one thing did he note that was suspicious, and that was Wentworth's suspicion of him. Next he tried sounding out Laura Sibley.

"Raw potatoes would cure everybody here," he remarked to the seeress. "I know it. I've seen it work before."

The flare of conviction in her eyes, followed by bitterness and hatred, told him the scent was warm.

"Why didn't you bring in a supply of fresh potatoes on the steamer?" he asked.

"We did. But coming up the river we sold them all out at a bargain at Fort Yukon. We had plenty of the evaporated kinds, and we knew they'd keep better. They wouldn't even freeze."

Smoke groaned. "And you sold them all?" he asked.

"Yes. How were we to know?"

"Now mightn't there have been a couple of odd sacks left?— accidentally, you know, mislaid on the steamer?"

She shook her head, as he thought, a trifle belatedly, then added, "We never found any."

"But mightn't there?" he persisted.

"How do I know?" she rasped angrily. "I didn't have charge of the commissary."

"And Amos Wentworth did," he jumped to the conclusion. "Very good. Now what is your private opinion—just between us two. Do you think Wentworth has any raw potatoes stored away somewhere?"

"No; certainly not. Why should he?"

"Why shouldn't he?"

She shrugged her shoulders.

Struggle as he would with her, Smoke could not bring her to admit the possibility.

"Wentworth's a swine," was Shorty's verdict, when Smoke told his suspicions.

"And so is Laura Sibley," Smoke added. "She believes he has the potatoes, and is keeping it quiet, and trying to get him to share with her."

"An' he won't come across, eh?" Shorty cursed frail human nature with one of his best flights, and caught his breath. "They both got their feet in the trough. May God rot them dead with scurvy for their reward, that's all I got to say, except I'm goin' right up now an' knock Wentworth's block off."

But Smoke stood out for diplomacy. That night, when the camp groaned and slept, or groaned and did not sleep, he went to Wentworth's unlighted cabin.

"Listen to me, Wentworth," he said. "I've got a thousand dollars in dust right here in this sack. I'm a rich man in this country, and I can afford it. I think I'm getting touched. Put a raw potato in my hand and the dust is yours. Here, heft it."

And Smoke thrilled when Amos Wentworth put out his hand in the darkness and hefted the gold. Smoke heard him fumble in the blankets, and then felt pressed into his hand, not the heavy gold-sack, but the unmistakable potato, the size of a hen's egg, warm from contact with the other's body.

Smoke did not wait till morning. He and Shorty were expecting at any time the deaths of their worst two cases, and to this cabin the partners went. Grated and mashed up in a cup, skin, and clinging specks of the earth, and all, was the thousand-dollar potato—a thick fluid, that they fed, several drops at a time, into the frightful orifices that had once been mouths. Shift by shift, through the long night, Smoke and Shorty relieved each other at administering the potato juice, rubbing it into the poor swollen gums where loose teeth rattled together and compelling the swallowing of every drop of the precious elixir.

By evening of the next day the change for the better in the two patients was miraculous and almost unbelievable. They were no longer the worst cases. In forty-eight hours, with the exhaustion of the potato, they were temporarily out of danger, though far from being cured.

"I'll tell you what I'll do," Smoke said to Wentworth. "I've got holdings in this country, and my paper is good anywhere. I'll give you five hundred dollars a potato up to fifty thousand dollars' worth. That's one hundred potatoes."

"Was that all the dust you had?" Wentworth queried.

"Shorty and I scraped up all we had. But, straight, he and I are worth several millions between us."

"I haven't any potatoes," Wentworth said finally. "Wish I had. That potato I gave you was the only one. I'd been saving it all the winter for fear I'd get the scurvy. I only sold it so as to be able to buy a passage out of the country when the river opens."

Despite the cessation of potato-juice, the two treated cases continued to improve through the third day. The untreated cases went from bad to worse. On the fourth morning, three horrible corpses were buried. Shorty went through the ordeal, then turned to Smoke.

"You've tried your way. Now it's me for mine."

He headed straight for Wentworth's cabin. What occurred there, Shorty never told. He emerged with knuckles skinned and bruised, and not only did Wentworth's face bear all the marks of a bad beating, but for a long time he carried his head, twisted and sidling, on a stiff neck. This phenomenon was accounted for by a row of four finger-marks, black and blue, on one side of the windpipe and by a single black-and-blue mark on the other side.

Next, Smoke and Shorty together invaded Wentworth's cabin, throwing him out in the snow while they turned the interior upside down. Laura Sibley hobbled in and frantically joined them in the search.

"You don't get none, old girl, not if we find a ton," Shorty assured her.

But she was no more disappointed than they. Though the very floor was dug up, they discovered nothing.

"I'm for roastin' him over a slow fire an' make 'm cough up," Shorty proposed earnestly.

Smoke shook his head reluctantly.

"It's murder," Shorty held on. "He's murderin' all them poor geezers just as much as if he knocked their brains out with an ax, only worse."

Another day passed, during which they kept a steady watch on Wentworth's movements. Several times, when he started out, water-bucket in hand, for the creek, they casually approached the cabin, and each time he hurried back without the water.

"They're cached right there in his cabin," Shorty said. "As sure as God made little apples, they are. But where? We sure overhauled it plenty." He stood up and pulled on his mittens. "I'm goin' to find 'em, if I have to pull the blame shack down a log at a time."

He glanced at Smoke, who, with an intent, absent face, had not heard him.

"What's eatin' you?" Shorty demanded wrathfully. "Don't tell me you've gone an' got the scurvy!"

"Just trying to remember something, Shorty."

"What?"

"I don't know. That's the trouble. But it has a bearing, if only I could remember it."

"Now you look here, Smoke; don't you go an' get bug-house," Shorty pleaded. "Think of me! Let your think-slats rip. Come on an' help me pull that shack down. I'd set her afire, if it wa'n't for roastin' them spuds."

"That's it!" Smoke exploded, as he sprang to his feet. "Just what I was trying to remember. Where's that kerosene-can? I'm with you, Shorty. The potatoes are ours."

"What's the game?"

"Watch me, that's all," Smoke baffled. "I always told you, Shorty, that a deficient acquaintance with literature was a handicap, even in the Klondike. Now what we're going to do came out of a book. I read it when I was a kid, and it will work. Come on."

Several minutes later, under a pale-gleaming, greenish aurora borealis, the two men crept up to Amos Wentworth's cabin. Carefully and noiselessly they poured kerosene over the logs, extra-drenching the door-frame and window-sash. Then the match was applied, and they watched the flaming oil gather headway. They drew back beyond the growing light and waited.

They saw Wentworth rush out, stare wildly at the conflagration, and plunge back into the cabin. Scarcely a minute elapsed when he emerged, this time slowly, half doubled over, his shoulders burdened by a sack heavy and unmistakable. Smoke and Shorty sprang at him like a pair of famished wolves. They hit him right and left, at the same instant. He crumpled down under the weight of the sack, which Smoke pressed over with his hands to make sure. Then he felt his knees clasped by Wentworth's arms as the man turned a ghastly face upward.

"Give me a dozen, only a dozen—half a dozen—and you can have the rest," he squalled. He bared his teeth and, with mad rage, half inclined his head to bite Smoke's leg, then he changed his mind and fell to pleading. "Just half a dozen," he wailed. "Just half a dozen. I was going to turn them over to you—to-morrow. Yes, to-morrow. That was my idea. They're life! They're life! Just half a dozen!"

"Where's the other sack?" Smoke bluffed.

"I ate it up," was the reply, unimpeachably honest. "That sack's all that's left. Give me a few. You can have the rest."

"Ate 'em up!" Shorty screamed. "A whole sack! An' them geezers dyin' for want of 'em! This for you! An' this! An' this! An' this! You swine! You hog!"

The first kick tore Wentworth away from his embrace of Smoke's knees. The second kick turned him over in the snow. But Shorty went on kicking.

"Watch out for your toes," was Smoke's only interference.

"Sure; I'm usin' the heel," Shorty answered. "Watch me. I'll cave his ribs in. I'll kick his jaw off. Take that! An' that! Wisht I could give you the boot instead of the moccasin. You swine!"

There was no sleep in camp that night. Hour after hour Smoke and Shorty went the rounds, doling the life-renewing potato-juice, a quarter of a spoonful at a dose, into the poor ruined mouths of the population. And through the following day, while one slept the other kept up the work.

There were no more deaths. The most awful cases began to mend with an immediacy that was startling. By the third day, men who had not been off their backs for weeks crawled out of their bunks and tottered around on crutches. And on that day, the sun, two months then on its journey into northern declination, peeped cheerfully over the crest of the canyon for the first time.

"Nary a potato," Shorty told the whining, begging Wentworth. "You ain't even touched with scurvy. You got outside a whole sack, an' you're loaded against scurvy for twenty years. Knowin' you, I've come to understand God. I always wondered why he let Satan live. Now I know. He let him live just as I let you live. But it's a cryin' shame, just the same."

"A word of advice," Smoke told Wentworth. "These men are getting well fast; Shorty and I are leaving in a week, and there will be nobody to protect you when these men go after you. There's the trail. Dawson's eighteen days' travel."

"Pull your freight, Amos," Shorty supplemented, "or what I done to you won't be a circumstance to what them convalescents'll do to you."

"Gentlemen, I beg of you, listen to me," Wentworth whined. "I'm a stranger in this country. I don't know its ways. I don't know the trail. Let me travel with you. I'll give you a thousand dollars if you'll let me travel with you."

"Sure," Smoke grinned maliciously. "If Shorty agrees."

"*Who*? *Me*?" Shorty stiffened for a supreme effort. "I ain't nobody. Woodticks ain't got nothin' on me when it comes to humility. I'm a worm, a maggot, brother to the pollywog an' child of the blow-fly. I ain't afraid or ashamed of nothin' that creeps or crawls or stinks. But travel with that mistake of creation! Go 'way, man. I ain't proud, but you turn my stomach."

And Amos Wentworth went away, alone, dragging a sled loaded with provisions sufficient to last him to Dawson. A mile down the trail Shorty overhauled him.

"Come here to me," was Shorty's greeting. "Come across. Fork over. Cough up."

"I don't understand," Wentworth quavered, shivering from recollection of the two beatings, hand and foot, he had already received from Shorty.

"That thousand dollars, d' ye understand that? That thousand dollars gold Smoke bought that measly potato with. Come through."

And Amos Wentworth passed the gold-sack over.

"Hope a skunk bites you an' you get howlin' hydrophoby," were the terms of Shorty's farewell.

X

A Flutter in Eggs

It was in the A. C. Company's big store at Dawson, on a morning of crisp frost, that Lucille Arral beckoned Smoke Bellew over to the dry-goods counter. The clerk had gone on an expedition into the storerooms, and, despite the huge, red-hot stoves, Lucille had drawn on her mittens again.

Smoke obeyed her call with alacrity. The man did not exist in Dawson who would not have been flattered by the notice of Lucille Arral, the singing soubrette of the tiny stock company that performed nightly at the Palace Opera House.

"Things are dead," she complained, with pretty petulance, as soon as they had shaken hands. "There hasn't been a stampede for a week. That masked ball Skiff Mitchell was going to give us has been postponed. There's no dust in circulation. There's always standing-room now at the Opera House. And there hasn't been a mail from the Outside for two whole weeks. In short, this burg has crawled into its cave and gone to sleep. We've got to do something. It needs livening—and you and I can do it. We can give it excitement if anybody can. I've broken with Wild Water, you know."

Smoke caught two almost simultaneous visions. One was of Joy Gastell; the other was of himself, in the midst of a bleak snow-stretch, under a cold arctic moon, being pot-shotted with accurateness and dispatch by the aforesaid Wild Water. Smoke's reluctance at raising excitement with the aid of Lucille Arral was too patent for her to miss.

"I'm not thinking what you are thinking at all, thank you," she chided, with a laugh and a pout. "When I throw myself at your head you'll have to have more eyes and better ones than you have now to see me."

"Men have died of heart disease at the sudden announcement of good fortune," he murmured in the unveracious gladness of relief.

"Liar," she retorted graciously. "You were more scared to death than anything else. Now take it from me, Mr. Smoke Bellew, I'm not going to make love to you, and if you dare to make love to me, Wild Water will take care of your case. You know *him*. Besides, I—I haven't really broken with him."

"Go on with your puzzles," he jeered. "Maybe I can start guessing what you're driving at after a while."

"There's no guessing, Smoke. I'll give it to you straight. Wild Water thinks I've broken with him, don't you see."

"Well, have you, or haven't you?"

"I haven't—there! But it's between you and me in confidence. He thinks I have. I made a noise like breaking with him, and he deserved it, too."

"Where do I come in, stalking-horse or fall-guy?"

"Neither. You make a pot of money, we put across the laugh on Wild Water and cheer Dawson up, and, best of all, and the reason for it all, he gets disciplined. He needs it. He's—well, the best way to put it is, he's too turbulent. Just because he's a big husky, because he owns more rich claims than he can keep count of—"

"And because he's engaged to the prettiest little woman in Alaska," Smoke interpolated.

"Yes, and because of that, too, thank you, is no reason for him to get riotous. He broke out last night again. Sowed the floor of the M. & M. with gold-dust. All of a thousand dollars. Just opened his poke and scattered it under the feet of the dancers. You've heard of it, of course."

"Yes; this morning. I'd like to be the sweeper in that establishment. But still I don't get you. Where do I come in?"

"Listen. He was too turbulent. I broke our engagement, and he's going around making a noise like a broken heart. Now we come to it. I like eggs."

"They're off!" Smoke cried in despair. "Which way? Which way?"

"Wait."

"But what have eggs and appetite got to do with it?" he demanded.

"Everything, if you'll only listen."

"Listening, listening," he chanted.

"Then for Heaven's sake listen. I like eggs. There's only a limited supply of eggs in Dawson."

"Sure. I know that, too. Slavovitch's restaurant has most of them. Ham and one egg, three dollars. Ham and two eggs, five dollars. That means two dollars an egg, retail. And only the swells and the Arrals and the Wild Waters can afford them."

"He likes eggs, too," she continued. "But that's not the point. I like them. I have breakfast every morning at eleven o'clock at Slavovitch's.

I invariably eat two eggs." She paused impressively. "Suppose, just suppose, somebody corners eggs."

She waited, and Smoke regarded her with admiring eyes, while in his heart he backed with approval Wild Water's choice of her.

"You're not following," she said.

"Go on," he replied. "I give up. What's the answer?"

"Stupid! You know Wild Water. When he sees I'm languishing for eggs, and I know his mind like a book, and I know how to languish, what will he do?"

"You answer it. Go on."

"Why, he'll just start stampeding for the man that's got the corner in eggs. He'll buy the corner, no matter what it costs. Picture: I come into Slavovitch's at eleven o'clock. Wild Water will be at the next table. He'll make it his business to be there. 'Two eggs, shirred,' I'll say to the waiter. 'Sorry, Miss Arral,' the waiter will say; 'they ain't no more eggs.' Then up speaks Wild Water, in that big bear voice of his, 'Waiter, six eggs, soft boiled.' And the waiter says, 'Yes, sir,' and the eggs are brought. Picture: Wild Water looks sideways at me, and I look like a particularly indignant icicle and summon the waiter. 'Sorry, Miss Arral,' he says, 'but them eggs is Mr. Wild Water's. You see, Miss, he owns 'em.' Picture: Wild Water, triumphant, doing his best to look unconscious while he eats his six eggs.

"Another picture: Slavovitch himself bringing two shirred eggs to me and saying, 'Compliments of Mr. Wild Water, Miss.' What can I do? What can I possibly do but smile at Wild Water, and then we make up, of course, and he'll consider it cheap if he has been compelled to pay ten dollars for each and every egg in the corner."

"Go on, go on," Smoke urged. "At what station do I climb onto the choo-choo cars, or at what water-tank do I get thrown off?"

"Ninny! You don't get thrown off. You ride the egg-train straight into the Union Depot. You make that corner in eggs. You start in immediately, to-day. You can buy every egg in Dawson for three dollars and sell out to Wild Water at almost any advance. And then, afterward, we'll let the inside history come out. The laugh will be on Wild Water. His turbulence will be some subdued. You and I share the glory of it. You make a pile of money. And Dawson wakes up with a grand ha! ha! Of course—if—if you think the speculation too risky, I'll put up the dust for the corner."

This last was too much for Smoke. Being only a mere mortal Western man, with queer obsessions about money and women, he declined with scorn the proffer of her dust.

"Hey! Shorty!" Smoke called across the main street to his partner, who was trudging along in his swift, slack-jointed way, a naked bottle with frozen contents conspicuously tucked under his arm. Smoke crossed over.

"Where have you been all morning? Been looking for you everywhere."

"Up to Doc's," Shorty answered, holding out the bottle. "Something's wrong with Sally. I seen last night, at feedin'-time, the hair on her tail an' flanks was fallin' out. The Doc says—"

"Never mind that," Smoke broke in impatiently. "What I want—"

"What's eatin' you?" Shorty demanded in indignant astonishment. "An' Sally gettin' naked bald in this crimpy weather! I tell you that dog's sick. Doc says—"

"Let Sally wait. Listen to me—"

"I tell you she can't wait. It's cruelty to animals. She'll be frost-bit. What are you in such a fever about anyway? Has that Monte Cristo strike proved up?"

"I don't know, Shorty. But I want you to do me a favor."

"Sure," Shorty said gallantly, immediately appeased and acquiescent. "What is it? Let her rip. Me for you."

"I want you to buy eggs for me—"

"Sure, an' Floridy water an' talcum powder, if you say the word. An' poor Sally sheddin' something scand'lous! Look here, Smoke, if you want to go in for high livin' you go an' buy your own eggs. Beans an' bacon's good enough for me."

"I am going to buy, but I want you to help me to buy. Now, shut up, Shorty. I've got the floor. You go right straight to Slavovitch's. Pay as high as three dollars, but buy all he's got."

"Three dollars!" Shorty groaned. "An' I heard tell only yesterday that he's got all of seven hundred in stock! Twenty-one hundred dollars for hen-fruit! Say, Smoke, I tell you what. You run right up and see the Doc. He'll tend to your case. An' he'll only charge you an ounce for the first prescription. So-long, I gotta to be pullin' my freight."

He started off, but Smoke caught his partner by the shoulder, arresting his progress and whirling him around.

"Smoke, I'd sure do anything for you," Shorty protested earnestly. "If you had a cold in the head an' was layin' with both arms broke, I'd set by your bedside, day an' night, an' wipe your nose for you. But I'll be everlastin'ly damned if I'll squander twenty-one hundred good iron dollars on hen-fruit for you or any other two-legged man."

"They're not your dollars, but mine, Shorty. It's a deal I have on. What I'm after is to corner every blessed egg in Dawson, in the Klondike, on the Yukon. You've got to help me out. I haven't the time to tell you of the inwardness of the deal. I will afterward, and let you go half on it if you want to. But the thing right now is to get the eggs. Now you hustle up to Slavovitch's and buy all he's got."

"But what'll I tell 'm? He'll sure know I ain't goin' to eat 'em."

"Tell him nothing. Money talks. He sells them cooked for two dollars. Offer him up to three for them uncooked. If he gets curious, tell him you're starting a chicken ranch. What I want is the eggs. And then keep on; nose out every egg in Dawson and buy it. Understand? Buy it! That little joint across the street from Slavovitch's has a few. Buy them. I'm going over to Klondike City. There's an old man there, with a bad leg, who's broke and who has six dozen. He's held them all winter for the rise, intending to get enough out of them to pay his passage back to Seattle. I'll see he gets his passage, and I'll get the eggs. Now hustle. And they say that little woman down beyond the sawmill who makes moccasins has a couple of dozen."

"All right, if you say so, Smoke. But Slavovitch seems the main squeeze. I'll just get an iron-bound option, black an' white, an' gather in the scatterin' first."

"All right. Hustle. And I'll tell you the scheme tonight."

But Shorty flourished the bottle. "I'm goin' to doctor up Sally first. The eggs can wait that long. If they ain't all eaten, they won't be eaten while I'm takin' care of a poor sick dog that's saved your life an' mine more 'n once."

Never was a market cornered more quickly. In three days every known egg in Dawson, with the exception of several dozen, was in the hands of Smoke and Shorty. Smoke had been more liberal in purchasing. He unblushingly pleaded guilty to having given the old man in Klondike City five dollars apiece for his seventy-two eggs. Shorty had bought most of the eggs, and he had driven bargains. He had given only two dollars an egg to the woman who made moccasins, and he prided himself that he had come off fairly well with Slavovitch, whose seven hundred and fifteen eggs he had bought at a flat rate of two dollars and a half. On the other hand, he grumbled because the little restaurant across the street had held him up for two dollars and seventy-five cents for a paltry hundred and thirty-four eggs.

The several dozen not yet gathered in were in the hands of two persons. One, with whom Shorty was dealing, was an Indian woman who lived in a cabin on the hill back of the hospital.

"I'll get her to-day," Shorty announced next morning. "You wash the dishes, Smoke. I'll be back in a jiffy, if I don't bust myself a-shovin' dust at her. Gimme a man to deal with every time. These blamed women— it's something sad the way they can hold out on a buyer. The only way to get 'em is sellin'. Why, you'd think them eggs of hern was solid nuggets."

In the afternoon, when Smoke returned to the cabin, he found Shorty squatted on the floor, rubbing ointment into Sally's tail, his countenance so expressionless that it was suspicious.

"What luck?" Shorty asked carelessly, after several minutes had passed.

"Nothing doing," Smoke answered. "How did you get on with the squaw?"

Shorty cocked his head triumphantly toward a tin pail of eggs on the table. "Seven dollars a clatter, though," he confessed, after another minute of silent rubbing.

"I offered ten dollars finally," Smoke said, "and then the fellow told me he'd already sold his eggs. Now that looks bad, Shorty. Somebody else is in the market. Those twenty-eight eggs are liable to cause us trouble. You see, the success of the corner consists in holding every last—"

He broke off to stare at his partner. A pronounced change was coming over Shorty—one of agitation masked by extreme deliberation. He closed the salve-box, wiped his hands slowly and thoroughly on Sally's furry coat, stood up, went over to the corner and looked at the thermometer, and came back again. He spoke in a low, toneless, and super-polite voice.

"Do you mind kindly just repeating over how many eggs you said the man didn't sell to you?" he asked.

"Twenty-eight."

"Hum," Shorty communed to himself, with a slight duck of the head of careless acknowledgment. Then he glanced with slumbering anger at the stove. "Smoke, we'll have to dig up a new stove. That fire-box is burned plumb into the oven so it blacks the biscuits."

"Let the fire-box alone," Smoke commanded, "and tell me what's the matter."

"Matter? An' you want to know what's the matter? Well, kindly please direct them handsome eyes of yourn at that there pail settin' on the table. See it?"

Smoke nodded.

"Well, I want to tell you one thing, just one thing. They's just exactly, preecisely, nor nothin' more or anythin' less'n twenty-eight eggs in the pail, an' they cost, every danged last one of 'em, just exactly seven great big round iron dollars a throw. If you stand in cryin' need of any further items of information, I'm willin' and free to impart."

"Go on," Smoke requested.

"Well, that geezer you was dickerin' with is a big buck Indian. Am I right?"

Smoke nodded, and continued to nod to each question.

"He's got one cheek half gone where a bald-face grizzly swatted him. Am I right? He's a dog-trader—right, eh? His name is Scar-Face Jim. That's so, ain't it? D'ye get my drift?"

"You mean we've been bidding—?"

"Against each other. Sure thing. That squaw's his wife, an' they keep house on the hill back of the hospital. I could 'a' got them eggs for two a throw if you hadn't butted in."

"And so could I," Smoke laughed, "if you'd kept out, blame you! But it doesn't amount to anything. We know that we've got the corner. That's the big thing."

Shorty spent the next hour wrestling with a stub of a pencil on the margin of a three-year-old newspaper, and the more interminable and hieroglyphic grew his figures the more cheerful he became.

"There she stands," he said at last. "Pretty? I guess yes. Lemme give you the totals. You an' me has right now in our possession exactly nine hundred an' seventy-three eggs. They cost us exactly two thousand, seven hundred an' sixty dollars, reckonin' dust at sixteen an ounce an' not countin' time. An' now listen to me. If we stick up Wild Water for ten dollars a egg we stand to win, clean net an' all to the good, just exactly six thousand nine hundred and seventy dollars. Now that's a book-makin' what is, if anybody should ride up on a dog-sled an' ask you. An' I'm in half on it! Put her there, Smoke. I'm that thankful I'm sure droolin' gratitude. Book-makin'! Say, I'd sooner run with the chicks than the ponies any day."

At eleven that night Smoke was routed from sound sleep by Shorty, whose fur parka exhaled an atmosphere of keen frost and whose hand was extremely cold in its contact with Smoke's cheek.

"What is it now?" Smoke grumbled. "Rest of Sally's hair fallen out?"

"Nope. But I just had to tell you the good news. I seen Slavovitch. Or Slavovitch seen me, I guess, because he started the seance. He says to me: 'Shorty, I want to speak to you about them eggs. I've kept it quiet. Nobody knows I sold 'em to you. But if you're speculatin', I can put you wise to a good thing.' An' he did, too, Smoke. Now what'd you guess that good thing is?"

"Go on. Name it."

"Well, maybe it sounds incredible, but that good thing was Wild Water Charley. He's lookin' to buy eggs. He goes around to Slavovitch an' offers him five dollars an egg, an' before he quits he's offerin' eight. An' Slavovitch ain't got no eggs. Last thing Wild Water says to Slavovitch is that he'll beat the head offen him if he ever finds out Slavovitch has eggs cached away somewheres. Slavovitch had to tell 'm he'd sold the eggs, but that the buyer was secret.

"Slavovitch says to let him say the word to Wild Water who's got the eggs. 'Shorty,' he says to me, 'Wild Water'll come a-runnin'. You can hold him up for eight dollars.' 'Eight dollars, your grandmother,' I says. 'He'll fall for ten before I'm done with him.' Anyway, I told Slavovitch I'd think it over and let him know in the mornin'. Of course we'll let 'm pass the word on to Wild Water. Am I right?"

"You certainly are, Shorty. First thing in the morning tip off Slavovitch. Have him tell Wild Water that you and I are partners in the deal."

Five minutes later Smoke was again aroused by Shorty.

"Say! Smoke! Oh, Smoke!"

"Yes?"

"Not a cent less than ten a throw. Do you get that?"

"Sure thing—all right," Smoke returned sleepily.

In the morning Smoke chanced upon Lucille Arral again at the dry-goods counter of the A. C. Store.

"It's working," he jubilated. "It's working. Wild Water's been around to Slavovitch, trying to buy or bully eggs out of him. And by this time Slavovitch has told him that Shorty and I own the corner."

Lucille Arral's eyes sparkled with delight. "I'm going to breakfast right now," she cried. "And I'll ask the waiter for eggs, and be so plaintive when there aren't any as to melt a heart of stone. And you know Wild Water's been around to Slavovitch, trying to buy the corner if it costs him one of his mines. I know him. And hold out for a stiff figure. Nothing less than ten dollars will satisfy me, and if you sell for anything less, Smoke, I'll never forgive you."

That noon, up in their cabin, Shorty placed on the table a pot of beans, a pot of coffee, a pan of sourdough biscuits, a tin of butter and a tin of condensed cream, a smoking platter of moose-meat and bacon, a plate of stewed dried peaches, and called: "Grub's ready. Take a slant at Sally first."

Smoke put aside the harness on which he was sewing, opened the door, and saw Sally and Bright spiritedly driving away a bunch of foraging sled-dogs that belonged to the next cabin. Also he saw something else that made him close the door hurriedly and dash to the stove. The frying-pan, still hot from the moose-meat and bacon, he put back on the front lid. Into the frying-pan he put a generous dab of butter, then reached for an egg, which he broke and dropped spluttering into the pan. As he reached for a second egg, Shorty gained his side and clutched his arm in an excited grip.

"Hey! What you doin'?" he demanded.

"Frying eggs," Smoke informed him, breaking the second one and throwing off Shorty's detaining hand. "What's the matter with your eyesight? Did you think I was combing my hair?"

"Don't you feel well?" Shorty queried anxiously, as Smoke broke a third egg and dexterously thrust him back with a stiff-arm jolt on the breast. "Or are you just plain loco? That's thirty dollars' worth of eggs already."

"And I'm going to make it sixty dollars' worth," was the answer, as Smoke broke the fourth. "Get out of the way, Shorty. Wild Water's coming up the hill, and he'll be here in five minutes."

Shorty sighed vastly with commingled comprehension and relief, and sat down at the table. By the time the expected knock came at the door, Smoke was facing him across the table, and, before each, was a plate containing three hot, fried eggs.

"Come in!" Smoke called.

Wild Water Charley, a strapping young giant just a fraction of an inch under six feet in height and carrying a clean weight of one hundred and ninety pounds, entered and shook hands.

"Set down an' have a bite, Wild Water," Shorty invited. "Smoke, fry him some eggs. I'll bet he ain't scoffed an egg in a coon's age."

Smoke broke three more eggs into the hot pan, and in several minutes placed them before his guest, who looked at them with so strange and strained an expression that Shorty confessed afterward his fear that Wild Water would slip them into his pocket and carry them away.

"Say, them swells down in the States ain't got nothin' over us in the matter of eats," Shorty gloated. "Here's you an' me an' Smoke gettin' outside ninety dollars' worth of eggs an' not battin' an eye."

Wild Water stared at the rapidly disappearing eggs and seemed petrified.

"Pitch in an' eat," Smoke encouraged.

"They—they ain't worth no ten dollars," Wild Water said slowly.

Shorty accepted the challenge. "A thing's worth what you can get for it, ain't it?" he demanded.

"Yes, but—"

"But nothin'. I'm tellin' you what we can get for 'em. Ten a throw, just like that. We're the egg trust, Smoke an' me, an' don't you forget it. When we say ten a throw, ten a throw goes." He mopped his plate with a biscuit. "I could almost eat a couple more," he sighed, then helped himself to the beans.

"You can't eat eggs like that," Wild Water objected. "It—it ain't right."

"We just dote on eggs, Smoke an' me," was Shorty's excuse.

Wild Water finished his own plate in a half-hearted way and gazed dubiously at the two comrades. "Say, you fellows can do me a great favor," he began tentatively. "Sell me, or lend me, or give me, about a dozen of them eggs."

"Sure," Smoke answered. "I know what a yearning for eggs is myself. But we're not so poor that we have to sell our hospitality. They'll cost you nothing—" Here a sharp kick under the table admonished him that Shorty was getting nervous. "A dozen, did you say, Wild Water?"

Wild Water nodded.

"Go ahead, Shorty," Smoke went on. "Cook them up for him. I can sympathize. I've seen the time myself when I could eat a dozen, straight off the bat."

But Wild Water laid a restraining hand on the eager Shorty as he explained. "I don't mean cooked. I want them with the shells on."

"So that you can carry 'em away?"

"That's the idea."

"But that ain't hospitality," Shorty objected. "It's—it's tradin'."

Smoke nodded concurrence. "That's different, Wild Water. I thought you just wanted to eat them. You see, we went into this for a speculation."

The dangerous blue of Wild Water's eyes began to grow more dangerous. "I'll pay you for them," he said sharply. "How much?"

"Oh, not a dozen," Smoke replied. "We couldn't sell a dozen. We're not retailers; we're speculators. We can't break our own market. We've got a hard and fast corner, and when we sell out it's the whole corner or nothing."

"How many have you got, and how much do you want for them?"

"How many have we, Shorty?" Smoke inquired.

Shorty cleared his throat and performed mental arithmetic aloud. "Lemme see. Nine hundred an' seventy-three minus nine, that leaves nine hundred an' sixty-two. An' the whole shootin'-match, at ten a throw, will tote up just about nine thousand six hundred an' twenty iron dollars. Of course, Wild Water, we're playin' fair, an' it's money back for bad ones, though they ain't none. That's one thing I never seen in the Klondike—a bad egg. No man's fool enough to bring in a bad egg."

"That's fair," Smoke added. "Money back for the bad ones, Wild Water. And there's our proposition—nine thousand six hundred and twenty dollars for every egg in the Klondike."

"You might play them up to twenty a throw an' double your money," Shorty suggested.

Wild Water shook his head sadly and helped himself to the beans. "That would be too expensive, Shorty. I only want a few. I'll give you ten dollars for a couple of dozen. I'll give you twenty—but I can't buy 'em all."

"All or none," was Smoke's ultimatum.

"Look here, you two," Wild Water said in a burst of confidence. "I'll be perfectly honest with you, an' don't let it go any further. You know Miss Arral an' I was engaged. Well, she's broken everything off. You know it. Everybody knows it. It's for her I want them eggs."

"Huh!" Shorty jeered. "It's clear an' plain why you want 'em with the shells on. But I never thought it of you."

"Thought what?"

"It's low-down mean, that's what it is," Shorty rushed on, virtuously indignant. "I wouldn't wonder somebody filled you full of lead for it, an' you'd deserve it, too."

Wild Water began to flame toward the verge of one of his notorious Berserker rages. His hands clenched until the cheap fork in one of them began to bend, while his blue eyes flashed warning sparks. "Now look here, Shorty, just what do you mean? If you think anything underhanded—"

"I mean what I mean," Shorty retorted doggedly, "an' you bet your sweet life I don't mean anything underhanded. Overhand's the only way to do it. You can't throw 'em any other way."

"Throw what?"

"Eggs, prunes, baseballs, anything. But Wild Water, you're makin' a mistake. They ain't no crowd ever sat at the Opery House that'll stand for it. Just because she's a actress is no reason you can publicly lambaste her with hen-fruit."

For the moment it seemed that Wild Water was going to burst or have apoplexy. He gulped down a mouthful of scalding coffee and slowly recovered himself.

"You're in wrong, Shorty," he said with cold deliberation. "I'm not going to throw eggs at her. Why, man," he cried, with growing excitement, "I want to give them eggs to her, on a platter, shirred— that's the way she likes 'em."

"I knowed I was wrong," Shorty cried generously, "I knowed you couldn't do a low-down trick like that."

"That's all right, Shorty," Wild Water forgave him. "But let's get down to business. You see why I want them eggs. I want 'em bad."

"Do you want 'em ninety-six hundred an' twenty dollars' worth?" Shorty queried.

"It's a hold-up, that's what it is," Wild Water declared irately.

"It's business," Smoke retorted. "You don't think we're peddling eggs for our health, do you?"

"Aw, listen to reason," Wild Water pleaded. "I only want a couple of dozen. I'll give you twenty apiece for 'em. What do I want with all the rest of them eggs? I've went years in this country without eggs, an' I guess I can keep on managin' without 'em somehow."

"Don't get het up about it," Shorty counseled. "If you don't want 'em, that settles it. We ain't a-forcin' 'em on you."

"But I do want 'em," Wild Water complained.

"Then you know what they'll cost you—ninety-six hundred an' twenty dollars, an' if my figurin's wrong, I'll treat."

"But maybe they won't turn the trick," Wild Water objected. "Maybe Miss Arral's lost her taste for eggs by this time."

"I should say Miss Arral's worth the price of the eggs," Smoke put in quietly.

"Worth it!" Wild Water stood up in the heat of his eloquence. "She's worth a million dollars. She's worth all I've got. She's worth all the dust in the Klondike." He sat down, and went on in a calmer voice. "But that ain't no call for me to gamble ten thousand dollars on a breakfast for her. Now I've got a proposition. Lend me a couple of dozen of them eggs. I'll turn 'em over to Slavovitch. He'll feed 'em to her with my compliments. She ain't smiled to me for a hundred years. If them eggs gets a smile for me, I'll take the whole boiling off your hands."

"Will you sign a contract to that effect?" Smoke said quickly; for he knew that Lucille Arral had agreed to smile.

Wild Water gasped. "You're almighty swift with business up here on the hill," he said, with a hint of a snarl.

"We're only accepting your own proposition," Smoke answered.

"All right—bring on the paper—make it out, hard and fast," Wild Water cried in the anger of surrender.

Smoke immediately wrote out the document, wherein Wild Water agreed to take every egg delivered to him at ten dollars per egg, provided that the two dozen advanced to him brought about a reconciliation with Lucille Arral.

Wild Water paused, with uplifted pen, as he was about to sign. "Hold on," he said. "When I buy eggs I buy good eggs."

"They ain't a bad egg in the Klondike," Shorty snorted.

"Just the same, if I find one bad egg you've got to come back with the ten I paid for it."

"That's all right," Smoke placated. "It's only fair."

"An' every bad egg you come back with I'll eat," Shorty declared.

Smoke inserted the word "good" in the contract, and Wild Water sullenly signed, received the trial two dozen in a tin pail, pulled on his mittens, and opened the door.

"Good-by, you robbers," he growled back at them, and slammed the door.

Smoke was a witness to the play next morning in Slavovitch's. He sat, as Wild Water's guest, at the table adjoining Lucille Arral's. Almost to the letter, as she had forecast it, did the scene come off.

"Haven't you found any eggs yet?" she murmured plaintively to the waiter.

"No, ma'am," came the answer. "They say somebody's cornered every egg in Dawson. Mr. Slavovitch is trying to buy a few just especially for you. But the fellow that's got the corner won't let loose."

It was at this juncture that Wild Water beckoned the proprietor to him, and, with one hand on his shoulder, drew his head down. "Look here, Slavovitch," Wild Water whispered hoarsely, "I turned over a couple of dozen eggs to you last night. Where are they?"

"In the safe, all but that six I have all thawed and ready for you any time you sing out."

"I don't want 'em for myself," Wild Water breathed in a still lower voice. "Shir 'em up and present 'em to Miss Arral there."

"I'll attend to it personally myself," Slavovitch assured him.

"An' don't forget—compliments of me," Wild Water concluded, relaxing his detaining clutch on the proprietor's shoulder.

Pretty Lucille Arral was gazing forlornly at the strip of breakfast bacon and the tinned mashed potatoes on her plate when Slavovitch placed before her two shirred eggs.

"Compliments of Mr. Wild Water," they at the next table heard him say.

Smoke acknowledged to himself that it was a fine bit of acting— the quick, joyous flash in the face of her, the impulsive turn of the head, the spontaneous forerunner of a smile that was only checked by a superb self-control which resolutely drew her face back so that she could say something to the restaurant proprietor.

Smoke felt the kick of Wild Water's moccasined foot under the table.

"Will she eat 'em?—that's the question—will she eat 'em?" the latter whispered agonizingly.

And with sidelong glances they saw Lucille Arral hesitate, almost push the dish from her, then surrender to its lure.

"I'll take them eggs," Wild Water said to Smoke. "The contract holds. Did you see her? Did you see her! She almost smiled. I know her. It's all fixed. Two more eggs to-morrow an' she'll forgive an' make up. If she wasn't here I'd shake hands, Smoke, I'm that grateful. You ain't a robber; you're a philanthropist."

Smoke returned jubilantly up the hill to the cabin, only to find Shorty playing solitaire in black despair. Smoke had long since learned that whenever his partner got out the cards for solitaire it was a warning signal that the bottom had dropped out of the world.

"Go 'way, don't talk to me," was the first rebuff Smoke received.

But Shorty soon thawed into a freshet of speech.

"It's all off with the big Swede," he groaned. "The corner's busted. They'll be sellin' sherry an' egg in all the saloons to-morrow at a dollar a flip. They ain't no starvin' orphan child in Dawson that won't be wrappin' its tummy around eggs. What d'ye think I run into?—a geezer with three thousan' eggs—d'ye get me? Three thousan', an' just freighted in from Forty Mile."

"Fairy stories," Smoke doubted.

"Fairy hell! I seen them eggs. Gautereaux's his name—a whackin' big, blue-eyed French-Canadian husky. He asked for you first, then took me to the side and jabbed me straight to the heart. It was our cornerin' eggs that got him started. He knowed about them three thousan' at Forty Mile an' just went an' got 'em. 'Show 'em to me,' I says. An' he did. There was his dog-teams, an' a couple of Indian drivers, restin' down the bank where they'd just pulled in from Forty Mile. An' on the sleds was soap-boxes—teeny wooden soap-boxes.

"We took one out behind a ice-jam in the middle of the river an' busted it open. Eggs!—full of 'em, all packed in sawdust. Smoke, you an' me lose. We've been gamblin'. D'ye know what he had the gall to say to me?—that they was all ourn at ten dollars a egg. D'ye know what he was doin' when I left his cabin?—drawin' a sign of eggs for sale. Said he'd give us first choice, at ten a throw, till 2 P. M., an' after that, if we didn't come across, he'd bust the market higher'n a kite. Said he wasn't no business man, but that he knowed a good thing when he seen it—meanin' you an' me, as I took it."

"It's all right," Smoke said cheerfully. "Keep your shirt on an' let me think a moment. Quick action and team play is all that's needed. I'll get Wild Water here at two o'clock to take delivery of eggs. You buy that Gautereaux's eggs. Try and make a bargain. Even if you pay ten dollars apiece for them, Wild Water will take them off our hands at the same price. If you can get them cheaper, why, we make a profit as well. Now go to it. Have them here by not later than two o'clock. Borrow Colonel Bowie's dogs and take our team. Have them here by two sharp."

"Say, Smoke," Shorty called, as his partner started down the hill. "Better take an umbrella. I wouldn't be none surprised to see the weather rainin' eggs before you get back."

Smoke found Wild Water at the M. & M., and a stormy half-hour ensued.

"I warn you we've picked up some more eggs," Smoke said, after Wild Water had agreed to bring his dust to the cabin at two o'clock and pay on delivery.

"You're luckier at finding eggs than me," Wild Water admitted. "Now, how many eggs have you got now?—an' how much dust do I tote up the hill?"

Smoke consulted his notebook. "As it stands now, according to Shorty's figures, we've three thousand nine hundred and sixty-two eggs. Multiply by ten—"

"Forty thousand dollars!" Wild Water bellowed. "You said there was only something like nine hundred eggs. It's a stickup! I won't stand for it!"

Smoke drew the contract from his pocket and pointed to the *Pay on Delivery*. "No mention is made of the number of eggs to be delivered. You agreed to pay ten dollars for every egg we delivered to you. Well, we've got the eggs, and a signed contract is a signed contract. Honestly, though, Wild Water, we didn't know about those other eggs until afterward. Then we had to buy them in order to make our corner good."

For five long minutes, in choking silence, Wild Water fought a battle with himself, then reluctantly gave in.

"I'm in bad," he said brokenly. "The landscape's fair sproutin' eggs. An' the quicker I get out the better. There might come a landslide of 'em. I'll be there at two o'clock. But forty thousand dollars!"

"It's only thirty-nine thousand six hundred an' twenty," Smoke corrected. "It'll weigh two hundred pounds," Wild Water raved on. "I'll have to freight it up with a dog-team."

"We'll lend you our teams to carry the eggs away," Smoke volunteered.

"But where'll I cache 'em? Never mind. I'll be there. But as long as I live I'll never eat another egg. I'm full sick of 'em."

At half-past one, doubling the dog-teams for the steep pitch of the hill, Shorty arrived with Gautereaux's eggs. "We dang near double our winnings," Shorty told Smoke, as they piled the soap-boxes inside the cabin. "I holds 'm down to eight dollars, an' after he cussed loco in French he falls for it. Now that's two dollars clear profit to us for each egg, an' they're three thousan' of 'em. I paid 'm in full. Here's the receipt."

While Smoke got out the gold-scales and prepared for business, Shorty devoted himself to calculation.

"There's the figgers," he announced triumphantly. "We win twelve thousan' nine hundred an' seventy dollars. An' we don't do Wild Water no harm. He wins Miss Arral. Besides, he gets all them eggs. It's sure a bargain-counter all around. Nobody loses."

"Even Gautereaux's twenty-four thousand to the good," Smoke laughed, "minus, of course, what the eggs and the freighting cost him. And if Wild Water plays the corner, he may make a profit out of the eggs himself."

Promptly at two o'clock, Shorty, peeping, saw Wild Water coming up the hill. When he entered he was brisk and businesslike. He took off his big bearskin coat, hung it on a nail, and sat down at the table.

"Bring on them eggs, you pirates," he commenced. "An' after this day, if you know what's good for you, never mention eggs to me again."

They began on the miscellaneous assortment of the original corner, all three men counting. When two hundred had been reached, Wild Water suddenly cracked an egg on the edge of the table and opened it deftly with his thumbs.

"Hey! Hold on!" Shorty objected.

"It's my egg, ain't it?" Wild Water snarled. "I'm paying ten dollars for it, ain't I? But I ain't buying no pig in a poke. When I cough up ten bucks an egg I want to know what I'm gettin'."

"If you don't like it, I'll eat it," Shorty volunteered maliciously.

Wild Water looked and smelled and shook his head. "No, you don't, Shorty. That's a good egg. Gimme a pail. I'm goin' to eat it myself for supper."

Thrice again Wild Water cracked good eggs experimentally and put them in the pail beside him.

"Two more than you figgered, Shorty," he said at the end of the count. "Nine hundred an' sixty-four, not sixty-two."

"My mistake," Shorty acknowledged handsomely. "We'll throw 'em in for good measure."

"Guess you can afford to," Wild Water accepted grimly. "Pass the batch. Nine thousan' six hundred an' twenty dollars. I'll pay for it now. Write a receipt, Smoke."

"Why not count the rest," Smoke suggested, "and pay all at once?"

Wild Water shook his head. "I'm no good at figgers. One batch at a time an' no mistakes."

Going to his fur coat, from each of the side pockets he drew forth two sacks of dust, so rotund and long that they resembled bologna sausages. When the first batch had been paid for, there remained in the gold-sacks not more than several hundred dollars.

A soap-box was carried to the table, and the count of the three thousand began. At the end of one hundred, Wild Water struck an egg sharply against the edge of the table. There was no crack. The resultant sound was like that of the striking of a sphere of solid marble.

"Frozen solid," he remarked, striking more sharply.

He held the egg up, and they could see the shell powdered to minute fragments along the line of impact.

"Huh!" said Shorty. "It ought to be solid, seein' it has just been freighted up from Forty Mile. It'll take an ax to bust it."

"Me for the ax," said Wild Water.

Smoke brought the ax, and Wild Water, with the clever hand and eye of the woodsman, split the egg cleanly in half. The appearance of the egg's interior was anything but satisfactory. Smoke felt a premonitory chill. Shorty was more valiant. He held one of the halves to his nose.

"Smells all right," he said.

"But it looks all wrong," Wild Water contended. "An' how can it smell when the smell's frozen along with the rest of it? Wait a minute."

He put the two halves into a frying-pan and placed the latter on the front lid of the hot stove. Then the three men, with distended, questing nostrils, waited in silence. Slowly an unmistakable odor began to drift through the room. Wild Water forbore to speak, and Shorty remained dumb despite conviction.

"Throw it out," Smoke cried, gasping.

"What's the good?" asked Wild Water. "We've got to sample the rest."

"Not in this cabin." Smoke coughed and conquered a qualm. "Chop them open, and we can test by looking at them. Throw it out, Shorty— Throw it out! Phew! And leave the door open!"

Box after box was opened; egg after egg, chosen at random, was chopped in two; and every egg carried the same message of hopeless, irremediable decay.

"I won't ask you to eat 'em, Shorty," Wild Water jeered, "an' if you don't mind, I can't get outa here too quick. My contract called for *good* eggs. If you'll loan me a sled an' team I'll haul them good ones away before they get contaminated."

Smoke helped in loading the sled. Shorty sat at the table, the cards laid before him for solitaire.

"Say, how long you been holdin' that corner?" was Wild Water's parting gibe.

Smoke made no reply, and, with one glance at his absorbed partner, proceeded to fling the soap boxes out into the snow.

"Say, Shorty, how much did you say you paid for that three thousand?" Smoke queried gently.

"Eight dollars. Go 'way. Don't talk to me. I can figger as well as you. We lose seventeen thousan' on the flutter, if anybody should ride up on a dog-sled an' ask you. I figgered that out while waitin' for the first egg to smell."

Smoke pondered a few minutes, then again broke silence. "Say, Shorty. Forty thousand dollars gold weighs two hundred pounds. Wild Water borrowed our sled and team to haul away his eggs. He came up the hill without a sled. Those two sacks of dust in his coat pockets weighed about twenty pounds each. The understanding was cash on delivery. He brought enough dust to pay for the good eggs. He never expected to pay for those three thousand. He knew they were bad. Now how did he know they were bad? What do you make of it, anyway?"

Shorty gathered the cards, started to shuffle a new deal, then paused. "Huh! That ain't nothin'. A child could answer it. We lose seventeen thousan'. Wild Water wins seventeen thousan'. Them eggs of Gautereaux's was Wild Water's all the time. Anything else you're curious to know?"

"Yes. Why in the name of common sense didn't you find out whether those eggs were good before you paid for them?"

"Just as easy as the first question. Wild Water swung the bunco game timed to seconds. I hadn't no time to examine them eggs. I had to hustle to get 'em here for delivery. An' now, Smoke, lemme ask you one civil question. What did you say was the party's name that put this egg corner idea into your head?"

Shorty had lost the sixteenth consecutive game of solitaire, and Smoke was casting about to begin the preparation of supper, when Colonel Bowie knocked at the door, handed Smoke a letter, and went on to his own cabin.

"Did you see his face?" Shorty raved. "He was almost bustin' to keep it straight. It's the big ha! ha! for you an' me, Smoke. We won't never dast show our faces again in Dawson."

The letter was from Wild Water, and Smoke read it aloud:

Dear Smoke and Shorty
    I write to ask, with compliments of the season, your
presence at a supper to-night at Slavovitch's joint. Miss
Arral will be there and so will Gautereaux. Him and me was

pardners down at Circle five years ago. He is all right and is going to be best man. About them eggs. They come into the country four years back. They was bad when they come in. They was bad when they left California. They always was bad. They stopped at Carluk one winter, and one winter at Nutlik, and last winter at Forty Mile, where they was sold for storage. And this winter I guess they stop at Dawson. Don't keep them in a hot room. Lucille says to say you and her and me has sure made some excitement for Dawson. And I say the drinks is on you, and that goes.

Respectfully your friend,
W. W.

"Well? What have you got to say?" Smoke queried. "We accept the invitation, of course?"

"I got one thing to say," Shorty answered. "An' that is Wild Water won't never suffer if he goes broke. He's a good actor—a gosh-blamed good actor. An' I got another thing to say: my figgers is all wrong. Wild Water wins seventeen thousan' all right, but he wins more 'n that. You an' me has made him a present of every good egg in the Klondike—nine hundred an' sixty-four of 'em, two thrown in for good measure. An' he was that ornery, mean cussed that he packed off the three opened ones in the pail. An' I got a last thing to say. You an' me is legitimate prospectors an' practical gold-miners. But when it comes to fi-nance we're sure the fattest suckers that ever fell for the get-rich-quick bunco. After this it's you an' me for the high rocks an' tall timber, an' if you ever mention eggs to me we dissolve pardnership there an' then. Get me?"

XI

The Town-Site of Tra-Lee

Smoke and Shorty encountered each other, going in opposite directions, at the corner where stood the Elkhorn saloon. The former's face wore a pleased expression, and he was walking briskly. Shorty, on the other hand, was slouching along in a depressed and indeterminate fashion.

"Whither away?" Smoke challenged gaily.

"Danged if I know," came the disconsolate answer. "Wisht I did. They ain't nothin' to take me anywheres. I've set two hours in the deadest game of draw—nothing excitin', no hands, an' broke even. Played a rubber of cribbage with Skiff Mitchell for the drinks, an' now I'm that languid for somethin' doin' that I'm perambulatin' the streets on the chance of seein' a dogfight, or a argument, or somethin'."

"I've got something better on hand," Smoke answered. "That's why I was looking for you. Come on along."

"Now?"

"Sure."

"Where to?"

"Across the river to make a call on old Dwight Sanderson."

"Never heard of him," Shorty said dejectedly. "An' never heard of no one living across the river anyway. What's he want to live there for? Ain't he got no sense?"

"He's got something to sell," Smoke laughed.

"Dogs? A gold-mine? Tobacco? Rubber boots?"

Smoke shook his head to each question. "Come along on and find out, because I'm going to buy it from him on a spec, and if you want you can come in half."

"Don't tell me it's eggs!" Shorty cried, his face twisted into an expression of facetious and sarcastic alarm.

"Come on along," Smoke told him. "And I'll give you ten guesses while we're crossing the ice."

They dipped down the high bank at the foot of the street and came out upon the ice-covered Yukon. Three-quarters of a mile away, directly opposite, the other bank of the stream uprose in precipitous bluffs hundreds of feet in height. Toward these bluffs, winding and twisting in and out among broken and upthrown blocks of ice, ran a slightly traveled trail. Shorty trudged at Smoke's heels, beguiling the time with guesses at what Dwight Sanderson had to sell.

"Reindeer? Copper-mine or brick-yard? That's one guess. Bear-skins, or any kind of skins? Lottery tickets? A potato-ranch?"

"Getting near it," Smoke encouraged. "And better than that."

"Two potato-ranches? A cheese-factory? A moss-farm?"

"That's not so bad, Shorty. It's not a thousand miles away."

"A quarry?"

"That's as near as the moss-farm and the potato-ranch."

"Hold on. Let me think. I got one guess comin'." Ten silent minutes passed. "Say, Smoke, I ain't goin' to use that last guess. When this thing you're buyin' sounds like a potato-ranch, a moss-farm, and a stone-quarry, I quit. An' I don't go in on the deal till I see it an' size it up. What is it?"

"Well, you'll see the cards on the table soon enough. Kindly cast your eyes up there. Do you see the smoke from that cabin? That's where Dwight Sanderson lives. He's holding down a town-site location."

"What else is he holdin' down?"

"That's all," Smoke laughed. "Except rheumatism. I hear he's been suffering from it."

"Say!" Shorty's hand flashed out and with an abrupt shoulder grip brought his comrade to a halt. "You ain't telling me you're buyin' a town-site at this fallin'-off place?"

"That's your tenth guess, and you win. Come on."

"But wait a moment," Shorty pleaded. "Look at it—nothin' but bluffs an' slides, all up-and-down. Where could the town stand?"

"Search me."

"Then you ain't buyin' it for a town?"

"But Dwight Sanderson's selling it for a town," Smoke baffled. "Come on. We've got to climb this slide."

The slide was steep, and a narrow trail zigzagged up it on a formidable Jacob's ladder. Shorty moaned and groaned over the sharp corners and the steep pitches.

"Think of a town-site here. They ain't a flat space big enough for a postage-stamp. An' it's the wrong side of the river. All the freightin' goes the other way. Look at Dawson there. Room to spread for forty thousand more people. Say, Smoke. You're a meat-eater. I know that.

An' I know you ain't buyin' it for a town. Then what in Heaven's name are you buyin' it for?"

"To sell, of course."

"But other folks ain't as crazy as old man Sanderson an' you."

"Maybe not in the same way, Shorty. Now I'm going to take this town-site, break it up in parcels, and sell it to a lot of sane people who live over in Dawson."

"Huh! All Dawson's still laughing at you an' me an' them eggs. You want to make 'em laugh some more, hey?"

"I certainly do."

"But it's too danged expensive, Smoke. I helped you make 'em laugh on the eggs, an' my share of the laugh cost me nearly nine thousan' dollars."

"All right. You don't have to come in on this. The profits will be all mine, but you've got to help me just the same."

"Oh, I'll help all right. An' they can laugh at me some more. But nary a ounce do I drop this time.

"What's old Sanderson holdin' it at? A couple of hundred?"

"Ten thousand. I ought to get it for five."

"Wisht I was a minister," Shorty breathed fervently.

"What for?"

"So I could preach the gosh-dangdest, eloquentest sermon on a text you may have hearn—to wit: a fool an' his money."

"Come in," they heard Dwight Sanderson yell irritably, when they knocked at his door, and they entered to find him squatted by a stone fireplace and pounding coffee wrapped in a piece of flour-sacking.

"What d'ye want?" he demanded harshly, emptying the pounded coffee into the coffee-pot that stood on the coals near the front of the fireplace.

"To talk business," Smoke answered. "You've a town-site located here, I understand. What do you want for it?"

"Ten thousand dollars," came the answer. "And now that I've told you, you can laugh, and get out. There's the door. Good-by."

"But I don't want to laugh. I know plenty of funnier things to do than to climb up this cliff of yours. I want to buy your town-site."

"You do, eh? Well, I'm glad to hear sense." Sanderson came over and sat down facing his visitors, his hands resting on the table and his eyes cocking apprehensively toward the coffee-pot. "I've told you my price, and I ain't ashamed to tell you again—ten thousand. And you can laugh or buy, it's all one to me."

To show his indifference he drummed with his knobby knuckles on the table and stared at the coffee-pot. A minute later he began to hum a monotonous "Tra-la-loo, tra-la-lee, tra-la-lee, tra-la-loo."

"Now look here, Mr. Sanderson," said Smoke. "This town-site isn't worth ten thousand. If it was worth that much it would be worth a hundred thousand just as easily. If it isn't worth a hundred thousand— and you know it isn't—then it isn't worth ten cents."

Sanderson drummed with his knuckles and hummed, "Tra-la-loo, tra-la-lee," until the coffee-pot boiled over. Settling it with a part cup of cold water, and placing it to one side of the warm hearth, he resumed his seat. "How much will you offer?" he asked of Smoke.

"Five thousand."

Shorty groaned.

Again came an interval of drumming and of tra-loo-ing and tra-lee-ing.

"You ain't no fool," Sanderson announced to Smoke. "You said if it wasn't worth a hundred thousand it wasn't worth ten cents. Yet you offer five thousand for it. Then it *is* worth a hundred thousand."

"You can't make twenty cents out of it," Smoke replied heatedly. "Not if you stayed here till you rot."

"I'll make it out of you."

"No, you won't."

"Then I reckon I'll stay an' rot," Sanderson answered with an air of finality.

He took no further notice of his guests, and went about his culinary tasks as if he were alone. When he had warmed over a pot of beans and a slab of sour-dough bread, he set the table for one and proceeded to eat.

"No, thank you," Shorty murmured. "We ain't a bit hungry. We et just before we come."

"Let's see your papers," Smoke said at last. Sanderson fumbled under the head of his bunk and tossed out a package of documents. "It's all tight and right," he said. "That long one there, with the big seals, come all the way from Ottawa. Nothing territorial about that. The national Canadian government cinches me in the possession of this town-site."

"How many lots you sold in the two years you've had it?" Shorty queried.

"None of your business," Sanderson answered sourly. "There ain't no law against a man living alone on his town-site if he wants to."

"I'll give you five thousand," Smoke said. Sanderson shook his head.

"I don't know which is the craziest," Shorty lamented. "Come outside a minute, Smoke. I want to whisper to you."

Reluctantly Smoke yielded to his partner's persuasions.

"Ain't it never entered your head," Shorty said, as they stood in the snow outside the door, "that they's miles an' miles of cliffs on both sides of this fool town-site that don't belong to nobody an' that you can have for the locatin' and stakin'?"

"They won't do," Smoke answered.

"Why won't they?"

"It makes you wonder, with all those miles and miles, why I'm buying this particular spot, doesn't it?"

"It sure does," Shorty agreed.

"And that's the very point," Smoke went on triumphantly. "If it makes you wonder, it will make others wonder. And when they wonder they'll come a-running. By your own wondering you prove it's sound psychology. Now, Shorty, listen to me; I'm going to hand Dawson a package that will knock the spots out of the egg-laugh. Come on inside."

"Hello," said Sanderson, as they re-entered. "I thought I'd seen the last of you."

"Now what is your lowest figure?" Smoke asked.

"Twenty thousand."

"I'll give you ten thousand."

"All right, I'll sell at that figure. It's all I wanted in the first place. But when will you pay the dust over?"

"To-morrow, at the Northwest Bank. But there are two other things I want for that ten thousand. In the first place, when you receive your money you pull down the river to Forty Mile and stay there the rest of the winter."

"That's easy. What else?"

"I'm going to pay you twenty-five thousand, and you rebate me fifteen of it."

"I'm agreeable." Sanderson turned to Shorty. "Folks said I was a fool when I come over here an' town-sited," he jeered. "Well, I'm a ten thousand dollar fool, ain't I?"

"The Klondike's sure full of fools," was all Shorty could retort, "an' when they's so many of 'em some has to be lucky, don't they?"

Next morning the legal transfer of Dwight Sanderson's town-site was made—"henceforth to be known as the town-site of Tra-Lee," Smoke incorporated in the deed. Also, at the Northwest Bank, twenty-five thousand of Smoke's gold was weighed out by the cashier, while half a dozen casual onlookers noted the weighing, the amount, and the recipient.

In a mining-camp all men are suspicious. Any untoward act of any man is likely to be the cue to a secret gold strike, whether the untoward act be no more than a hunting trip for moose or a stroll after dark to observe the aurora borealis. And when it became known that so prominent a figure as Smoke Bellew had paid twenty-five thousand dollars to old Dwight Sanderson, Dawson wanted to know what he had paid it for. What had Dwight Sanderson, starving on his abandoned town-site, ever owned that was worth twenty-five thousand? In lieu of an answer, Dawson was justified in keeping Smoke in feverish contemplation.

By mid-afternoon it was common knowledge that several score of men had made up light stampeding-packs and cached them in the convenient saloons along Main Street. Wherever Smoke moved, he was the observed of many eyes. And as proof that he was taken seriously, not one man of the many of his acquaintance had the effrontery to ask him about his deal with Dwight Sanderson. On the other hand, no one mentioned eggs to Smoke. Shorty was under similar surveillance and delicacy of friendliness.

"Makes me feel like I'd killed somebody, or had smallpox, the way they watch me an' seem afraid to speak," Shorty confessed, when he chanced to meet Smoke in front of the Elkhorn. "Look at Bill Saltman there acrost the way—just dyin' to look, an' keepin' his eyes down the street all the time. Wouldn't think he'd knowed you an' me existed, to look at him. But I bet you the drinks, Smoke, if you an' me flop around the corner quick, like we was goin' somewheres, an' then turn back from around the next corner, that we run into him a-hikin' hell-bent."

They tried the trick, and, doubling back around the second corner, encountered Saltman swinging a long trail-stride in pursuit.

"Hello, Bill," Smoke greeted. "Which way?"

"Hello. Just a-strollin'," Saltman answered, "just a-strollin'. Weather's fine, ain't it?"

"Huh!" Shorty jeered. "If you call that strollin', what might you walk real fast at?"

When Shorty fed the dogs that evening, he was keenly conscious that from the encircling darkness a dozen pairs of eyes were boring in upon him. And when he stick-tied the dogs, instead of letting them forage free through the night, he knew that he had administered another jolt to the nervousness of Dawson.

According to program, Smoke ate supper downtown and then proceeded to enjoy himself. Wherever he appeared, he was the center of interest, and he purposely made the rounds. Saloons filled up after his entrance and emptied following upon his departure. If he bought a stack of chips at a sleepy roulette-table, inside five minutes a dozen players were around him. He avenged himself, in a small way, on Lucille Arral, by getting up and sauntering out of the Opera House just as she came on to sing her most popular song. In three minutes two-thirds of her audience had vanished after him.

At one in the morning he walked along an unusually populous Main Street and took the turning that led up the hill to his cabin. And when he paused on the ascent, he could hear behind him the crunch of moccasins in the snow.

For an hour the cabin was in darkness, then he lighted a candle, and, after a delay sufficient for a man to dress in, he and Shorty opened the door and began harnessing the dogs. As the light from the cabin flared out upon them and their work, a soft whistle went up from not far away. This whistle was repeated down the hill.

"Listen to it," Smoke chuckled. "They've relayed on us and are passing the word down to town. I'll bet you there are forty men right now rolling out of their blankets and climbing into their pants."

"Ain't folks fools," Shorty giggled back. "Say, Smoke, they ain't nothin' in hard graft. A geezer that'd work his hands these days is a—well, a geezer. The world's sure bustin' full an' dribblin' over the edges with fools a-honin' to be separated from their dust. An' before we start down the hill I want to announce, if you're still agreeable, that I come in half on this deal."

The sled was lightly loaded with a sleeping- and a grub-outfit. A small coil of steel cable protruded inconspicuously from underneath a grub-sack, while a crowbar lay half hidden along the bottom of the sled next to the lashings.

Shorty fondled the cable with a swift-passing mitten, and gave a last affectionate touch to the crowbar. "Huh!" he whispered. "I'd sure do some tall thinking myself if I seen them objects on a sled on a dark night."

They drove the dogs down the hill with cautious silence, and when, emerged on the flat, they turned the team north along Main Street toward the sawmill and directly away from the business part of town, they observed even greater caution. They had seen no one, yet when this change of direction was initiated, out of the dim starlit darkness behind arose a whistle. Past the sawmill and the hospital, at lively speed, they went for a quarter of a mile. Then they turned about and headed back over the ground they had just covered. At the end of the first hundred yards they barely missed colliding with five men racing along at a quick dog-trot. All were slightly stooped to the weight of stampeding-packs. One of them stopped Smoke's lead-dog, and the rest clustered around.

"Seen a sled goin' the other way?" was asked.

"Nope," Smoke answered. "Is that you, Bill?"

"Well, I'll be danged!" Bill Saltman exclaimed in honest surprise. "If it ain't Smoke!"

"What are you doing out this time of night?" Smoke inquired. "Strolling?"

Before Bill Saltman could make reply, two running men joined the group. These were followed by several more, while the crunch of feet on the snow heralded the imminent arrival of many others.

"Who are your friends?" Smoke asked. "Where's the stampede?"

Saltman, lighting his pipe, which was impossible for him to enjoy with lungs panting from the run, did not reply. The ruse of the match was too obviously for the purpose of seeing the sled to be misunderstood, and Smoke noted every pair of eyes focus on the coil of cable and the crowbar. Then the match went out.

"Just heard a rumor, that's all, just a rumor," Saltman mumbled with ponderous secretiveness.

"You might let Shorty and me in on it," Smoke urged.

Somebody snickered sarcastically in the background.

"Where are *you* bound?" Saltman demanded.

"And who are you?" Smoke countered. "Committee of safety?"

"Just interested, just interested," Saltman said.

"You bet your sweet life we're interested," another voice spoke up out of the darkness.

"Say," Shorty put in, "I wonder who's feelin' the foolishest?"

Everybody laughed nervously.

"Come on, Shorty; we'll be getting along," Smoke said, mushing the dogs.

The crowd formed in behind and followed.

"Say, ain't you-all made a mistake?" Shorty gibed. "When we met you you was goin', an' now you're comin' without bein' anywheres. Have you lost your tag?"

"You go to the devil," was Saltman's courtesy. "We go and come just as we danged feel like. We don't travel with tags."

And the sled, with Smoke in the lead and Shorty at the pole, went on down Main Street escorted by three score men, each of whom, on his back, bore a stampeding-pack. It was three in the morning, and only the all-night rounders saw the procession and were able to tell Dawson about it next day.

Half an hour later, the hill was climbed and the dogs unharnessed at the cabin door, the sixty stampeders grimly attendant.

"Good-night, fellows," Smoke called, as he closed the door.

In five minutes the candle was put out, but before half an hour had passed Smoke and Shorty emerged softly, and without lights began harnessing the dogs.

"Hello, Smoke!" Saltman said, stepping near enough for them to see the loom of his form.

"Can't shake you, Bill, I see," Smoke replied cheerfully. "Where're your friends?"

"Gone to have a drink. They left me to keep an eye on you, and keep it I will. What's in the wind anyway, Smoke? You can't shake us, so you might as well let us in. We're all your friends. You know that."

"There are times when you can let your friends in," Smoke evaded, "and times when you can't. And, Bill, this is one of the times when we can't. You'd better go to bed. Good-night."

"Ain't goin' to be no good-night, Smoke. You don't know us. We're woodticks."

Smoke sighed. "Well, Bill, if you *will* have your will, I guess you'll have to have it. Come on, Shorty, we can't fool around any longer."

Saltman emitted a shrill whistle as the sled started, and swung in behind. From down the hill and across the flat came the answering whistles of the relays. Shorty was at the gee-pole, and Smoke and Saltman walked side by side.

"Look here, Bill," Smoke said. "I'll make you a proposition. Do you want to come in alone on this?"

Saltman did not hesitate. "An' throw the gang down? No, sir. We'll all come in."

"You first, then," Smoke exclaimed, lurching into a clinch and tipping the other into deep snow beside the trail.

Shorty hawed the dogs and swung the team to the south on the trail that led among the scattered cabins on the rolling slopes to the rear of Dawson. Smoke and Saltman, locked together, rolled in the snow. Smoke considered himself in gilt-edged condition, but Saltman outweighed him by fifty pounds of clean, trail-hardened muscle and repeatedly mastered him. Time and time again he got Smoke on his back, and Smoke lay complacently and rested. But each time Saltman attempted to get off him and get away, Smoke reached out a detaining, tripping hand that brought about a new clinch and wrestle.

"You can go some," Saltman acknowledged, panting at the end of ten minutes, as he sat astride Smoke's chest. "But I down you every time."

"And I hold you every time," Smoke panted back. "That's what I'm here for, just to hold you. Where do you think Shorty's getting to all this time?"

Saltman made a wild effort to go clear, and all but succeeded. Smoke gripped his ankle and threw him in a headlong tumble. From down the hill came anxious questioning whistles. Saltman sat up and whistled a shrill answer, and was grappled by Smoke, who rolled him face upward and sat astride his chest, his knees resting on Saltman's biceps, his hands on Saltman's shoulders and holding him down. And in this position the stampeders found them. Smoke laughed and got up.

"Well, good-night, fellows," he said, and started down the hill, with sixty exasperated and grimly determined stampeders at his heels.

He turned north past the sawmill and the hospital and took the river trail along the precipitous bluffs at the base of Moosehide Mountain. Circling the Indian village, he held on to the mouth of Moose Creek, then turned and faced his pursuers.

"You make me tired," he said, with a good imitation of a snarl.

"Hope we ain't a-forcin' you," Saltman murmured politely.

"Oh, no, not at all," Smoke snarled with an even better imitation, as he passed among them on the back-trail to Dawson. Twice he attempted to cross the trailless icejams of the river, still resolutely followed, and both times he gave up and returned to the Dawson shore. Straight down Main Street he trudged, crossing the ice of Klondike River to Klondike City and again retracing to Dawson. At eight o'clock, as gray dawn began to show, he led his weary gang to Slavovitch's restaurant, where tables were at a premium for breakfast.

"Good-night fellows," he said, as he paid his reckoning.

And again he said good-night, as he took the climb of the hill. In the clear light of day they did not follow him, contenting themselves with watching him up the hill to his cabin.

For two days Smoke lingered about town, continually under vigilant espionage. Shorty, with the sled and dogs, had disappeared. Neither travelers up and down the Yukon, nor from Bonanza, Eldorado, nor the Klondike, had seen him. Remained only Smoke, who, soon or late, was certain to try to connect with his missing partner; and upon Smoke everybody's attention was centered. On the second night he did not leave his cabin, putting out the lamp at nine in the evening and setting the alarm for two next morning. The watch outside heard the alarm go off, so that when, half an hour later, he emerged from the cabin, he found waiting for him a band, not of sixty men, but of at least three hundred. A flaming aurora borealis lighted the scene, and, thus hugely escorted, he walked down to town and entered the Elkhorn. The place was immediately packed and jammed by an anxious and irritated multitude that bought drinks, and for four weary hours watched Smoke play cribbage with his old friend Breck. Shortly after six in the morning, with an expression on his face of commingled hatred and gloom, seeing no one, recognizing no one, Smoke left the Elkhorn and went up Main Street, behind him the three hundred, formed in disorderly ranks, chanting: "Hay-foot! Straw-foot! Hep! Hep! Hep!"

"Good-night, fellows," he said bitterly, at the edge of the Yukon bank where the winter trail dipped down. "I'm going to get breakfast and then go to bed."

The three hundred shouted that they were with him, and followed him out upon the frozen river on the direct path he took for Tra-Lee. At seven in the morning he led his stampeding cohort up the zigzag trail, across the face of the slide, that led to Dwight Sanderson's cabin. The light of a candle showed through the parchment-paper window, and smoke curled from the chimney. Shorty threw open the door.

"Come on in, Smoke," he greeted. "Breakfast's ready. Who-all are your friends?"

Smoke turned about on the threshold. "Well, good-night, you fellows. Hope you enjoyed your pasear!"

"Hold on a moment, Smoke," Bill Saltman cried, his voice keen with disappointment. "Want to talk with you a moment."

"Fire away," Smoke answered genially.

"What'd you pay old Sanderson twenty-five thousan' for? Will you answer that?"

"Bill, you give me a pain," was Smoke's reply. "I came over here for a country residence, so to say, and here are you and a gang trying to cross-examine me when I'm looking for peace an' quietness an' breakfast. What's a country residence good for, except for peace and quietness?"

"You ain't answered the question," Bill Saltman came back with rigid logic.

"And I'm not going to, Bill. That affair is peculiarly a personal affair between Dwight Sanderson and me. Any other question?"

"How about that crowbar an' steel cable then, what you had on your sled the other night?"

"It's none of your blessed and ruddy business, Bill. Though if Shorty here wants to tell you about it, he can."

"Sure!" Shorty cried, springing eagerly into the breach. His mouth opened, then he faltered and turned to his partner. "Smoke, confidentially, just between you an' me, I don't think it *is* any of their darn business. Come on in. The life's gettin' boiled outa that coffee."

The door closed and the three hundred sagged into forlorn and grumbling groups.

"Say, Saltman," one man said, "I thought you was goin' to lead us to it."

"Not on your life," Saltman answered crustily. "I said Smoke would lead us to it."

"An' this is it?"

"You know as much about it as me, an' we all know Smoke's got something salted down somewheres. Or else for what did he pay Sanderson the twenty-five thousand? Not for this mangy town-site, that's sure an' certain."

A chorus of cries affirmed Saltman's judgment.

"Well, what are we goin' to do now?" someone queried dolefully.

"Me for one for breakfast," Wild Water Charley said cheerfully. "You led us up a blind alley this time, Bill."

"I tell you I didn't," Saltman objected. "Smoke led us. An' just the same, what about them twenty-five thousand?"

At half-past eight, when daylight had grown strong, Shorty carefully opened the door and peered out. "Shucks," he exclaimed. "They-all's hiked back to Dawson. I thought they was goin' to camp here."

"Don't worry; they'll come sneaking back," Smoke reassured him. "If I don't miss my guess you'll see half Dawson over here before we're done with it. Now jump in and lend me a hand. We've got work to do."

"Aw, for Heaven's sake put me on," Shorty complained, when, at the end of an hour, he surveyed the result of their toil—a windlass in the corner of the cabin, with an endless rope that ran around double logrollers.

Smoke turned it with a minimum of effort, and the rope slipped and creaked. "Now, Shorty, you go outside and tell me what it sounds like."

Shorty, listening at the closed door, heard all the sounds of a windlass hoisting a load, and caught himself unconsciously attempting to estimate the depth of shaft out of which this load was being hoisted. Next came a pause, and in his mind's eye he saw the bucket swinging short to the windlass. Then he heard the quick lower-away and the dull sound as of the bucket coming to abrupt rest on the edge of the shaft. He threw open the door, beaming.

"I got you," he cried. "I almost fell for it myself. What next?"

The next was the dragging into the cabin of a dozen sled-loads of rock. And through an exceedingly busy day there were many other nexts.

"Now you run the dogs over to Dawson this evening," Smoke instructed, when supper was finished. "Leave them with Breck. He'll take care of them. They'll be watching what you do, so get Breck to go to the A. C. Company and buy up all the blasting-powder—there's only several hundred pounds in stock. And have Breck order half a dozen hard-rock drills from the blacksmith. Breck's a quartz-man, and he'll give the blacksmith a rough idea of what he wants made. And give Breck these location descriptions, so that he can record them at the gold commissioner's to-morrow. And finally, at ten o'clock, you be on Main Street listening. Mind you, I don't want them to be too loud. Dawson must just hear them and no more than hear them. I'll let off three, of different quantities, and you note which is more nearly the right thing."

At ten that night Shorty, strolling down Main Street, aware of many curious eyes, his ears keyed tensely, heard a faint and distant explosion. Thirty seconds later there was a second, sufficiently loud to attract the attention of others on the street. Then came a third, so violent that it rattled the windows and brought the inhabitants into the street.

"Shook 'em up beautiful," Shorty proclaimed breathlessly, an hour afterward, when he arrived at the cabin on Tra-Lee. He gripped Smoke's hand. "You should a-saw 'em. Ever kick over a ant-hole? Dawson's just like that. Main Street was crawlin' an' hummin' when I pulled my freight. You won't see Tra-Lee to-morrow for folks. An' if they ain't some a-sneakin' acrost right now I don't know minin' nature, that's all."

Smoke grinned, stepped to the fake windlass, and gave it a couple of creaking turns. Shorty pulled out the moss-chinking from between the logs so as to make peep-holes on every side of the cabin. Then he blew out the candle.

"Now," he whispered at the end of half an hour.

Smoke turned the windlass slowly, paused after several minutes, caught up a galvanized bucket filled with earth and struck it with slide and scrape and grind against the heap of rocks they had hauled in. Then he lighted a cigarette, shielding the flame of the match in his hands.

"They's three of 'em," Shorty whispered. "You oughta saw 'em. Say, when you made that bucket-dump noise they was fair quiverin'. They's one at the window now tryin' to peek in."

Smoke glowed his cigarette, and glanced at his watch.

"We've got to do this thing regularly," he breathed. "We'll haul up a bucket every fifteen minutes. And in the meantime—"

Through triple thicknesses of sacking, he struck a cold-chisel on the face of a rock.

"Beautiful, beautiful," Shorty moaned with delight. He crept over noiselessly from the peep-hole. "They've got their heads together, an' I can almost see 'em talkin'."

And from then until four in the morning, at fifteen-minute intervals, the seeming of a bucket was hoisted on the windlass that creaked and ran around on itself and hoisted nothing. Then their visitors departed, and Smoke and Shorty went to bed.

After daylight, Shorty examined the moccasin-marks. "Big Bill Saltman was one of them," he concluded. "Look at the size of it."

Smoke looked out over the river. "Get ready for visitors. There are two crossing the ice now."

"Huh! Wait till Breck files that string of claims at nine o'clock. There'll be two thousand crossing over."

"And every mother's son of them yammering 'mother-lode,'" Smoke laughed. "'The source of the Klondike placers found at last.'"

Shorty, who had clambered to the top of a steep shoulder of rock, gazed with the eye of a connoisseur at the strip they had staked.

"It sure looks like a true fissure vein," he said. "A expert could almost trace the lines of it under the snow. It'd fool anybody. The slide fills the front of it an' see them outcrops? Look like the real thing, only they ain't."

When the two men, crossing the river, climbed the zigzag trail up the slide, they found a closed cabin. Bill Saltman, who led the way, went softly to the door, listened, then beckoned Wild Water Charley up to him. From inside came the creak and whine of a windlass bearing a heavy load. They waited at the final pause, then heard the lower-away and the impact of a bucket on rock. Four times, in the next hour, they heard the thing repeated. Then Wild Water knocked on the door. From inside came low furtive noises, then silences, and more furtive noises, and at the end of five minutes Smoke, breathing heavily, opened the door an inch and peered out. They saw on his face and shirt powdered rock-fragments. His greeting was suspiciously genial.

"Wait a minute," he added, "and I'll be with you."

Pulling on his mittens, he slipped through the door and confronted the visitors outside in the snow. Their quick eyes noted his shirt, across the shoulders, discolored and powdery, and the knees of his overalls that showed signs of dirt brushed hastily but not quite thoroughly away.

"Rather early for a call," he observed. "What brings you across the river? Going hunting?"

"We're on, Smoke," Wild Water said confidentially. "An' you'd just as well come through. You've got something here."

"If you're looking for eggs—" Smoke began.

"Aw, forget it. We mean business."

"You mean you want to buy lots, eh?" Smoke rattled on swiftly. "There's some dandy building sites here. But, you see, we can't sell yet. We haven't had the town surveyed. Come around next week, Wild Water, and for peace and quietness, I'll show you something swell, if you're anxious to live over here. Next week, sure, it will be surveyed. Good-by. Sorry I can't ask you inside, but Shorty—well, you know him. He's peculiar. He says he came over for peace and quietness, and he's asleep now. I wouldn't wake him for the world."

As Smoke talked he shook their hands warmly in farewell. Still talking and shaking their hands, he stepped inside and closed the door.

They looked at each other and nodded significantly.

"See the knees of his pants?" Saltman whispered hoarsely.

"Sure. An' his shoulders. He's been bumpin' an' crawlin' around in a shaft." As Wild Water talked, his eyes wandered up the snow-covered ravine until they were halted by something that brought a whistle to his lips. "Just cast your eyes up there, Bill. See where I'm pointing? If that ain't a prospect-hole! An' follow it out to both sides—you can see where they tramped in the snow. If it ain't rim-rock on both sides I don't know what rim-rock is. It's a fissure vein, all right."

"An' look at the size of it!" Saltman cried. "They've got something here, you bet."

"An' run your eyes down the slide there—see them bluffs standin' out an' slopin' in. The whole slide's in the mouth of the vein as well."

"And just keep a-lookin' on, out on the ice there, on the trail," Saltman directed. "Looks like most of Dawson, don't it?"

Wild Water took one glance and saw the trail black with men clear to the far Dawson bank, down which the same unbroken string of men was pouring.

"Well, I'm goin' to get a look-in at that prospect-hole before they get here," he said, turning and starting swiftly up the ravine.

But the cabin door opened, and the two occupants stepped out.

"Hey!" Smoke called. "Where are you going?"

"To pick out a lot," Wild Water called back. "Look at the river. All Dawson's stampeding to buy lots, an' we're going to beat 'em to it for the choice. That's right, ain't it, Bill?"

"Sure thing," Saltman corroborated. "This has the makin's of a Jim-dandy suburb, an' it sure looks like it'll be some popular."

"Well, we're not selling lots over in that section where you're heading," Smoke answered. "Over to the right there, and back on top of the bluffs are the lots. This section, running from the river and over the tops, is reserved. So come on back."

"That's the spot we've gone and selected," Saltman argued.

"But there's nothing doing, I tell you," Smoke said sharply.

"Any objections to our strolling, then?" Saltman persisted.

"Decidedly. Your strolling is getting monotonous. Come on back out of that."

"I just reckon we'll stroll anyways," Saltman replied stubbornly. "Come on, Wild Water."

"I warn you, you are trespassing," was Smoke's final word.

"Nope, just strollin'," Saltman gaily retorted, turning his back and starting on.

"Hey! Stop in your tracks, Bill, or I'll sure bore you!" Shorty thundered, drawing and leveling two Colt's forty-fours. "Step another step in your steps an' I let eleven holes through your danged ornery carcass. Get that?"

Saltman stopped, perplexed.

"He sure got me," Shorty mumbled to Smoke. "But if he goes on I'm up against it hard. I can't shoot. What'll I do?"

"Look here, Shorty, listen to reason," Saltman begged.

"Come here to me an' we'll talk reason," was Shorty's retort.

And they were still talking reason when the head of the stampede emerged from the zigzag trail and came upon them.

"You can't call a man a trespasser when he's on a town-site lookin' to buy lots," Wild Water was arguing, and Shorty was objecting: "But they's private property in town-sites, an' that there strip is private property, that's all. I tell you again, it ain't for sale."

"Now we've got to swing this thing on the jump," Smoke muttered to Shorty. "If they ever get out of hand—"

"You've sure got your nerve, if you think you can hold them," Shorty muttered back. "They's two thousan' of 'em an' more a-comin'. They'll break this line any minute."

The line ran along the near rim of the ravine, and Shorty had formed it by halting the first arrivals when they got that far in their invasion. In the crowd were half a dozen Northwest policemen and a lieutenant. With the latter Smoke conferred in undertones.

"They're still piling out of Dawson," he said, "and before long there will be five thousand here. The danger is if they start jumping claims. When you figure there are only five claims, it means a thousand men to a claim, and four thousand out of the five will try to jump the nearest claim. It can't be done, and if it ever starts, there'll be more dead men here than in the whole history of Alaska. Besides, those five claims were recorded this morning and can't be jumped. In short, claim-jumping mustn't start."

"Right-o," said the lieutenant. "I'll get my men together and station them. We can't have any trouble here, and we won't have. But you'd better get up and talk to them."

"There must be some mistake, fellows," Smoke began in a loud voice. "We're not ready to sell lots. The streets are not surveyed yet. But next week we shall have the grand opening sale."

He was interrupted by an outburst of impatience and indignation.

"We don't want lots," a young miner cried out. "We don't want what's on top of the ground. We've come for what's under the ground."

"We don't know what we've got under the ground," Smoke answered. "But we do know we've got a fine town-site on top of it."

"Sure," Shorty added. "Grand for scenery an' solitude. Folks lovin' solitude come a-flockin' here by thousands. Most popular solitude on the Yukon."

Again the impatient cries arose, and Saltman, who had been talking with the later comers, came to the front.

"We're here to stake claims," he opened. "We know what you've did—filed a string of five quartz claims on end, and there they are over there running across the town-site on the line of the slide and the canyon. Only you misplayed. Two of them entries is fake. Who is Seth Bierce? No one ever heard of him. You filed a claim this mornin' in his name. An' you filed a claim in the name of Harry Maxwell. Now Harry Maxwell ain't in the country. He's down in Seattle. Went out last fall. Them two claims is open to relocation."

"Suppose I have his power of attorney?" Smoke queried.

"You ain't," Saltman answered. "An' if you have you got to show it. Anyway, here's where we relocate. Come on, fellows."

Saltman, stepping across the dead-line, had turned to encourage a following, when the police lieutenant's voice rang out and stopped the forward surge of the great mass.

"Hold on there! You can't do that, you know!"

"Can't, eh?" said Bill Saltman. "The law says a fake location can be relocated, don't it?"

"Thet's right, Bill! Stay with it!" the crowd cheered from the safe side of the line.

"It's the law, ain't it?" Saltman demanded truculently of the lieutenant.

"It may be the law," came the steady answer. "But I can't and won't allow a mob of five thousand men to attempt to jump two claims. It would be a dangerous riot, and we're here to see there is no riot. Here, now, on this spot, the Northwest police constitute the law. The next man who crosses that line will be shot. You, Bill Saltman, step back across it."

Saltman obeyed reluctantly. But an ominous restlessness became apparent in the mass of men, irregularly packed and scattered as it was over a landscape that was mostly up-and-down.

"Heavens," the lieutenant whispered to Smoke. "Look at them like flies on the edge of the cliff there. Any disorder in that mass would force hundreds of them over."

Smoke shuddered and got up. "I'm willing to play fair, fellows. If you insist on town lots, I'll sell them to you, one hundred apiece, and you can raffle locations when the survey is made." With raised hand he stilled the movement of disgust. "Don't move, anybody. If you do, there'll be hundreds of you shoved over the bluff. The situation is dangerous."

"Just the same, you can't hog it," a voice went up. "We don't want lots. We want to relocate."

"But there are only two disputed claims," Smoke argued. "When they're relocated where will the rest of you be?"

He mopped his forehead with his shirt-sleeve, and another voice cried out:

"Let us all in, share and share alike!"

Nor did those who roared their approbation dream that the suggestion had been made by a man primed to make it when he saw Smoke mop his forehead.

"Take your feet out of the trough an' pool the town-site," the man went on. "Pool the mineral rights with the town-site, too."

"But there isn't anything in the mineral rights, I tell you," Smoke objected.

"Then pool them with the rest. We'll take our chances on it."

"Fellows, you're forcing me," Smoke said. "I wish you'd stayed on your side of the river."

But wavering indecision was so manifest that with a mighty roar the crowd swept him on to agreement. Saltman and others in the front rank demurred.

"Bill Saltman, here, and Wild Water don't want you all in," Smoke informed the crowd. "Who's hogging it now?"

And thereat Saltman and Wild Water became profoundly unpopular.

"Now how are we going to do it?" Smoke asked. "Shorty and I ought to keep control. We discovered this town-site."

"That's right!" many cried. "A square deal!" "It's only fair!"

"Three-fifths to us," Smoke suggested, "and you fellows come in for two-fifths. And you've got to pay for your shares."

"Ten cents on the dollar!" was a cry. "And non-assessable!"

"And the president of the company to come around personally and pay you your dividends on a silver platter," Smoke sneered. "No, sir. You fellows have got to be reasonable. Ten cents on the dollar will help start things. You buy two-fifths of the stock, hundred dollars par, at ten dollars. That's the best I can do. And if you don't like it, just start jumping the claims. I can't stand more than a two-fifths gouge."

"No big capitalization!" a voice called, and it was this voice that crystallized the collective mind of the crowd into consent.

"There's about five thousand of you, which will make five thousand shares," Smoke worked the problem aloud. "And five thousand is two-fifths of twelve thousand, five hundred. Therefore The Tra-Lee Town-Site Company is capitalized for one million two hundred and fifty thousand dollars, there being twelve thousand, five hundred shares, hundred par, you fellows buying five thousand of them at ten dollars apiece. And I don't care a whoop whether you accept it or not. And I call you all to witness that you're forcing me against my will."

With the assurance of the crowd that they had caught him with the goods on him, in the shape of the two fake locations, a committee was formed and the rough organization of the Tra-Lee Town-Site Company effected. Scorning the proposal of delivering the shares next day in Dawson, and scorning it because of the objection that the portion of Dawson that had not engaged in the stampede would ring in for shares, the committee, by a fire on the ice at the foot of the slide, issued a receipt to each stampeder in return for ten dollars in dust duly weighed on two dozen gold-scales which were obtained from Dawson.

By twilight the work was accomplished and Tra-Lee was deserted, save for Smoke and Shorty, who ate supper in the cabin and chuckled at the list of shareholders, four thousand eight hundred and seventy-four strong, and at the gold-sacks, which they knew contained approximately forty-eight thousand seven hundred and forty dollars.

"But you ain't swung it yet," Shorty objected.

"He'll be here," Smoke asserted with conviction. "He's a born gambler, and when Breck whispers the tip to him not even heart disease would stop him."

Within the hour came a knock at the door, and Wild Water entered, followed by Bill Saltman. Their eyes swept the cabin eagerly, coming to rest on the windlass elaborately concealed by blankets.

"But suppose I did want to vote twelve hundred shares," Wild Water was arguing half an hour later. "With the other five thousand sold to-day it'd make only sixty-two hundred shares. That'd leave you and Shorty with sixty-three hundred. You'd still control."

"But what d' you want with all that of a town-site?" Shorty queried.

"You can answer that better 'n me," Wild Water replied. "An' between you an' me," his gaze drifted over the blanket-draped windlass, "it's a pretty good-looking town-site."

"But Bill wants some," Smoke said grudgingly, "and we simply won't part with more than five hundred shares."

"How much you got to invest?" Wild Water asked Saltman.

"Oh, say five thousand. It was all I could scare up."

"Wild Water," Smoke went on, in the same grudging, complaining voice, "if I didn't know you so well, I wouldn't sell you a single besotted share. And, anyway, Shorty and I won't part with more than five hundred, and they'll cost you fifty dollars apiece. That's the last word, and if you don't like it, good-night. Bill can take a hundred and you can have the other four hundred."

Next day Dawson began its laugh. It started early in the morning, just after daylight, when Smoke went to the bulletin-board outside the A. C. Company store and tacked up a notice. Men gathered and were reading and snickering over his shoulder ere he had driven the last tack. Soon the bulletin-board was crowded by hundreds who could not get near enough to read. Then a reader was appointed by acclamation, and thereafter, throughout the day, many men were acclaimed to read in loud voice the notice Smoke Bellew had nailed up. And there were numbers of men who stood in the snow and heard it read several times in order to memorize the succulent items that appeared in the following order:

The Tra-Lee Town-Site Company keeps its accounts on the wall. This is its first account and its last.

Any shareholder who objects to donating ten dollars to the Dawson General Hospital may obtain his ten dollars on personal application to Wild Water Charley, or, failing that, will absolutely obtain it on application to Smoke Bellew.

Moneys Received and Disbursed

From 4874 shares at $10.00	$48,740.00
To Dwight Sanderson for Town-Site of Tra-Lee	10,000.00
To incidental expenses, to wit: powder, drills, windlass, gold commissioner's office, etc.	1,000.00
To Dawson General Hospital	37,740.00
Total	$48,740.00

From Bill Saltman, for 100 shares privately purchased at $50.00	$5,000.00
From Wild Water Charley, for 400 shares privately purchased at $50.00	20,000.00
To Bill Saltman, in recognition of services as volunteer stampede promoter..................	5,000.00
To Dawson General Hospital	3,000.00
To Smoke Bellew and Jack Short, balance in full on egg deal and morally owing................	17,000.00
	————
Total	$25,000.00

Shares remaining to account for 7126. These shares, held by Smoke Bellew and Jack Short, value nil, may be obtained gratis, for the asking, by any and all residents of Dawson desiring change of domicile to the peace and solitude of the town of Tra-Lee.

(Note: Peace and solitude always and perpetually guaranteed in town of Tra-Lee)

(Signed) SMOKE BELLEW, President.
(Signed) JACK SHORT, Secretary.

XII

Wonder of Woman

"J ust the same, I notice you ain't tumbled over yourself to get married," Shorty remarked, continuing a conversation that had lapsed some few minutes before.

Smoke, sitting on the edge of the sleeping-robe and examining the feet of a dog he had rolled snarling on its back in the snow, did not answer. And Shorty, turning a steaming moccasin propped on a stick before the fire, studied his partner's face keenly.

"Cock your eye up at that there aurora borealis," Shorty went on. "Some frivolous, eh? Just like any shilly-shallyin', shirt-dancing woman. The best of them is frivolous, when they ain't foolish. And they's cats, all of 'em, the littlest an' the biggest, the nicest and the otherwise. They're sure devourin' lions an' roarin' hyenas when they get on the trail of a man they've cottoned to."

Again the monologue languished. Smoke cuffed the dog when it attempted to snap his hand, and went on examining its bruised and bleeding pads.

"Huh!" pursued Shorty. "Mebbe I couldn't 'a' married if I'd a mind to! An' mebbe I wouldn't 'a' been married without a mind to, if I hadn't hiked for tall timber. Smoke, d'you want to know what saved me? I'll tell you. My wind. I just kept a-runnin'. I'd like to see any skirt run me outa breath."

Smoke released the animal and turned his own steaming, stick-propped moccasins. "We've got to rest over to-morrow and make moccasins," he vouchsafed. "That little crust is playing the devil with their feet."

"We oughta keep goin' somehow," Shorty objected. "We ain't got grub enough to turn back with, and we gotta strike that run of caribou or them white Indians almighty soon or we'll be eatin' the dogs, sore feet an' all. Now who ever seen them white Indians anyway? Nothin' but hearsay. An' how can a Indian be white? A black white man'd be as natural. Smoke, we just oughta travel to-morrow. The country's plumb dead of game. We ain't seen even a rabbit-track in a week, you know that. An' we gotta get out of this dead streak into somewhere that meat's runnin'."

"They'll travel all the better with a day's rest for their feet and moccasins all around," Smoke counseled. "If you get a chance at any low divide, take a peep over at the country beyond. We're likely to strike open rolling country any time now. That's what La Perle told us to look for."

"Huh! By his own story, it was ten years ago that La Perle come through this section, an' he was that loco from hunger he couldn't know what he did see. Remember what he said of whoppin' big flags floatin' from the tops of the mountains? That shows how loco *he* was. An' he said himself he never seen any white Indians—that was Anton's yarn. An', besides, Anton kicked the bucket two years before you an' me come to Alaska. But I'll take a look to-morrow. An' mebbe I might pick up a moose. What d' you say we turn in?"

Smoke spent the morning in camp, sewing dog-moccasins and repairing harnesses. At noon he cooked a meal for two, ate his share, and began to look for Shorty's return. An hour later he strapped on his snow-shoes and went out on his partner's trail. The way led up the bed of the stream, through a narrow gorge that widened suddenly into a moose-pasture. But no moose had been there since the first snow of the preceding fall. The tracks of Shorty's snow-shoes crossed the pasture and went up the easy slope of a low divide. At the crest Smoke halted. The tracks continued down the other slope. The first spruce-trees, in the creek bed, were a mile away, and it was evident that Shorty had passed through them and gone on. Smoke looked at his watch, remembered the oncoming darkness, the dogs, and the camp, and reluctantly decided against going farther. But before he retraced his steps he paused for a long look. All the eastern sky-line was saw-toothed by the snowy backbone of the Rockies. The whole mountain system, range upon range, seemed to trend to the northwest, cutting athwart the course to the open country reported by La Perle. The effect was as if the mountains conspired to thrust back the traveler toward the west and the Yukon. Smoke wondered how many men in the past, approaching as he had approached, had been turned aside by that forbidding aspect. La Perle had not been turned aside, but, then, La Perle had crossed over from the eastern slope of the Rockies.

Until midnight Smoke maintained a huge fire for the guidance of Shorty. And in the morning, waiting with camp broken and dogs harnessed for the first break of light, Smoke took up the pursuit. In the narrow pass of the canyon, his lead-dog pricked up its ears and whined. Then Smoke came upon the Indians, six of them, coming toward him.

They were traveling light, without dogs, and on each man's back was the smallest of pack outfits. Surrounding Smoke, they immediately gave him several matters for surprise. That they were looking for him was clear. That they talked no Indian tongue of which he knew a word was also quickly made clear. They were not white Indians, though they were taller and heavier than the Indians of the Yukon basin. Five of them carried the old-fashioned, long-barreled Hudson Bay Company musket, and in the hands of the sixth was a Winchester rifle which Smoke knew to be Shorty's.

Nor did they waste time in making him a prisoner. Unarmed himself, Smoke could only submit. The contents of the sled were distributed among their own packs, and he was given a pack composed of his and Shorty's sleeping-furs. The dogs were unharnessed, and when Smoke protested, one of the Indians, by signs, indicated a trail too rough for sled-travel. Smoke bowed to the inevitable, cached the sled end-on in the snow on the bank above the stream, and trudged on with his captors. Over the divide to the north they went, down to the spruce-trees which Smoke had glimpsed the preceding afternoon. They followed the stream for a dozen miles, abandoning it when it trended to the west and heading directly eastward up a narrow tributary.

The first night was spent in a camp which had been occupied for several days. Here was cached a quantity of dried salmon and a sort of pemmican, which the Indians added to their packs. From this camp a trail of many snow-shoes led off—Shorty's captors, was Smoke's conclusion; and before darkness fell he succeeded in making out the tracks Shorty's narrower snow-shoes had left. On questioning the Indians by signs, they nodded affirmation and pointed to the north.

Always, in the days that followed, they pointed north; and always the trail, turning and twisting through a jumble of upstanding peaks, trended north. Everywhere, in this bleak snow-solitude, the way seemed barred, yet ever the trail curved and coiled, finding low divides and avoiding the higher and untraversable chains. The snow-fall was deeper than in the lower valleys, and every step of the way was snow-shoe work. Furthermore, Smoke's captors, all young men, traveled light and fast; and he could not forbear the prick of pride in the knowledge that he easily kept up with them. They were travel-hardened and trained to snow-shoes from infancy; yet such was his condition that the traverse bore no more of ordinary hardship to him than to them.

In six days they gained and crossed the central pass, low in comparison with the mountains it threaded, yet formidable in itself and not possible for loaded sleds. Five days more of tortuous winding, from lower altitude to lower altitude, brought them to the open, rolling, and merely hilly country La Perle had found ten years before. Smoke knew it with the first glimpse, on a sharp cold day, the thermometer forty below zero, the atmosphere so clear that he could see a hundred miles. Far as he could see rolled the open country. High in the east the Rockies still thrust their snowy ramparts heavenward. To the south and west extended the broken ranges of the projecting spur-system they had crossed. And in this vast pocket lay the country La Perle had traversed—snow-blanketed, but assuredly fat with game at some time in the year, and in the summer a smiling, forested, and flowered land.

Before midday, traveling down a broad stream, past snow-buried willows and naked aspens, and across heavily timbered flats of spruce, they came upon the site of a large camp, recently abandoned. Glancing as he went by, Smoke estimated four or five hundred fires, and guessed the population to be in the thousands. So fresh was the trail, and so well packed by the multitude, that Smoke and his captors took off their snow-shoes and in their moccasins struck a swifter pace. Signs of game appeared and grew plentiful—tracks of wolves and lynxes that without meat could not be. Once, one of the Indians cried out with satisfaction and pointed to a large area of open snow, littered with fang-polished skulls of caribou, trampled and disrupted as if an army had fought upon it. And Smoke knew that a big killing had been made by the hunters since the last snow-flurry.

In the long twilight no sign was manifested of making camp. They held steadily on through a deepening gloom that vanished under a sky of light—great, glittering stars half veiled by a greenish vapor of pulsing aurora borealis. His dogs first caught the noises of the camp, pricking their ears and whining in low eagerness. Then it came to the ears of the humans, a murmur, dim with distance, but not invested with the soothing grace that is common to distant murmurs. Instead, it was in a high, wild key, a beat of shrill sound broken by shriller sounds—the long wolf-howling of many wolf-dogs, a screaming of unrest and pain, mournful with hopelessness and rebellion. Smoke swung back the crystal of his watch and by the feel of finger-tips on the naked hands made out eleven o'clock. The men about him quickened. The legs that had lifted through a dozen strenuous hours lifted in a still swifter pace that was half a run and mostly a running jog. Through a dark spruce-flat they burst upon an abrupt glare of light from many fires and upon an abrupt increase of sound. The great camp lay before them.

And as they entered and threaded the irregular runways of the hunting-camp, a vast tumult, as in a wave, rose to meet them and rolled on with them—cries, greetings, questions and answers, jests and jests thrust back again, the snapping snarl of wolf-dogs rushing in furry projectiles of wrath upon Smoke's stranger dogs, the scolding of squaws, laughter, the whimpering of children and wailing of infants, the moans of the sick aroused afresh to pain, all the pandemonium of a camp of nerveless, primitive wilderness folk.

Striking with clubs and the butts of guns, Smoke's party drove back the attacking dogs, while his own dogs, snapping and snarling, awed by so many enemies, shrank in among the legs of their human protectors, and bristled along stiff-legged in menacing prance.

They halted in the trampled snow by an open fire, where Shorty and two young Indians, squatted on their hams, were broiling strips of caribou meat. Three other young Indians, lying in furs on a mat of spruce-boughs, sat up. Shorty looked across the fire at his partner, but with a sternly impassive face, like those of his companions, made no sign and went on broiling the meat.

"What's the matter?" Smoke demanded, half in irritation. "Lost your speech?"

The old familiar grin twisted on Shorty's face. "Nope," he answered. "I'm a Indian. I'm learnin' not to show surprise. When did they catch you?"

"Next day after you left."

"Hum," Shorty said, the light of whimsy dancing in his eyes. "Well, I'm doin' fine, thank you most to death. This is the bachelors' camp." He waved his hand to embrace its magnificence, which consisted of a fire, beds of spruce-boughs laid on top of the snow, flies of caribou skin, and wind-shields of twisted spruce and willow withes. "An' these are the bachelors." This time his hand indicated the young men, and he spat a few spoken gutturals in their own language that brought the white flash of acknowledgment from eyes and teeth. "They're glad to meet you, Smoke. Set down an' dry your moccasins, an' I'll cook up some grub. I'm gettin' the hang of the lingo pretty well, ain't I? You'll have to come to it, for it looks as if we'll be with these folks a long time. They's another white man here. Got caught six years ago. He's a Irishman they picked up over Great Slave Lake way. Danny McCan is what he goes by. He's settled down with a squaw. Got two kids already, but he'll skin out if ever the chance opens up. See that low fire over there to the right? That's his camp."

Apparently this was Smoke's appointed domicile, for his captors left him and his dogs, and went on deeper into the big camp. While he attended to his foot-gear and devoured strips of hot meat, Shorty cooked and talked.

"This is a sure peach of a pickle, Smoke—you listen to me. An' we got to go some to get out. These is the real, blowed-in-the-glass, wild Indians. They ain't white, but their chief is. He talks like a mouthful of hot mush, an' if he ain't full-blood Scotch they ain't no such thing as Scotch in the world. He's the hi-yu, skookum top-chief of the whole caboodle. What he says goes. You want to get that from the start-off. Danny McCan's been tryin' to get away from him for six years. Danny's all right, but he ain't got go in him. He knows a way out—learned it on huntin' trips—to the west of the way you an' me came. He ain't had the nerve to tackle it by his lonely. But we can pull it off, the three of us. Whiskers is the real goods, but he's mostly loco just the same."

"Who's Whiskers?" Smoke queried, pausing in the wolfing-down of a hot strip of meat.

"Why, he's the top geezer. He's the Scotcher. He's gettin' old, an' he's sure asleep now, but he'll see you to-morrow an' show you clear as print what a measly shrimp you are on his stompin'-grounds. These grounds belong to him. You got to get that into your noodle. They ain't never been explored, nor nothin', an' they're hisn. An' he won't let you forget it. He's got about twenty thousand square miles of huntin' country here all his own. He's the white Indian, him an' the skirt. Huh! Don't look at me that way. Wait till you see her. Some looker, an' all white, like her dad—he's Whiskers. An' say, caribou! I've saw 'em. A hundred thousan' of good running meat in the herd, an' ten thousan' wolves an' cats a-followin' an' livin' off the stragglers an' the leavin's. We leave the leavin's. The herd's movin' to the east, an' we'll be followin' 'em any day now. We eat our dogs, an' what we don't eat we smoke 'n cure for the spring before the salmon-run gets its sting in. Say, what Whiskers don't know about salmon an' caribou nobody knows, take it from me."

"Here comes Whiskers lookin' like he's goin' somewheres," Shorty whispered, reaching over and wiping greasy hands on the coat of one of the sled-dogs.

It was morning, and the bachelors were squatting over a breakfast of caribou-meat, which they ate as they broiled. Smoke glanced up and saw a small and slender man, skin-clad like any savage, but unmistakably white, striding in advance of a sled team and a following of a dozen Indians. Smoke cracked a hot bone, and while he sucked out the steaming marrow gazed at his approaching host. Bushy whiskers and yellowish gray hair, stained by camp smoke, concealed most of the face, but failed wholly to hide the gaunt, almost cadaverous, cheeks. It was a healthy leanness, Smoke decided, as he noted the wide flare of the nostrils and the breadth and depth of chest that gave spaciousness to the guaranty of oxygen and life.

"How do you do," the man said, slipping a mitten and holding out his bare hand. "My name is Snass," he added, as they shook hands.

"Mine's Bellew," Smoke returned, feeling peculiarly disconcerted as he gazed into the keen-searching black eyes.

"Getting plenty to eat, I see."

Smoke nodded and resumed his marrow-bone, the purr of Scottish speech strangely pleasant in his ears.

"Rough rations. But we don't starve often. And it's more natural than the hand-reared meat of the cities."

"I see you don't like cities," Smoke laughed, in order to be saying something; and was immediately startled by the transformation Snass underwent.

Quite like a sensitive plant, the man's entire form seemed to wilt and quiver. Then the recoil, tense and savage, concentered in the eyes, in which appeared a hatred that screamed of immeasurable pain. He turned abruptly away, and, recollecting himself, remarked casually over his shoulder:

"I'll see you later, Mr. Bellew. The caribou are moving east, and I'm going ahead to pick out a location. You'll all come on to-morrow."

"Some Whiskers, that, eh?" Shorty muttered, as Snass pulled on at the head of his outfit.

Again Shorty wiped his hands on the wolf-dog, which seemed to like it as it licked off the delectable grease.

Later on in the morning Smoke went for a stroll through the camp, busy with its primitive pursuits. A big body of hunters had just returned, and the men were scattering to their various fires. Women and children were departing with dogs harnessed to empty toboggan-sleds, and women and children and dogs were hauling sleds heavy with meat fresh from the killing and already frozen. An early spring cold-snap was on, and the wildness of the scene was painted in a temperature of thirty below zero. Woven cloth was not in evidence. Furs and soft-tanned leather clad all alike. Boys passed with bows in their hands, and quivers of bone-barbed arrows; and many a skinning-knife of bone or stone Smoke saw in belts or neck-hung sheaths. Women toiled over the fires, smoke-curing the meat, on their backs infants that stared round-eyed and sucked at lumps of tallow. Dogs, full-kin to wolves, bristled up to Smoke to endure the menace of the short club he carried and to whiff the odor of this newcomer whom they must accept by virtue of the club.

Segregated in the heart of the camp, Smoke came upon what was evidently Snass's fire. Though temporary in every detail, it was solidly constructed and was on a large scale. A great heap of bales of skins and outfit was piled on a scaffold out of reach of the dogs. A large canvas fly, almost half-tent, sheltered the sleeping- and living-quarters. To one side was a silk tent—the sort favored by explorers and wealthy big-game hunters. Smoke had never seen such a tent, and stepped closer. As he stood looking, the flaps parted and a young woman came out. So quickly did she move, so abruptly did she appear, that the effect on Smoke was as that of an apparition. He seemed to have the same effect on her, and for a long moment they gazed at each other.

She was dressed entirely in skins, but such skins and such magnificently beautiful fur-work Smoke had never dreamed of. Her parka, the hood thrown back, was of some strange fur of palest silver. The mukluks, with walrus-hide soles, were composed of the silver-padded feet of many lynxes. The long-gauntleted mittens, the tassels at the knees, all the varied furs of the costume, were pale silver that shimmered in the frosty light; and out of this shimmering silver, poised on slender, delicate neck, lifted her head, the rosy face blonde as the eyes were blue, the ears like two pink shells, the light chestnut hair touched with frost-dust and coruscating frost-glints.

All this and more, as in a dream, Smoke saw; then, recollecting himself, his hand fumbled for his cap. At the same moment the wonder-stare in the girl's eyes passed into a smile, and, with movements quick and vital, she slipped a mitten and extended her hand.

"How do you do," she murmured gravely, with a queer, delightful accent, her voice, silvery as the furs she wore, coming with a shock to Smoke's ears, attuned as they were to the harsh voices of the camp squaws.

Smoke could only mumble phrases that were awkwardly reminiscent of his best society manner.

"I am glad to see you," she went on slowly and gropingly, her face a ripple of smiles. "My English you will please excuse. It is not good. I am English like you," she gravely assured him. "My father he is Scotch. My mother she is dead. She is French, and English, and a little Indian, too. Her father was a great man in the Hudson Bay Company. Brrr! It is cold." She slipped on her mitten and rubbed her ears, the pink of which had already turned to white. "Let us go to the fire and talk. My name is Labiskwee. What is your name?"

And so Smoke came to know Labiskwee, the daughter of Snass, whom Snass called Margaret.

"Snass is not my father's name," she informed Smoke. "Snass is only an Indian name."

Much Smoke learned that day, and in the days that followed, as the hunting-camp moved on in the trail of the caribou. These were real wild Indians—the ones Anton had encountered and escaped from long years before. This was nearly the western limit of their territory, and in the summer they ranged north to the tundra shores of the Arctic, and eastward as far as the Luskwa. What river the Luskwa was Smoke could not make out, nor could Labiskwee tell him, nor could McCan. On occasion Snass, with parties of strong hunters, pushed east across the Rockies, on past the lakes and the Mackenzie and into the Barrens. It was on the last traverse in that direction that the silk tent occupied by Labiskwee had been found.

"It belonged to the Millicent-Adbury expedition," Snass told Smoke.

"Oh! I remember. They went after musk-oxen. The rescue expedition never found a trace of them."

"I found them," Snass said. "But both were dead."

"The world still doesn't know. The word never got out."

"The word never gets out," Snass assured him pleasantly.

"You mean if they had been alive when you found them—?"

Snass nodded. "They would have lived on with me and my people."

"Anton got out," Smoke challenged.

"I do not remember the name. How long ago?"

"Fourteen or fifteen years," Smoke answered.

"So he pulled through, after all. Do you know, I've wondered about him. We called him Long Tooth. He was a strong man, a strong man."

"La Perle came through here ten years ago."

Snass shook his head.

"He found traces of your camps. It was summer time."

"That explains it," Snass answered. "We are hundreds of miles to the north in the summer."

But, strive as he would, Smoke could get no clew to Snass's history in the days before he came to live in the northern wilds. Educated he was, yet in all the intervening years he had read no books, no newspapers. What had happened in the world he knew not, nor did he show desire to know. He had heard of the miners on the Yukon, and of the Klondike strike. Gold-miners had never invaded his territory, for which he was glad. But the outside world to him did not exist. He tolerated no mention of it.

Nor could Labiskwee help Smoke with earlier information. She had been born on the hunting-grounds. Her mother had lived for six years after. Her mother had been very beautiful—the only white woman Labiskwee had ever seen. She said this wistfully, and wistfully, in a thousand ways, she showed that she knew of the great outside world on which her father had closed the door. But this knowledge was secret. She had early learned that mention of it threw her father into a rage.

Anton had told a squaw of her mother, and that her mother had been a daughter of a high official in the Hudson Bay Company. Later, the squaw had told Labiskwee. But her mother's name she had never learned.

As a source of information, Danny McCan was impossible. He did not like adventure. Wild life was a horror, and he had had nine years of it. Shanghaied in San Francisco, he had deserted the whaleship at Point Barrow with three companions. Two had died, and the third had abandoned him on the terrible traverse south. Two years he had lived with the Eskimos before raising the courage to attempt the south traverse, and then, within several days of a Hudson Bay Company post, he had been gathered in by a party of Snass's young men. He was a small, stupid man, afflicted with sore eyes, and all he dreamed or could talk about was getting back to his beloved San Francisco and his blissful trade of bricklaying.

"You're the first intelligent man we've had," Snass complimented Smoke one night by the fire. "Except old Four Eyes. The Indians named him so. He wore glasses and was short-sighted. He was a professor of zoology." (Smoke noted the correctness of the pronunciation of the word.) "He died a year ago. My young men picked him up strayed from an expedition on the upper Porcupine. He was intelligent, yes; but he was also a fool. That was his weakness—straying. He knew geology, though, and working in metals. Over on the Luskwa, where there's coal, we have several creditable hand-forges he made. He repaired our guns and taught the young men how. He died last year, and we really missed him. Strayed—that's how it happened—froze to death within a mile of camp."

It was on the same night that Snass said to Smoke:

"You'd better pick out a wife and have a fire of your own. You will be more comfortable than with those young bucks. The maidens' fires—a sort of feast of the virgins, you know—are not lighted until full summer and the salmon, but I can give orders earlier if you say the word."

Smoke laughed and shook his head.

"Remember," Snass concluded quietly, "Anton is the only one that ever got away. He was lucky, unusually lucky."

Her father had a will of iron, Labiskwee told Smoke.

"Four Eyes used to call him the Frozen Pirate—whatever that means— the Tyrant of the Frost, the Cave Bear, the Beast Primitive, the King of the Caribou, the Bearded Pard, and lots of such things. Four Eyes loved words like these. He taught me most of my English. He was always making fun. You could never tell. He called me his cheetah-chum after times when I was angry. What is cheetah? He always teased me with it."

She chattered on with all the eager naivete of a child, which Smoke found hard to reconcile with the full womanhood of her form and face.

Yes, her father was very firm. Everybody feared him. He was terrible when angry. There were the Porcupines. It was through them, and through the Luskwas, that Snass traded his skins at the posts and got his supplies of ammunition and tobacco. He was always fair, but the chief of the Porcupines began to cheat. And after Snass had warned him twice, he burned his log village, and over a dozen of the Porcupines were killed in the fight. But there was no more cheating. Once, when she was a little girl, there was one white man killed while trying to escape. No, her father did not do it, but he gave the order to the young men. No Indian ever disobeyed her father.

And the more Smoke learned from her, the more the mystery of Snass deepened.

"And tell me if it is true," the girl was saying, "that there was a man and a woman whose names were Paolo and Francesca and who greatly loved each other?"

Smoke nodded.

"Four Eyes told me all about it," she beamed happily. "And so he did not make it up, after all. You see, I was not sure. I asked father, but, oh, he was angry. The Indians told me he gave poor Four Eyes an awful talking to. Then there were Tristan and Iseult—two Iseults. It was very sad. But I should like to love that way. Do all the young men and women in the world do that? They do not here. They just get married. They do not seem to have time. I am English, and I will never marry an Indian—would you? That is why I have not lighted my maiden's fire. Some of the young men are bothering father to make me do it. Libash is one of them. He is a great hunter. And Mahkook comes around singing songs. He is funny. To-night, if you come by my tent after dark, you will hear him singing out in the cold. But father says I can do as I please, and so I shall not light my fire. You see, when a girl makes up her mind to get married, that is the way she lets young men know. Four Eyes always said it was a fine custom. But I noticed he never took a wife. Maybe he was too old. He did not have much hair, but I do not think he was really very old. And how do you know when you are in love?—like Paolo and Francesca, I mean."

Smoke was disconcerted by the clear gaze of her blue eyes. "Why, they say," he stammered, "those who are in love say it, that love is dearer than life. When one finds out that he or she likes somebody better than everybody else in the world—why, then, they know they are in love. That's the way it goes, but it's awfully hard to explain. You just know it, that's all."

She looked off across the camp-smoke, sighed, and resumed work on the fur mitten she was sewing. "Well," she announced with finality, "I shall never get married anyway."

"Once we hit out we'll sure have some tall runnin'," Shorty said dismally.

"The place is a big trap," Smoke agreed.

From the crest of a bald knob they gazed out over Snass's snowy domain. East, west, and south they were hemmed in by the high peaks and jumbled ranges. Northward, the rolling country seemed interminable; yet they knew, even in that direction, that half a dozen transverse chains blocked the way.

"At this time of the year I could give you three days' start," Snass told Smoke that evening. "You can't hide your trail, you see. Anton got away when the snow was gone. My young men can travel as fast as the best white man; and, besides, you would be breaking trail for them. And when the snow is off the ground, I'll see to it that you don't get the chance Anton had. It's a good life. And soon the world fades. I have never quite got over the surprise of finding how easy it is to get along without the world."

"What's eatin' me is Danny McCan," Shorty confided to Smoke. "He's a weak brother on any trail. But he swears he knows the way out to the westward, an' so we got to put up with him, Smoke, or you sure get yours."

"We're all in the same boat," Smoke answered.

"Not on your life. It's a-comin' to you straight down the pike."

"What is?"

"You ain't heard the news?"

Smoke shook his head.

"The bachelors told me. They just got the word. To-night it comes off, though it's months ahead of the calendar."

Smoke shrugged his shoulders.

"Ain't interested in hearin'?" Shorty teased.

"I'm waiting to hear."

"Well, Danny's wife just told the bachelors," Shorty paused impressively. "An' the bachelors told me, of course, that the maidens' fires is due to be lighted to-night. That's all. Now how do you like it?"

"I don't get your drift, Shorty."

"Don't, eh? Why, it's plain open and shut. They's a skirt after you, an' that skirt is goin' to light a fire, an' that skirt's name is Labiskwee. Oh, I've been watchin' her watch you when you ain't lookin'. She ain't never lighted her fire. Said she wouldn't marry a Indian. An' now, when she lights her fire, it's a cinch it's my poor old friend Smoke."

"It sounds like a syllogism," Smoke said, with a sinking heart reviewing Labiskwee's actions of the past several days.

"Cinch is shorter to pronounce," Shorty returned. "An' that's always the way—just as we're workin' up our get-away, along comes a skirt to complicate everything. We ain't got no luck. Hey! Listen to that, Smoke!"

Three ancient squaws had halted midway between the bachelors' camp and the camp of McCan, and the oldest was declaiming in shrill falsetto.

Smoke recognized the names, but not all the words, and Shorty translated with melancholy glee.

"Labiskwee, the daughter of Snass, the Rainmaker, the Great Chief, lights her first maiden's fire to-night. Maka, the daughter of Owits, the Wolf-Runner—"

The recital ran through the names of a dozen maidens, and then the three heralds tottered on their way to make announcement at the next fires.

The bachelors, who had sworn youthful oaths to speak to no maidens, were uninterested in the approaching ceremony, and to show their disdain they made preparations for immediate departure on a mission set them by Snass and upon which they had planned to start the following morning. Not satisfied with the old hunters' estimates of the caribou, Snass had decided that the run was split. The task set the bachelors was to scout to the north and west in quest of the second division of the great herd.

Smoke, troubled by Labiskwee's fire-lighting, announced that he would accompany the bachelors. But first he talked with Shorty and with McCan.

"You be there on the third day, Smoke," Shorty said. "We'll have the outfit an' the dogs."

"But remember," Smoke cautioned, "if there is any slip-up in meeting me, you keep on going and get out to the Yukon. That's flat. If you make it, you can come back for me in the summer. If I get the chance, I'll make it, and come back for you."

McCan, standing by his fire, indicated with his eyes a rugged mountain where the high western range out-jutted on the open country.

"That's the one," he said. "A small stream on the south side. We go up it. On the third day you meet us. We'll pass by on the third day. Anywhere you tap that stream you'll meet us or our trail."

But the chance did not come to Smoke on the third day. The bachelors had changed the direction of their scout, and while Shorty and McCan plodded up the stream with their dogs, Smoke and the bachelors were sixty miles to the northeast picking up the trail of the second caribou herd. Several days later, through a dim twilight of falling snow, they came back to the big camp. A squaw ceased from wailing by a fire and darted up to Smoke. Harsh tongued, with bitter, venomous eyes, she cursed him, waving her arms toward a silent, fur-wrapped form that still lay on the sled which had hauled it in.

What had happened, Smoke could only guess, and as he came to McCan's fire he was prepared for a second cursing. Instead, he saw McCan himself industriously chewing a strip of caribou meat.

"I'm not a fightin' man," he whiningly explained. "But Shorty got away, though they're still after him. He put up a hell of a fight. They'll get him, too. He ain't got a chance. He plugged two bucks that'll get around all right. An' he croaked one square through the chest."

"Yes, I know," Smoke answered. "I just met the widow."

"Old Snass'll be wantin' to see you," McCan added. "Them's his orders. Soon as you come in you was to go to his fire. I ain't squealed. You don't know nothing. Keep that in mind. Shorty went off on his own along with me."

At Snass's fire Smoke found Labiskwee. She met him with eyes that shone with such softness and tenderness as to frighten him.

"I'm glad you did not try to run away," she said. "You see, I—" She hesitated, but her eyes didn't drop. They swam with a light unmistakable. "I lighted my fire, and of course it was for you. It has happened. I like you better than everybody else in the world. Better than my father. Better than a thousand Libashes and Mahkooks. I love. It is very strange. I love as Francesca loved, as Iseult loved. Old Four Eyes spoke true. Indians do not love this way. But my eyes are blue, and I am white. We are white, you and I."

Smoke had never been proposed to in his life, and he was unable to meet the situation. Worse, it was not even a proposal. His acceptance was taken for granted. So thoroughly was it all arranged in Labiskwee's mind, so warm was the light in her eyes, that he was amazed that she did not throw her arms around him and rest her head on his shoulder. Then he realized, despite her candor of love, that she did not know the pretty ways of love. Among the primitive savages such ways did not obtain. She had had no chance to learn.

She prattled on, chanting the happy burden of her love, while he strove to grip himself in the effort, somehow, to wound her with the truth. This, at the very first, was the golden opportunity.

"But, Labiskwee, listen," he began. "Are you sure you learned from Four Eyes all the story of the love of Paolo and Francesca?"

She clasped her hands and laughed with an immense certitude of gladness. "Oh! There is more! I knew there must be more and more of love! I have thought much since I lighted my fire. I have—"

And then Snass strode in to the fire through the falling snowflakes, and Smoke's opportunity was lost.

"Good evening," Snass burred gruffly. "Your partner has made a mess of it. I am glad you had better sense."

"You might tell me what's happened," Smoke urged.

The flash of white teeth through the stained beard was not pleasant. "Certainly, I'll tell you. Your partner has killed one of my people. That sniveling shrimp, McCan, deserted at the first shot. He'll never run away again. But my hunters have got your partner in the mountains, and they'll get him. He'll never make the Yukon basin. As for you, from now on you sleep at my fire. And there'll be no more scouting with the young men. I shall have my eye on you."

Smoke's new situation at Snass's fire was embarrassing. He saw more of Labiskwee than ever. In its sweetness and innocence, the frankness of her love was terrible. Her glances were love glances; every look was a caress. A score of times he nerved himself to tell her of Joy Gastell, and a score of times he discovered that he was a coward. The damnable part of it was that Labiskwee was so delightful. She was good to look upon. Despite the hurt to his self-esteem of every moment spent with her, he pleasured in every such moment. For the first time in his life he was really learning woman, and so clear was Labiskwee's soul, so appalling in its innocence and ignorance, that he could not misread a line of it. All the pristine goodness of her sex was in her, uncultured by the conventionality of knowledge or the deceit of self-protection. In memory he reread his Schopenhauer and knew beyond all cavil that the sad philosopher was wrong. To know woman, as Smoke came to know Labiskwee, was to know that all woman-haters were sick men.

Labiskwee was wonderful, and yet, beside her face in the flesh burned the vision of the face of Joy Gastell. Joy had control, restraint, all the feminine inhibitions of civilization, yet, by the trick of his fancy and the living preachment of the woman before him, Joy Gastell was stripped to a goodness at par with Labiskwee's. The one but appreciated the other, and all women of all the world appreciated by what Smoke saw in the soul of Labiskwee at Snass's fire in the snow-land.

And Smoke learned about himself. He remembered back to all he knew of Joy Gastell, and he knew that he loved her. Yet he delighted in Labiskwee. And what was this feeling of delight but love? He could demean it by no less a name. Love it was. Love it must be. And he was shocked to the roots of his soul by the discovery of this polygamous strain in his nature. He had heard it argued, in the San Francisco studios, that it was possible for a man to love two women, or even three women, at a time. But he had not believed it. How could he believe it when he had not had the experience? Now it was different. He did truly love two women, and though most of the time he was quite convinced that he loved Joy Gastell more, there were other moments when he felt with equal certainty that he loved Labiskwee more.

"There must be many women in the world," she said one day. "And women like men. Many women must have liked you. Tell me."

He did not reply.

"Tell me," she insisted.

"I have never married," he evaded.

"And there is no one else? No other Iseult out there beyond the mountains?"

Then it was that Smoke knew himself a coward. He lied. Reluctantly he did it, but he lied. He shook his head with a slow indulgent smile, and in his face was more of fondness than he dreamed as he noted Labiskwee's swift joy-transfiguration.

He excused himself to himself. His reasoning was jesuitical beyond dispute, and yet he was not Spartan enough to strike this child-woman a quivering heart-stroke.

Snass, too, was a perturbing factor in the problem. Little escaped his black eyes, and he spoke significantly.

"No man cares to see his daughter married," he said to Smoke. "At least, no man of imagination. It hurts. The thought of it hurts, I tell you. Just the same, in the natural order of life, Margaret must marry some time."

A pause fell; Smoke caught himself wondering for the thousandth time what Snass's history must be.

"I am a harsh, cruel man," Snass went on. "Yet the law is the law, and I am just. Nay, here with this primitive people, I am the law and the justice. Beyond my will no man goes. Also, I am a father, and all my days I have been cursed with imagination."

Whither his monologue tended, Smoke did not learn, for it was interrupted by a burst of chiding and silvery laughter from Labiskwee's tent, where she played with a new-caught wolf-cub. A spasm of pain twitched Snass's face.

"I can stand it," he muttered grimly. "Margaret must be married, and it is my fortune, and hers, that you are here. I had little hopes of Four Eyes. McCan was so hopeless I turned him over to a squaw who had lighted her fire twenty seasons. If it hadn't been you, it would have been an Indian. Libash might have become the father of my grandchildren."

And then Labiskwee came from her tent to the fire, the wolf-cub in her arms, drawn as by a magnet, to gaze upon the man, in her eyes the love that art had never taught to hide.

"Listen to me," said McCan. "The spring thaw is here, an' the crust is comin' on the snow. It's the time to travel, exceptin' for the spring blizzards in the mountains. I know them. I would run with no less a man than you."

"But you can't run," Smoke contradicted. "You can keep up with no man. Your backbone is limber as thawed marrow. If I run, I run alone. The world fades, and perhaps I shall never run. Caribou meat is very good, and soon will come summer and the salmon."

Said Snass: "Your partner is dead. My hunters did not kill him. They found the body, frozen in the first of the spring storms in the mountains. No man can escape. When shall we celebrate your marriage?"

And Labiskwee: "I watch you. There is trouble in your eyes, in your face. Oh, I do know all your face. There is a little scar on your neck, just under the ear. When you are happy, the corners of your mouth turn up. When you think sad thoughts they turn down. When you smile there are three and four wrinkles at the corners of your eyes. When you laugh there are six. Sometimes I have almost counted seven. But I cannot count them now. I have never read books. I do not know how to read. But Four Eyes taught me much. My grammar is good. He taught me. And in his own eyes I have seen the trouble of the hunger for the world. He was often hungry for the world. Yet here was good meat, and fish in plenty, and the berries and the roots, and often flour came back for the furs through the Porcupines and the Luskwas. Yet was he hungry for the world. Is the world so good that you, too, are hungry for it? Four Eyes had nothing. But you have me." She sighed and shook her head. "Four Eyes died still hungry for the world. And if you lived here always would you, too, die hungry for the world? I am afraid I do not know the world. Do you want to run away to the world?"

Smoke could not speak, but by his mouth-corner lines was she convinced.

Minutes of silence passed, in which she visibly struggled, while Smoke cursed himself for the unguessed weakness that enabled him to speak the truth about his hunger for the world while it kept his lips tight on the truth of the existence of the other woman.

Again Labiskwee sighed.

"Very well. I love you more than I fear my father's anger, and he is more terrible in anger than a mountain storm. You told me what love is. This is the test of love. I shall help you to run away back to the world."

SMOKE AWAKENED SOFTLY AND WITHOUT movement. Warm small fingers touched his cheek and slid gently to a pressure on his lips. Fur, with the chill of frost clinging in it, next tingled his skin, and the one word, "Come," was breathed in his ear. He sat up carefully and listened. The hundreds of wolf-dogs in the camp had lifted their nocturnal song, but under the volume of it, close at hand, he could distinguish the light, regular breathing of Snass.

Labiskwee tugged gently at Smoke's sleeve, and he knew she wished him to follow. He took his moccasins and German socks in his hand and crept out into the snow in his sleeping moccasins. Beyond the glow from the dying embers of the fire, she indicated to him to put on his outer foot-gear, and while he obeyed, she went back under the fly where Snass slept.

Feeling the hands of his watch Smoke found it was one in the morning. Quite warm it was, he decided, not more than ten below zero. Labiskwee rejoined him and led him on through the dark runways of the sleeping camp. Walk lightly as they could, the frost crunched crisply under their moccasins, but the sound was drowned by the clamor of the dogs, too deep in their howling to snarl at the man and woman who passed.

"Now we can talk," she said, when the last fire had been left half a mile behind.

And now, in the starlight, facing him, Smoke noted for the first time that her arms were burdened, and, on feeling, discovered she carried his snowshoes, a rifle, two belts of ammunition, and his sleeping-robes.

"I have everything fixed," she said, with a happy little laugh. "I have been two days making the cache. There is meat, even flour, matches, and skees, which go best on the hard crust and, when they break through, the webs will hold up longer. Oh, I do know snow-travel, and we shall go fast, my lover."

Smoke checked his speech. That she had been arranging his escape was surprise enough, but that she had planned to go with him was more than he was prepared for. Unable to think immediate action, he gently, one by one, took her burdens from her. He put his arm around her and pressed her close, and still he could not think what to do.

"God is good," she whispered. "He sent me a lover."

Yet Smoke was brave enough not to suggest his going alone. And before he spoke again he saw all his memory of the bright world and the sun-lands reel and fade.

"We will go back, Labiskwee," he said. "You will be my wife, and we shall live always with the Caribou People."

"No! no!" She shook her head; and her body, in the circle of his arm, resented his proposal. "I know. I have thought much. The hunger for the world would come upon you, and in the long nights it would devour your heart. Four Eyes died of hunger for the world. So would you die. All men from the world hunger for it. And I will not have you die. We will go on across the snow mountains on the south traverse."

"Dear, listen," he urged. "We must go back."

She pressed her mitten against his lips to prevent further speech. "You love me. Say that you love me."

"I do love you, Labiskwee. You are my wonderful sweetheart."

Again the mitten was a caressing obstacle to utterance.

"We shall go on to the cache," she said with decision. "It is three miles from here. Come."

He held back, and her pull on his arm could not move him. Almost was he tempted to tell her of the other woman beyond the south traverse.

"It would be a great wrong to you to go back," she said. "I—I am only a wild girl, and I am afraid of the world; but I am more afraid for you. You see, it is as you told me. I love you more than anybody else in the world. I love you more than myself. The Indian language is not a good language. The English language is not a good language. The thoughts in my heart for you, as bright and as many as the stars—there is no language for them. How can I tell you them? They are there—see?"

As she spoke she slipped the mitten from his hand and thrust the hand inside the warmth of her parka until it rested against her heart. Tightly and steadily she pressed his hand in its position. And in the long silence he felt the beat, beat of her heart, and knew that every beat of it was love. And then, slowly, almost imperceptibly, still holding his hand, her body began to incline away from his and toward the direction of the cache. Nor could he resist. It was as if he were drawn by her heart itself that so nearly lay in the hollow of his hand.

So firm was the crust, frozen during the night after the previous day's surface-thaw, that they slid along rapidly on their skees.

"Just here, in the trees, is the cache," Labiskwee told Smoke.

The next moment she caught his arm with a startle of surprise. The flames of a small fire were dancing merrily, and crouched by the fire was McCan. Labiskwee muttered something in Indian, and so lashlike was the sound that Smoke remembered she had been called "cheetah" by Four Eyes.

"I was minded you'd run without me," McCan explained when they came up, his small peering eyes glimmering with cunning. "So I kept an eye on the girl, an' when I seen her caching skees an' grub, I was on. I've brought my own skees an' webs an' grub. The fire? Sure, an' it was no danger. The camp's asleep an' snorin', an' the waitin' was cold. Will we be startin' now?"

Labiskwee looked swift consternation at Smoke, as swiftly achieved a judgement on the matter, and spoke. And in the speaking she showed, child-woman though she was in love, the quick decisiveness of one who in other affairs of life would be no clinging vine.

"McCan, you are a dog," she hissed, and her eyes were savage with anger. "I know it is in your heart to raise the camp if we do not take you. Very well. We must take you. But you know my father. I am like my father. You will do your share of the work. You will obey. And if you play one dirty trick, it would be better for you if you had never run."

McCan looked up at her, his small pig-eyes hating and cringing, while in her eyes, turned to Smoke, the anger melted into luminous softness.

"Is it right, what I have said?" she queried.

Daylight found them in the belt of foothills that lay between the rolling country and the mountains. McCan suggested breakfast, but they held on. Not until the afternoon thaw softened the crust and prevented travel would they eat.

The foothills quickly grew rugged, and the stream, up whose frozen bed they journeyed, began to thread deeper and deeper canyons. The signs of spring were less frequent, though in one canyon they found foaming bits of open water, and twice they came upon clumps of dwarf willow upon which were the first hints of swelling buds.

Labiskwee explained to Smoke her knowledge of the country and the way she planned to baffle pursuit. There were but two ways out, one west, the other south. Snass would immediately dispatch parties of young men to guard the two trails. But there was another way south. True, it did no more than penetrate half-way into the high mountains, then, twisting to the west and crossing three divides, it joined the regular trail. When the young men found no traces on the regular trail they would turn back in the belief that the escape had been made by the west traverse, never dreaming that the runaways had ventured the harder and longer way around.

Glancing back at McCan, in the rear, Labiskwee spoke in an undertone to Smoke. "He is eating," she said. "It is not good."

Smoke looked. The Irishman was secretly munching caribou suet from the pocketful he carried.

"No eating between meals, McCan," he commanded. "There's no game in the country ahead, and the grub will have to be whacked in equal rations from the start. The only way you can travel with us is by playing fair."

By one o'clock the crust had thawed so that the skees broke through, and before two o'clock the web-shoes were breaking through. Camp was made and the first meal eaten. Smoke took stock of the food. McCan's supply was a disappointment. So many silver fox-skins had he stuffed in the bottom of the meat bag that there was little space left for meat.

"Sure an' I didn't know there was so many," he explained. "I done it in the dark. But they're worth good money. An' with all this ammunition we'll be gettin' game a-plenty."

"The wolves will eat you a-plenty," was Smoke's hopeless comment, while Labiskwee's eyes flashed their anger.

Enough food for a month, with careful husbanding and appetites that never blunted their edge, was Smoke's and Labiskwee's judgment. Smoke apportioned the weight and bulk of the packs, yielding in the end to Labiskwee's insistence that she, too, should carry a pack.

Next day the stream shallowed out in a wide mountain valley, and they were already breaking through the crust on the flats when they gained the harder surface of the slope of the divide.

"Ten minutes later and we wouldn't have got across the flats," Smoke said, when they paused for breath on the bald crest of the summit. "We must be a thousand feet higher here."

But Labiskwee, without speaking, pointed down to an open flat among the trees. In the midst of it, scattered abreast, were five dark specks that scarcely moved.

"The young men," said Labiskwee.

"They are wallowing to their hips," Smoke said. "They will never gain the hard footing this day. We have hours the start of them. Come on, McCan. Buck up. We don't eat till we can't travel."

McCan groaned, but there was no caribou suet in his pocket, and he doggedly brought up the rear.

In the higher valley in which they now found themselves, the crust did not break till three in the afternoon, at which time they managed to gain the shadow of a mountain where the crust was already freezing again. Once only they paused to get out McCan's confiscated suet, which they ate as they walked. The meat was frozen solid, and could be eaten only after thawing over a fire. But the suet crumbled in their mouths and eased the palpitating faintness in their stomachs.

Black darkness, with an overcast sky, came on after a long twilight at nine o'clock, when they made camp in a clump of dwarf spruce. McCan was whining and helpless. The day's march had been exhausting, but in addition, despite his nine years' experience in the arctic, he had been eating snow and was in agony with his parched and burning mouth. He crouched by the fire and groaned, while they made the camp.

Labiskwee was tireless, and Smoke could not but marvel at the life in her body, at the endurance of mind and muscle. Nor was her cheerfulness forced. She had ever a laugh or a smile for him, and her hand lingered in caress whenever it chanced to touch his. Yet, always, when she looked at McCan, her face went hard and pitiless and her eyes flashed frostily.

In the night came wind and snow, and through a day of blizzard they fought their way blindly, missing the turn of the way that led up a small stream and crossed a divide to the west. For two more days they wandered, crossing other and wrong divides, and in those two days they dropped spring behind and climbed up into the abode of winter.

"The young men have lost our trail, an' what's to stop us restin' a day?" McCan begged.

But no rest was accorded. Smoke and Labiskwee knew their danger. They were lost in the high mountains, and they had seen no game nor signs of game. Day after day they struggled on through an iron configuration of landscape that compelled them to labyrinthine canyons and valleys that led rarely to the west. Once in such a canyon, they could only follow it, no matter where it led, for the cold peaks and higher ranges on either side were unscalable and unendurable. The terrible toil and the cold ate up energy, yet they cut down the size of the ration they permitted themselves.

One night Smoke was awakened by a sound of struggling. Distinctly he heard a gasping and strangling from where McCan slept. Kicking the fire into flame, by its light he saw Labiskwee, her hands at the

Irishman's throat and forcing from his mouth a chunk of partly chewed meat. Even as Smoke saw this, her hand went to her hip and flashed with the sheath-knife in it.

"Labiskwee!" Smoke cried, and his voice was peremptory.

The hand hesitated.

"Don't," he said, coming to her side.

She was shaking with anger, but the hand, after hesitating a moment longer, descended reluctantly to the sheath. As if fearing she could not restrain herself, she crossed to the fire and threw on more wood. McCan sat up, whimpering and snarling, between fright and rage spluttering an inarticulate explanation.

"Where did you get it?" Smoke demanded.

"Feel around his body," Labiskwee said.

It was the first word she had spoken, and her voice quivered with the anger she could not suppress.

McCan strove to struggle, but Smoke gripped him cruelly and searched him, drawing forth from under his armpit, where it had been thawed by the heat of his body, a strip of caribou meat. A quick exclamation from Labiskwee drew Smoke's attention. She had sprung to McCan's pack and was opening it. Instead of meat, out poured moss, spruce-needles, chips—all the light refuse that had taken the place of the meat and given the pack its due proportion minus its weight.

Again Labiskwee's hand went to her hip, and she flew at the culprit only to be caught in Smoke's arms, where she surrendered herself, sobbing with the futility of her rage.

"Oh, lover, it is not the food," she panted. "It is you, your life. The dog! He is eating you, he is eating you!"

"We will yet live," Smoke comforted her. "Hereafter he shall carry the flour. He can't eat that raw, and if he does I'll kill him myself, for he will be eating your life as well as mine." He held her closer. "Sweetheart, killing is men's work. Women do not kill."

"You would not love me if I killed the dog?" she questioned in surprise.

"Not so much," Smoke temporized.

She sighed with resignation. "Very well," she said. "I shall not kill him."

THE PURSUIT BY THE YOUNG men was relentless. By miracles of luck, as well as by deduction from the topography of the way the runaways must take, the young men picked up the blizzard-blinded trail and clung to it. When the snow flew, Smoke and Labiskwee took the most improbable courses, turning east when the better way opened south or west, rejecting a low divide to climb a higher. Being lost, it did not matter. Yet they could not throw the young men off. Sometimes they gained days, but always the young men appeared again. After a storm, when all trace was lost, they would cast out like a pack of hounds, and he who caught the later trace made smoke signals to call his comrades on.

Smoke lost count of time, of days and nights and storms and camps. Through a vast mad phantasmagoria of suffering and toil he and Labiskwee struggled on, with McCan somehow stumbling along in the rear, babbling of San Francisco, his everlasting dream. Great peaks, pitiless and serene in the chill blue, towered about them. They fled down black canyons with walls so precipitous that the rock frowned naked, or wallowed across glacial valleys where frozen lakes lay far beneath their feet. And one night, between two storms, a distant volcano glared the sky. They never saw it again, and wondered whether it had been a dream.

Crusts were covered with yards of new snow, that crusted and were snow-covered again. There were places, in canyon- and pocket-drifts, where they crossed snow hundreds of feet deep, and they crossed tiny glaciers, in drafty rifts, wind-scurried and bare of any snow. They crept like silent wraiths across the faces of impending avalanches, or roused from exhausted sleep to the thunder of them. They made fireless camps above timber-line, thawing their meat-rations with the heat of their bodies ere they could eat. And through it all Labiskwee remained Labiskwee. Her cheer never vanished, save when she looked at McCan, and the greatest stupor of fatigue and cold never stilled the eloquence of her love for Smoke.

Like a cat she watched the apportionment of the meager ration, and Smoke could see that she grudged McCan every munch of his jaws. Once, she distributed the ration. The first Smoke knew was a wild harangue of protest from McCan. Not to him alone, but to herself, had she given a smaller portion than to Smoke. After that, Smoke divided the meat himself. Caught in a small avalanche one morning after a night of snow, and swept a hundred yards down the mountain, they emerged half-stifled and unhurt, but McCan emerged without his pack in which was all the flour. A second and larger snow-slide buried it beyond hope of recovery. After that, though the disaster had been through no fault of his, Labiskwee never looked at McCan, and Smoke knew it was because she dared not.

It was a morning, stark still, clear blue above, with white sun-dazzle on the snow. The way led up a long, wide slope of crust. They moved like weary ghosts in a dead world. No wind stirred in the stagnant, frigid calm. Far peaks, a hundred miles away, studding the backbone of the Rockies up and down, were as distinct as if no more than five miles away.

"Something is going to happen," Labiskwee whispered. "Don't you feel it?—here, there, everywhere? Everything is strange."

"I feel a chill that is not of cold," Smoke answered. "Nor is it of hunger."

"It is in your head, your heart," she agreed excitedly. "That is the way I feel it."

"It is not of my senses," Smoke diagnosed. "I sense something, from without, that is tingling me with ice; it is a chill of my nerves."

A quarter of an hour later they paused for breath.

"I can no longer see the far peaks," Smoke said.

"The air is getting thick and heavy," said Labiskwee. "It is hard to breathe."

"There be three suns," McCan muttered hoarsely, reeling as he clung to his staff for support.

There was a mock sun on either side of the real sun.

"There are five," said Labiskwee; and as they looked, new suns formed and flashed before their eyes.

"By Heaven, the sky is filled with suns beyant all countin'," McCan cried in fear.

Which was true, for look where they would, half the circle of the sky dazzled and blazed with new suns forming.

McCan yelped sharply with surprise and pain. "I'm stung!" he cried out, then yelped again.

Then Labiskwee cried out, and Smoke felt a prickling stab on his cheek so cold that it burned like acid. It reminded him of swimming in the salt sea and being stung by the poisonous filaments of Portuguese men-of-war. The sensations were so similar that he automatically brushed his cheek to rid it of the stinging substance that was not there.

And then a shot rang out, strangely muffled. Down the slope were the young men, standing on their skees, and one after another opened fire.

"Spread out!" Smoke commanded. "And climb for it! We're almost to the top. They're a quarter of a mile below, and that means a couple of miles the start of them on the down-going of the other side."

With faces prickling and stinging from invisible atmospheric stabs, the three scattered widely on the snow surface and toiled upward. The muffled reports of the rifles were weird to their ears.

"Thank the Lord," Smoke panted to Labiskwee, "that four of them are muskets, and only one a Winchester. Besides, all these suns spoil their aim. They are fooled. They haven't come within a hundred feet of us."

"It shows my father's temper," she said. "They have orders to kill."

"How strange you talk," Smoke said. "Your voice sounds far away."

"Cover your mouth," Labiskwee cried suddenly. "And do not talk. I know what it is. Cover your mouth with your sleeve, thus, and do not talk."

McCan fell first, and struggled wearily to his feet. And after that all fell repeatedly ere they reached the summit. Their wills exceeded their muscles, they knew not why, save that their bodies were oppressed by a numbness and heaviness of movement. From the crest, looking back, they saw the young men stumbling and falling on the upward climb.

"They will never get here," Labiskwee said. "It is the white death. I know it, though I have never seen it. I have heard the old men talk. Soon will come a mist—unlike any mist or fog or frost-smoke you ever saw. Few have seen it and lived."

McCan gasped and strangled.

"Keep your mouth covered," Smoke commanded.

A pervasive flashing of light from all about them drew Smoke's eyes upward to the many suns. They were shimmering and veiling. The air was filled with microscopic fire-glints. The near peaks were being blotted out by the weird mist; the young men, resolutely struggling nearer, were being engulfed in it. McCan had sunk down, squatting, on his skees, his mouth and eyes covered by his arms.

"Come on, make a start," Smoke ordered.

"I can't move," McCan moaned.

His doubled body set up a swaying motion. Smoke went toward him slowly, scarcely able to will movement through the lethargy that weighed his flesh. He noted that his brain was clear. It was only the body that was afflicted.

"Let him be," Labiskwee muttered harshly.

But Smoke persisted, dragging the Irishman to his feet and facing him down the long slope they must go. Then he started him with a shove, and McCan, braking and steering with his staff, shot into the sheen of diamond-dust and disappeared.

Smoke looked at Labiskwee, who smiled, though it was all she could do to keep from sinking down. He nodded for her to push off, but she came near to him, and side by side, a dozen feet apart, they flew down through the stinging thickness of cold fire.

Brake as he would, Smoke's heavier body carried him past her, and he dashed on alone, a long way, at tremendous speed that did not slacken till he came out on a level, crusted plateau. Here he braked till Labiskwee overtook him, and they went on, again side by side, with diminishing speed which finally ceased. The lethargy had grown more pronounced. The wildest effort of will could move them no more than at a snail's pace. They passed McCan, again crouched down on his skees, and Smoke roused him with his staff in passing.

"Now we must stop," Labiskwee whispered painfully, "or we will die. We must cover up—so the old men said."

She did not delay to untie knots, but began cutting her pack-lashings. Smoke cut his, and, with a last look at the fiery death-mist and the mockery of suns, they covered themselves over with the sleeping-furs and crouched in each other's arms. They felt a body stumble over them and fall, then heard feeble whimpering and blaspheming drowned in a violent coughing fit, and knew it was McCan who huddled against them as he wrapped his robe about him.

Their own lung-strangling began, and they were racked and torn by a dry cough, spasmodic and uncontrollable. Smoke noted his temperature rising in a fever, and Labiskwee suffered similarly. Hour after hour the coughing spells increased in frequency and violence, and not till late afternoon was the worst reached. After that the mend came slowly, and between spells they dozed in exhaustion.

McCan, however, steadily coughed worse, and from his groans and howls they knew he was in delirium. Once, Smoke made as if to throw the robes back, but Labiskwee clung to him tightly.

"No," she begged. "It is death to uncover now. Bury your face here, against my parka, and breathe gently and do no talking—see, the way I am doing."

They dozed on through the darkness, though the decreasing fits of coughing of one invariably aroused the other. It was after midnight, Smoke judged, when McCan coughed his last. After that he emitted low and bestial moanings that never ceased.

Smoke awoke with lips touching his lips. He lay partly in Labiskwee's arms, his head pillowed on her breast. Her voice was cheerful and usual. The muffled sound of it had vanished.

"It is day," she said, lifting the edge of the robes a trifle. "See, O my lover. It is day; we have lived through; and we no longer cough. Let us look at the world, though I could stay here thus forever and always. This last hour has been sweet. I have been awake, and I have been loving you."

"I do not hear McCan," Smoke said. "And what has become of the young men that they have not found us?"

He threw back the robes and saw a normal and solitary sun in the sky. A gentle breeze was blowing, crisp with frost and hinting of warmer days to come. All the world was natural again. McCan lay on his back, his unwashed face, swarthy from camp-smoke, frozen hard as marble. The sight did not affect Labiskwee.

"Look!" she cried. "A snow bird! It is a good sign."

There was no evidence of the young men. Either they had died on the other side of the divide or they had turned back.

There was so little food that they dared not eat a tithe of what they needed, nor a hundredth part of what they desired, and in the days that followed, wandering through the lone mountain-land, the sharp sting of life grew blunted and the wandering merged half into a dream. Smoke would become abruptly conscious, to find himself staring at the never-ending hated snow-peaks, his senseless babble still ringing in his ears. And the next he would know, after seeming centuries, was that again he was roused to the sound of his own maunderings. Labiskwee, too, was light-headed most of the time. In the main their efforts were unreasoned, automatic. And ever they worked toward the west, and ever they were baffled and thrust north or south by snow-peaks and impassable ranges.

"There is no way south," Labiskwee said. "The old men know. West, only west, is the way."

The young men no longer pursued, but famine crowded on the trail.

Came a day when it turned cold, and a thick snow, that was not snow but frost crystals of the size of grains of sand, began to fall. All day and night it fell, and for three days and nights it continued to fall. It was impossible to travel until it crusted under the spring sun, so they lay in their furs and rested, and ate less because they rested. So small was the ration they permitted that it gave no appeasement to the hunger pang that was much of the stomach, but more of the brain. And Labiskwee, delirious, maddened by the taste of her tiny portion, sobbing and mumbling, yelping sharp little animal cries of joy, fell upon the next day's portion and crammed it into her mouth.

Then it was given to Smoke to see a wonderful thing. The food between her teeth roused her to consciousness. She spat it out, and with a great anger struck herself with her clenched fist on the offending mouth.

It was given to Smoke to see many wonderful things in the days yet to come. After the long snow-fall came on a great wind that drove the dry and tiny frost-particles as sand is driven in a sand-storm. All through the night the sand-frost drove by, and in the full light of a clear and wind-blown day, Smoke looked with swimming eyes and reeling brain upon what he took to be the vision of a dream. All about towered great peaks and small, lone sentinels and groups and councils of mighty Titans. And from the tip of every peak, swaying, undulating, flaring out broadly against the azure sky, streamed gigantic snow-banners, miles in length, milky and nebulous, ever waving lights and shadows and flashing silver from the sun.

"Mine eyes have seen the glory of the coming of the Lord," Smoke chanted, as he gazed upon these dusts of snow wind-driven into sky-scarves of shimmering silken light.

And still he gazed, and still the bannered peaks did not vanish, and still he considered that he dreamed, until Labiskwee sat up among the furs.

"I dream, Labiskwee," he said. "Look. Do you, too, dream within my dream?"

"It is no dream," she replied. "This have the old men told me. And after this will blow the warm winds, and we shall live and win west."

Smoke shot a snow-bird, and they divided it. Once, in a valley where willows budded standing in the snow, he shot a snowshoe rabbit. Another time he got a lean, white weasel. This much of meat they encountered, and no more, though, once, half-mile high and veering toward the west and the Yukon, they saw a wild-duck wedge drive by.

"It is summer in the lower valleys," said Labiskwee. "Soon it will be summer here."

Labiskwee's face had grown thin, but the bright, large eyes were brighter and larger, and when she looked at him she was transfigured by a wild, unearthly beauty.

The days lengthened, and the snow began to sink. Each day the crust thawed, each night it froze again; and they were afoot early and late, being compelled to camp and rest during the midday hours of thaw when the crust could not bear their weight. When Smoke grew snow-blind, Labiskwee towed him on a thong tied to her waist. And when she was so blinded, she towed behind a thong to his waist. And starving, in a deeper dream, they struggled on through an awakening land bare of any life save their own.

Exhausted as he was, Smoke grew almost to fear sleep, so fearful and bitter were the visions of that mad, twilight land. Always were they of food, and always was the food, at his lips, snatched away by the malign deviser of dreams. He gave dinners to his comrades of the old San Francisco days, himself, with whetting appetite and jealous eye, directing the arrangements, decorating the table with crimson-leafed runners of the autumn grape. The guests were dilatory, and while he greeted them and all sparkled with their latest cleverness, he was frantic with desire for the table. He stole to it, unobserved, and clutched a handful of black ripe olives, and turned to meet still another guest. And others surrounded him, and the laugh and play of wit went on, while all the time, hidden in his closed hand, was this madness of ripe olives.

He gave many such dinners, all with the same empty ending. He attended Gargantuan feasts, where multitudes fed on innumerable bullocks roasted whole, prying them out of smoldering pits and with sharp knives slicing great strips of meat from the steaming carcasses. He stood, with mouth agape, beneath long rows of turkeys which white-aproned shopmen sold. And everybody bought save Smoke, mouth still agape, chained by a leadenness of movement to the pavement. A boy again, he sat with spoon poised high above great bowls of bread and milk. He pursued shy heifers through upland pastures and centuries of torment in vain effort to steal from them their milk, and in noisome dungeons he fought with rats for scraps and refuse. There was no food that was not a madness to him, and he wandered through vast stables, where fat horses stood in mile-long rows of stalls, and sought but never found the bran-bins from which they fed.

Once, only, he dreamed to advantage. Famishing, shipwrecked or marooned, he fought with the big Pacific surf for rock-clinging mussels, and carried them up the sands to the dry flotsam of the spring tides. Of this he built a fire, and among the coals he laid his precious trove. He watched the steam jet forth and the locked shells pop apart, exposing the salmon-colored meat. Cooked to a turn—he knew it; and this time there was no intruding presence to whisk the meal away. At last—so he dreamed within the dream—the dream would come true. This time he would eat. Yet in his certitude he doubted, and he was steeled for the inevitable shift of vision until the salmon-colored meat, hot and savory, was in his mouth. His teeth closed upon it. He ate! The miracle had happened! The shock aroused him. He awoke in the dark, lying on his back, and heard himself mumbling little piggish squeals and grunts of joy. His jaws were moving, and between his teeth meat was crunching. He did not move, and soon small fingers felt about his lips, and between them was inserted a tiny sliver of meat. And in that he would eat no more, rather than that he was angry, Labiskwee cried and in his arms sobbed herself to sleep. But he lay on awake, marveling at the love and the wonder of woman.

THE TIME CAME WHEN THE last food was gone. The high peaks receded, the divides became lower, and the way opened promisingly to the west. But their reserves of strength were gone, and, without food, the time quickly followed when they lay down at night and in the morning did not arise. Smoke weakly gained his feet, collapsed, and on hands and knees crawled about the building of a fire. But try as she would Labiskwee sank back each time in an extremity of weakness. And Smoke sank down beside her, a wan sneer on his face for the automatism that had made him struggle for an unneeded fire. There was nothing to cook, and the day was warm. A gentle breeze sighed in the spruce-trees, and from everywhere, under the disappearing snow, came the trickling music of unseen streamlets.

Labiskwee lay in a stupor, her breathing so imperceptible that often Smoke thought her dead. In the afternoon the chattering of a squirrel aroused him. Dragging the heavy rifle, he wallowed through the crust that had become slush. He crept on hands and knees, or stood upright and fell forward in the direction of the squirrel that chattered its wrath and fled slowly and tantalizingly before him. He had not the strength for a quick shot, and the squirrel was never still. At times Smoke sprawled in the wet snow-melt and cried out of weakness. Other times the flame of his life flickered, and blackness smote him. How long he lay in the last faint he did not know, but he came to, shivering in the chill of evening, his wet clothing frozen to the re-forming crust. The squirrel was gone, and after a weary struggle he won back to the side of Labiskwee. So profound was his weakness that he lay like a dead man through the night, nor did dreams disturb him.

The sun was in the sky, the same squirrel chattering through the trees, when Labiskwee's hand on Smoke's cheek awakened him.

"Put your hand on my heart, lover," she said, her voice clear but faint and very far away. "My heart is my love, and you hold it in your hand."

A long time seemed to go by, ere she spoke again.

"Remember always, there is no way south. That is well known to the Caribou People. West—that is the way—and you are almost there—and you will make it."

And Smoke drowsed in the numbness that is near to death, until once more she aroused him.

"Put your lips on mine," she said. "I will die so."

"We will die together, sweetheart," was his answer.

"No." A feeble flutter of her hand checked him, and so thin was her voice that scarcely did he hear it, yet did he hear all of it. Her hand fumbled and groped in the hood of her parka, and she drew forth a pouch that she placed in his hand. "And now your lips, my lover. Your lips on my lips, and your hand on my heart."

And in that long kiss darkness came upon him again, and when again he was conscious he knew that he was alone and he knew that he was to die. He was wearily glad that he was to die.

He found his hand resting on the pouch. With an inward smile at the curiosity that made him pull the draw-string, he opened it. Out poured a tiny flood of food. There was no particle of it that he did not recognize, all stolen by Labiskwee from Labiskwee—bread-fragments saved far back in the days ere McCan lost the flour; strips and strings of caribou-meat, partly gnawed; crumbles of suet; the hind-leg of the snowshoe rabbit, untouched; the hind-leg and part of the fore-leg of the white weasel; the wing dented still by her reluctant teeth, and the leg of the snow-bird—pitiful remnants, tragic renunciations, crucifixions of life, morsels stolen from her terrible hunger by her incredible love.

With maniacal laughter Smoke flung it all out on the hardening snow-crust and went back into the blackness.

He dreamed. The Yukon ran dry. In its bed, among muddy pools of water and ice-scoured rocks, he wandered, picking up fat nugget-gold. The weight of it grew to be a burden to him, till he discovered that it was good to eat. And greedily he ate. After all, of what worth was gold that men should prize it so, save that it was good to eat?

He awoke to another sun. His brain was strangely clear. No longer did his eyesight blur. The familiar palpitation that had vexed him through all his frame was gone. The juices of his body seemed to sing, as if the spring had entered in. Blessed well-being had come to him. He turned to awaken Labiskwee, and saw, and remembered. He looked for the food flung out on the snow. It was gone. And he knew that in delirium and dream it had been the Yukon nugget-gold. In delirium and dream he had taken heart of life from the life sacrifice of Labiskwee, who had put her heart in his hand and opened his eyes to woman and wonder.

He was surprised at the ease of his movements, astounded that he was able to drag her fur-wrapped body to the exposed thawed gravel-bank, which he undermined with the ax and caved upon her.

THREE DAYS, WITH NO FURTHER food, he fought west. In the mid third day he fell beneath a lone spruce beside a wide stream that ran open and which he knew must be the Klondike. Ere blackness conquered him, he unlashed his pack, said good-by to the bright world, and rolled himself in the robes.

Chirping, sleepy noises awoke him. The long twilight was on. Above him, among the spruce boughs, were ptarmigan. Hunger bit him into instant action, though the action was infinitely slow. Five minutes passed before he was able to get his rifle to his shoulder, and a second five minutes passed ere he dared, lying on his back and aiming straight upward, to pull the trigger. It was a clean miss. No bird fell, but no bird flew. They ruffled and rustled stupidly and drowsily. His shoulder pained him. A second shot was spoiled by the involuntary wince he made as he pulled trigger. Somewhere, in the last three days, though he had no recollection how, he must have fallen and injured it.

The ptarmigan had not flown. He doubled and redoubled the robe that had covered him, and humped it in the hollow between his right arm and his side. Resting the butt of the rifle on the fur, he fired again, and a bird fell. He clutched it greedily and found that he had shot most of the meat out of it. The large-caliber bullet had left little else than a mess of mangled feathers. Still the ptarmigan did not fly, and he decided that it was heads or nothing. He fired only at heads. He reloaded and reloaded the magazine. He missed; he hit; and the stupid ptarmigan, that were loath to fly, fell upon him in a rain of food—lives disrupted that his life might feed and live. There had been nine of them, and in the end he clipped the head of the ninth, and lay and laughed and wept he knew not why.

The first he ate raw. Then he rested and slept, while his life assimilated the life of it. In the darkness he awoke, hungry, with strength to build a fire. And until early dawn he cooked and ate, crunching the bones to powder between his long-idle teeth. He slept, awoke in the darkness of another night, and slept again to another sun.

He noted with surprise that the fire crackled with fresh fuel and that a blackened coffee-pot steamed on the edge of the coals. Beside the fire, within arm's length, sat Shorty, smoking a brown-paper cigarette and intently watching him. Smoke's lips moved, but a throat paralysis seemed to come upon him, while his chest was suffused with the menace of tears. He reached out his hand for the cigarette and drew the smoke deep into his lungs again and again.

"I have not smoked for a long time," he said at last, in a low calm voice. "For a very long time."

"Nor eaten, from your looks," Shorty added gruffly.

Smoke nodded and waved his hand at the ptarmigan feathers that lay all about.

"Not until recently," he returned. "Do you know, I'd like a cup of coffee. It will taste strange. Also flapjacks and a strip of bacon."

"And beans?" Shorty tempted.

"They would taste heavenly. I find I am quite hungry again."

While the one cooked and the other ate, they told briefly what had happened to them in the days since their separation.

"The Klondike was breakin' up," Shorty concluded his recital, "an' we just had to wait for open water. Two polin' boats, six other men— you know 'em all, an' crackerjacks—an' all kinds of outfit. An' we've sure been a-comin'—polin', linin' up, and portagin'. But the falls'll stick 'em a solid week. That's where I left 'em a-cuttin' a trail over the tops of the bluffs for the boats. I just had a sure natural hunch to keep a-comin'. So I fills a pack with grub an' starts. I knew I'd find you a-driftin' an' all in."

Smoke nodded, and put forth his hand in a silent grip. "Well, let's get started," he said.

"Started hell!" Shorty exploded. "We stay right here an' rest you up an' feed you up for a couple of days."

Smoke shook his head.

"If you could just see yourself," Shorty protested.

And what he saw was not nice. Smoke's face, wherever the skin showed, was black and purple and scabbed from repeated frost-bite. The cheeks were fallen in, so that, despite the covering of beard, the upper rows of teeth ridged the shrunken flesh. Across the forehead and about the deep-sunk eyes, the skin was stretched drum-tight, while the scraggly beard, that should have been golden, was singed by fire and filthy with camp-smoke.

"Better pack up," Smoke said. "I'm going on."

"But you're feeble as a kid baby. You can't hike. What's the rush?"

"Shorty, I am going after the biggest thing in the Klondike, and I can't wait. That's all. Start packing. It's the biggest thing in the world. It's bigger than lakes of gold and mountains of gold, bigger than adventure, and meat-eating, and bear-killing."

Shorty sat with bulging eyes. "In the name of the Lord, what is it?" he queried huskily. "Or are you just simple loco?"

"No, I'm all right. Perhaps a fellow has to stop eating in order to see things. At any rate, I have seen things I never dreamed were in the world. I know what a woman is,—now."

Shorty's mouth opened, and about the lips and in the light of the eyes was the whimsical advertisement of the sneer forthcoming.

"Don't, please," Smoke said gently. "You don't know. I do."

Shorty gulped and changed his thought. "Huh! I don't need no hunch to guess *her* name. The rest of 'em has gone up to the drainin' of Surprise Lake, but Joy Gastell allowed she wouldn't go. She's stickin' around Dawson, waitin' to see if I come back with you. An' she sure swears, if I don't, she'll sell her holdin's an' hire a army of gun-fighters, an' go into the Caribou Country an' knock the everlastin' stuffin' outa old Snass an' his whole gang. An' if you'll hold your horses a couple of shakes, I reckon I'll get packed up an' ready to hike along with you."

A Note About the Author

Jack London (1876–1916) was an American novelist and journalist. Born in San Francisco to Florence Wellman, a spiritualist, and William Chaney, an astrologer, London was raised by his mother and her husband, John London, in Oakland. An intelligent boy, Jack went on to study at the University of California, Berkeley before leaving school to join the Klondike Gold Rush. His experiences in the Klondike—hard labor, life in a hostile environment, and bouts of scurvy—both shaped his sociopolitical outlook and served as powerful material for such works as "To Build a Fire" (1902), *The Call of the Wild* (1903), and *White Fang* (1906). When he returned to Oakland, London embarked on a career as a professional writer, finding success with novels and short fiction. In 1904, London worked as a war correspondent covering the Russo-Japanese War and was arrested several times by Japanese authorities. Upon returning to California, he joined the famous Bohemian Club, befriending such members as Ambrose Bierce and John Muir. London married Charmian Kittredge in 1905, the same year he purchased the thousand-acre Beauty Ranch in Sonoma County, California. London, who suffered from numerous illnesses throughout his life, died on his ranch at the age of 40. A lifelong advocate for socialism and animal rights, London is recognized as a pioneer of science fiction and an important figure in twentieth century American literature.

A Note from the Publisher

Spanning many genres, from non-fiction essays to literature classics to children's books and lyric poetry, Mint Edition books showcase the master works of our time in a modern new package. The text is freshly typeset, is clean and easy to read, and features a new note about the author in each volume. Many books also include exclusive new introductory material. Every book boasts a striking new cover, which makes it as appropriate for collecting as it is for gift giving. Mint Edition books are only printed when a reader orders them, so natural resources are not wasted. We're proud that our books are never manufactured in excess and exist only in the exact quantity they need to be read and enjoyed.

bookfinity™

Discover more of your favorite classics with Bookfinity™.

- Track your reading with custom book lists.
- Get great book recommendations for your personalized Reader Type.
- Add reviews for your favorite books.
- AND MUCH MORE!

Visit **bookfinity.com** and take the fun Reader Type quiz to get started.

Enjoy our classic and modern companion pairings!

Classic & Modern

Printed in the USA
CPSIA information can be obtained
at www.ICGtesting.com
JSHW022324140824
68134JS00019B/1286

9 781513 270227